A Boy in a
Storm

A Boy in a Storm

Oliver Crane

First published in 2022 by TBLOD
publishing@tblod.com

This book is a work of fiction. Names,
characters, businesses, places, events and
incidents are either the product of the author's
imagination or used in a fictitious manner. Any
resemblance to actual persons, living or dead,
or actual events is purely coincidental.

ISBN: 978-1-7397969-0-7
eBook 978-1-7397969-1-4

DEDICATION

To those who deserve something
better

ACKNOWLEDGMENTS

The seeds for this story were sown decades ago. My thanks, therefore, to those who by accompanying me on a lifetime of adventure, have helped inspire the tale.

And my gratitude to the group I can best describe as cheerleaders. Their help over the 5 years taken to write the book has been invaluable, reading manuscripts, suggesting changes, listening to me witter on about the characters and filling in the knowledge gaps to make A Boy in a Storm as authentic as possible. In no special order: Georgie, Kirsty, Helen, Adele, Colin, Laura, Linda, Mike, Chris, Marie-Laure and others.

Finally, my mum. It seems you were right!

CHAPTER 1

Hamish sat with the engine running while Miriam placed her and Nicholas's bags alongside his leather holdall and closed the boot.

As she got in beside him, he forced a yawn, then checked the wing mirror and pulled away.

'Have you got everything now?' he asked.

'Yes, I think so,' and without thinking, added, 'I was just preparing a snack for Nicholas to eat during the journey.'

When he failed to reply with his usual derision she realised he was distracted by a woman about her age walking along the pavement opposite, a gold-trimmed clutch tucked under her arm. Dressed in a well-cut short coat buttoned up against the February chill, and with black tights and heels, she looked typical of an employee from one of the professional services firms proliferating in Edinburgh's New Town.

Miriam wondered whether she was another of her husband's conquests, but when the woman glanced at the car, then dismissively at the driver and back to the pavement ahead, it was obvious she neither knew nor was interested in Hamish Fraser.

Torn between schadenfreude at the woman's snub, and relief that she wasn't another source of humiliation, Miriam moved her thoughts to the half-term weekend ahead. With snow forecast, perhaps she and Nicholas would go sledging, as she used to do with her father. Passing the Botanic Gardens, she peered in through the tall wrought-iron gates, hoping to keep with memories from a happier time.

But her husband brought her back to the present. 'I told you to keep Nicholas at home today. Now we'll be caught in the traffic.'

'It's the last day of term. He was looking forward to Golden Time. What would he have done stuck in the house all day?' she asked.

'Well, let's think about that …'

But before he finished, his mobile rang. The dashboard displayed *Rachael HR* and a number ending in *2030*.

What an easy number, thought Miriam, mindful that she could never remember her own.

She sensed her husband hesitate before pressing Answer.

'Has she gone?' he demanded.

'It's not that straightforward,' replied an equally abrupt female voice. 'We should be following due process. Technically, she hasn't done anything wrong. She'll say she was speaking up for the good of the business.'

Miriam tried to picture the caller: early thirties maybe, assertive and from northern England certainly. Manchester, perhaps.

'I don't give a toss about that,' he replied. 'I'm

not having people question my authority. It's your job to sort this out. Dig up some dirt or pay her off if you must, but I don't want to see that woman in the office again. Have I made myself clear?'

'Perfectly.'

A tense silence followed. Miriam saw her husband glance at the display. 'Is that everything?' he asked, the finality in his voice indicating he wanted to close the call.

'Where are you going?' came the reply, her admonitory tone revealing that this was personal.

'I'm spending the weekend in Auchenmore – it's half-term.'

'You're with your family, then?'

Hamish twitched. 'I'll speak to you next week,' and turned the phone off.

'Who was that?' Miriam asked.

'Just someone from the office,' and as they swept through the school gates, it occurred to Miriam that whoever *Rachael HR* was, the mighty Hamish was wary of her.

Ms English sat perched on the edge of her desk, taking a moment of respite while her classroom assistant supervised Golden Time. Her mind returned to her charges, and as was often the case, her eyes came to rest on the little boy, Nicholas Fraser.

Ms English had been the class teacher for six months, and whereas most of the children were building in confidence, eight-year-old Nicholas was retreating further into himself.

She pondered whether to speak to his mother, a

woman she'd observed when covering the end-of-day playground duty. Ms English had seen from the way Mrs Fraser avoided the other mothers that she was uncomfortable in their presence. Not surprising, given the way the women whispered and exchanged glances behind her back. However, the headmistress's words of caution held her back. 'Whereas I fully subscribe to the principle of "Getting it right for every child", we need to remember who pays the bills. With that in mind, don't say anything that might antagonise the parents, especially the mothers. You know what a pernicious lot they are, even amongst themselves.'

Her thoughts were cut by the warbling phone on her desk.

'Nicholas, Mummy's here. Gather your things, and I'll take you to her.'

Nicholas continued as though he hadn't heard, content kneeling on the floor at a small table littered with building blocks. He preferred to play alone, ever since one of the other children had told him, 'My mummy says your daddy sleeps with other women.'

Ms English signalled to the assistant that she would be away for a few minutes, and then repeated her request, 'Come along, Nicholas. One of the other children will tidy your toys.'

He reluctantly stood up, collected his satchel and followed her out of the classroom. As he passed, he lifted his coat from the peg with his name. The peg with a picture of a face she had asked him to redraw, 'with a happy face this time, Nicholas'.

They walked down a corridor decorated with the children's artwork, and as they neared the entrance hall, Ms English could see Mrs Fraser hovering.

'Is everything alright, Mrs Fraser?'

Mrs Fraser glanced at the front door then turned to her son, 'Yes, quite alright,' she replied, taking Nicholas's satchel from him.

Ms English patted Nicholas on the shoulder. 'Enjoy the holiday weekend, Nicholas,' and he returned a forced smile, looked towards the main doors, then faltered at the sight of his father's car through the glass.

Ms English noticed. 'Run along,' she encouraged, then turned to his mother. 'Mrs Fraser, I wonder whether we could meet next week – to discuss Nicholas?'

Mrs Fraser stiffened. 'I have a lot on. I'll call you if I can,' then scurried off, adding to the teacher's suspicions.

Nicholas climbed into the back of the car, his mother fussing over him, securing his seat belt and handing him a bag containing a sandwich, a bottle of juice and a biscuit.

'For the journey,' she whispered, kissing him on the cheek.

The door closed with a solid thump, cutting off the sound from the outside world, and his mother got into the front. Nicholas immediately felt different, his stomach tight and his body weak. He looked up to see his father watching him through the rear-view mirror, his face devoid of kindness. Sensing danger,

Nicholas looked down at his hands, now trembling as he held the paper bag.

His eyes still on Nicholas, Hamish took a small box from his jacket pocket and removed a cigar from within. The boxes intrigued Nicholas, with their picture of a woman dancing in a swirling red dress.

He lit the cigar, filling the car with smoke, then started the engine and pulled away down the leafy drive.

Nicholas stifled a cough and his mother opened her window slightly, but nothing was said; they both knew the consequences of speaking up.

The car swung onto the main road, forcing a white van to brake, and blare its horn. Banging his fist on the steering wheel, his father blasted a reply.

'Please, Hamish, don't go there,' his mother whispered.

He snapped back, 'Don't go where?' But they all knew the dark place she was referring to.

The cars ahead were showing their brake lights. Slowing to a crawl, his father noticed Nicholas drinking his juice. 'If you didn't spoil him, he wouldn't be wetting his bed. An eight-year-old, bed-wetting. The child's a bloody embarrassment.'

His mother came to his defence. 'He can't help it. You know why he does that.'

'And exactly why is that?'

'Because he's anxious.'

It's what Nicholas had heard the doctor tell Mummy. *Nicholas is suffering from anxiety.* He remembered her telling the doctor that it was because of her husband, and then she'd cried. The doctor had said she should speak to someone, but Mummy had said she could manage.

His father scowled. 'Are you saying it's my fault?'

'That's not what I meant.'

'And you're such a bloody perfect mother, aren't you?'

Nicholas knew that his father was talking about the secret thing. He didn't know what it was, only that it scared Mummy, and she would now go quiet.

They sat in silence, then Mummy asked, 'Hamish, why are you coming to Auchenmore if you don't want to be with us?'

He laughed. 'Now you decide you don't want to go. Can you not make up your bloody mind for once?

'Please don't speak to me like that in front of Nicholas,' she replied, but his father didn't seem to hear.

They followed the road out of Edinburgh, and as they crossed a large grey bridge Nicholas looked down to the water below. He took a toy Land Rover from his satchel. The one Mummy had bought him after he had seen his father hit her.

'Don't say anything to anyone about what happened. It was only a game,' she had said. But Nicholas knew that it was wrong to hit people and it frightened him. Then Mummy bought him the little Land Rover they had seen in the toy shop window. 'Remember, it's our secret, Nicholas.' After that, he always had a sore tummy when he heard his father shouting, scared he would hurt Mummy again.

The light was fading as they passed a loch with a castle on an island.

'That's Loch Leven Castle,' said Mummy. 'Mary Queen of Scots was imprisoned there. A brave boy called Willie Douglas helped her to escape.'
Nicholas wondered if one day he would be brave like Willie Douglas, and help Mummy escape.

A message sign read: *Snow Forecast, Drive with Care*, and geese flew overhead in a giant V, free to go where they pleased.

They inched past a police car. The policeman gave Nicholas a little wave and Nicholas waved back.

'Don't look at him,' his father said.

'Why? He waved to me.'

'Don't argue with me.'

Now his parents were arguing about their house. His father said that it should be in his name, not Mummy's. But she said her father had given it to her, not him.

They passed a sign – *Welcome to Perth* – and continued north. Nicholas saw a triangular picture of a deer with huge antlers.

He was feeling sleepy. On the right, a line of steel giants plodded one behind the other, tied together by wire ropes like the climbers he had seen in a picture book. He dreamt that he was riding high on the back of one. His father was prowling below, but the giant was protecting Nicholas from him.

It was late when they reached the chalet. Nicholas sat at the kitchen table drinking a mug of hot chocolate and eating something Mummy had prepared in the microwave.

When he had finished she brought her eyes close to his. 'You'll be a good boy this weekend, won't you, Nicholas? Keep out of Daddy's way and he won't be in a bad mood.' Then she threw her arms around him, hugged tight and whispered, 'I'm so sorry, Nicholas. This isn't what I wanted for us. One day we'll get away from him. I promise.'

She was crying again.

Nicholas got out of bed and ran to the window. It had snowed overnight, turning the world fluffy white. Animal tracks crisscrossed then disappeared into the trees beyond. He pushed himself up on the windowsill, trying to see further, but the woods refused to reveal their secrets.

Mummy appeared. 'Let's get you dressed, and then we'll have breakfast together.'

From the sitting-room door, he could see the woodstove had been lit and his father on his mobile phone.

'Come on, Nicholas,' Mummy said, ushering him to the kitchen. There was a glass of orange juice and a bowl of cereal waiting. Mummy sat with him, drinking her cup of coffee and eating a slice of toast.

After breakfast, she helped him into his ski jacket, boots, hat and gloves. 'Stay near the chalet,' she called as he ran off to build his snowman.

Rolling it forward, what started as a snowball quickly grew until it was too large to move. He scooped and patted handfuls of snow, increasing the body and forming the head. Having dressed it with twigs for arms, pinecone eyes and an old woollen hat, he stepped back to admire his work. He smiled and the snowman smiled back – but not enough. So using his mittened hand, he made the smile bigger.

However, soon the snowman was looking beyond him, into the woods. Nicholas followed his gaze to the pine trees on the boundary. *Go on, have a look*, the snowman said. So Nicholas made his way to the first tree, put his gloved hand on the orange-brown bark, and peered through the trees. The ground was carpeted with pine needles topped with a dusting of fine snow and illuminated by rays of yellow sunlight filtering down; the entrance to the Magic Kingdom!

He glanced back to the chalet and then to the snowman. *Go on,* the snowman encouraged, *you can do it*. So he made his way to the second tree. It was quieter here, the snowman and chalets gone from view. He looked further into the trees and moved on. By the fifth tree, he was in a different world. He sat on the ground, his back against a pine. It was peaceful and for once, he felt safe.

Miriam put the last of the cups into the dishwasher and lifted the door shut. Readying to go outside, she took her coat from a chair but was distracted by a distant buzz. A familiar sound, yet somehow out of place. Her eyes scanned the cooker, radio, and back to the dishwasher, but nothing seemed untoward. Finally, they landed on her bag sitting at the end of the table.

A moment of panic: *It's the school – Nicholas has had an accident*, then the realisation that it couldn't be. She calmed but went to check on him anyway. He was playing with his snowman. Returning to the kitchen she paused, trying to recall what had sent her out, and then remembered the phone.

Rummaging through her bag she saw its winking light signalling a message.

Hello Miriam. Your husband is having another affair. Have a nice family weekend.

Despite what she knew about her husband, the message still gripped her: an intrusion onto her phone and into her personal life.

In the other room, Hamish was still making calls, laughing and joking with a crony about a game of golf next week and dinner in the club afterwards.

'Just tell the little lady that it's business,' he was saying.

Clutching the phone with trembling fingers, and in a state of utter confusion, Miriam tried to connect the text to a person, time or place. Yet despite a flood of painful memories, there seemed nothing in particular with which to attribute this. Until her eyes came to rest on the sender's number. A number ending in 2030.

Delete the message, switch off the phone, or do as I always do and deny that any of this is happening.

From the sitting room, Hamish's tone of voice changed. 'Angus, something's cropped up. I need to go.'

The chalet went quiet. Miriam's eyes lifted to the door as Hamish appeared. He looked at the phone in her hand, and she looked at the phone in his, then their eyes met. 'She says she sent you a text. Ignore it. She's a crazy bitch.'

Miriam stood firm, her grip tightening around the phone. 'Oh, another one. I don't believe you.'

'Believe what you want. She'll be here soon enough. Or so she says.'

'You disgust me,' said Miriam, her face contorting with anger. 'And to think I ever had sex with you.'

He smirked. 'Is that what you called it? Remind me to swap notes with that other fellow you had. What was his name again?'

Grabbing her coat and bag her look changed to one of loathing. 'You really are a vulgar man. If she's coming here, I'm not staying to witness it. I'm leaving. I'm going to call my father and have him collect Nicholas and me.'

He gave a mocking laugh. 'The great Archibald Stewart to the rescue. I'm sure your delightful mother will be very supportive of that – especially when the gossip starts to circulate. Face it, Miriam, I'm all you and that boy have.'

Lying on his back, Nicholas stared dreamily up through the swaying branches to the blue sky above. A crow cawed in the distance. The world looked so different from here.

He heard Mummy call. 'Nicholas, where are you?'

She called again, louder this time and with a voice telling him she was worried.

He called back, 'Coming,' then stood up and followed his snowy footprints out of the woods. A twig arm had fallen from the snowman. He was about to replace it when Mummy took his hand.

'Leave it for now. We're going into town.'

A white car with a grey box on the roof arrived and they sat in the back.

'Where to?' asked the driver.

'Somewhere in Auchenmore where we can get lunch.'

Nicholas saw the driver look at them through the mirror and was about to look away as he did with his father, but the driver smiled and Nicholas smiled back.

'What's the box on the roof for?' he asked.

'Skis,' the man replied. 'Can you ski?'

'I've tried it once. Mummy says we might go tomorrow.'

'We'll see,' she said, in a way he knew meant they wouldn't.

They stopped in front of a café. Mummy handed the driver some money and he gave her a card. 'Just give me a call when you're ready to return.'

The café was busy with families staying for the long weekend. A lady showed them to a table. Nicholas watched a family beside them as Mummy chose from the menu. A boy his age and his older sister were sitting with their mummy and daddy. The daddy was smiling and putting out his hand for the boy to try and catch. It looked like an easy game, with the boy able to win each time. Nicholas remembered his own father's hand and the way it had struck out when he had spilt his drink over some papers.

A waitress arrived with a milkshake for him and a coffee for Mummy.

'Can we go sledging this afternoon?' he asked.

'No. I'm afraid we can't. Listen, Nicholas, I need to make a telephone call. Be a good boy and stay here for a few minutes will you?'

He nodded and Mummy asked the family to keep an eye on him. The lady smiled, and then waved to Nicholas. 'You can come and sit with us if you like?' and the children beckoned him.

But, starting to feel uncertain about the day, he shook his head and looked for Mummy. She wouldn't usually leave him like this – not on his own. Then he saw her near the door, speaking on her phone. She was gesturing with her hand, as though trying to make someone listen to her. It wasn't long before she came back.

While Nicholas ate his macaroni cheese, Miriam reread the anonymous text, unsure whether it was in the hope of seeing something new, or that returning to the message would somehow immunise her from its cruelty. She let out a nervous laugh at the irony of the situation. A woman who by any normal measure would be marked as a threat had given her what she needed: the impetus to challenge the mighty Hamish and free her and her child from his malevolent force.

She lowered her eyes, level with Nicholas's. 'I need to speak to you, Nicholas. What I have to say is very important.'

He looked back with a doleful expression, awaiting her words.

'Grandpa is coming to collect us. We are going to stay with him and Grandma for a while.'

Nicholas poked the food on his plate. 'I thought you didn't like Grandma?'

Bridling at the memory of what her mother had put her through, she drew a breath.

'We won't be there for long. Just until we get the house to ourselves.'

'Will Daddy be coming to Grandpa's?' he asked, without looking up.

'No, he won't.'

She watched Nicholas ease and put another forkful of food into his mouth. The family at the next table were now on their ice creams: elaborate creations topped with brightly coloured sauces and eaten with long spoons from tall glasses. Miriam saw the woman laughing with her husband. Delighting in the presence of her family.

'Could we get an ice cream?' Nicholas asked, following her gaze.

'Of course.'

Too soon, they returned to the chalet.

'You have visitors,' said the driver. Miriam didn't reply as her mind worked through the implications of the open chalet door and the unfamiliar red car parked outside.

She looked at her watch. They had been away for nearly three hours. Her father would be arriving soon. It had been a mistake to arrange to meet him here, but difficult to change now. Mobile phones and Archibald were just too many worlds apart.

The taxi pulled away, leaving them standing by the steps. Loud voices could be heard from within.

Nicholas peered through the door, then to his snowman. 'Can I go and fix his arm now?'

'Yes, but don't go too far and don't come in until I call you. Do you understand?'

He nodded and trotted off to his new-found friend.

Miriam climbed the steps and stood listening to the voice she'd heard in the car the previous day.

'You bastard! You promised me you'd leave her. But oh no. You leave *me* and take up with another woman.'

'I promised you no such thing. You've been given a well-paid job beyond your ability. What more do you want?'

'RESPECT,' she shouted back and Hamish let out a ridiculing laugh.

Emboldened by the woman's defiance, Miriam walked softly through the chalet, and stopped short of the kitchen door, listening to the man she called her husband quarrel with his scorned lover. Piecing together the fragments, it seemed that she and Rachael had experienced a similar induction into the world of Hamish Fraser: wined and dined by a congenial and successful executive holding the grand title of Finance Director; a whirlwind of expensive hotels in exotic – albeit not far-flung – locations; and then awkward sex, taken to the boundaries of consent. But here their paths diverged. Whereas Rachael was cast aside to rue the day she'd ever got into bed with the man, Miriam had continued into the world of someone she'd come to learn was a violent and possessive abuser.

Still, from the way the conversation was going, Miriam could tell that Rachael would soon be seeing the darker side of his character.

'I'm telling you now, Rachael, turn and leave here and be grateful for what I've given you.'

'Grateful for what you've given me?' she screamed. 'Grateful for letting a misogynist like you get his sleazy hands on my body? I don't know what I ever saw in you and I'm going to make you pay. If you think me telling your wife has brought you trouble, just wait until I get to back Edinburgh and tell the rest of the world about you. I'll expose you for what you are! Not just your sordid affairs, but all the financial shenanigans that I've covered up for you and that cabal of yours.'

From his lack of response, Miriam could sense Hamish's shifting mien: his eyes would be darkening and the veins on his forehead starting to bulge. For a moment she thought of alerting Rachael to the danger, but she was too late. The familiar sound of a hand connecting with a head echoed through the door, quickly followed by a crash as the woman collapsed onto the tiled floor. Miriam moved forward to see Rachael on the ground propped up by her right arm, her legs bent, and shaking her head as though not believing what had just happened. As she rose unsteadily to her feet, it seemed the enormity of what Hamish had done was dawning on her.

Looking up, her fists clenched, she yowled in a voice born of fury, 'You bastard, you fucking bastard. You think you can hit me?'

In an explosion of movement, she lunged towards his face. Hamish lifted his hands to protect his eyes as her fingers tore at him. He tried to hit back but the ferocity of her attack forced him to hold his guard.

Whether to protect the woman or driven by the sheer absurdity of the situation, Miriam stepped into the kitchen. 'Stop this!' she shouted.

But enraged, Rachael persisted, pulling open a nearby drawer, grabbing a large knife from within and lunging at Hamish. Miriam leapt into the fray, but it was too late. The knife struck home and Hamish made one last strike, missing his mark and yet again hitting Miriam.

Detaching himself from the sound of shouting adults, Nicholas added more snow to the body of his friend. 'I'll get a scarf to keep you warm tonight,' he said.

The shouting stopped. Nicholas paused what he was doing and looked expectantly towards the door then heard a sound that terrified, but at the same time, drew him rushing to its source. A primal groan, like that of a wounded beast in its final throes.

As he ran towards the house, a woman appeared, got into the red car and drove off.

Nicholas entered the kitchen and froze, his mind grappling with the horror before him; his father doubled over, one hand on the table to support himself, the other holding a knife that protruded from his stomach. Blood trickled from the wound, running down his hand and onto the floor. As if realising the futility of his actions, his father stopped, looked at Nicholas, and then collapsed – the release of pressure from the wound increasing the flow that pooled on the tiles.

Nicholas shouted for his mother, but she didn't reply so he ran to the sitting room to find her in a chair, her head bowed. 'Are you hurt, Mummy?'

She shook her head without looking up and Nicholas ran back to the kitchen.

The sight of the man who caused so much fear lying helpless confused him. He thought of returning to the sitting room for comfort or running out of the door and into the woods, but instead, he knelt on the floor beside his father, fearful of his reaction, but drawn to his plight.

'What can I do?' he pleaded, his fumbling hands covered in blood as they tried to help. Taking a tea towel, he pressed it against the wound. His father yelled in pain, lifting a hand. Nicholas flinched, but Hamish just pushed him away.

'Get help,' he groaned.

He ran into the hallway and onto the porch. A car parked further down the lane drew him to the adjacent chalet, where he banged on the door. An elderly man in slippers answered, startled by the sight of a distraught child with blood on his hands.

'He's hurt, he's hurt,' Nicholas cried, through his sobs.

Pulling on boots that sat by the door, the neighbour dashed towards their chalet, but Nicholas stayed where he was. He looked across to the snowman; it looked back at him, and shouted, 'Run Nicholas, run!' So he ran, as fast as he could, past the snowman, to tree number one, on to five, and far beyond.

PC Eilidh Grant looked down at her German Shepherd, Blue, sitting beside her. For Blue to find the boy he would need to be let loose to follow scents carried in the air and self-reliant until his distinctive bark summoned her. Trained for duties across the spectrum of police work, Blue would need to interpret his find. Had he been seeking an undesirable in a bleak industrial estate on a cold night, Eilidh would have had few qualms. However, this was a vulnerable and scared child. How would the boy react to the large animal approaching? If the child panicked, would Blue understand?

Eilidh assessed the situation. The child could have travelled a considerable distance and although dressed for the weather, he was probably lost, perhaps injured and unlikely to survive a February night in the open. She looked down at Blue – his ears pricked as he stared into the woods – and asked the question, 'If he were my child out there, would I trust you?'

Thirty minutes later, Blue's bark sounded and Eilidh made her way to find Nicholas sitting under a large tree, cold and distressed 'Well done,' she said, relaxing the dog, as she crouched beside the child. 'Hello, Nicholas, I'm Eilidh, and this is Blue. We came to find you.'

Blue approached the child and sniffed the bloodied hands he was holding fearfully away from himself. Eilidh drew the dog back. 'Let's clean you up,' she said.

Wearing latex gloves, she poured water from her bottle over the hands and wiped them clean with a swab from her pouch.

'Is Mummy alright?' Nicholas asked.

'Yes, she's fine,' and was going to reassure him about his father when her mother's intuition held her back.

'Is she angry with me?'

'No. She's not angry. She was worried about you, Nicholas. We all were. But she's not angry. There, this will keep you warm,' putting a foil blanket around him.

With pleading eyes, Nicholas looked at Eilidh. 'I don't want to go back to the chalet.'

'Let's stay here for a wee bit then.'

With Nicholas taking comfort from the dog now lying beside him, she discreetly updated the control room and received her instructions.

As they drew up, Nicholas recognised the woman and child waiting to greet them. She was Mary and would occasionally look after him when his parents went out. The little girl with long red hair and clutching a soft toy was her daughter, Tracy.

Eilidh encouraged him forward. 'This is Nicholas,' she said. 'Once we get things sorted out his granddad will be along to collect him.'

'Yes, we know Nicholas. We'll look after him,' Mary said, putting her arm around his shoulder.

'I know you will,' replied Eilidh. Then switching

to a loud whisper she leant towards Mary, 'He's been through a lot today. The paramedics said that he saved his father's life.'

Mary closed the front door and led the way into the sitting room.

'Come through and sit down, my wee man,' she said, 'Tracy, you stay with Nicholas and I'll get him some dry clothes, and then I'll make us all a mug of hot milk.'

Nicholas sat on the edge of the settee, looking around an impeccably tidy room. He felt insecure knowing that his mother, for tonight at least, was incapable of looking after him, and lurking beneath it sat the horror of what he had witnessed. He felt as if he'd woken from a night terror. Worst of all was the dreadful feeling that what he had experienced at the chalet signified a change. A move to an altogether different type of awfulness. He sensed that life would never be the same.

The little girl with red hair stood watching him as she waited for her mother's return. Looking at the boy she had met once or twice at the chalet, the boy who had arrived in need of help.

'Would you like to hold Floppy Rabbit?' she asked, knowing the value of a good companion at such a time.

'Thank you,' he replied, taking the soft toy and holding it next to his face.

'You can come and live with us if you'd like to?' she offered.

Mary returned with an assortment of clothes. They drank their hot milk while Mary made them scrambled eggs on toast. Afterwards, she set up paper and crayons on the kitchen table. The little girl drew a picture of herself and her mummy, and Nicholas drew a picture of himself and a dog in a dark wood.

Later on, his granddad arrived to take him back to Edinburgh.

'Will he visit us again?' the little girl asked as they waved goodbye from the front door.

'I doubt it, not now.'

Nicholas returned a meek wave and a forced smile through the car window and then disappeared.

That's a pity, thought the little girl. *He was nice.*

CHAPTER 2

Dragging his feet, Nicholas walked past the Georgian townhouses of Moray Circle. Arriving at Number 33 he looked up at the building that felt less and less like home. Despite the difficulties with his father, his mother had always made him feel wanted. But something had changed. Although she hadn't overtly said it, he could sense that she was anxious for him to move on. A year at college repeating Highers, but with little to show, had left them both wondering, where next?

He mounted the steps that bridged the basement vestibule, entered, and hung his coat by the door. The light and sounds from the kitchen confirmed his mother was home, but he didn't announce his arrival. His coat and the creaking floor in his bedroom would tell her soon enough. It was what they had learnt to do: use fragments of sight, sound and habit as a substitute for words that were just too awkward.

Slumping into the swivel chair at his desk he booted up the PlayStation.

From the kitchen below came the odd knock of a cupboard door and background voices from the radio. Noises he associated with his mother living her routine when just the two of them, and entirely different to those heard when his father was home.

The screen settled and he flicked through a series of games to see who was active. But the friends with whom he had once escaped into a virtual world had moved on with their lives: university, gap years in foreign locations, or for a few, family businesses. Giving up on the console, he lay down on the bed, staring at the ceiling until his eyes became heavy and the tall pines swayed in the wind.

His mother was calling from the chalet. 'Nicholas, Nicholas!' Moments later he was awake. 'Nicholas, I'm not calling you again. Supper is on the table.'

With customary apprehension, he descended to the kitchen where she had already started on a small portion of whatever ready meal she had managed to spoil. Tonight it looked Italian, but he couldn't be sure. Taking his place he glanced at her, his stomach tightening at the sight of a bruise on her cheek.

'You shouldn't let him do that to you,' he said, shaking his head and looking back at his plate.

She put her hand up to cover it, wincing as her fingers made contact. 'It was the cupboard door.'

'Sure it was,' he replied, the contempt in his voice once again highlighting to Miriam the dilemma she faced.

She changed the subject. 'What did you do today?'

'Not much,' turning his food with his fork to inspect the underside.

'Oh. Did you speak to the people in the shop I

was telling you about? You like the outdoors; I'm sure you would be very good at selling.'

'I spoke to them, but they said they didn't need anyone at the moment. Maybe at Christmas.'

She tried to sound optimistic. 'Well, that could be promising. Did they take your number?'

He shook his head, and then at the end of the table spotted a cigarillo box with an image of a flamenco dancer.

'When is he back?' Nicholas asked.

Miriam tensed. 'Not until Friday night,' then put her fork down and looked at the son who barely acknowledged her presence, picking at his food.

'Nicholas. I've been thinking. It's not good for you here. You need to get on with your life.'

'Do you think I don't know that?' he said.

She gathered herself. 'Perhaps you should go up to Auchenmore for a while. You can stay in the chalet and have time to work out what you want to do. I'm sure with all the tourists there you'll find work. And there's the skiing … you like that, don't you?'

His eyes stayed down. 'You want me to go away, is that it?'

She shook her head. 'Of course I don't. But staying here isn't healthy. I have the money that Grandpa left me, so I can help you out until you find something.'

His breathing quickened with the implication of what she was saying. The bond they had forged to survive the brutality of Hamish Fraser was about to be severed. A bond that had, up to now, endured despite the awkwardness that lay between them.

'But I don't know what I want to do … And I don't feel ready to be on my own,' he said, floundering to express his near-panic.

She went to rub his hand but he pulled away and stood up.

'Fine, I'll go if that's what you want,' and stormed out of the kitchen.

Miriam pushed her plate away and stared blankly out over the darkened garden, to the yellow light burning in the service lane beyond. She knew that what she had said had left her son feeling rejected. Yet what was the choice? The need to protect him that throughout his childhood had demanded she keep him close, now compelled her to cast him off. In the wake of that awful day at the chalet, Hamish had reached an uneasy accommodation with the boy who had saved his life. However, now she sensed something stirring within her tormentor's primal psyche. Nicholas was a young man and starting to question the life they led. Hamish would deem him a threat. It was no longer safe for him here.

***

Tracy lowered the sachets of boil-in-the-bag rice into the saucepan and double-checked the cooking time on the side of the box.

Hearing the front door open she called through, 'Hi Mum, supper's nearly ready.'

Mary made her way along their hallway to join

her daughter. She could see that Tracy had prepared their usual places at the table, but tonight there was also a conspicuous brown envelope in front of Mary's setting.

'Is this for me?' Mary asked, but Tracy didn't answer.

She had planned to busy herself with the cooking as if everything was normal. 'Yes, that's for you,' she would say, then carry on, taking the Italian meatballs out of the oven.

But something was going badly wrong with her plan, something she hadn't anticipated. Mary sensed it straight away.

'What's wrong, lass?' she asked, moving over to her daughter.

Taken by her emotions Tracy turned around and hugged her mum as she had when seeking comfort as a child, and enveloping her in red hair. Being taller than Mum, and much more athletic in build made no difference to the warmth she felt.

Concerned, Mary asked, 'What's happened? Is there a problem at work?'

Mary could feel Tracy shake her head. 'No, it's nothing like that,' she eventually replied, then said what she usually said on such occasions, 'I must look a right mess.'

She went to the wall mirror, wiped her eyes and tidied her make-up while Mary looked again at the envelope, wondering what part it played in this.

'Go on, Mum, open it,' Tracy beckoned. 'It was meant to be a nice surprise, but it's all gone wrong.'

She watched as Mary sat at her place, lifted the

envelope and opened it. Inside were twenty-pound notes, lots of them.

Mary looked at Tracy and shook her head. 'No, Tracy. It's kind of you, but this isn't right. I can't take it.'

Aware that were she to try and explain she would return to tears, Tracy didn't answer. Instead, she put the meatballs on the table. Mary sat quietly as Tracy served the rice onto two plates, brought them over and sat down in her usual place. As the two of them added meatballs to the nests of rice and started to eat, their eyes returned to the envelope.

Mary spoke first. 'Don't think I'm not grateful, Tracy. I am, but it's your first pay packet. You don't want to give me all this after you've worked so hard for it.'

Tracy put down her knife and fork and, having composed herself, was once again the girl who said things as they were.

'Mum, what are you saying, *me* working hard? Don't you think I know how difficult things have been for you all these years?'

Finding the conversation tough she picked up her knife and fork and continued eating, her eyes now on her food.

'You don't owe me anything, Tracy. I did everything I did because I wanted to and if I could have done more for you, I would have gladly done so. Don't feel you're indebted or that you've somehow been a burden. I would hate to think I ever made you feel that way.'

Tracy shook her head. 'No, I've never felt that …

ever.'

'Well, how about you give me a monthly contribution towards our housekeeping and keep the rest for yourself. Would that work?'

Tracy nodded and smiled, and the two of them returned to their meal.

Later on, with the table cleared and Mum curled up on the sofa watching television, Tracy tucked a little pile of notes under the teapot beside the microwave, and the next day, on her way to work, deposited most of the remainder at the bank – a high-interest account, of course. With what she kept back, she bought the pair of sheepskin-lined snow boots she had seen in the window of Auchenmore Outdoor Sports, from last year's collection with 60 per cent off.

***

By four o'clock, Nicholas was driving the small car, bought with money gifted by Grandad, up the lane to the chalet. With endless roadworks on the A9, the journey from Edinburgh had been slow, and a leaden sky was drawing an early close to the day. His heart sank further as the chalet came into view. With weeds taken root in the gravel, the porch littered with leaves from the autumn fall, and flaking paintwork, it carried the faded appearance of the unloved.

Using his foot, he brushed aside the debris from the bottom of the front door and placed his key in the lock. A shoogle released the swollen door from the constraints of its frame, to open a few inches, then jam on a piece of junk mail. Squeezing his leg around, he trapped the leaflet under his shoe and pulled the door free. A few hesitant steps and he was inside, swiping at a cobweb that touched his face.

Pausing to allow fresh air to make its mark on the stale atmosphere, he noticed his breath swirl. As anticipated, the chalet still carried a sinister feel – the legacy of that dreadful day from his childhood. It all seemed so familiar, yet so different. He had never arrived on his own, or without a purpose, even if it was limited to surviving their stay. His eyes roamed: ahead to the kitchen, left, to the staircase leading up to the bedrooms, right to the sitting room, then back to the kitchen. As he entered, his eyes instinctively looked to the floor where his father had lain, bleeding to death. *Why the hell did I help him?*

Returning to the front door he looked over to the other properties, all closed up; their owners foregoing soulless months in their second homes in favour of work, or for some, taking advantage of closed season deals on Mediterranean beaches.

His gaze shifted to a chalet down the lane, his thoughts wandering to a scene long ago in which a little boy banged frantically on the door. Then he looked to where the snowman had stood, urging him on, *Run Nicholas, run*, and further still to the woods. He started towards the trees and onwards, pushing between overgrown branches and stepping over mossy hummocks until he reached a Scots pine, smaller than he recalled, but undoubtedly the same one.

Lying on his back he looked up through its swaying canopy to the darkness above, and realised that this time there would be no one calling him home. He was alone

***

A flash of lightning coincided with the rumble of thunder and the heavens opened, sending rods of rain to splatter on the ground.

Coerced by an imminent drenching, Tracy and Dani pulled their jackets over their bowed heads and dashed to the Institute Hall. Donated in the early 1900s by the absentee laird, the hall served members of the community from cradle to grave, with the Mothers and Toddlers Club at one end of life, and the senior citizens' Christmas lunch and the occasional wake at the other.

The girls took shelter under the incongruous red-brick porch. Taking off their wet layers and shaking them, they started to laugh at how they must have appeared. A Scottish Country Dance Club poster caught Dani's attention. 'Do you remember when we used to come to this?'

Tracy nodded. 'How could I forget? It was where we first met. What were we – about thirteen? Your dad brought you through from Inverness.'

'Yes, and sat embarrassing me from a bench at the side.'

Tracy looked curious. 'I never asked – why did he

bring you to Auchenmore? Was there nowhere closer?'

'Because of the dance teacher, Miss McKenzie,' said Dani. 'I didn't know at the time, but apparently, she'd been Mum's dance partner and I think Dad hoped she would be able to make a dancer of me. Little did he know.'

Tracy looked at the poster then back to Dani. 'Ah, yes, Miss McKenzie. Where did she disappear to?'

'New Zealand, I think. I heard she met a guy from there and followed him back home.'

Tracy smiled recalling Miss McKenzie trying in vain to teach Dani the pas de basque step. 'You might not have been much of a dancer, Dani, but I was so jealous of you.'

'Why? It was you who won all the prizes, not me.'

'I maybe won the prizes, but it was you who got the boys, wasn't it? Remember that lad Jamie from my school? I was smitten by him, but it was you he asked to dance.'

Dani shook her head. 'I think that was only because he could lark about with me.'

But Tracy looked despondent. 'No, Dani. There's more to it than that. You seem to be able to attract people, whereas me, I don't think I interest them.'

Dani looked at her friend, wondering why Tracy was always putting herself down. Could it have anything to do with her dad? Tracy had only mentioned him once, simply saying, 'I never knew my father,' then changing the subject. Dani knew what it was like, growing up without one of your parents – it was something else that had brought the two of them together. But she did at least have photos of her mother and the treasured wedding video. More than Tracy had ever had.

'Tracy, don't think of yourself that way. People like you. Look at our nights out with the others. It's you who gets us all going. And you're smart. Look who's been offered a trainee manager's role at the supermarket, while I'm going up the mountain to freeze my butt off teaching skiing. And what about you becoming a Special with the police? Don't tell me that doesn't take courage.'

Tracy challenged her. 'You *like* being up on the mountains, Dani.'

'Well, maybe I do,' Dani conceded. 'But the point I'm making is that you're a great person and you're my best friend, so I don't want to hear you putting yourself down. Do you hear me?'

'I hear you, but it's hard to change the way you feel about yourself, isn't it?'

'Oh, come here,' said Dani, pulling her into a warm hug.

With the cloudburst spent, shafts of sunlight started to show, promising something better for the evening.

'Why don't we grab a hot chocolate?' said Dani. 'Then we can see if there's anyone we know at the ice rink.'

***

While the valley was showing off the last of its autumnal browns and greens, high up on the ski area, the pisters were making the most of early-season snow, eking it out to cover the narrow runs bordered by snow fences that typified Scottish skiing.

Nicholas glanced at his watch – 12.30 – then looked about to see if anyone he knew had turned up. A party of schoolchildren were tentatively following their instructor down the piste towards him, zigzagging the full width of the run, and a few couples and individuals were taking advantage of the weekday quiet, but no one he recognised.

He recalled past visits to the mountain, hanging out with schoolfriends. The days had never seemed long enough and a welcome diversion from his parents and the chalet. Now, here alone under an overcast sky, his heart just wasn't in it. But what was the alternative? A wander around Auchenmore, or return to the chalet and the PlayStation?

A few more runs, then a bite to eat in the café. By now the instructor and her class were close, so he slid back on his skis to let them through. 'Thanks,' she called, leading the group to execute a turn on the opposite side. The last child, a boy, crossed diagonally, causing him to pick up speed and end up in a heap in the snow.

The instructor stopped further down and the remainder of the party gathered beside her.

'Come on, Mikey,' called one of the children, intimating it wasn't the first time Mikey had held them up.

'I can't, I'm stuck,' he shouted back.

Seeing the instructor taking off her skis for a laborious plod back up, Nicholas set off across the slope to offer his help.

'Are you OK?' he asked.

The boy looked helplessly up at him. 'Yes, but I can't move. My skis are buried.'

Nicholas removed his own and released the boy's bindings.

'Give me your hand,' he said, then pulled the boy to his feet.

The boy reached down to pick up his skis and carry them. 'I'm not doing this again.'

'Why?' Nicholas asked.

'Because I end up going too fast and crashing.'

'That's only because you don't turn enough. Have another go and keep turning until you're crossing the slope.'

They refitted the skis. 'Thanks, mister,' said the boy as Nicholas handed him the poles, then he departed, making huge turns to arrive at the instructor. She looked up the mountain to wave her thanks to the person who had saved her a climb, but he was gone.

Having wiped the steamed-up window with his forearm, Nicholas peered outside, reflectively chomping on a greasy sausage roll. Apart from two piste workers in conversation, there was nothing to see. He turned back to his phone. A friend had messaged, inviting him to join them for a night out in Edinburgh.

'Too busy skiing, mate,' he replied, trying to sound upbeat but knowing Edinburgh was no longer an option – unless he found someone's floor to sleep on. The sausage roll finished, he left the café, collected his skis from the rack and headed towards the T-bar tow. *A couple of runs to fill in the afternoon, then into town, pick up something for supper and back to the chalet.*

The T-bar was designed to sit behind a pair of skiers' backsides and haul them up the hill. However, when used alone it felt unbalanced, its red gloss paint adding to the likelihood of slipping off on the steep sections. Standing ready for a solo ride, Nicholas became aware of someone arriving beside him. 'We can pair up if you don't mind?' the girl said. A glance at her bright red ski suit told him she was an instructor, but catching the approaching T-bar took his attention and the next thing they were underway.

For twenty metres or so, they travelled with only the wooshing sound of snow passing under their skis. Then the girl spoke.

'Thanks for helping Mikey this morning.'

Nicholas twisted his body to look at her. She was shorter than him and wearing a two-piece combination with the name of an outdoor centre embroidered on the front. With her goggles and helmet, it was hard to make out her face, except that it was round, she had freckles and was smiling.

'Oh, that's OK,' he replied. 'Where are they now?'

'They're doing half-days. There's another group somewhere on the mountain doing the full ski week but my group are on multi-activities. I've got a couple of afternoons off – lucky me.'

'Are you a full-time instructor?' he asked.

'Trying to be. It's my first year since I got my ski qualifications. What about you, are you up here for the day?'

'Well actually, I'm here for the winter. We have a chalet on the back road.'

They were nearing the top and Nicholas became aware that when they arrived, the girl would ski off on her own, taking her company with her. 'I'm Nicholas, Nicholas Fraser.'

'And I'm Dani,' she replied.

When they got off at the top, Dani bent down to adjust the tension on her boot. When she stood up again, Nicholas was still there.

She pointed to the other side of the tow. 'You probably already know this, but the best snow after a fresh fall is usually in the Flour Bowl over the ridge.'

'I didn't know that,' Nicholas replied, being frugal with the truth.

'I'll show you if you like?'

The afternoon passed in a flash as they whizzed down the mountain and chatted their way up. Back at the car park, Dani looked over to the minibus where they were loading skis into a backdoor carrier. 'That was a brilliant afternoon. Thank you,' she said.

Nicholas smiled. 'Yes, it was fun. Let me get you a hot chocolate for showing me around. They're *really* good.'

'Thanks. I'll just dump my skis at the minibus so they don't leave without me.'

He went to the serving hatch of the gourmet coffee van cannily positioned to take advantage of the end of day business.

'The usual?' asked the barista.

'Make it two, and large. Oh, and can you add chantilly cream?'

'Sure,' she said, already heating a stainless-steel jug of milk with a hissing steam jet.

Having left her skis and swapped her helmet and goggles for a thick woollen beanie, Dani was soon back beside him, watching the girl swirl the whipped cream onto the hot chocolate.

Nicholas lifted their drinks from the counter and turned to hand Dani hers. His heart skipped a beat as he looked into her hazel eyes for the first time.

'What is it?' she asked, seeing his look, but he didn't reply.

She took a sip, then ran her tongue over her lip to remove the cream. 'This is delicious. Thank you, Nicholas.'

He smiled. 'I was wondering whether …'

But a honk from the minibus horn distracted her. 'I need to go. Thanks again for this,' she said, holding up the drink.

Nicholas watched her scurry across the car park, balancing her cup in front. She climbed up beside the driver, laughing with the occupants as she did so. Then just before closing the door she looked back at him and waved.

Nicholas watched the van disappear.

'Everyone likes Dani,' said the barista, who was now leaning on the counter and following his gaze.

***

Dani leant her bike against the wall at the side of the house, knocked on the front door and without waiting for an answer, entered. Mary looked through from where she was ironing in the kitchen.

'Hello, Dani. Tracy's just having a shower.'

'Hi, Mary,' Dani replied, taking off her damp trainers and hanging her ski jacket on a peg by the door before wandering through.

'Have you had your supper?' Mary asked without looking up from the steaming iron she was passing to and fro over a pillowslip. 'We've had ours, but I can make you a sandwich?'

'That's OK,' Dani replied, looking for any evidence of a meal having been recently eaten, but as usual with Mary, the kitchen was immaculate. 'I ate with the children. Fish fingers, beans and mash.'

Dani looked on as Mary added the ironed slip to the others on a small pile then laid the next on the board.

'How's the job going?' Mary continued.

'Good … apart from the pay. The children are fun and it's nice to be doing something you enjoy, isn't it?'

Mary smiled. 'I suppose it must be. I can't honestly say that my ambition was ever to clean hotel rooms.'

'I'm sure you're good at it though,' Dani replied, mindful of the long hours Mary worked to make a living.

A door could be heard opening upstairs, and Tracy called down, 'Mum, have we got a dry towel?'

'I'll take it up to her,' said Dani, and Mary handed her one from the pile.

Wearing a white bathrobe, Tracy met her on the landing. She gathered her wet hair and wrapped the towel around it. 'Come through and tell me what's so exciting,' referring to the intriguing text Dani had sent.

Tracy sat at her dressing table trying to untangle the knotted hairdryer lead while Dani jumped onto the bed, propping herself up with pillows and looking around the room: the familiar boy-band poster, Tracy's toiletries laid out neatly on the dressing table and the chest of drawers with teddies on top. The bedroom smelt of talc, and seemed so feminine and organised compared with the room she shared with another instructor at the centre – cluttered with rucksacks and outdoor gear and smelling of climbing boots.

Tracy looked at Dani in the mirror. 'Well, are you going to tell me then?'

Dani pulled her knees up to her chest and gathered them in her arms. Her eyes brightened. 'I've met this boy.'

'And?' Tracy asked, curious about this sudden turn of events.

'And he's really nice. We skied together. He's from Edinburgh.'

Tracy ran through the people she knew from Edinburgh, but apart from an older couple who had retired to the town, she drew a blank. 'Is he on holiday?'

'He's up here for winter. His parents have one of those chalets on the back road.'

'Where does he work?'

'I don't think he does.'

'Well, he can't be a student – unless he's taken a term off, which I doubt. So he's either older, unemployed or super-rich.' Tracy said, her imagination working through the implications of the latter.

Dani looked thoughtful, realising that this hadn't occurred to her but perhaps it should have. 'I don't know – except that he looks our age.'

'Typical,' replied Tracy, then turning on her seat, 'Tell me what you do know about him.'

Now with her friend's full attention, Dani shared all she had gleaned during the afternoon's skiing.

'His name is Nicholas and his family have one of the chalets on the back road.'

Tracy gave an impatient sigh. 'Yes, you told me that bit … And?'

'And, he seems friendly: a little shy, but he's nice. He was interested in my work and what we do at the outdoor centre. He said he's been coming up here on and off since he was a child, but I didn't recognise him. Oh, and at the end of the day he bought me a hot chocolate with whipped cream on top from that little van in the car park.'

Tracy rolled her eyes to the ceiling. 'Well, he

must be serious if he did that. When are you seeing him next?' now suspecting her outdoorsy friend had more than a casual interest in this boy called Nicholas.

Dani's face dropped. 'I don't know … we didn't arrange anything and we didn't swap numbers. The minibus was leaving so I had to rush off.'

'At least we know where he lives,' said Tracy, a little more settled that she was not about to lose her best friend to some guy from Edinburgh called Nicholas.

CHAPTER 3

A heavy fall of snow during the week and sunny weather forecast for the weekend had brought an influx of visitors to Auchenmore. Tracy looked at her watch – *an hour to go* – then to the dwindling stack of trollies by the door and on to the car park, where vehicles were still arriving. 'I'll do a sweep and see what I can find,' she told her manager, and putting on her hi-vis coat and woollen hat and gloves, she headed out.

It didn't take long to find her quarry. Trollies abandoned between cars, in parking bays and stuck in snowbanks created by earlier clearing. Stacking each onto a crocodile secured with a long strap, she gathered what seemed a manageable number and began the traverse across the incline of the car park back to the store. The slippery conditions caused people to shuffle penguin-like, inadvertently hampering her way. Tracy soon found the crocodile rotating left, downhill towards parked cars, and on the slippery surface it seemed impossible to stop them.

A large German SUV pulled into a bay ahead and a severe-looking man with dark curly hair got out of the driver's side. She could hear him talk harshly to a boy she assumed to be his son, who had alighted from the passenger side. The boy was about her age, and wearing loose jeans, trainers and a T-shirt, was wrestling with a baggy hoodie. There was a familiarity about him that caught her attention.

The father was haranguing his son. 'Listen, laddie. If you have a problem, talk to your mother about it, because being here with you isn't my idea of a good weekend.' He then glanced over to Tracy struggling with the trollies and gave what she took to be a contemptuous look before heading towards the shop. She took an instant dislike to him. *It will serve you right if you slip on your arse*, she thought, while at the same time wondering why, yet again, she was letting someone like that bother her.

The boy had now sorted his hoodie and also noticed her struggling. He made brief eye contact then dashed to the front of the crocodile.

'I'm on it,' he said, halting their descent then pulling the front of the stack towards the shop.

Relieved, Tracy thanked him, adding, 'I thought I'd had it there.'

'No worries,' he replied as they continued to the safety of the supermarket canopy.

'Thanks again. I can manage now,' Tracy said, but he had already unclipped the strap and was pushing batches of trollies into the storage bays.

'Are you on holiday?' she asked, having lost interest in what she was there for.

'Mm, not really,' he replied, pushing the last trolley into the stack. 'I'm staying up here for a few months. We have one of those chalets on the back road.'

The job completed, he put his hands in his trouser pockets looked down at his feet, then shyly up at her.

She reached out a gloved hand. 'I'm Tracy.'

'And I'm Nicholas, Nicholas Fraser,' shaking her hand.

'Oh … I think you might know my friend, Dani?'

'Dani, from the outdoor centre who teaches skiing?'

'Yes, that's her.'

He was about to speak when his father reappeared. 'What the hell do you think you're doing? I don't have all night.'

Looking acutely embarrassed, Nicholas turned and followed him obediently into the shop. Tracy watched him go, then found a task to strategically position herself near the checkouts, waiting for him to reappear. She eventually spotted him and his father at one of the further away stations, looking glum as he helped to pack their shopping. Nicholas looked furtively through the milling customers and spotted her, then averted his gaze.

She spent the rest of her shift wondering about this boy who had shown her kindness. He must have known the trouble it would get him into, yet he'd still gone out of his way to help. But there was Dani. How serious was she about him?

Dani and Tracy's expectations heightened as loud music, bursts of laughter and raucous voices streamed down the steps that led up to The Alpine.

'It's busy for the time of year,' Dani noted, receiving a nod from Tracy. They entered through the door beside the bar, into the large, rectangular lounge. Constructed with an A-frame ceiling and dormer windows down either side, the room was fitted out with built-in cushion seats, round tables and stools. At the far end, huge windows gave a panoramic view onto moonlit mountains below a starry sky.

Dani looked around to see who was there. She acknowledged a few local faces but for once her interest was more in the visitors.

Tracy spotted a vacant table between a couple browsing the bar supper menu and a group poring over a map. 'There's space there,' she said, and Dani gave up her search and followed her.

'It's my round. The usual?' Tracy asked. Dani nodded then sat down to occupy herself with her phone.

'Hello, Dani!' Startled, she looked up to see Nicholas standing there, dressed in a grey sweatshirt and navy blue outdoor trousers with black patches.

Her heart skipped a beat. 'Oh, hiya,' she said. For some reason, words had become difficult to find, and she lamely completed the sentence with, 'I like your trousers.'

He glanced down in case of anything untoward – the zip perhaps – then back to Dani. 'I bought them in Edinburgh.'

'Oh,' she said, and they both smiled, aware that this was not the conversation they had anticipated.

'Did you ski this week?' she asked, looking for a

topic to share.

He nodded. 'I saw you on the hill.'

'You should have come and said hello. Why didn't you?'

'I was going to, but you seemed busy with your group.'

She looked mischievous. 'That wouldn't have stopped me having a chat.'

Tracy returned clutching two spritzers. Initially surprised to see her, Nicholas then remembered Tracy mention her friendship with Dani when they'd met at the supermarket. Recalling how his father had embarrassed him in front of her, he suddenly felt uncomfortable.

'Hi, Tracy,' he said, trying to avoid eye contact.

With drinks in hand, she looked at Nicholas, and then Dani, assuming Nicholas's awkwardness was on account of her arrival.

'Am I interrupting?'

He shook his head. 'No, I saw Dani and just came over to say hello.'

He was about to say more when a loud girl at the bar called over, 'Nicholas, are you coming back … or have you turned native with the yokels?' looking at Dani and Tracy in turn.

Somebody in the group said something to the girl. 'What? It's just an expression,' she protested.

Nicholas fidgeted. 'Rebecca's always like that,' but Tracy was now exchanging looks with the girl.

'So she's a friend of yours, is she?' Tracy asked.

'We were at school together,' he replied. Then looking at Dani, he plucked up the courage. 'Would you be up for a ski this week?'

'Tuesday's my day off – if you're free then?'

'I'll make sure I am.'

'Great,' she said. 'Nine o'clock in front of the café. I can get a lift up with the minibus.'

He was about to say it would be an early start for him but opted for, 'I look forward to it. Let me give you my number – just in case.'

He gave her his number and she dialled it then hung up as soon as it rang in his pocket.

With a drink too many, Rebecca at the bar was becoming obstreperous and the group were readying to leave.

'I'd better go,' said Nicholas. 'See you on Tuesday.'

Sensing that Tracy felt left out, Dani tried to reassure her. 'He would have asked you along, but you don't ski.'

'He doesn't know that though, does he?' she replied.

However, Dani was no longer listening as she entered 'Nicholas' to the number on her phone.

Nicholas spotted the outdoor centre minibus. An instructor was handing out skis to a group of apprehensive-looking teenagers, but there was no sign of Dani. He wondered whether she had been put off by the overcast sky – despite the fresh fall of snow it had brought. Or perhaps she was already waiting? Then he saw her, crouched down as she sorted her boots.

He parked a little way off and after hurried

preparations, was outside the café for her arrival.

'You've not been waiting long have you?' she asked with a cheeky grin, then added, 'I saw you arrive.'

He glanced at his watch, wondering whether he was late, then realised Dani was teasing. 'Come on,' she said. 'Let's get some runs in before the fresh snow's tracked out.'

Once again time went by in a blur as they chatted their way up the tows then searched for increasingly elusive patches of fresh snow to descend. It seemed to Nicholas that the girl in the coffee van was right: Dani was popular. Everywhere they went, someone would say, 'Hi, Dani,' and she would introduce Nicholas, making him feel a part of the scene.

By one o'clock the clouds were starting to relent. 'Are you hungry?' he asked. 'I can get us something from the café.' But Dani had a packed lunch, dashing his hopes of treating her.

'I've plenty for two of us,' she said, and suggested a place to stop.

They sat on an outcrop of rocks. Dani took off her helmet, shook out her bob of hair and put on her beanie. She had applied a little mascara and as Nicholas's eyes met hers she smiled. He smiled back, and then looked away, self-conscious at how good she made him feel. She was something wonderful, in a life that, he suddenly realised, had felt empty for a long time.

She took a paper bag from her backpack and handed him a cheese and pickle sandwich and a small carton of juice. He started on the sandwich.

'Do you not use the café?' he asked.

Dani shook her head, 'Not on my wages. Besides, I like eating cheese and pickle sandwiches every day.'

'So do I,' he said, a little too keenly to be credible.

'Liar,' she said, with a smile.

Her sandwich finished, she gathered a handful of snow into a ball and threw it.

Nicholas tried the same but his fell short, much to her amusement.

'You're rubbish,' she laughed, then noticing his coy expression, wondered whether he had deliberately let her win.

She snapped a biscuit in two and offered him half.

'That's OK,' he said.

'Take it,' she insisted. 'What did you do before you came to Auchenmore?'

'Oh, not much, I was at college in Edinburgh, but it didn't work out.'

'What were you studying?'

'The same subjects as the year before at school. Then some stuff happened with my parents – well, my dad actually – so Mum thought it best if I came here.'

'Do you not get on with your dad?' remembering Tracy's mention of Nicholas, his father and the supermarket.

'No, not really.'

'What does he do?' she asked.

'He's the financial director for a company in Edinburgh.'

She put what was left from the lunch into her pack. 'He sounds very important.'

'He thinks he is. What about your dad? What does he do?'

'He has a bike shop in Inverness.'

'Do you get on with him?'

Dani smiled. 'Yes, we get on well. But we have to – there's only the two of us. Mum died when I was born.'

'Oh, I'm so sorry. That must be tough.'

'I'm used to it. I'll show you her picture if you like,' and before he had a chance to answer, Dani had her phone out and was showing him the image of a photograph.

'What was her name?' Nicholas asked as he looked at the young woman in a floral dress.

'Isla,' replied Dani. 'My middle name.'

Nicholas continued looking at the picture and the resemblance to Dani. 'She's really pretty,' and as he looked at Dani, he once again felt feelings he had never felt before. It excited him, but at the same time, left him a bit scared. He stood up. 'Let's get some more runs in, and then I'll buy us both a hot chocolate.'

'You don't need to do that,' she said, putting her helmet back on. 'But you can if you want to!'

He reached out and pulled her back onto her feet. 'I want to.'

'Thanks,' she said, clipping her boots back into her bindings. 'And thanks for the nice thing you said about my mum. I'm working tomorrow morning but free in the afternoon. You're probably busy though?'

Nicholas texted first thing to say he'd bring their lunch, and they met at the rocky outcrop, Dani still wearing her instructor jacket.

'I didn't want to keep you waiting,' she said. 'What have you got there?' her eyes on the two paper bags he had laid out. He handed her one.

'It's cheese and pickle: I know how much you like them. Mine's pastrami and salad.'

She lunged for his bag and he lay back on the snow keeping it from her grasp, so she reached further, her body touching his as she scrabbled for the prize. 'I surrender,' he said, both of them now laughing. 'There's no cheese and pickle. Coronation chicken or pastrami. You choose.'

Dani was tucking in when Nicholas's phone rang. She watched him check the screen then cancel the call.

'Who was that?' she mumbled through a mouthful of pastrami and rye.

'My mum.'

'What if it's important?'

'Then she'll text me.'

He pocketed the phone and to Dani's delight, retrieved more goodies from his pack. As they munched on cereal bars, Dani spotted something.

'Look,' she whispered, pointing to another outcrop of rocks. 'Don't move or you'll scare her.'

Nicholas craned his neck to see what she had seen and then spotted a movement.

'It's a ptarmigan,' Dani said, taking in the snow-white bird with feathery legs.

'You don't see many of those in Edinburgh,' he joked.

'No, you wouldn't,' as though he was serious. 'She belongs in the mountains. If you took her away from here, her heart would break. She would never survive.'

The little bird puffed her feathers, flicked her head into the snow and reappeared with a sprig of heather in her beak.

Dani giggled. 'Isn't she gorgeous? Just perfect.'

But Nicholas wasn't looking at the ptarmigan; it was Dani, her pretty face lit up with excitement, that had his attention. *Yes, you are*, his heart was saying.

A skier passed by, waving to Dani and breaking the moment. Dani waved back and then turned to Nicholas. 'I've got an idea. I have two days off next week. Have you ever been to Waterfall Bothy?'

He shook his head. 'No. I've heard of it, but never been.'

'Would you like to go? It only takes a few hours to get there. We could do it in a day, or stay the night? It will be quite cold, but I can get everything we need from the centre. What do you think?'

'I think it's a brilliant idea.'

Still wearing her coat, Tracy stared absently out of the coffee shop window as she waited for Dani. The high winds and snow that had closed the mountain were nothing more than a depressing drizzle down in Auchenmore. She empathised with the disappointment on people's faces as they wandered about burdened with skis, rucksacks and dashed hopes.

I should have gone shopping in Inverness, rather than wasting my day off here. Better still, moved to Inverness and made something of my life.

'A penny for your thoughts,' said the man behind the counter, but before she could answer, a bedraggled group entered with a kerfuffle of wet coats being removed and the shifting of chairs.

The door opened again and Dani entered.

'Sorry I'm a bit late,' she said. 'One of the kids lost a shoe and held us up.'

'It's OK, I'm not going anywhere,' Tracy replied. 'Would you like a hot chocolate?'

'I'll get them,' offered Dani.

But Tracy insisted, 'No, my treat.'

Standing at the counter, she looked back at Dani, who was laughing at something on her phone and tapping away on the keyboard. *Nicholas Fraser, no doubt.* Her gloom deepened. *How, with no effort, did Dani meet someone? And how, out of all the people who visit Auchenmore, did he turn out to be the same boy I met?*

Back at the table, she went straight to what was on her mind. 'How're things with Nicholas?' her fleeting glance at the phone telling Dani she knew who she was messaging.

Dani shifted in her seat. 'Oh, fine. We're just friends, though. That's all,' feeling that she needed to clarify the point.

However, from the upbeat look on her face, Tracy concluded that either there was, or soon would be, more to it.

'Well, I hope he's not like his father.'

'What do you mean by that?' Dani asked.

'The time I told you about when I met them at the supermarket. The way his dad put him down. It was so embarrassing. Anyway, I suppose it's none of my business. Do you fancy a night out on Friday?'

'Oh … I thought you were working?'

'I was, but they've changed the rota.'

Dani looked at her hands wrapped around her mug, then awkwardly up at Tracy. 'I'm afraid I can't. I've arranged to spend the night at Waterfall Bothy … with Nicholas.'

Tracy moved sharply back in her seat. 'Spend the night together? You just told me you were only friends.'

'We are,' protested Dani. 'It's a bothy trip, that's all. You can come too if you want? I just thought it wasn't your type of thing.'

'My type of thing? Like the skiing, I suppose.'

Dani looked disappointed. 'I thought you would be pleased for me?'

Tracy calmed down. 'I'm sorry. I am pleased for you, Dani. It's just that I'm feeling a bit rubbishy at the moment. I thought leaving school and starting a job would lead to something exciting. But it's not worked out that way. And seeing how well you get on with Nicholas doesn't help. I thought when I met him that time, he might be someone *I* could get along with. Then I find out that you beat me to it.'

'Would you prefer I didn't go with him? If it's upsetting you, Tracy, I can make an excuse.'

'No, don't do that on my account. I'll get past it –

I always do. But I'm starting to wonder – is this it? Working at a supermarket and going home to Mum every night?'

'But you've got other interests.'

'Such as?'

'Well, your police work. You enjoy being a Special, don't you?'

Tracy forced a smile. 'Running around in a police car isn't exactly a substitute for a boyfriend, is it? I'll be OK, Dani. It's probably just this weather.' But she knew the reason behind her despondency was the knowledge that Nicholas had chosen Dani over her. *He clearly isn't interested in me. Am I that boring?*

Dani appeared at the front door of the centre carrying a large rucksack.

'I know,' she said, seeing Nicholas eye its size. 'Big for one night, isn't it?'

But when he opened the hatchback she realised her rucksack was minuscule compared to his.

'What have you got there?' she asked.

'Oh, just a few bits and bobs for comfort, but the biggest item is the wood.'

'I said we'd need *some* wood, not a forest,' she joked. 'It'll be a nightmare carrying that.'

They drove to the car park next to the snow gates, and leaving some of the wood behind, took a footpath diagonally up through the trees, chatting as they went. With the route steepening they soon felt overdressed. Stopping to remove a layer, they shared a cereal bar then pushed onwards. The path eventually reached a gorge where it became a scramble. A slip would see a fall of over sixty feet into the boulder-strewn stream below. They paused to catch their breath and watch the cascading water, its spray swirling in the air.

Thirty minutes later the forest thinned, with the few remaining trees stunted by the alpine tundra. Shortly after, they reached a deer fence. They passed through a tall gate for walkers and on to heathery scrubland before the gradient eased and they met the snow. Ahead, lay a series of cairns marking the way, but otherwise the blanket of white was unbroken.

'Why are there so many?' Nicholas asked.

'In case the weather closes in. Have you ever been in a whiteout?'

He shook his head, so Dani explained. 'It's frightening. You can't see a thing, not even the ground beneath your feet. Even with a map and compass, it would be easy to get lost.'

'Has that ever happened?' he asked, and Dani nodded.

'A few years ago two people got caught out not far from here. It was really sad,' but she didn't elaborate.

Dani took the lead until up ahead, sitting on a small hummock, was Waterfall Bothy.

A simple stone-built affair with a grey corrugated iron roof, a door in the middle, and symmetrically placed windows on either side, it blended with the landscape as though part of the original creation. Nicholas cleared the snow from the entrance with an old shovel left for the purpose, and then pressed the latch and the two of them entered.

He looked around the sparse interior formed by a rough floor and stone walls. 'Do they do room service?' he asked, gazing up to the exposed trusses that supported the gabled roof and receiving a smile back from Dani.

On the right were two wooden chairs and a rudimentary table marked with countless scores and burns, and built into the gable wall was a fireplace with a simple grate and a heavy metal poker. The stone mantelpiece supported an accumulation of wine bottles with initials written on their labels and now serving as wax-laden candlestick holders. 'Those must be the names of the visitors who brought them here,' Nicholas observed.

At the opposite end of the room was a rudimentary wooden sleeping platform. Looking to catch the remaining light, Dani opened the flimsy curtains. They emptied their rucksacks of everything they would need for the evening then set off to explore the nearby waterfall.

By eight o'clock they had heated and eaten the ready meals bought from a climbing shop in Auchenmore, followed by a trifle. Nicholas opened a surprise bottle of wine and put another of their hard-earned pieces of wood onto the fire. Wearing their jackets, they pulled their chairs close and sat catching its warmth while the flickering flames danced light and shadows across the room.

Dani sipped the wine from her mug. 'This is lovely,' she commented. 'Not the vinegar I usually end up with. What is it?'

'Chateau Lagrange,' he replied.

None the wiser, she retrieved the stub of a pencil from the mantelpiece and scribbled the initials DB and NF – together with two smiley faces – onto the label. 'There. We're now part of the history of Waterfall Bothy.'

Pulling her chair a little closer to Nicholas's, she sat down again and he decided now was the moment to talk. 'One of the reasons I came to Auchenmore was to think about what I want to do in the future. I have an idea that I'd like to share with you.'

'Go on. Tell me,' intrigued as to what it might be.

'I've been looking into setting up an outdoor business. Something small to start with, hiring out mountain bikes. I was wondering whether you would like to join me? You must know so much about bikes, with your dad having a shop.'

She looked sceptical. 'Where would I get the money? Getting it off the ground would cost a small fortune, and I've got my job to think about.'

'I've given it a lot of thought and written a plan. I've even been to the bank. They're prepared to lend most of the money if I get a guarantor. I'm going to Edinburgh next week to see if Mum will do that.'

'Do you think she will?'

'I hope so. If Grandad were alive he definitely would, and Mum's quite like him. If she agrees, I could get everything organised here, then perhaps when the season finishes we could squeeze in a few weeks' skiing in Chamonix before we start.'

Dani looked at him, smiled, and then returned to the fire. 'Stop teasing me, Nicholas.'

'I'm not teasing you … We could ski the Vallée

Blanche.'

Her eyes widened. 'Skiing the Vallée Blanche is one of my dreams. Have you done it?'

He nodded. 'On a school trip.'

'What was it like?'

'Magical! You take two cable cars to the top of the Midi, and then descend a don't-look-down type of rope and ski off into the valley. It's the most amazing place ever. A sea of snow and ice surrounded by huge mountains. I remember stopping at some rocks for lunch and just staring at the scenery.'

He looked at Dani. 'I wanted that moment to last forever,' then turned away, flustered at having shared a feeling so close to how he felt being beside her now.

She looked at him, thinking of Chamonix and the Vallée Blanche and what it would be like to be there, with him. 'Just say we did go, where would we stay?'

'Oh, there are lots of hostels and places like that. Maybe we could get an old van and kit it out as a camper?'

'Well, let's see what your parents say.'

'My mum,' he corrected.

'Not your dad then?'

He took a sip of wine and stared at the fire. 'My dad's not nice, Dani. I know I shouldn't say that about my father, but it's true.'

She linked her arm through Nicholas's and rested her head on his shoulder. 'Well let's see what your mum says then.'

And as he sat with the girl he was falling in love with, Nicholas had the feeling that for the first time in his life someone believed in him.

***

He laid the papers he had prepared out on the kitchen table and talked through his idea. 'What do you think, Mum? Do you like it? I've been working on this all winter.'

She looked at the rows of numbers neatly printed in little boxes, the brochures for bikes, the map and a copy of the email Nicholas had received from the bank. *He may have finally found something to which he can apply himself. He must be serious, to make it worth the trip from Auchenmore and the risk of an encounter with Hamish.*

'It sounds like a good idea, Nicholas, and it does look as though you've put a lot of thought into it, but I'm not sure it would be wise for either of us to do this without your father knowing.'

'I'm not asking for much money,' he pressed. 'The main thing I need is for you to act as guarantor.'

He could see from the way she was shifting between him, the papers and the door that she felt compromised. 'Does he even have to know, Mum?'

'Nicholas, what if it goes wrong? No, it's better for both of us if Hamish knows about this.'

He started to gather the papers. 'I might as well forget it then,' he said flatly. Would the hold his father had over them never end?

'You don't know that for certain,' she said, but they both knew that, given an opportunity to work against them, Hamish would take it.

They heard the front door opening then banging shut. 'That'll be him,' Miriam stated. But Nicholas already knew. Years of sensing Hamish's whereabouts and anticipating his moods and moves had tuned Nicholas's awareness of him to a high pitch. Besides, who else would it be? Nicholas visualised him going through his ritual: putting his briefcase down on the hall chair, removing his scarf, then coat, and hanging them on the stand by the door.

They heard him shout through. 'I won't be having supper. I'm going out.'

'Hamish, Nicholas is here,' Miriam called from the kitchen door. 'He has something he wants our opinion on,' her deferential voice hoping to appease.

'I know he is. I'm not stupid. I saw his mess.'

'See?' said Nicholas, but Miriam persisted.

'Hamish, come through for a moment, will you? He's here especially to show us.'

At the sound of his approaching steps, Miriam moved to the end of the table.

'What?' he grunted, standing tall in the doorway in his pinstriped suit and white shirt, his gold silk tie hanging loose.

Nicholas looked cautiously at him, his stomach tightening at the sight of his face. 'I was wondering whether I could talk you through an idea I have. It won't take long.'

Without speaking, Hamish moved to the table, picked up the spreadsheet and with a display of superiority ran his eyes along the bottom line.

'Huh, no chance,' he said, tossing the paper down. 'You'd be better putting your money on the dogs. No doubt you want my money for this nonsense?'

'I don't need much money. The main thing I need is a guarantor for a bank loan. Can I talk you through the plan?'

'Was I not clear? The answer is no.'

His mother interjected. 'Hamish, how do you know it's not a good idea if you haven't listened to him?'

'Leave it, Mum, it doesn't matter.'

Hamish gave his wife a menacing look then turned to Nicholas. 'I know it will fail, because you always fail.'

Miriam interjected. 'That's not fair, Hamish.'

'Isn't it?' he said, his eyes now squarely on Nicholas. 'You come out of school with two Ds for Highers – a bloody mess after we spent a small fortune on your education – and then think you can set up a business.'

Miriam didn't challenge him, even though they all knew her father had covered the school fees.

Nicholas tried to explain why this would be different. 'I know about this. It's what I enjoy; I can be good at it. The Higher subjects weren't my thing. Remember, I wanted to do Graphic Design and Environmental Science? I would have done well in those, even the teachers said so. But you wanted me to do Maths and Economics. They were your subjects, not mine. I tried, I did, but I couldn't get my head around them.'

'Ah, my fault,' Hamish mocked. 'Never yours, is it?'

Nicholas took a deep breath, 'I'm not saying that,' and Miriam tried to speak up for him.

'He did try, Hamish. You saw the effort he put in. Perhaps we should have taken the teachers' advice.'

Hamish returned to Miriam, 'Shut up,' then rounded on Nicholas. 'You can't add two numbers, but you put a half-arsed spreadsheet together and expect me to waste my time looking at it?'

Knowing this wasn't going anywhere, Miriam stepped in. 'Perhaps we'll talk about it another time,' but Hamish wanted the final word. 'I'm not sure which part of this you don't understand, Miriam. I said no. Now I'm going to get changed. You've held me up long enough with this stupidity.'

As he left the room, Nicholas muttered to his mother, 'I told you so.'

Hamish overheard, turned on his heel and came back. 'What did you say?'

'I just said, "I told you so".'

'Told her what?' he questioned, sensing a fight he was determined to win.

'That you wouldn't listen to me,' replied Nicholas.

'I never listen to you? Nobody ever bloody listens to you, do they? Well, you listen here, laddie, you're a fucking embarrassment and always have been.'

Nicholas remained passive, but his mother could

see his hands shaking and eyes reddening.

'And you've never embarrassed me?' he said, looking down at the papers.

Sensing imminent danger, Miriam spoke up. 'Hamish, you get changed. Nicholas, you can have supper, then I think it's best if you head back north this evening.'

But Nicholas hadn't finished.

'When I was at prep school, one of the boys said, "Your father sleeps with other women." It's what he had heard his mother say. Was that not embarrassing for me? And what about Mum? How do you think your affairs have made her feel?'

On the cusp of being overwhelmed, Nicholas continued, determined to release what he had stifled for years.

'That was when I was eight years old. At senior school, they referred to you as, "The Shagger". How do you think that made me feel?'

Hamish's eyes darkened and Miriam realised that if Nicholas went any further, she would be powerless to protect him. 'Please, stop it NOW, Nicholas,' she warned.

But he continued. 'Do you think people don't know that you abuse us? That you beat your wife and your son? And you call *me* an embarrassment?'

A hand swung towards him, he tried to duck, but his reaction was too slow, his head taking the full impact of the blow.

Through a foggy mind, he could hear his mother screaming and then her distant voice. 'Nicholas! Nicholas! What have you done, Hamish? What have you done?'

His father was shouting back. 'Don't be so bloody self-righteous, woman. You tried to kill him yourself before he was even born. You never wanted the child, and neither did I. Now for your own sake, make sure he keeps his mouth shut.'

The front door banged, then silence. As his head cleared, Nicholas realised he was on the floor with his mother holding a damp tea towel to the side of his face. He tried to get up but couldn't. 'Is he still here?' he asked, trying to search past her.

'No, he's left. But Nicholas, you need to go. Let me help you up.'

He got unsteadily to his feet and sat on a kitchen chair. Bewildered by what he had heard, he asked, 'Is it true, Mum? Did you try to do that?'

'Do what?' she asked, but he could tell from her frightened look and the way her eyes avoided his that she knew what he was talking about. 'Nicholas, it's not safe for you here. You need to go.'

'I want to go, Mum. I've never felt safe here. But tell me, did you try to do that?'

She wouldn't answer his question, her thoughts returning to her habitual fear. 'You won't say anything about this to anyone, will you, Nicholas?'

'That's the problem. We never say anything. We just suffer in silence. But everyone knows. He's an evil bastard, Mum, that's all he is. An evil bastard.'

She started to prepare a sandwich for him to take with him, but her shaking hand was unable to hold the knife. Banging it down in frustration, she bowed her head, squeezing her eyes closed to shut out the awfulness. And as Nicholas looked at her he thought how saving Hamish's life had only prolonged their misery. He reached forward to touch her arm, wanting to tell her how desperately sorry he was for what he had done, and of the never-ending pain that knowledge was causing him, but he couldn't get the words out.

She took some notes from her purse and thrust them into his hand.

'Take this. It might be safer for you to stay in a hotel tonight rather than drive north.'

He put the money on the table. 'I don't want it this time,' remembering the little Land Rover she had given him as a bribe the first time he had witnessed his father hit her.

Standing at the front door he looked back at her. 'You want to know why I pushed him? It's because I can't stand this anymore. I want it to end, and if he had hit me a bit harder, it would have.

CHAPTER 4

Dani looked anxiously across the car park for Nicholas then glanced at her watch. He was late. That wasn't like him. Then again, it had taken three texts to get a reply, and even though he'd agreed to join her and her friends, he'd seemed reluctant.

She was about to give up when he appeared, shoulders hunched and hands pushed deep into his jacket pockets, walking slowly from the direction of the station.

She waved and set off across the car park to meet him, but he didn't respond, adding to her suspicion that something was wrong. Gone was his usual cheery greeting. He looked pale, his woollen hat pulled down over his ears and his collar turned up.

'Happy twentieth,' she said, kissing him on the cheek.

He forced a smile, and then looked away.

'Are you OK?' she asked.

'I'm fine.'

'Why didn't you answer my calls? I was starting to worry about you.'

'I was busy. Shall we go inside?'

'Well, can you at least tell me how you got on in

Edinburgh? I've been thinking about your idea for the bikes. I'm excited about it. Did your mum agree to help?'

'Can we talk about that later?' he said, then walked off towards the door.

For a moment she stood watching him, and then followed, trying to figure out what was happening. Only a week ago they had sat together in Waterfall Bothy, excited about plans for Chamonix and an outdoor business. Now, it didn't seem to matter to him.

The others were sitting around a table looking at menus. Tracy glanced at Nicholas, then turned her attention to Dani. 'I've kept a seat for you,' waving at a single stool opposite her.

'Thanks,' Dani replied, taking off her jacket and putting it on the floor. Conscious that Nicholas was looking lost, she collected another stool from nearby and put it beside her own – an act she knew wouldn't be lost on Tracy.

Still wearing his hat and coat, Nicholas sat down, barely acknowledging the others as they wished him a happy birthday. Dani handed him a menu then shortly afterwards nudged to get his attention.

'What is it?' he asked.

'I said if you took your hat off, perhaps you'd hear me.'

Reaching out, she playfully tried to grab the hat, dislodging it. Seeing it coming he swiftly raised his arm to stop her, then pulled the hat back down, but not before she saw the deep-blue bruise running from the bottom of his ear upwards. She looked at him in shock and he looked back, ashamed. Aware of the kerfuffle, the others in the group stopped talking. His emotions building, Nicholas looked around, unsure who had seen what, and then stood up and rushed out.

Dani grabbed her jacket and followed him.

'Nicholas! Nicholas!'

He carried on walking until she caught up, then stopped and leaned against a wall, staring at the ground.

'What happened?' she asked, but he didn't answer, his eyes closed, as though blocking the world out.

She persisted, 'Who did that to you?' Then, putting together all she had heard, added, 'It was your father, wasn't it?'

She noticed his hands now shaking uncontrollably and his shoulders moving up and down in little rhythmic motions. He was crying.

'Oh Nicholas, it breaks my heart to see you like this,' she said, putting her arms around him and pressing her head against his chest. She could feel his jacket against her face and smell the woody freshness of his aftershave and smoke from the chalet stove.

He didn't respond, as though disconnected from the world.

Eventually, she let go. He took a tissue from his pocket and blew his nose.

'Please, Dani, I don't want to talk about it.'

'But I can help you, Nicholas. If you've been hit, we should tell someone.'

He shook his head. 'No, I don't want to do that. No one can help. Look at me, Dani, I'm a mess.'

Then he took her hand. 'I'm sorry for raising your hopes, but the plans we talked about are dead, all of them. I wasn't even meant to be here.'

'What are you saying, Nicholas? What do you mean by that?'

'My father's an evil man who destroys everything good. That's all he knows. Go back inside, and please, don't say anything to the others; tell them I felt unwell.' Just as his mother had taught him.

Dani nodded. 'If you don't want to go back in then that's OK, I'll come with you.'

He shook his head. 'No, you don't have to do that.'

'I know I don't, but that's what friends do. They look out for each other, don't they?'

He managed a faint smile.

'Thanks, Dani, you *are* a good friend, I know that, but stay here.'

She watched him walk away, a forlorn and dejected figure, till he disappeared. Something had broken in him, she knew it. Then she looked up at the night sky and saw the moon encircled by a halo: a sign of an impending storm and, as mythology would have it, an omen of great upheaval.

After a week of hearing nothing from Nicholas, a text inviting her to a belated birthday party at the chalet was the last thing Dani had expected.

She called him and when he eventually answered she asked, 'How are you feeling?'

'Fine,' he replied, as if to say, 'Why wouldn't I be?'

'I just thought that …' but he brushed her off.

'I'm in a bit of a hurry, Dani – getting things ready for the party.'

She tried to work it out. Was the incident with his father an accident? Or did Nicholas now think he had overreacted? Maybe his parents had had a change of heart and agreed to help him, or he'd come up with another plan. Whatever it was, she hoped they could still go to Chamonix and figure the rest out afterwards.

She cadged a lift from the centre minibus as it went about the Saturday evening chip shop run.

'It's forecast to snow later. Give me a phone if you need a lift back,' the driver offered. 'Or maybe you plan to stop over?'

'Thanks, I'll let you know,' she said, evading his mischievous look.

'Well, it looks as though you'll have a good time,' he continued, eyeing the abundance of parked cars and curtains pulsating with light.

Wearing a ski-themed sweatshirt, jeans and snow boots, Dani had decided to be true to her personality rather than dressing to impress. A schoolfriend who ran a home salon had tidied her bob and she'd applied a little make-up to highlight her features.

Standing outside, she was surprised by the appearance of the place. For a family she had assumed were well-to-do, it all looked rather run-down. A heap of skis lay dumped on the wooden terrace, the damp rusting their edges. *What a way to treat your stuff*, Dani thought, moving a pair that impeded the doorway.

The mix of music and competing voices from inside drowned her knock, so she made her entrance, shuffling a group from behind the door as it opened. The party seemed well underway, the hall bustling with people, some with drinks in hand, some already drunk and others pushing past to get to the toilet. Strobes lit the sitting room to her right, synchronised to music conjured by a local guy with two laptops who DJ'd in his spare time. The furniture had been set to one side, allowing for dancers who threw their hands into the air and shouted something indecipherable on the DJ's command.

She took off her coat, dumped it on a pile in the corner, and set about looking amongst the throng for Nicholas. She spotted him in the kitchen at the far end of the hall, holding a beer bottle and engrossed in an animated conversation with a group she presumed to be friends from Edinburgh. After all the time they had spent together, it was odd not having him to herself. She felt uneasy about joining them, so instead, sidled up to an acquaintance who worked as a receptionist in a local hotel.

'Do you know any of these people?' she asked.

'I know *of* them,' came the reply. 'Most have stayed with us at one time or another.' The girl pointed to several individuals, citing their mainly double-barrelled names. Surprised by how different they sounded from the names of people she knew, Dani asked, 'Does anybody have a normal name?'

'No, no, no,' said the girl, wagging a reproaching

finger and pursuing her lips for effect. 'A simple name would never be good enough. It would be far too common,' leaving Dani feeling even more out of place.

A girl wearing a cream-coloured off-the-shoulder jumper and an expensive blow-dry looked down from where she was sitting on the stairs. Recognising her as the noisy Rebecca from Nicholas's group in The Alpine, Dani attempted a smile but regretted her overtures when the girl returned a disparaging look, her nostrils pinched as if smelling something disagreeable.

The evening marched on with plenty to drink and a pizza delivery large enough to satisfy a full festival.

Dani made forced conversation with a few of the revellers while becoming increasingly irked that Nicholas seemed to have time for everyone but her.

'Hang fire, I'll be back in a moment,' he said when she caught him passing

She watched as he laughed and joked in a manner at odds with the Nicholas she knew; his behaviour seemed contrived and fuelled by alcohol.

A bristly-faced guy wearing cargo trousers and a half-zip Aran sweater wandered over to her.

'Having fun?' he asked.

'Not really,' she said, glancing at him before returning her gaze to the room.

'I thought not. I'm Herb, an old friend of Nicholas.'

'And I'm Dani.'

Herb gulped from his bottle. 'Nicholas and I go

back to prep school.'

'You've known him a long time then?' her interest piqued.

'About ten years. How about you?'

'I thought I'd known him since December, but after the last week, I don't think I know him at all. Do you know his family?'

'I know his parents, if that's what you mean. His mum's nice but she doesn't say much. Not surprising with the husband she's got.'

Dani picked up the implication. 'I only hear bad stuff about his dad,' her discretion curbed by her disgruntled mood.

Herb nodded and took a long slug to finish the bottle. 'He's not a nice man, Dani. He really isn't.' Then he looked straight at her. 'With one thing and another, Nicholas isn't in a great place right now. Anyway, I'm off in search of beer. Can I get you anything?'

'No, that's OK. This isn't my scene; I'm going to head ...'

She was donning her coat when Nicholas finally appeared. 'Hey, Dani, what's up? Why are you going so soon?'

She looked at him, contrasting who she had met and fallen for with what now stood before her: a drunk with slurred speech.

'I'm going home, Nicholas. This isn't what I expected from you or the party.'

From the depths of his inebriated haze, he sensed her disappointment. 'I know what you're thinking. I'm sorry. Stay a bit longer. We can go and talk upstairs, away from this lot. Then if you want to leave I'll call a taxi … What have you got to lose?'

She thought for a moment, then put her coat back on the pile. 'Well, OK, for a bit,' her decision swayed by her need to understand what was happening between them.

'Great, I'll grab us a drink.'

She touched his arm. 'No, don't. I think you've had enough.'

He accepted her advice and led the way upstairs, missing the second step and landing on his hands before continuing to his parents' bedroom.

Dani sat awkwardly beside him on the settee, clasping her hands away from his reach and looking out through the large patio doors and across a frozen pond to the woods and mountains beyond. From downstairs came the bass notes of homogeneous tracks, thumping like a tribal ritual.

'Tell me, what's going on between us, Nicholas?'

'What do you mean by "going on"?' he asked, as though it were some kind of guessing game.

She pulled herself away to get a better look at him.

'You know what I mean,' irritated that he was making a difficult conversation even harder.

'No, I don't.'

Her mood stiffened further. 'Well, let me spell it out for you. We spend a night together at Waterfall Bothy, where you raise my hopes. You talk about us going to Chamonix and afterwards setting up a business together. We lie together on the bunk in our sleeping bags, kissing, and you saying that you care for me. Afterwards, you go to Edinburgh and come back a mess but won't say what happened. Now you're partying as though you haven't got a care in the world. What's more, you invite me here then ignore me as though I mean nothing to you.' She looked hard at him, her voice straining. 'Was all that stuff you said just a load of nonsense to string me along, and now you're bored with me? Is that it? Because I can't see any other reason.'

He stared out of the window, the look on his face telling Dani that he wasn't sure what to say.

'Come on, Nicholas, level with me. What's this all about?' she pressed.

'Maybe it was a load of nonsense. Shit happens, Dani. You know that.'

She stood up, her face tight and eyes narrowing. 'I believed in you, Nicholas. I trusted you. But you're an idiot, just like those friends of yours.'

'Chill, Dani,' he said, jovially reaching to try and take her hand, but she pulled back, her eyes flashed with anger.

'Don't touch me.'

'Come on, Dani. Don't be like this,' he said, standing up and moving towards her. She stepped further back so he reached quickly, grabbing her hand and pulling her towards him.

Finding herself in a situation that suddenly felt out of control, she lashed out, connecting with his face, 'I said, DON'T!'

He recoiled, falling backwards into the settee, and she rushed to the door and leapt down the stairs.

Herb saw her grab her coat from the pile. 'What's

happened, Dani? Are you OK?' He looked up to the bedroom door, expecting Nicholas to appear. From what he knew of his schoolfriend, none of this made sense.

Dani shook her head, unable to talk, feeling confused and distressed. *How did this happen?*

A now rough-looking Rebecca gawked from the sitting room where she lay recumbent on a settee being groped by a boy with acne. 'Home to Mummy?' Rebecca mocked.

Herb glared at her. 'Shut it,' and Dani's anger followed.

'Get stuffed, bitch,' she shouted, then left, banging the front door shut behind her.

It was now snowing heavily. PC Claire Campbell glanced at SPC Tracy Shaw, not only her buddy-up for the evening but a girl to whom she had taken a liking. Tracy was reliable, and chatty company during what could otherwise be a tedious shift – a young officer whose personality withstood the uniform.

'Have you got anything fun lined up for tomorrow?' Claire asked.

Tracy shook her head. 'Not really. Mum's working, so I'll probably have a duvet day.'

Claire slowed as they drove past the lane end.

'Hopefully, no one's thinking of driving home,' she commented, seeing the cars parked outside the Frasers' chalet and lights from within.

'They're stupid enough to,' Tracy replied, resentful of the party, yet mindful that it was her choice not to attend.

'Do you know Nicholas Fraser?' Claire asked as she flicked the wipers to clear the snow.

'Yes, but he's not my type. Too posh for me.'

Claire gave her a questioning look. 'What do you mean by that?'

'Oh, nothing, let's leave it.'

They carried on, Claire switching to full beam then returning to dip as the light glared back from the voluptuous snowflakes. 'What have we got here?' she asked, peering to get a better look at footprints in the snow.

Flicking back to full beam, they saw a figure standing at the side of the road, poised as if ready to disappear into the woods. 'They won't know who we are,' said Claire, and after a single flash of their blue lights, the figure settled.

Tracy lowered her window. 'Dani, what are you doing out here?'

'Heading home,' she replied, clearly relieved to see their friendly faces.

Tracy looked questioningly. 'Is everything OK?'

'Yes. I'm fine. I was at the party but it wasn't my thing, that's all.'

'Jump in, we'll take you,' Claire offered.

Dani got into the nearside back seat. The car was warm. She could see a police radio blinking on the dashboard and hear Scottish music playing in the background.

Claire's eyes met hers through the rear-view mirror. 'We've been up to Kinloch Bridge. Can you believe a tourist reported deer on the road? I mean, what the …?'

The officers laughed and Tracy chipped in. 'Aye, and snow on the mountains.'

The police radio was now issuing a Lookout Request for a white Transit van stolen from the Inverness area. Dani looked around. She could see a bright red seat belt cutter attached to the dashboard and a control panel for the various emergency lights. It felt safe, being with them. They seemed good-humoured – even though they were working a Saturday night.

As they made their way, Dani sang along softly with the Gaelic song now playing on the radio, comforting after what had happened at the chalet.

'I'll be fluent by the end of the shift,' said Tracy, with a sideways look to make sure Claire had taken it in.

'*Am biodh sin cho dona?*' Claire asked, receiving a blank stare in return.

Dani translated. 'Claire says, "Would that be so bad?"'

Claire caught Dani's eyes again in the mirror. 'Ah, I see you've got the mother tongue.'

'My mum spoke Gaelic,' she replied, as though that would explain it.

Tracy didn't comment and Claire's attention returned to the snowy road. Dani often said things like that, implying some sort of relationship with her departed mother.

They continued, the snow crunching under the tyres and the three of them accompanying the lyrics as best they could and humming where all else failed. 'Good practice for my Gaelic class on Monday,' said Claire.

As Dani looked out of the window into the snowy woods, she reflected on how a life that had seemed so promising when she had left school had since gone into rapid decline. She had hankered after a boy who had now bitterly disappointed her, and no matter how hard she tried, her career seemed to be going nowhere.

'Thanks ever so much,' she said, as they pulled up outside the centre.

'I'll get the door,' said Tracy. 'You can't open it from the inside.'

Tracy now stood in front of her. 'Did something happen between you and Nicholas?' she asked, already knowing the answer.

Dani said nothing so Tracy continued, quietly enough not to be overheard by Claire.

'He could be such a nice guy, but instead, he's an arse. And those idiot friends of his treat everyone like shite.'

Dani nodded. 'I know. Thanks for stopping.'

Tracy now saw that her friend had been crying.

'Oh, come here, lass,' putting her arms around her, but encumbered by all the gear protruding from her stab vest. 'If you want to talk, I'm here for you.'

'There's nothing to talk about, Tracy. Whatever there was between me and Nicholas is over.'

Tracy glared at Nicholas with all the menace she could bring to bear. 'Look what the cat's dragged in,' she said.

Dani followed her stare and immediately regretted being persuaded to come out. Nicholas was at a table with a girl: a pretty girl slightly older than him with her long dark hair tied back. Dani felt her heart skip and her chest tighten as she looked on, transfixed by the sight of the boy she thought she had known so well with another girl. The girl looked friendly; certainly not the pretentious type Dani had witnessed at the party. Nicholas glanced in Dani's direction and she caught his eye, but it was as though he was completely blanking her.

She watched as the girl rubbed his shoulder, and sensed Tracy speaking, like a distant voice in a bad dream. However, the sight of Nicholas and all the accompanying emotions threatened to overwhelm her, so she turned and left.

Tracy seized the moment to confront him.

'You're a real bastard, Nicholas Fraser. You might come from a wealthy family but as a person, you're nobody. You know the value of nothing; Dani's friendship was the best thing you had, and you blew it. How could you have been so nasty to her?'

He didn't respond so the pretty girl with dark hair calmly spoke on his behalf. 'You've made your point, now please go away.'

Tracy left, meeting Dani in the car park. 'I thought you said you weren't bothered about him?' she asked.

'I didn't think I was, but the sight of him with someone else. I mean, he didn't waste any time, did he?'

'He's not worth it, Dani.'

'I know that now,' she said, confused by the contradiction between what she was saying and how she felt. 'Can we just go to your house?'

'Sure.'

They made their way to Tracy's, where Mary prepared them cheese on toast which they ate snuggled up under a duvet on the settee.

***

The last customer left the shop armed with a spare inner tube for their Great Glen cycle ride. Dani locked the door, turned the sign to closed and rearranged a couple of bikes that had been pulled out to view, while Rory cashed up the till.

'That's the best day we've had for a while,' he said. 'It makes a difference having a young face in the shop.'

Summoning the courage, she approached the counter. 'Dad, there's something I need to speak to you about.' Catching her tone, he stopped what he was doing and looked up.

'What is it, Dani?'

'Well …' she started, fidgeting the way she had as a child when she had something awkward to say. 'I've been thinking about my career, and I'm not sure now what future there is in being an outdoor instructor.'

'Well, that's not the end of the world. You can help me here while you think about what really interests you. Perhaps a college course in September? There's still time to apply.'

'I've already decided, Dad.'

'Oh. Well, what is it then?'

'I want to join the police.'

Rory put his palms down on the counter and looked curiously at his daughter. 'The police? Where did this idea come from?'

'I've been thinking about it ever since Tracy joined as a Special. It's a good, steady career with lots of opportunities.'

'That's true. It's just that I've never heard you mention it before. But perhaps it's not such a bad idea. It's a regular income compared to running a bicycle shop. And you'll get plenty of days off to spend in the hills and glens.'

'That's the thing, Dad …'

Her manner told him that he was about to hear something he wouldn't like. 'What *thing*?'

'I've applied for Thames Valley.'

There was a long pause while the implications sank in, then Rory stood up straight.

'You can't go – I won't allow it.'

She stepped forward and took his hand. 'Dad, I'm not your little girl anymore. You can't stop me.'

But Rory wasn't listening. 'This is because of that friend of yours. The one you were so excited about going into business with and then we heard nothing more about. It's why you left that job and came home, isn't it?'

'It's nothing to do with him.'

'Oh, so it's a *him,* is it? A boyfriend. That

explains everything. Just you let me have his name and I'll get this all sorted.'

Despite his bluster, Dani could see her father was upset. She came around to the other side of the counter and put her arm around him. 'I know this is difficult for both of us. We've always been such a tight little team, you and me. But I'm not Mum. I'm not your wife. I'm your daughter and I need to get on with my life.'

***

Claire pulled up in front of the chalet, her thoughts returning to her first visit years before, and the scene of a man with a knife wound, a woman with a concussion and a missing child. Strange to think that child was now the young man she was here to see.

By the smoke rising from the chimney she deduced that Nicholas was home, but his wellbeing needed to be verified.

She knocked and was surprised when a young woman answered.

'Oh, hello. Is Nicholas here? I'd like a word with him – nothing to worry about.'

The young woman stepped outside and pulled the door closed.

'Is this to do with the girl, Dani?' she asked. 'Because if it is, I can tell you now that Nicholas didn't do anything. He's not like that.'

Claire looked inquisitive. 'No, it's nothing to do with her. Is there something I should know about?'

Regretting having mentioned it, the woman shook her head. 'No, there isn't.'

'Well, can I see Nicholas then?' Claire repeated. 'I presume he's here?'

The woman opened the front door and led the way to the sitting room. 'Nicholas, there's a police officer to see you.'

He looked up at Claire from where he was sitting in an armchair, but said nothing.

'Hello, Nicholas. Your mother called us. She's worried about you. She says that you haven't been answering your phone. I'm just here to check that everything's alright.'

He nodded and without looking at Claire, added, 'You can tell her there's nothing to worry about.'

'OK. You're old enough to look after yourself. I'll leave you to it.'

The woman led Claire back to the front door and once again stepped outside and closed it. 'I'm sorry, I should have introduced myself properly. I'm Tess, a friend of Nicholas's from Edinburgh. I think you should know that Nicholas has had some type of breakdown. He won't go and see a doctor so I'm staying up here for a few days to look after him.'

'Oh, I didn't realise. Are you a nurse?'

'No. I'm studying counselling, but I'm not here in a professional capacity – just as a friend.'

'Well, that's good of you,' said Claire. 'I suppose it's my turn to ask, is this to do with the person you mentioned earlier?'

Tess shook her head. 'It goes back much further than that, but Nicholas would need to tell you himself. I'll give his mother a call and let her know he's alright. Thanks for your concern.'

'That's alright, it's what we're here for. His mother will be getting a call from us anyway, but as Nicholas is an adult, what we pass on will be limited.'

Claire was about to leave when Tess stopped her. 'What Nicholas needs is something to build his self-esteem. I shouldn't say this, but it's his father you should be speaking to. That man has done a great job of making his son feel worthless.'

From what she had witnessed years before, Claire wasn't surprised. 'Is Nicholas going to be here for a while?' she asked.

Tess nodded. 'At the moment he has nowhere else to go, but it's not good for him moping around here. What he needs is something positive to focus on.'

Claire unhooked the car keys from her radio aerial. 'Let me ask around. My husband, Geoff, works in a place where they help kids with complex needs; an extra pair of hands might be useful. If not, he may know of somewhere.'

Geoff handed Nicholas the climbing harnesses. 'We need to fit each child with one of these. Make sure it's the right size and the belt is tightened. Then Julie and I will check them.'

Nicholas nodded to say that he understood and Julie grabbed the helmets and hooked the chin straps over her arms. Dressed in outdoor wear and with a cheery nature, she reminded him of Dani.

The trio set off across the yard towards the High

Ropes course, passing an old, short-wheelbase Land Rover on their way. A For Sale sign in the window caught Nicholas's eye.

'It's mine,' said Geoff, noting his curiosity. 'Claire won't let me keep it. She says it's a bottomless money pit.'

'What are you asking for it?'

Geoff scratched his beard. 'You won't thank me for selling you that thing. The engine's fine, but the chassis needs welding and there's a problem with the electrics.'

The High Ropes consisted of ropes, wires and logs strung and suspended at height amongst the trees. Nicholas and Julie laid out the safety equipment and shortly afterwards the children arrived, led by a fit-looking teacher with balding spiky hair and dressed in a tracksuit.

'Give me a moment,' he said to the instructors, then gathered the children. 'Right, quiet everyone. I'm not happy about what happened last night. If I catch any of you smoking in the dormitory again, it will be straight back to Edinburgh. Do you understand me?'

A boy at the rear called, 'Can we just go home today?'

The group looked at him and laughed, making it clear that it wasn't the joke they found funny, but the boy himself. The boy squinted back at them through a pair of thick glasses that sat lopsided on his face, the bridge bound with sellotape, and then wandered off to sit on his own.

The teacher didn't respond, and Geoff and Julie

stepped forward to start the session.

'This activity is called the Leap of Faith,' Geoff announced. He explained that it involved pairs of children being clipped onto safety ropes and climbing a 20-metre ladder of logs. Once up, the children would leap off a platform and grab hold of a trapeze, whereupon they would be lowered to the ground by their instructor. 'There's a prize for anyone who can swing forward, let go and grab the second trapeze,' he added, to murmurs of 'Fuck that' from the children, now craning their necks to see the challenge.

The first pair set off, with Geoff and Julie holding their ropes. They faltered halfway up, but encouraged by the instructors, made it to the top. A half-hearted leap forward on a tight safety rope saw them miss the first trapeze and lowered back to the ground.

Nicholas watched from the side, then, keen to be useful, wandered over to the teacher, who was taking a break.

'Is that lad not doing it?' he asked, indicating the boy with glasses sitting on the grass.

A nearby child overheard and answered on the teacher's behalf. 'Stookie's a crapper.'

The children laughed and Stookie poked the ground with a stick.

'That's enough,' said the teacher, then turned to Nicholas. 'He has a trust issue.'

'Do you mind if I talk to him?' Nicholas asked.

The teacher looked sceptical. 'Listen, son. I don't want to sound rude, but the two of you won't have much in common. You'll be wasting your time, but be my guest.'

Nicholas went over to the boy. 'Is Stookie your proper name?' he asked.

'It's what they call me,' the boy replied without looking up.

'I'm Nicholas.'

The boy stopped what he was doing and cast a critical eye over Nicholas. 'You sound posh,' then resumed his preoccupation with the stick.

Nicholas looked at the boy's hands, the skin flaking with eczema, and then at his clothes, which seemed to be hand-me-downs. Grey flannel trousers that were too short, a school sweatshirt too big and scuffed black shoes.

The group were now goading a hysterical girl who had become stuck at the top of the ladder and convinced herself that she was about to meet her maker.

Nicholas sat himself down beside the boy. 'Why don't you give the ladder a go?'

'Because I don't want to.'

'In case you get stuck?'

The boy didn't answer, so Nicholas suggested another reason. 'Or is it because of them?' he asked, looking towards the group.

As they watched the reprieved girl being lowered, Nicholas asked another question. 'Do you not get sick of other people telling you what you're capable of?'

With still no answer, he made an offer. 'Why don't we give it a go together, you and me, once the others have gone?'

Geoff gave Nicholas a subtle wink as he and Stookie fitted their harnesses.

They climbed the ladder, throwing their arms over the log above and pulling themselves up, while Geoff and Julie kept the safety lines tight. At the top, they carefully stood up, side by side, on what now appeared to be an alarmingly narrow plank, and looked over to the first trapezes just out of reach. Beyond these were the second set, but it would require a monumental swing from the first to reach them.

'After three?' suggested Nicholas, and Stookie confirmed.

On the count, they made their leap of faith. Nicholas grabbed his trapeze with both hands, swung slightly forward, then – with his momentum gone – swung back to a halt. It was a relief to feel the safety rope go tight and Julie lowering him down.

Back on the ground, he looked up to see Stookie still hanging on, his legs flailing as he tried to swing his body to reach the second trapeze. A shoe fell off, dropping to the ground, but still, he persevered until it was hopeless. Without the momentum, he too stalled out and Geoff took the strain to lower him down.

The boy retrieved his shoe, took off his gear and peered up, shading his eyes with his hand. He turned to Geoff. 'I'm sure I could make it to the second one if I swung out a bit harder. Can I have another try?' Geoff made a play of saying if the boy believed something was possible, then it most likely was, and they should give it a go; but tomorrow, when they were fresh.

The boy agreed then turned to Nicholas. 'My name's Calum.'

'Nice to meet you, Calum,' said Nicholas, politely shaking his hand.

Calum looked at him quizzically. 'You're quite cool for a posh guy,' then ran off to tell the others of his victory.

The teacher thanked them for the session and was about to leave, but stopped and turned to Nicholas.

'It was good of you to take the time with Calum. These kids can be awkward. They carry a lot of baggage.'

'Oh, that's OK,' said Nicholas, picking up their harnesses. 'He's a nice lad. I was impressed by how he refused to give up.' Then puzzled by what the boy had just said, he asked, 'If his name's Calum, why do they call him Stookie?'

'Because at one time he seemed to be permanently wearing one.' He could see that Nicholas wasn't following. 'A stookie … it's what they call a plaster cast.'

'Ah, I get it. He was accident-prone.'

The teacher shook his head. 'No. His father is violent. Before they locked him up he used to batter the boy and his mother to a pulp. That's why Calum's self-esteem is so low. Still, I've got to hand it to the lad, despite the impression he sometimes gives, he's making a real effort to move on with his life.'

***

As Claire looked around to see why the landowner had called the police, two boys crawled from the tent. The site looked immaculate: a carrier bag contained their rubbish, there were no signs of a fire and there was a trowel to deal with the call of nature.

'What have we done wrong?' one of the boys asked. 'I thought wild camping was legal in Scotland?'

'It is, and by the look of things you're doing everything by the book. Where are you from?'

'Kilmarnock,' replied the other. 'We took the train to Pitlochry and are hiking to Glencoe. You can go ahead and check us out if you want to, but you won't find anything,' in a manner that told her it wasn't the first time they had been questioned for no reason other than their age.

'That won't be necessary,' Claire replied, miffed at the police being used to do the bidding of a landowner who refused to accept Right to Roam legislation. 'Enjoy your expedition, lads, and take care of yourselves.'

As she turned to leave, her earpiece came to life. An accident ten miles south on the A9. Multiple casualties. A member of the public administering CPR on one, and another trapped in an overturned vehicle.

She pressed transmit. 'Control from Three One Echo, will attend also,' adding herself to those en route.

With blue lights flashing and siren wailing Claire

weaved the Ford Kuga in and out of the southbound flow, her mind concentrating on the road but her emotions preparing for the awfulness to come. The number of northbound vehicles soon petered out and she arrived at a queue of stationary traffic. Drivers now standing in the road to see what had happened stepped to one side as she advanced slowly down the northbound carriageway to the locus.

Fire tenders, ambulances and police cars created a scene of flashing blue, fluorescent yellow and red. Claire got out of her car, donned her hi-vis jacket and walked closer. Even though she knew what to expect, she was sickened by the smell that always accompanied serious road accidents: oil vaporising on a hot engine, acrid burning and mutilated human beings.

At the bottom of a gouged embankment was the mangled wreckage of an overturned vehicle. What had been a car was now a confusion of torn and compacted steel, the roof crushed down. Pieces of broken plastic, glass and personal effects from the vehicle lay strewn about.

The legs of a paramedic protruded from the passenger side as they worked on a casualty in the front of the vehicle. Firefighters wearing thick beige suits and yellow helmets with visors were using hydraulic shears through what had been the windscreen.

A traffic officer approached Claire. 'Not good,' he said, answering her inevitable question. 'There were four in the car. From what we gather the driver tried to sprint past a line of vehicles at the end of the dual carriageway but messed up. They clipped that parcel lorry,' indicating a small truck in front of which a pale-looking man wearing a company uniform was giving a statement. 'There's a lad trapped inside the car – he's in a bad way – and two walking-wounded. God knows how they survived that,' gesturing back towards the wreckage.

'And a fatality?' Claire asked, referring to what she had heard over the radio.

'I'm afraid so. She suffered a partial ejection – you know how common they are in rollover accidents. Thrown half out of the side window but caught by her seatbelt. She didn't stand a chance. A broken neck, according to the paramedics. They all live in Edinburgh, but from what we gather, they *weekend* up your way.'

Claire knew the implications. Word of the accident would quickly circulate and people would speculate to fill the gaps. *What if the deceased's family hear through the grapevine or someone else is wrongly informed?*

They walked over to where a mobile screen had been erected to shield the body. At Claire's signal, a paramedic pulled back the blanket just far enough to expose the face of a girl, a pretty girl with long dark hair, and Claire's heart sank.

***

Geoff and Julie were hanging up buoyancy aids when Nicholas entered.

'I'll finish up here,' said Julie, knowing that Geoff would want to talk to him. She gave a little wave, 'Take care, Nicholas.'

He smiled. 'And you, Julie.'

Geoff led the way as they walked slowly along the woodland path back to the car park. 'Well, Nicholas, it hasn't been an easy run for you, has it?'

Nicholas shook his head. 'No, it hasn't – but Tess would want me to carry on.'

'Yes, she would, and despite losing your friend, I've seen you grow during your time here.'

'Thanks, Geoff, but that hasn't been down to me. Working with you guys and the children has taught me a lot. I need to stand on my own two feet now. Do you understand that?'

Geoff smiled. 'Time to grab that second trapeze, eh?'

'Something like that.'

Geoff reached into his pocket. 'We had a meeting last night and it was agreed that although you're a volunteer, you deserve a little something for your efforts. It will get you started in France.'

Nicholas looked at the envelope then back at Geoff. 'I don't think I can take this.'

'Of course you can. We see it as our investment in you. Just as you invested yourself in the children. What goes around comes around, Nicholas.'

They arrived at the car park where Nicholas had the Land Rover loaded and ready for the journey.

Geoff patted the bonnet of his old friend. 'Look after each other,' he said, then hugged Nicholas. 'And come back in one piece.'

CHAPTER 5

Rory stared at the envelope propped up by a ketchup bottle on the kitchen table: an envelope postmarked Auchenmore and made out to his daughter, Dani.

He ran through the facts. Although postmarked Auchenmore, whoever sent it must be unaware that Dani had left two weeks earlier. The writing was neat – not the bubbly hand of Tracy, whose card dropped through the letterbox each Christmas – but missing the title Ms or Miss afforded to strangers. And Dani's birthday was still months away.

Perhaps it's someone from the centre wishing her well with her new career?

No, it's him. The boy who caused all of this, and with a resolve forged by resentment, he grabbed the envelope, opened the flap and took out a card. A note fell to the floor but he left it lying as he read the card. *To Dani, I'm so sorry for how I behaved. Please forgive me, Nicholas.*

I knew it, a moment of validation and then foreboding as his own deeds from years before came rushing back. With Isla now in his thoughts, he gathered the fallen note, read the first line, but found himself riven with guilt. Blocking anything further from his mind, he stuffed the card and note back into the envelope and put them into the sideboard drawer below the picture of Isla.

***

Through the passenger window of the patrol car Dani watched the residents getting on with their lives. It seemed that every house had someone either sponge-washing a vehicle or parading up and down a meagre square of grass with a lawnmower.

The last shift, a late, had ended badly when she'd found herself separated from her colleagues and jostled by a milling group outside an emptying nightclub. Having come to her aid, an experienced officer had then berated her in front of the others. 'It wasn't clever going off on your own like that, Dani. You put yourself and the team at risk,' he had said. Afterwards, she was advised by someone more sympathetic not to take it to heart. 'He's an arse, always looking for an opportunity to put people down,' but it was something else to knock Dani's confidence and add to her growing sense that she wasn't cut out for police work.

Still, nothing much was likely to happen today. It was Sunday. The neds would be nursing hangovers, the roads quiet and houses prone to break-ins whilst their owners were at work, occupied.

'Everything OK?' Marshall asked as he slowed to allow a boy to retrieve his ball from between two parked cars.

Marshall Pickering was a popular officer; confident, funny and cool under pressure. So much so he'd earned the title of Gucci.

'I'm fine,' Dani replied. 'A bit tired, that's all.'

'Well don't let the job or others in the team get to you. Do what you have to do and go home. We can grab a coffee if you like? Help wake you up.'

She attempted a smile, thankful he was prepared to go along with her excuse.

The radio chirped into life.

'Control to Three Two Charlie.'

She remained passive as Marshall pressed his transmit button. 'Three Two Charlie, go ahead.'

'Three Two. We have a report of a sudden death. A male, early fifties at 42 Anderson Drive. Paramedics on scene.'

'Yes, yes. Will attend.'

Dani felt her stress level rise as Marshall drove quickly to the end of the suburban street then activated the blue lights, changed down a gear and sped off towards Anderson Drive.

Number 42 was like all the other houses in the road: a two-storey red-brick semi-detached. On the drive at the side stood the family car and caravan. An ambulance and a yellow and green Volvo with Emergency Doctor written in reverse across the bonnet were parked on the road outside.

Pulling up in front of the ambulance, Marshall informed Control of their arrival. Once out of the car they set questioning eyes on a group of bashful onlookers, causing them to melt away, then turned their attention to a man exiting the caravan. In his thirties, wearing cords, a pink shirt with sleeves rolled up and carrying a medical bag, he had the downbeat look of someone who had just lost a battle.

'Jeremy Smith. I'm the emergency doctor today but I'm afraid there's nothing I could do to help the chap,' he said, in a southern English voice with clearly articulated consonants. 'The deceased is a Stuart Murdoch, aged fifty-two. He's in the caravan. His wife and daughter are there also, together with a paramedic.'

The officers pulled out their handheld devices and Marshall ran through a series of questions: the doctor's details, time pronounced dead, and so on. The doctor then passed on what else he knew. 'It was the daughter who found him. From what I gather, he didn't respond to calls for lunch so she came out and there he was, poor fellow. I'd say that by the time I arrived he'd been dead for … what …' He paused, glanced at his watch then looked at the sky as if to aid his calculations. 'Yes, about thirty minutes. By the look of him, the probable cause of death was a cardiac arrest, but don't quote me.'

'Do you have the wife and daughter's details?' Marshall asked.

'His wife's name is Jean and the daughter's Heather. Scottish family from a place called Dunkeld. I was up there for a stag do last year. Nice little village not too far into the Highlands. I managed to catch a salmon even with the mother of all headaches. Too much of the amber nectar, if you know what I mean.'

Neither officer added that to their notes, but with the mention of Dunked, Dani felt the sudden death encroaching on her heartland.

Marshall entered the cramped caravan with Dani two steps behind. They acknowledged Mrs Murdoch with sympathetic comments while placing themselves as unobtrusively as possible near the entrance.

Heather was engrossed with her father. 'Dad, Dad, wake up,' she whispered in a gentle Highland accent, all too familiar to Dani.

The paramedic attempted to console her as he tidied Stuart Murdoch ready for the stretcher. Mrs Murdoch explained to the officers, 'We've arranged to meet friends in Dunkeld. It's where Stuart was born. He's been looking forward to it for a long time,' in the forlorn hope that the situation might somehow correct itself and normal life resume. The realisation that her husband would not be going back to Dunkeld as intended was yet to sink in.

Dani knew well the pretty village with its street of quaint shops and bridge that crossed the River Tay. To the north lay the crag where she'd led her first climb: a clean and straightforward route called Anon. That day near Dunkeld had reinforced what she had once wanted to do with her life, and how she had wanted to feel. She recalled sitting at the top of the route, with a glowing sense of achievement. Below lay the shining river and a magnificent canopy of silver birches, rowans and Scots pines – a generous reward for her efforts. Sitting there with the sun on her face, life had felt so good. School would soon be over and a world of adventure beckoned.

The contrast between then and now was palpable. It felt as though her heart would burst from her chest and flee back to Scotland, leaving her body abandoned. Once more, all she could think was, *Is this really for me?*

A flurry of incidents meant that by lunchtime, Dani's team were stretched to the limit. Over her earpiece, she heard Response Units being asked to attend shopliftings, minor traffic incidents, males behaving suspiciously ... It seemed endless. She wondered what the others thought of the menial task she'd been assigned as they rushed about more serious business.

Distracted by the search for an obscure address, she only caught the end of the latest call, ' ... Three Foxtrot'.

Was that for me? She waited for another unit to respond, but none came back.

'Control to Two Three Foxtrot,' less patient now.

'Two Three Foxtrot, go ahead,' she replied, attempting an air of confidence.

'Two Three Foxtrot. We've received a report of a male behaving strangely at the Southern Viaduct. Appreciate you're on other duties; however, all units are tied up.'

'Shite,' she muttered when certain her finger was clear of the transmit button.

'Yes, yes, pass me the details.'

Control came back. 'The caller reports a male, twentyish, dark hair, blue top, behaving in what they describe as "an odd fashion" near the viaduct. No other details at this time.'

'Yes, yes, will attend.'

Don't worry; it'll be fine.

The viaduct spanned a valley between gently rolling hills. Consisting of twenty or so red-brick arches supporting a two-line track, it was over one hundred feet tall at its highest point. Each end adjoined steep grass embankments that carried the lines their final metres to level ground.

Turning off the main road, Dani took a dirt track, careful to avoid the potholes and wincing each time the car bottomed out on the central hump. Nothing seemed untoward as she approached the viaduct. No young male; in fact, no one at all.

'Control, Two Three Foxtrot at the locus.'

'Acknowledged.'

It seemed that this was another tick-box exercise for an unsubstantiated report. However, it had been drummed into her to take nothing for granted before reporting No Trace.

She carried on under an end arch then followed the track as it turned sharply left. Parking on a grassy verge, she got out of the vehicle and looked around. The hedgerows made it difficult to see much, but a set of concrete steps with galvanised handrails ascended in two tiers to the tracks. A vantage point. She climbed swiftly.

At the top, a small gantry and a padlocked gate led onto the line. She peered over, looking right – nothing – then left, and was startled by the sight of someone sitting about a quarter of the way along, his feet dangling over the edge: a young man in his twenties fitting the description given earlier. He was making slight lunging motions as though summoning the moment to make the final move to launch himself into oblivion. The situation looked terrible, heightened by the likelihood of a high-speed train passing at any moment.

Dani fumbled for her transmit button and blurted out a situation report, a request for an immediate line closure and back-up.

'Yes, yes. Stand by.'

The radio went eerily silent as other units, hearing a drama unfold, sought to avoid cluttering the channel.

What now? With the line open, venturing onto the tracks was inconceivable. A fast train wouldn't be able to stop and she wouldn't get clear. *But what when Control say the line's closed?*

There seemed to be no obvious answer. Waiting for back-up risked watching the young man jump to certain death, but what was the alternative?

Her time to think was short as Control quickly came back, confirming the line closed.

'Yes, yes,' Dani replied, and without further thought, she climbed over the small locked gate and started along the line.

The position high above ground felt exposed, made worse by an unimpeded breeze. With no footway and the slimmest of balustrades on either side, she strode awkwardly from wooden sleeper to sleeper, slippery from years of grease and waste fallen or flushed from the trains. Every twenty-five metres a metal stance perched over the edge, staggered either side; havens should a worker be caught by an approaching locomotive. At each stance she felt a little safer. *What if Control got this wrong?*

Having tried to make her approach heard, she arrived within a few metres of the young man and stopped. With no obvious place to settle, she sat down on one of the tracks, seeking to level their eye contact. However, the young man seemed oblivious to her presence. Her radio was now passing a profusion of messages – calls for units to attend and senior officers requesting specialist support. Without thinking, she took out her earpiece and hooked it over the stubby aerial.

'Hello, my name's Dani. What's yours?' But the young man remained silent.

She tried again. 'Can I talk to you?' Still no response.

The situation had escalated. With no reaction, she knew that there was a danger of making matters worse, and a scene from her training played across her mind – a clip in which a casualty gently launched herself into space as two officers tried to negotiate. It had shocked the class and seemed to be an antecedent to today. Feeling out of her depth and with only a basic skill set, she felt like an impostor about to be unmasked. *Why didn't I wait?*

Her gaze moved to the valley, where a meandering stream cut its way through green meadows. Beyond sat a small hill with a Norman church on top. A tractor ploughed one of the slopes accompanied by a circling flock of black-headed gulls, the driver turned to observe his perfectly straight lines. It seemed absurd, the tractor dutifully going about its day-to-day business, ploughing and planting for the future, while a young man thought of his life in seconds, perhaps minutes, but no further.

'I go to quiet places when I need to think,' she said, still looking over the valley. Then a thought crossed her mind. *This is quite a nice spot, not dissimilar to Scotland.*

The young man sensed her peace and looked briefly at her. She caught his eye and smiled, making a brief connection before he looked away.

'Hi, I'm Dani,' she said, starting over. 'Can we talk?' and with his eyes still fixed to the ground, he spoke.

'There isn't anything to talk about. I just want to be with her again.'

He seemed oddly polite in turning her down but also fatigued, as though he had had enough.

'Who would you like to be with?' she asked.

'Katie,' he replied.

Dani wondered who Katie was. *A girlfriend, perhaps?*

'Tell me about Katie,' she asked, but he didn't reply.

She tried a different question. 'What's your name? So I can get to know you.'

'It's Jason.'

Knowing the need for people to find purpose when hope was lost, Dani continued.

'Jason, there will be people who care about you. Who are they?' she asked.

His body tensed and he clenched his fists. Dani prepared to leap forward and grab him, but with only the balustrade to cling onto, he would likely pull her over. He squeezed his eyes shut as though blocking out the world, just as she had seen Nicholas do on the wall, and then he relaxed.

'I know my little girl, Molly, does.'

'Where is Molly at the moment?' Dani asked, her concern for the wellbeing of the child betrayed in her voice.

'She's safe, with her grandparents.'

He sounded genuine, so Dani returned to him. 'Tell me about Molly, I'd like to know about her.'

Jason described his daughter: when she was born, how happy her arrival had made him and Katie, and their times together. And he told of how a road accident had taken their Katie away, how much they missed her, and his subsequent struggle to cope.

Dani listened to his story unfold, and with it, his language became more reasoned and his demeanour calmer. She looked out towards the field where the tractor was about to complete its task, then turned to Jason.

'Molly sounds like a lovely girl, and it's a terrible thing to lose your mum. You need to be with her and give her the assurance and love she needs. Dads are special for girls. I can tell you that from my own experience. My mum died when I was born and I can't think what I would have done without my dad. I know losing a wife is hard. I've seen it. But the two of you are here for each other, to care for each other. I think it's what Katie would have wanted, is it not?'

Jason nodded.

'Shall we go and see Molly then, and let her know how much you love her?'

And with that, he was ready to return. He worked himself cautiously back from the edge and stood up, Dani there to steady him.

She hadn't noticed the group form at the end of the viaduct and on the road below: an ambulance, police vehicles, even a solitary fireman with his yellow helmet. Two paramedics calmly walked forward and put a blanket over Jason's shoulders. One of them looked at Dani, smiled and nodded as if to say, 'Well done. We'll take it from here,' and led him down the steps to the waiting ambulance.

It was then that she noticed her sergeant, Sandra Cameron. Her concerned look brought on a sinking feeling as Dani returned to her world of an hour ago. A world of self-doubts and failings.

'I'm sorry. I shouldn't have gone on my own, should I?' Dani said as her eyes started to fill.

Sandra bent down. 'Hey, hey, look at me, Dani. You did great; you did exactly the right thing.'

Dani looked up, her expression telling Sandra that she doubted what she was hearing.

'If you hadn't intervened, that young man might not be here. You have to think on your feet in this job, and that's what you did.'

Dani regained her composure and tried to explain. 'His name's Jason, he has a daughter …' but Sandra interrupted.

'Yes, we know. The daughter's fine, she's with her grandparents. They phoned us, concerned about

Jason.' Then she looked at Dani's radio. 'We tried to call you …'

Dani looked down at her earpiece still hooked over its stubby aerial. 'Oh … sorry,' putting it back around her ear.

'Anyway, it wouldn't have made any difference,' Sandra continued, her attention moving to the steep embankment. 'I'll help you write this up later. Then we'll pass it to Community to follow up. Now, can we please get down from here? I don't like heights.'

Back in the car, Dani took a deep breath and looked at her hands, wondering what she would see. They were steady. *I can do this*, she thought, *I can make a difference*. It was the first time since joining the shift that she'd felt the satisfaction of a job well done.

She looked over to where Jason was sitting in the ambulance, the paramedics fussing over him, then felt her mobile vibrating in her pocket.

'Hi, Dani. It's Marshall. Are you OK?'

'Yes, I'm fine.'

'I'm glad. You had us all worried … What would you say to a drink tonight?

CHAPTER 6

From his position fifty metres down the street and beyond Auchenmore's last street lamp, Seamus O'Doile could still make out who was coming and going from her house, but with little chance of being seen.

He took an anonymous pay-as-you-go from the glove box and scrolled through a string of sent messages: 'I'm watching you' … 'Think you can get away from me?' … 'Guess who?' then tapped in another. 'I'm outside.' He hovered over send, then pressed delete.

She knew the texts were from him, and so did the police. They just couldn't prove it. Who else would be that sick?

Now bored with the vigil, he turned his attention to his gaunt face in the rear-view mirror. An approaching van with something on the roof – a police lightbar perhaps – sent him down into his seat, then once it passed, quickly back up. A builder's van with a ladder rack, but time for plan B. Make her jealous with a younger girl, a better-looking one.

Tracy looked over to the rain splattering on her

bedroom window. *How could I have been so stupid?* she thought, annoyed with herself for what she now saw as an infatuation with a boy who had ignored her. *Time to be like Dani and move on with my life.* She had been dismissive of Kirsty Jones's text suggesting a girls night out. Previous ones had felt flat – as if something exciting was meant to happen but never quite did. However, perhaps it was worth giving it another go with a more positive mindset.

They arranged to meet on Friday evening at the Ultra Violet – Auchenmore's version of a nightclub. Tracy pulled together an outfit of white leggings, a bottle-green satin top and a gold belt. Although the venue was busy, the girls were able to shift two lads from their corner position on a built-in seat.

'Can you put a good word in for me with your dad?' one of them asked Kirsty, hoping to curry favour with his employer.

'Don't worry, Cammy, I'll do that,' she assured with a sweet smile, before giving her friends a look of, 'Aye, that'll be right.'

They joined two rectangular drinks tables and rounded up additional stools until everyone was seated. The evening started well, with a kitty established and a loud conversation, catching up on the gossip.

'She didn't, did she?'

'Yes, she did, and such a quiet lass at school. Who would've thought it?' That type of thing. It was a laugh.

A few local lads chanced their mitt asking girls up for a staid dance as red, green and blue pools of light moved predictably around the dance floor. Tracy was asked up by a boy she knew from the college, a nice lad who lived locally and whose girlfriend was a trainee nurse in Inverness.

'Tonight's the last of her late shifts; I'm going up to see her tomorrow so she can hear the new sound system in my Corsa,' he said.

'That'll be fun for her, I'm sure,' Tracy replied.

'Do you think so?' Her sarcasm had missed its mark.

His duty complete, he thanked her for the dance and headed back to his mates at the bar and a discussion as to whether the cheap-and-loud aftermarket exhaust systems they'd fitted to their cars were street legal.

Tracy and Kirsty were chatting when they realised the rest of the group had gone quiet.

'Good evening, girls. Can I give you the pleasure of my company?'

They looked up to see Seamus O'Doile leering at them and one of the girls pulled uncomfortably at the top of her dress. O'Doile was notorious in Auchenmore. He'd arrived from somewhere in Ireland and taken up with a local woman. However, things had turned sour between them and he had been served a Non-Harassment Order.

'Not really,' replied one of the girls, triggering a furtive giggle from the others.

Tracy saw from his response that it wasn't a clever reply; then again, no matter what they said, it would end badly with a character like O'Doile.

The grin left his face. 'What do mean by that?'

his tone putting the girl on edge.

One of the others sought to defuse the situation. 'It's our night out. A girls' thing. We want to be on our own if you don't mind.'

'A girls' thing, is it? I suppose that's why she was dancing with him?' pointing to Tracy, then the lad from the college. 'Come on, give us a dance. I don't care which one of you lovelies it is.' With no takers, he persisted. 'One dance, then I'll go away. Otherwise, I'll join you,' looking at a space between two of the group.

Kirsty Jones felt particularly wary. O'Doile worked for her father, who rued the day he had taken him on. O'Doile looked at her. 'Oh, little Miss Feisty. Do you think Daddy would like us to get together?' waggling his tongue at her.

She turned away, a look of disgust on her face.

'Not good enough, am I? Is that the problem?'

Tracy sensed the situation getting out of control. O'Doile wasn't getting his way, but he clearly wouldn't back down.

'Come on then, let's have that one dance,' she said, standing up and leading O'Doile away from the group.

He followed, attempting to rub a sweaty hand on Kirsty's cheek as he passed, then tilted his head to make a show of inspecting Tracy's backside. The group watched uneasily as Tracy suffered the dance, pushing O'Doile's hands away as he tried to touch her.

'One more,' he urged at the end.

'No, I said *one* dance, and that was *one* dance.'

Then for reasons incomprehensible, he unbuttoned his shirt, stripped it off and swung it about his head. The doorman stepped in and O'Doile was asked to leave. Conceding, he made his way to the exit but stopped short and pointed two fingers at Tracy as though aiming a pistol.

'Pow,' he mimed.

The girls quivered. 'That guy is such a creep,' said one.

Kirsty's eyes stayed on the door until she was sure he was gone. Then she turned to Tracy. 'Dad says he's a dangerous man. I think you should keep your distance from him.'

'I think you're forgetting my hobby,' Tracy replied.

Kirsty, a streetwise girl who'd lived in Glasgow till recently, shook her head. 'That will make no difference to him whatsoever.'

Heading towards the door marked Staff Only, Tracy looked around to see who was in the supermarket, a habit adopted since O'Doile had entered her life. It now seemed that wherever she went, he would appear.

As she hung her coat in her locker, a colleague called over. 'Hi, Tracy. Your boyfriend was in earlier asking what shifts you were working.'

'Boyfriend?'

'I'm being sarcastic. It was that sleazebag, O'Doile. He did say he was your boyfriend, though.'

Her stomach tightened. 'You didn't tell him, did you?'

'Of course not, but he was quite determined. Anyway, have a good shift.'

Throughout the evening her mind kept returning to O'Doile. *Why is he so persistent? What have I done to deserve this?* A sick feeling settled in the pit of her stomach, as though she had been possessed by something evil.

At the end of the shift, with heightened vigilance, she started the walk home. Her eyes jumped from side to side, ahead, then over her shoulder for any sign of him. Avoiding her usual route through the houses, she kept to the main street, until she reached a short connecting road. First looking around, she turned and started briskly down the fifty-metre stretch. About halfway her pace quickened further, encouraged by the sight of passing cars and pedestrians on the road ahead.

'Ah, here she is. I've been waiting to see you all week.' O'Doile appeared from nowhere.

Her body tensed and her heartbeat climbed. Her mind raced as she kept moving towards safety.

He kept pace beside her. 'Are you not talking to me tonight?'

Still looking ahead, she challenged him. 'Are you stalking me? If you are, it's a serious offence.'

'Oh, I'm not allowed out now, is that it?'

'Did you go into my work and tell someone you were my boyfriend?'

His finger went to his mouth and he looked up as though pondering. 'I might have said I was a boy and a friend, but to be honest, I can't remember exactly. Am I not your friend then? And am I not a boy?

Which makes me a boyfriend, does it not?'

'No, you're not my boyfriend and you're not a friend. Be clear about that,' she replied, eyes fixed on the final metres to safety.

But he kept in step and his tone flipped. 'Well, what am I then? Some guy you think you can string along and treat like shit?'

Tracy didn't answer so he pushed his face in front of hers. She could smell his breath, sour with the odour of cigarettes. 'Well, what am I?' As she pulled to one side, away from him, he pushed her hard into a gateway and behind a tall wall, then grasped her upper arms in his hands, squeezing them tight.

'You're disrespecting me,' no longer trying to mask his malice.

Through reflex, she drove her hands up between his arms then thrust them outwards, breaking his grip, as she had been taught during police officer safety training.

'Get off!' she shouted, hoping to draw attention from one of the houses.

Surprised, he looked around, and she ran.

'This isn't the end of it,' he called, and she knew it was only a matter of time before he threatened her again.

'You're quiet this evening. What's up?' Claire asked.

Tracy straightened her shoulders and turned to face her partner. 'Claire—'

'Control to Three One Echo.'

Claire let out a sigh of frustration as she picked up

the call. A group camping by the loch had lit a campfire that was now out of control. Firefighters were on their way, but, unsure as to their reception, had asked for a police presence.

'Here we go again,' she said. These things were happening too frequently.

It turned out that the campers were equally concerned, flailing with fire beaters and deploying an extinguisher from their car to try to rein things in. While pairs of firefighters dampened the area with wide sprays from their hoses, Claire and Tracy took details, ensuring the unintentional fireraisers felt suitably contrite.

The event temporarily took Tracy's mind off O'Doile, but later that evening they received a call that brought matters to a head: an abusive ex-partner breaking a Non-Harassment Order at a known address.

Claire was about to respond when Tracy interrupted. 'Can we let another unit go? There's something I need to tell you.'

Claire knew straight away that it was serious and pulled into a lay-by.

'What is it, Tracy? What's happened?' and Tracy was brought to tears as the tension of the last few weeks poured out.

Back at the station, they were joined by one of the two shift sergeants and the area inspector. Tracy ran through what had happened to her, how she had been intimidated, and the incident the other night when she'd been walking home after work.

'I thought I was able to deal with it, but I can see

now that I was out of my depth. I'm sorry I didn't speak up sooner.'

The inspector shook his head. 'There's nothing to be sorry about. Men like O'Doile are dangerous. They don't behave reasonably.' He turned to the sergeant. 'I want him brought in – make sure he's cautioned first and inform the duty solicitor. Breaching the Non-Harassment Order is enough to hold him for now, and we've got Tracy's statement. But I'd like to see him remanded until his trial. For that, we need the mobile he's using for the texts. Can you arrange a search warrant for wherever he's staying and his place of work? We've already got grounds for the car.'

'On it,' replied the sergeant, heading for the door.

Then he turned to Tracy. 'I want you to go home. Claire will give you a lift. And don't worry. O'Doile won't be bothering you again.'

'Tracy, Dani's here to see you,' Mary called up, feigning surprise.

Tracy wasn't fooled.

'What did you do that for?' she shouted down, and then slammed her bedroom door shut.

Mary looked at Dani and shrugged apologetically. Tracy knew them both too well – Dani wouldn't have just turned up without talking to Tracy first unless Mary had asked her to.

Dani looked at the stairs. 'Do you mind if I go and see her myself?'

'You do that; I'll tidy up here,' leaving Dani to wonder, as always, what there was to do in such an immaculate house.

She made her way softly up, respectful with her intrusion. On the door were the familiar five alphabet figures spelling *Tracy*. Painted as smiling clowns, they signified more than the name of the occupant. They symbolised a bygone era. She thought of all the time the two of them had spent together in that room, sharing secrets, listening to music, laughing, playing and planning their lives.

Now she stood at the door in an entirely different mood. Time had moved on for both of them, and life had become so much more complicated.

She knocked lightly. 'Tracy, it's me. Can I come in?'

A faint sound came from inside, but no answer. She knocked again; still nothing. She considered trying the handle but it felt wrong so she settled down on the floor across the door, her back against one side of the frame, her feet on the other, and waited.

'I'll sit here until you're ready. Take your time.'

Dani looked around, at the ceiling, the lampshade, the pictures, the trainers on her feet, before occupying herself with twiddling an elastic hair tie in her fingers. She hummed this tune and that – anything that came into her mind – before arriving at a song they both knew and loved, 'The Tiree Love Song'. It was a song they'd learnt through Mary, on a rare occasion when she'd played a CD from her small collection. Dani could tell it held memories by the distant look in Mary's eyes. On such occasions, the girls would busy themselves, giving Mary a moment with whatever cherished thoughts had overtaken her.

A click of the door lock told Dani she had permission to enter. The room was a mess, the curtains closed, things scattered all over the floor. Tracy's nearly spent sobs could be heard from under the duvet and Floppy Rabbit's ears and locks of Tracy's beautiful red hair protruded onto the pillow. Dani climbed onto the bed and lay next to her friend, taking her and the duvet into her arms and holding them tightly.

'Oh, Tracy, what's happened?'

They lay like that for a while, as Tracy slowly calmed. When her tears eased, Dani felt it was safe to get up and do something about the room – it couldn't be helping. She half-opened the curtains, then set about tidying, picking things up and putting them back in their familiar places.

'I remember buying you this,' she commented, as she set the little Nessie in red tartan back on the dressing table: a present from a field trip to Loch Ness.

They shared the memory of each item, Tracy sitting up in bed holding Floppy.

'It's a piece of glass, that's all,' said Dani, seeing Tracy look at the broken mirror. She took a poster of some long-forgotten boy band off the wall to prop in front of it.

'There. We can look at them instead,' she said, standing back and viewing the picture. 'Nah, second thoughts,' and chucked a towel over the lot.

Tracy gave a meek laugh, blew her nose and

wiped her eyes with a tissue.

Around lunchtime, they set off for a walk and a chat. Tracy wore sunglasses to hide her red eyes, a woolly hat and her puffer jacket with furry hood. 'You look like one of those rappers,' Dani joked. 'I need to give you a huge gold dollar sign to hang around your neck, as they wear in London.' She grinned as she received a sniffled laugh back.

It was a cold, bright day. The girls talked about trivia as they made their way to the little community woodland on the outskirts of town. You could always find peace there.

At the far end was a bench set back from the path and they took a seat. Mary had given Dani some snacks, as though they were going on a school outing. Dani passed Tracy a favourite cereal bar.

'She hasn't eaten much for days,' Mary had said, handing over what seemed an excess of food for the short walk.

Dani opened a can of Irn Bru and took a sip. 'I've missed this,' she said, then looked at the scenery and over to the mountains beyond. 'All of it.'

Then she turned her attention to Tracy. 'Tell me what you can, I'll just listen.'

'I think there's something wrong with me,' Tracy started. 'I'm so messed up; I feel like I'm worthless and can't stop crying.'

Dani took her hand.

'It's the way we respond when we're struggling to cope. I did the same when I was struggling with my job. You remember, when you helped me?'

Tracy paused, then nodded slowly. 'It started with

that creep, O'Doile, the way he treated me. Afterwards, I had nightmares and now I'm afraid to sleep. I mean, I can't even bring myself to go to work!'

'Have you spoken to anyone about it?'

Tracy shook her head.

'Do you want to tell me?' and Tracy went on to explain everything that had happened and the feeling of violation that seemed to have settled deep inside her.

'You know, Tracy, you need to remember you're the victim here, not the cause. O'Doile is a predator. If it hadn't been you, then it might well have been someone else. You said yourself that there had already been a complaint made against him. If you're OK with it, let's get someone who knows about these things, a professional, to talk with you.'

Tracy pulled back, frowning.

'I tell you, Tracy, they won't judge, they work with this type of thing all the time. I see it with my job, frequently. They'll help. I'll come with you if you like; we'll get through it together.'

'Would you?' Tracy asked, wiping her eyes.

'Yes, of course, like you were there for me when I felt so low. I couldn't have got through it without you. Helping each other, that's what friends do, isn't it?'

'You're better now though, aren't you?' Tracy asked, thinking back to how difficult Dani had found the transition south.

'I'm getting on with the job … and the people are fine. I'm just not sure I want to become too much a part of it. Perhaps I should have been more persistent and become a bigger part of this,' she said, looking around.

Tracy squeezed Dani's hand. 'I miss you, Dani.'

'I know … And I miss you. It's not easy being away from each other, is it?'

Tracy shook her head.

'You could have joined up in Scotland. We could have done shifts together, it would have been fun.'

Dani laughed. 'A carry-on, more like.'

Tracy gave another sniffled laugh, then looked serious. 'Was it because of what happened with Nicholas Fraser? Is that why you left?'

Dani looked at the ground as she allowed herself to examine her feelings. It was strange, being back in Auchenmore and hearing Nicholas's name.

'It was part of it, I suppose. But to be honest, Tracy, I think I had to leave to grow up – to find myself. When I was here, I was always Daddy's little girl. He made my decisions, or at least I made decisions he would approve of. I had to leave to stand on my own two feet.'

'I never realised that,' Tracy said.

'No, neither did I, but I felt it.'

'What about this guy you mentioned, is it serious?'

Dani smiled. 'I don't know yet. His name's Marshall – we were on shift together for a while.'

'What's he like?'

'Quite calm and ordinary. He's popular, confident and he doesn't get flustered … none of the drama.' The contrast with the chaotic world of Nicholas was obvious to them both. 'We're hoping to come up in February, so you'll get to meet him.'

Dani looked again at the mountains and the hill above the loch where Waterfall Bothy sat. 'Has anyone heard from Nicholas?' she asked.

Tracy shook her head. 'No, he's gone. Claire says he's in France. I don't think we'll ever see him again. You know, Dani, I was so jealous of you and Nicholas. It seems silly now, but I was.'

Dani didn't respond.

***

Tracy gathered a couple of mementoes from around her bedroom – the little Nessie, a picture with her mum on the Greig Street Bridge in Inverness – and then she came to the little rabbit with the big ears lying on top of the chest of drawers.

She turned to Mary. 'Would you mind if I left Floppy here? He's been a good friend, but I think he needs a rest.'

'Of course. I'll make sure he doesn't get up to any mischief,' Mary replied, busying herself with packing to prevent her emotions getting the better of her.

However, Tracy knew her well. 'Mum, I'll be ten minutes down the road. You can come and see me whenever you want. I'll even let you do my ironing! How's that for a deal?'

Mary hugged her daughter. 'I know. It's just that I've never been on my own. When I left home you were a toddler. But you're doing the right thing, lass – standing on your own two feet. Let's leave the rest of the packing for tomorrow or it will be too late for a cycle.'

Tracy chose a well-made path around the loch where silver birches glowed in their late-autumn colours, contrasting with the darker browns of bracken and the omnipresent greens. However, there was something else that had brought her here, a tranquillity that she hoped would make the question she had easier to ask.

They arrived at the head of the loch and sat down on a familiar bench.

'What is it, Tracy?' Mary asked, sensing her daughter's pensive mood and taking her hand in hers.

Tracy gathered herself, and with eyes cast down the loch, she broached a subject that she had always taken for granted, but now needed to understand.

'Mum, we've never talked about this, but can you tell me about my dad?'

Mary paused, preparing her words, so Tracy continued. 'Was I a …?' then stopped. Perhaps she didn't want to know after all. How would she cope with the knowledge that she was a child who was never supposed to be?

'Were you an accident, is that what you want to ask me?'

Tracy nodded, her eyes still on the view but her mind focused on the answer.

'Tracy, I was in love with your father, and you came from that love. I would never have conceived you if I had not been in love, even if that love was for far too short a time, and I was too young to understand my feelings and how to manage them. That aside, you know that you've always meant everything to me.'

'I know that, Mum. I suppose I want to know what my dad was like. Am I like him?'

'You're like yourself; a bit like me, a bit like your dad, but mostly you are you, Tracy Shaw. I'll tell you about your father as best I can, but don't go looking for yourself there.'

Tracy listened as Mum told her about the summer when she was sixteen, recounting the details up to the moment on his final evening when Mary had made love for the first and last time.

'Will you tell me where you were that evening?' Tracy asked.

Mary took her daughter's hand and held it.

'I will tell you it was a beautiful place, but would you let me keep that bit for myself for just a while longer? When I'm ready, I'll take you there. I promise. Your father didn't know that I was pregnant, neither of us did. He left without saying goodbye. At the time, that was what hurt the most – him disappearing without a word.'

'Did you look for him?'

'I thought about it, but what was I to do? Find him and force him back? Would that have worked?'

'But if he didn't know?'

'Tracy, I was so young and there were a lot of people giving me their advice, telling me what I must and mustn't do. I didn't know which way to turn for the best.'

'It's easy to fall in love, isn't it?' Tracy said, thinking how head over heels she still was about a boy she hardly knew – she couldn't deny those feelings, no matter how hard she tried to tell herself it had been a mere infatuation.

'Sometimes it seems that way, and sometimes finding love is the hardest thing of all.'

'Do you think he was in love with you, Mum?'

'Perhaps briefly, but then there is a difference between being in love with someone, and showing that you love them. When the person you think is right for you arrives in your life, take your time and be sure of his heart as well as your own.'

'You never heard from him again?'

'No, and I've given up hoping.'

CHAPTER 7

Careful with his footing, Nicholas continued down the snow-covered road, knocking on doors and depositing a slip of paper into each of the standardised La Poste letterboxes. 'Reliable snow clearing, wood stacking and general help,' written in French and English, and accompanied by a French mobile number.

Finding work was proving a challenge and things were now hand-to-mouth. *Different from late summer*, he mused, when there had seemed to be a constant stream of odd jobs as people tidied their gardens and put away outdoor furniture in readiness for the winter freeze. Earlier that day an elderly couple at the top of the road had given him an hour's work clearing snow and moving wood from a stack to the shelter of their porch. The woman had offered him ten euros, but seeing her search through the coins in her purse, he'd declined the cash and instead accepted a container of homemade tartiflette – the hearty Savoyard dish of cheese, potatoes and onions would stretch to three meals if accompanied with bread and he wasn't greedy.

Casting an eye over each property, he evaluated

the potential for work. Chalets with immaculately cleared drives would be either self-sufficient or have arrangements in hand. Those with closed shutters and knee-deep snow might lead to a rush-job when the owners returned. The best chance stood with the lavish chalets of cash-rich/time-poor weekenders from Geneva, or rental chalets preparing for arrivals.

The next chalet seemed different; more traditional, with the stone-built ground floor and the floor above constructed of wood. One end appeared to be set into the hillside.

As he got close, Nicholas smelt cigarette smoke hanging in the cold afternoon air, then noticed a woman in her mid-thirties sitting on a stone bench in the entrance alcove. Wearing a thick coat, large sunglasses and a woollen hat she stared up to the mountains while drawing hard on the cigarette. Beside her on the bench was the packet, a tin ashtray and a small cup of black coffee. A young German Shepherd lying at her feet eyed Nicholas's approach.

'Good afternoon,' Nicholas offered in now-practised French.

She glanced fleetingly at him as though caught by his voice, and then returned her gaze to the mountains.

'A beautiful chalet you have,' he continued.

'It's not a chalet, it's a grange,' she replied, making clear she had wearied of explaining this. 'It's very different from a chalet. It has a history, unlike those monstrosities,' pointing her fingers with the cigarette dismissively at the chocolate-box chalets opposite. Bleached-wood affairs with hearts and pine trees cut through the planks of their balconies. As she gestured, Nicholas noticed her hand trembling.

He stepped back and looked at the grange's lime-rendered walls on which occasional feature-stones had been left exposed. 'Yes, this has much more character,' then dipped into his pocket for a paper slip and reached forward to hand it to her.

'If you need any help, here is my number. I'll work hard and take whatever you're prepared to pay.'

The woman took the slip, and without looking at it, placed it on the bench. She then took another long, slow draw to finish her cigarette and stubbed the butt into the ashtray. As she emptied her lungs, exhaling the smoke, he sensed a melancholy. A resignation he knew from his mother.

She lifted her cup and sipped from it. 'You're from Scotland, aren't you?' she continued, now in English.

'Yes, I am. Edinburgh. How did you know?' reverting to his native language.

'Your accent and your neck scarf with the saltires. You Scots are a proud people, aren't you?'

He nodded as his thumb and forefinger caressed the neckerchief. 'I suppose we are. My name is Nicholas, Nicholas Fraser,' and for a moment he was distracted as he recalled saying that same thing to Dani at that first meeting on the T-bar.

When he looked back at the woman, her eyes were searching him. 'And I'm Corinne. It's forecast to snow tonight. Be here tomorrow morning at nine and I will have some work for you. I pay seven euros an hour. Are you happy with that?'

'Yes, that's brilliant, thank you, Corinne.'

She forced a smile then, taking another cigarette from the packet, looked back to the mountains. 'If you will excuse me now, I'd like to be on my own. *À demain,* Nicholas Fraser.'

Next morning, he followed Corinne and her dog to the back of the grange, their steps kicking up puffs of fresh snow that glistened like tiny mirrors in the sunlight. Nicholas couldn't help but notice how thin she was, her physique accentuated by the size of her sheepskin-lined snowboots.

'You'll find a shovel in the mazot over there,' she said in French. 'I'm expecting a delivery of firewood. The driver is what you call *a grumpy sort,*' her use of the English expression surprising him. 'But his wood is dry: the best in the valley. It needs to be stacked,' indicating a spot under the eaves. 'If you need anything, I will be upstairs preparing for the visitors.'

Raised above the snow on large stones, with thick log walls and a roof of wooden shingles, the mazot resembled a miniature old-world chalet. At the front sat a tiny balcony leading to an undersized arched door with a square window on one side.

As Nicholas retrieved the aluminium shovel, he saw that the interior had once been inhabited. However, the bedframe was turned on its side and the furniture scattered as though the place had been ransacked. From habit, he stood up two chairs that had been knocked over, then left.

Once he had cleared the top parking area and paths, he moved his Land Rover from where he had left it beside the road. Soon afterwards, the firewood arrived and as he had been warned, and despite his attempts at diplomacy, the driver dumped it unceremoniously onto the most awkward position possible.

Taking bundles of wood in his arms he made his way back and forth, shifting the delivery. A small van arrived and the driver, a man of similar age to Corinne, unshaven and wearing a down jacket, got out. Nicholas saw him look at the Land Rover's registration plate then glance in his direction before heading to an open door.

'Corinne, are you here? It's Jerome,' he heard the man call.

'What do you want now?' she replied, clearly irritated by his appearance.

'I need to talk to you, Corinne. We must talk. Why are you shutting me out? Why don't you let me help? You didn't need to take on a British,' he heard the man say.

'Don't you dare tell me what I can and can't do,' she shouted back.

Nicholas took the shovel and moved to the path at the far end of the chalet, uncomfortable knowing this wasn't a conversation he should be hearing and that Jerome was irked by his presence. Shortly afterwards he heard an engine start and the van leave.

The wood stacked and the rest of the snow cleared, he put the shovel back in the mazot and looked at his watch. Four and a half hours. The

German Shepherd appeared at the chalet door and having finished his work, Nicholas called him over. 'Come on, fella,' and the dog obliged with a high, wagging tail. Nicholas rubbed his head playfully. 'What's your name, then?' he asked.

'He's called Sandy,' he heard in English, and Nicholas looked up to see Corinne approaching with a tray bearing a saucisson half baguette, a glass of orange juice and a small black coffee.

'Ah, a Scottish name,' Nicholas said, still playing with the dog.

'Not necessarily,' Corinne contradicted.

'I suppose not,' said Nicholas, thinking it wise to agree.

She put the tray down. 'Those are for you,' indicating the baguette and juice, then went into her pocket and took out fifty euros.

Nicholas was about to remind her what they had agreed, but she cut in. 'I know what I said, but you've worked hard. Keep it.'

He thanked her and started on the food while she took a cigarette from the packet and lit it. 'Tell me about Edinburgh and if you don't mind, speak English,' she said, inhaling the cigarette and looking up to the mountains. Nicholas rambled on about the world he had left behind: the city, his school and the Edinburgh Festival. As he spoke and she stared at the mountains, one arm across her chest as if for comfort, it occurred to him that it wasn't Edinburgh she was interested in, but the sound of his voice.

Before long, Nicholas had a weekly routine: a day

and a half helping Corinne, a couple of days of ad hoc work with other customers and, weather permitting, the rest of the time spent skiing. His domestic chores, such as shopping, usually took second place, which invariably meant getting caught up in a lengthy checkout queue when the skiers descended at the day's end.

As he left the supermarket one day, clutching a carton of UHT milk, a small bag of potatoes and a packet of sausages, he met Corinne at the door.

'Can you believe, I've run out of coffee,' she said.

'You should have texted me. I'd have brought it up tomorrow.'

'Merci, Nicholas, but I need cigarettes as well.' Those wouldn't wait, he knew.

'Did you have a good ski today?' she asked politely.

'Yes. Well, yes and no. I found what I thought was an off-piste track, but it took me too far away from the slopes and I had to climb back.'

She looked concerned. 'Were you on your own?'

Nicholas gave a contrite nod, knowing Corinne wouldn't approve of him going too far off the piste. He wasn't expecting her furious response though.

'Merde, Nicholas Fraser! You are a stupid boy. Do you know how dangerous that is?'

By now people were looking, tourists at both of them, and locals focused on him.

'I know, Corinne. It was silly of me. I won't do it again.'

'Silly? Do you call that silly? I don't think you do understand. I tell you, Nicholas, if you ever do that again, that will be the end of our working arrangement. Have I made myself clear?' But before he could answer, she had stormed off into the shop.

The next morning he arrived at the grange expecting a frosty reception, but apart from refusing to converse in English, it seemed Corinne had moved on. He had become accustomed to her speaking mainly French for work-related conversation then switching to English for everything else. It appeared to be a small indulgence in a life that otherwise looked joyless.

'I've guests arriving tonight so there's plenty to do, Nicholas. Let's get on with it.' He spent the next few hours alone, clearing snow, stacking wood and cleaning the stove.

By mid-morning, they were outside shaking the dust from blankets, with Nicholas at one end and Corinne the other. Assuming it a game, Sandy jumped up trying to catch the edge, but Nicholas was too quick for him. For a moment Corinne smiled – something he rarely saw – and he realised just how attractive she was. Then it was gone, the arrival of Jerome's car killing the moment.

'Tell him the skis are in the cellar,' she said, taking the blanket and disappearing back into the chalet.

Nicholas had noticed that despite her hostility towards Jerome, Corinne still promoted his services to clients who wanted to ski the Vallée Blanche or one of the other off-piste areas. 'He's a guide,' she told Nicholas, 'and the clients like him.'

On the rare occasions when Nicholas observed

Jerome at work, he saw a very different man from the one he witnessed when Corinne was present. He exuded an aura that quickly won the clients' respect, as Nicholas had seen with the better instructors in Auchenmore. Corinne would invariably keep out of his way and Nicholas thought it prudent to do likewise, although today he had to pass on her message. But Jerome didn't seem interested in the skis.

'You're from Scotland then?' he asked.

Nicholas was cautious but thought it best to play along. 'Yes, Edinburgh. Have you been there?'

Jerome shook his head. 'No, I haven't,' then looked towards the fence as though in thought. He turned back to Nicholas. 'It's not what you think it is between me and Corinne.'

Nicholas felt uncomfortable. 'It's none of my business.'

Jerome returned an understanding nod and moved the subject on again. 'I'm surprised you're still here. Most seasonal workers offer to help, then disappear. But you've stayed and Corinne seems happy with you.'

Nicholas smiled then picked up the shovel he had propped against the wall, saying 'I'd better get on.'

But Jerome hadn't finished with him. 'Have you skied the Vallée Blanche?'

'Yes, when I was at school. We had a trip to Chamonix and a group of the better skiers got to do it. It's an amazing place.'

'Well, if you are free tomorrow you can help me. I have a group of English clients who want lunch included. If you can ski with a rucksack and help out, then I'll pay for your lift pass and give you forty euros. What do you think?'

'I'd do it for nothing!' said Nicholas, a little too quick off the mark.

Jerome smiled. 'No, I'll pay you. Be at the téléphérique station at eight o'clock and don't be late.'

'I won't be. My name is Nicholas.'

'Yes, I know, and I'm sure Corinne will have told you mine!'

Once Jerome had left, Nicholas wondered whether he had been hasty in accepting the offer. Would Corinne think him disloyal? Was it a good idea to go into the mountains in the company of a man with whom she had issues? So he asked her and to his surprise, she said she had no problem with it and Jerome was a safe pair of hands – as long as Nicholas did as he was told.

The clients were three young couples from the Home Counties. Jerome introduced himself and Nicholas, then fitted each person with an avalanche transceiver. 'Now we can find you if you disappear to the pub,' he said, before leading off to the shuffling queue for the téléphérique.

The first cable car offered an unremarkable ascent over the forest, the highlights being the sight of the buildings in Chamonix diminishing into specks and the swing of the cabin as it rode over its pylons drawing oohs and aahs from the passengers as their stomachs took exception. The second was altogether more intimidating, with a near-vertical climb up the imposing north side of the Midi. The clients looked in awe at a pair of climbers on a breathtaking arête.

'That's the Frendo Spur,' offered Jerome. 'First climbed in 1941.' But the audience's attention had switched to a paraglider soaring effortlessly in the thermals on the other side of the valley.

At the top, Jerome roped them together and with the aid of a fixed handline, they made their way cautiously down a daunting ridge to a flattish area from where skiing commenced. Before setting off he issued three instructions. 'Ski only where I ski. Stop immediately when I tell you. And don't take off your skis, as you might be standing over a crevasse a hundred metres deep.'

Chastened by the thought of disappearing into the void, they set off with Jerome leading and Nicholas in the rear. The route consisted of twenty kilometres of pristine snow through stunning high-mountain scenery. Jerome knew plenty of detours off the beaten track, offering the clients the opportunity to ski huge S-turns in untouched powder and to negotiate some tricky passages through towering ice formations.

'You need to keep moving through these parts in case they collapse,' he said, winking discreetly at Nicholas as he added drama to the run and a good story for the clients to tell in the bar later.

Arriving at their lunch stop Nicholas recognised a cluster of rocks: the place he had described to Dani at Waterfall Bothy, and where he had hoped to bring her before everything fell apart.

Jerome handed out three small blankets for the clients to sit on and Nicholas served a selection of charcuteries, cheeses, quiches, fresh baguettes and drinks while making pleasant conversation and flattering them on their skiing. With the clients settled into their meal and discussing soaring London property prices and their various career moves, Nicholas took his plate and retreated to a quiet spot.

'Do you mind if I join you?' Jerome asked, and Nicholas shuffled along to make room.

Feeling insignificant against the grandeur of the place, they ate their lunch gazing across the sea of snow to the huge mountains beyond.

Jerome spoke first. 'This place makes you forget that there is anything else going on in the world. But of course, there is. You know that she's angry with me, don't you Nicholas?' There was no need to elaborate.

'I sensed there was something between you,' he replied, and Jerome laughed.

'You British are so – as you say – understated?'

Nicholas smiled. 'I know what you mean,' then looked serious. 'She was angry with me as well.'

Jerome gave him a friendly knock with his elbow. 'And you know why that was, don't you?'

'Because I was stupid,' his mind going back to the night Dani had said how disappointed she was in him.

Jerome shook his head. 'No, it's because she cares about you. If she didn't, she wouldn't have been angry, would she?'

'I suppose not. Is that why she asked you to bring

me along today?'

'Ah, you figured that out. Yes, it is.'

'I thought so. That was nice of her, and you.'
Then he asked Jerome a question that was building
in significance. 'What happened between the two of
you?'

'That's a long story, Nicholas. And a sad one. But
not what you think. Corinne will need to tell you
herself.'

The clients were getting restless. Having ticked
the Vallée Blanche box, they were eager to return to
Chamonix with its hot tubs and après-ski. Jerome
stood up and made amiable noises in their direction,
then turned back to Nicholas.

'I can give you more work helping to look after
my clients. Listen to me, and I can show you how to
stay alive in the mountains. Would that interest
you?'

'Yes, it would, thank you. And you can tell
Corinne that I've learnt my lesson.'

The *drip, drip, drip* from melting snow on the mazot
roof heralded the arrival of spring. Nicholas sat on
the step scribbling in a jotter while his ski gear dried
in the evening sun. Corinne had asked him to clean
and paint the inside. It was to have been rented out
for the summer, but once complete, she had lost
interest in the idea and offered it to him. 'You'll give
me the going rate,' she had said – a rate that seemed
reasonable compared to what he paid for the
cramped attic in which he had overwintered.

Sandy appeared from the chalet door and came

loping towards him, followed by Corinne holding a letter. Whereas Sandy dutifully followed his mistress about her work, when he saw Nicholas he became positively excited.

'Hello, fella,' he said, ruffling the dog's head, then looked over to Corinne as she approached in her flip-flops, shorts and running vest. There seemed to be even less of her now: she looked all spindly arms and legs and pronounced chest bones.

'This is for you, Nicholas,' she said, handing him the envelope.

He took it and looked at the handwriting. 'It's from Mum.'

'Ah, if she's gone to the trouble of writing she must be missing you.'

Nicholas put the letter down. 'Maybe, but my dad won't be.'

'You don't get on with him, do you?' asked Corinne.

'No. He's a bully.'

'I'm sorry to hear that,' but Nicholas just shrugged.

'What are you drawing?' she asked.

'It's a sketch,' and he stood up to show her. 'My dream is to set up an outdoor centre in Scotland. I'd given up on the idea, but living here and going into the mountains with Jerome has inspired me.'

'Ah, dreams,' she said wistfully. 'Do you mind if I look inside?' her eyes now on the mazot door.

Nicholas gestured her towards it. 'Go ahead,' and Corinne went to peer inside. He watched as she took in the room, looking at each item in turn: the tiny sink and gas stove, an old table and two chairs. Her eyes settled on the wooden bed.

'Go in,' he offered and without replying, she stepped in, moved over to the bed and sat down on the edge.

He could tell that she was in her faraway place again, however, from where she was perched there were no mountains to disappear into, so she looked at Nicholas, her expression telling him that there was something she wanted to share.

'What is it?' he asked.

'This was his dream. The chalet, the mazot, the life here, all of it.'

Nicholas turned one of the wooden chairs to face her and sat down.

'Whose dream was it, Corinne?'

'Alexander, my partner. We were engaged to be married but he died in the mountains last winter.'

Sitting on the edge of the bed, her eyes now full of tears, she looked completely helpless. It was a pain Nicholas recognised from the night in Auchenmore when his shame had made him reject Dani's efforts to comfort him, and he had felt so alone. He recalled also the feeling of devastation when Claire had come to the chalet and told him that Tess was dead.

He picked up one of Corinne's limp hands in his own. 'How did it happen?'

Corinne wiped a tear from her cheek with the back of her free hand. 'He was ski-touring with Jerome when a group ahead were caught in an avalanche. Alexander rushed forward to help but a serac at the top of the slope broke loose and he was killed, struck by a block of ice.'

'Is that why you're angry with Jerome?'

Head bowed, she nodded. 'Jerome said he tried to stop him. He said he warned Alexander that the slope was still dangerous but Alexander wouldn't listen.'

Nicholas's eyes went down to Corinne's hand in his. 'And do you believe Jerome?'

Corinne sniffled, then took a paper hanky from her shorts pocket and blew her nose. 'Alexander was always trying to help people. It's what he would have done: put himself in harm's way to help another. But if Jerome had stopped him, if he had insisted that Alexander waited, I wouldn't be suffering all this pain, would I?'

He took her hand again and gave it a little squeeze. 'Sometimes life can be so unfair. Jerome will be thinking the same thing … you should talk to him.'

'I know, but it's so difficult to face him and forgive.' Her eyes went to the door as though contemplating, and back to Nicholas. 'Alexander came from Scotland.'

He wasn't surprised. There were just too many familiar items around the place and too much of a connection between him and Corinne.

She then looked at him with despairing eyes. 'I've now accepted that he's gone and there's nothing anyone can do about it. But it's so lonely knowing that I will never have him holding me in his arms again.'

Driven by a wave of compassion, Nicholas got up from his seat, moved to the bed, and wrapped his arms gently around her.

The smell of Corinne's cooking and the heat from the stove filled the wood-panelled room.

'You must be looking forward to seeing Scotland again and getting on with your project,' said Jerome as he and Nicholas waited for their hostess to return with the box of *gâteries* keeping cool on the upstairs balcony.

'Yes and no,' replied Nicholas.

'Oh?'

'I'll get to the project, but first I need to see Mum.' There was a pregnant pause while he turned a dessert fork in his hand. 'When I left Scotland I wasn't in a great place with my life. I want to go back now – see if I can sort things out and perhaps help Mum.'

Jerome returned an understanding smile.

Then Nicholas asked a question that had been nagging him. 'Do you remember that day when you suggested we ski across the couloir to save time?'

Jerome completed the question. 'You're going to ask me whether I was testing you.' Nicholas nodded.

'That couloir was dangerous, so the decision to avoid it was the right one. I spend my life in the mountains – they are the place that I love – but no mountain is worth a life. Don't misunderstand me, Nicholas, Alexander's decision was different. He was trying to *save* a life.'

'So you think Alexander did the right thing?'

'He did what he believed was right at the time and I respect him for that. Sometimes all we can do is follow our instincts and hope for the best. But remember, we and others bear the consequences of our decisions.'

The door opened and a waft of wintry air entered the room followed by Corinne holding the box. Dressed in a thick-knitted jumper and woollen scarf, she now looked happier, had put on a little weight, and had even cut down on her smoking. However, since the afternoon when she had bared her soul to Nicholas, things had changed between them. There was an intimacy derived from a deeper level of understanding, but he also sensed awkwardness on her part, born not of what she had disclosed that afternoon in the mazot, but of what had followed physically between them afterwards.

Jerome popped the champagne cork and charged their flutes while Corinne opened the box to display the handmade delicacies. Jerome was about to make a toast when Corinne spoke up.

'Before we toast, I'd like to say something. Firstly, I'd like a thought for Alexander, the man from Scotland whom I loved and will always love. Alexander is gone, but he will forever be an inspiration.'

Nicholas and Jerome clapped gently, but knowing that Corinne hadn't finished, their flutes stayed on the table.

'Jerome. We've now talked about what happened. I don't blame you and never did. Thank you for being patient with me.'

Jerome got to his feet, went around the table and hugged Corinne.

Then she turned to Nicholas. 'A year ago, *un petit écossais* appeared at my door looking for work. He introduced himself as Nicholas Fraser. At the time I felt completely alone; as though I had lost everything of any value. Since that day, Nicholas, you have shown me great kindness and become a good friend. I've also seen you grow as a person, gaining confidence, and according to Jerome, you're now an alpinist in the making. It is time for us all to move forward. You're returning to Scotland, and with Jerome's help, I am going to carry on building what I started here with Alexander. So, for now, Nicholas Fraser, it's *au revoir*.'

He swallowed hard to hold back his emotions and as he looked into Corinne's eyes he could tell that she was doing the same. They raised their flutes and sipped the tingling champagne. 'There's one last thing, Nicholas. I have given this a lot of thought and I know Alexander would approve. Would you like to take Sandy with you?'

CHAPTER 8

'How long have you been a police officer?' Rory asked from his stance next to the sideboard.

'Five years, come May,' Marshall replied. 'Before that, I worked in a bank.'

Rory held up a bottle of single malt. 'This is a special wee number, an eighteen-year-old Speyside. A customer who works in a distillery gave it to me a couple of years ago.'

'Not for me,' said Dani, familiar with the ritual her dad reserved for guests of honour.

Marshall gave an appreciative smile from his armchair. 'That's very kind of you, Mr Bruce.'

'Oh, it's the least I can do for our visitor from the south. And call me Rory.' He poured equal measures into two crystal tumblers and added a little water from a jug. 'Dani tells me you're a keen skier. Have you skied in Scotland before?'

Marshall shook his head. 'No. France and Italy, and once in Canada. Off-piste, mainly. I'm keen to see what Scotland has to offer.'

'Well compared to all that you might find our skiing a little underwhelming,' Rory replied, passing his guest a tumbler. He lifted his own to eye level, catching the flickering flames from the fire through the whisky. 'But don't underestimate it. The mountains here can be quite unforgiving – especially for those foolish enough to take them for granted.'

'Dad,' protested Dani, thinking his comment might be accurate but a little too pointed. Besides, at work Marshall seemed enviably unfazed by tricky situations, and had declared himself an accomplished skier.

'All I'm saying is, be careful,' Rory continued. 'There's a storm forecast for tomorrow night. You want to be well clear of the mountain by then.'

Marshall also held up his glass and looked discerningly at the contents. 'Don't worry, Rory, we can handle it. We'll be well clear by the time the storm arrives. Besides, I was hoping to take you and Dani somewhere nice for dinner tomorrow evening.'

'Aye, that would be nice. *Slange var.*'

With her screen angled so they could both see, Erin McKay scrolled through her portfolio of property and land for sale. A woman in her mid-forties with auburn hair cut stylishly short and with immaculately manicured nails, she appeared as fastidious with her appearance as she did in demonstrating her knowledge of the local market. Nicholas vaguely remembered her and was relieved to find the recognition wasn't reciprocated.

'We have a few industrial units on the outskirts of Auchenmore,' she said, pausing to look at what had once been a laundry, 'but nothing within your price bracket that sits on its own. Not at the moment, anyway. However, things change quickly. It's a case of being patient and ready. I'll make sure you're notified the moment I hear of anything. Are there any other areas you're considering? If you're flexible I could speak to my colleagues in our other branches?'

He considered her suggestion. *Perhaps not a bad idea.* Being part of the original plan, Auchenmore had seemed the natural place to start, but now he was here it felt uncomfortable, even hostile, with this impending storm.

He was about to ask about the Great Glen when he noticed she was distracted by something outside. He turned to see dense snow swirling in the light of the shopfront.

Erin looked at her watch. 'Three-thirty. The storm's arrived much earlier than expected. If you're driving back to Edinburgh I suggest you leave now, before they close the snow gates. Do you have a four-by-four?'

'Yes, but I'd better push on. I'll give you a call tomorrow.'

The mobile on her desk vibrated, her eyes dropping to check the caller ID.

'Can you excuse me a moment?'

She answered the call, and as she listened, her expression changed to one of concern.

'Keep me posted,' she said, and hung up.

'That was my son. He's a member of the local rescue team. They think someone is lost on the mountain. A local girl.'

Nicholas immediately asked, 'Do you know

who?'

'A girl by the name of Dani Bruce. She used to work—' but Nicholas was out of his seat and heading for the door.

Storms always brought extra work for the police, so Tracy finished work early and phoned to volunteer. Wearing her hat and gloves, and with her jacket zipped to the neck, she made the short walk to the police station. A shift felt meaningful in a life that had so recently gone from turbulent to terrifying. Although things were back under control, Tracy's world still lacked the sensual and emotional heart that adulthood had promised.

She changed into her uniform, logged in with Control, then made her way to the muster room. The 17.00 team briefing was normally a quiet affair. A sergeant would update everyone on recent events and issue roles and instructions. Given the right assemblage, the atmosphere would often be lightened by friendly banter. But that also depended on what was happening in the section. Tonight the mood was solemn as officers waited expectantly, already wearing their jackets, hats and winter boots. One of them turned to Tracy, 'I suppose you've heard the news?' But before she could ask, the sergeant called them to order.

'Right, let's get on with this,' she said, beaming the briefing onto a screen, and casting an eye over them to ensure she had everyone's attention.

'You've probably already heard that one of our own, Dani Bruce, has been reported missing on the mountain. At this point details are sketchy but we've ascertained that she was skiing off-piste with a colleague …' She glanced at a piece of paper, 'A Marshall Pickering?' then looked questioningly over to Tracy.

'Her boyfriend,' she answered, as her mind went into freefall.

The sergeant continued. 'They were caught out by the weather and became separated. The boyfriend was picked up by a party returning from the corries. A lucky break for him as he was heading in the wrong direction,' provoking murmurs from the climbers in the team. 'As usual, Mountain Rescue will take care of this but we need to put a point on the gates.'

She looked again at Tracy. 'Can you take this? I know Dani's your friend so if you don't feel up to it …'

'Yes, I want to be useful,' Tracy replied, knowing how agonising it would be returning to her flat and waiting to hear.

'Good. Just make sure nobody gets through. We don't want a repeat of that last fiasco,' referring to the previous storm, when a visitor more accustomed to the urban school run had circumvented the barriers then become stuck, prolonging the road closure.

'I'll make sure,' Tracy replied, trying to sound focused, but distracted by the enormity of what she'd heard.

High on the ridge, Dani felt close to panic. *How did I*

lose sight of him like that? Why did I not see this coming?

One moment Marshall was clearly in sight, only metres ahead, the next he had vanished, consumed by the storm. Throwing snowballs ahead in case of a sudden drop, she shuffled along on her skis to where she thought she had last seen him, but there was no sign, not even a ski track. 'Marshall, Marshall,' she yelled against the screeching wind.

Foreboding thoughts entered her mind: he might have taken a slide into the corrie; he might have fallen over rocks; he might even have been blown away. She continued to search, but, barely able to make out the tips of her skis in the whiteout, and with the fading light, it was hopeless.

Keep calm and think this through. Should I go for help or carry on looking? I could make my way down, keeping the wind to my left until the slope lessens. But it will take hours for help to return. In the meantime, Marshall will be looking for me and might not survive being caught out.

She took out her phone. *Damn.* It was dead. *Why now?* She remembered the transceivers and took her own from inside her jacket. Setting it to receive she checked the screen in case he was close. Nothing. *Keep looking, keep looking.*

Traversing what seemed to be an innocuous slope she felt an ominous thud reverberate below her feet then sensed herself coming off balance, as though a carpet were being pulled from under her. A moment later, the carpet was gone and she was dropping through space. The drop became a tumble as the accelerating avalanche gathered mass to form a suffocating turmoil of snow, noise and energy. Engulfed, Dani found herself thrown violently. She fought to cover her face but the momentum of the snow grabbed at her hands, then wrenched the pack from her back.

Kick your skis off, swim to the top. Kick your skis off, swim to the top. Kick—. The words resounded in her head, but all the theories she'd learnt seemed impossible now. Then a searing pain from a wrenched knee, and finally, stillness and dark.

In less than thirty seconds it was over and Dani lay exhausted and confused, unable to make sense of where she was. *What's that touching my face?* She went to remove it, but unaccountably, her arms held fast.

Through a hazy mind, bewildering questions emerged. *Why can't I move? Why can't I see anything? A dream, surely?*

As her head cleared, it dawned on Dani that this was a prelude to something far more sinister: a real-world nightmare from which there would be no awakening. A world in which it would only be a matter of time before asphyxia or hypothermia prevailed.

I'm going to die here.

The rescue base was a wooden structure with a sheet-metal roof. Nicholas parked the Land Rover then looked over his shoulder into the back. 'You stay here, Sandy,' he said as he got out. He walked through the deepening snow to the front door. A sign, *AMR Control Room*, directed him along a corridor to an open door where he stopped and peered in.

The room had an air of composed efficiency, its walls hosting maps and whiteboards, titled to signify their function. The furthest wall housed a bench desk with blue swivel chairs and two laptops. Fixed to the wall above sat a bank of monitors. One, labelled 'Satellite,' displayed a live weather image of a huge swirl of seething cloud engulfing Scotland. 'M1' and 'M2' were clearly webcams sited on the mountain. M1 was greyed out. However, M2, positioned beside a floodlight, displayed an arctic scene of horizontally driven snow, reminiscent of a polar survival movie. The last monitor showed the garage and equipment store, where silent figures were readying a Land Rover in the brightly lit bay.

On the left, standing beside a plotting table and deep in discussion, was a man Nicholas recognised as the team leader, Ryan Peterson, and another team member, Tulla, who worked at the ski centre. A large red oblong had been drawn onto a laminated map, encircling the ridge and surrounding area.

Tulla was speaking. 'The last signal from her mobile was two hours ago. We can't get an accurate fix from that.'

'What about her boyfriend – Marshall, isn't it? Why didn't he call immediately?' asked Ryan as he pored over the map.

Despite knowing whatever he and Dani had had was over, Nicholas felt a stab of disappointment.

Tulla shrugged. 'He said he couldn't get a signal,

but he's pretty vague about the whole thing. In shock, most likely.'

Ryan scratched at his stubble. 'If we send a party out now without knowing where to look, they're unlikely to find her. The visibility will be two metres at best. They'll struggle to get anywhere against that wind, and the avalanche risk on the steeper ground is unacceptable.' He paused for thought, then continued, 'We need to wait until either the weather lets up, or we get further information. That way, we can get three strong groups on the hill and use the dogs to cover the area properly.'

'You can't just leave her there!' protested Nicholas from the door.

Tulla immediately recognised him. Confused, she said, 'Nicholas, I didn't realise you were back. Were you with Dani today?'

Concern written across his face, he shook his head. 'No, I wasn't. I just happened to be in Auchenmore when I heard that she's in trouble. You're going to help her aren't you?'

Tulla looked cautiously to Ryan for direction and Ryan addressed Nicholas. 'I don't know what you've heard, so let me explain the situation. We think Dani is still on the mountain but we're not sure where. We're getting the team together but need a better fix on her position, or a break in the weather, or daylight before we move. If we go now the teams will be exhausted before dawn – or casualties themselves.'

Nicholas didn't like what he was hearing. 'Can you not at least try?'

Ryan snapped back. 'Look, son, there's not a

team member who wouldn't go right now if asked to.' His own frustration with the delay was obvious.

'That's not what I meant,' Nicholas replied, his tone signalling that he wasn't questioning their commitment.

'I know it wasn't,' Ryan conceded. 'I'm sorry. I didn't mean to be abrupt. You're worried about Dani, we all are. If you want to help, we would appreciate your assistance.' He looked at his watch. 'There'll be a briefing in the common room in forty minutes. As soon as the conditions change, we'll move without hesitation.' Then, pointing to the garage monitor, 'You can see our vehicles are all set to go. For now though, the best thing you can do to help is to go through and meet the others. There are soup and sandwiches to keep you going. I'll see you at the briefing.'

Making it clear there would be no more debate, he returned to Tulla and continued their discussion.

Nicholas headed out of the building, stopping under the porch canopy to zip up his jacket against the biting cold and retrieve his hat from a pocket. The scene across the car park was almost tranquil, the sodium floodlights colouring everything a syrupy yellow. Large snowflakes drifted diagonally to the ground, accumulating into a thick blanket that muffled any sound there might have been.

It was as though the world had come to a stop, yet when he looked up to the top of the trees blowing in the wind, he was reminded that there was a storm raging and that somewhere on the mountain, Dani was in danger.

His mind raced; none of this made any sense. He had scarcely arrived back in Scotland, and had heard nothing from anyone in all the time he had been away. Now, while visiting Auchenmore for only one day, he found himself pulled into a crisis. Thinking no further than his next action, he crossed the car park, took snow chains from the back of his vehicle and fitted them onto the tyres. The task complete, he climbed aboard and headed towards the mountain.

Tracy parked beside the gates then sat with the engine running and the 'at scene' blue and red lights flickering, sending multicoloured bursts to create the effect of an enormous glitterball.

She turned up the heater and felt the warm air wash over her, but the comfort was short-lived as she thought of Dani, then toggled through the radio channels to Roam, so that she could hear communications from throughout the division.

Her phone pinged: a text message from Mum. *I've heard about Dani. Please keep me updated.* Tracy replied, *I know, it's terrible, will let you know as soon as I hear anything.* At one point she dialled Dani's number, then regretted it as she heard her friend's cheery voice. 'Hi, Dani here. Leave a message and I'll call you back.' If Dani had been able to call, she would have done so hours ago.

Glancing up, she saw headlights approaching but, expecting the vehicle to turn off, returned to her phone. When she next looked it was still advancing, eventually stopping at the closed gates. Even with its headlights blazing, she could tell it was a Land

Rover and that the driver was getting out. *For fuck sake*, she thought, preparing to state the obvious, then putting on her hat, she too got out.

Her hand raised to shield her eyes from the glare, she yelled over the wind, 'The road's closed. Can you not turn off your headlights?'

'Tracy? Is that you?' came the reply.

Even with the storm raging, Tracy instantly recognised his voice. For a moment she stood, stunned, and then, gathering herself, shouted, 'Nicholas Fraser, what the hell are you doing here?'

He walked purposefully towards her, stopping a metre short. 'It's Dani, she's in trouble. I'm going to try and find her,' he blurted, as though he and Tracy had last spoken earlier that day.

But Tracy was guarded as memories came flooding back. She remembered what he had put her and Dani through before he left. And yet when he'd finally disappeared, she'd hurt. He'd been so nice the first time they'd met, but after that, he'd only had eyes for Dani. Then when he left, she'd felt as if she'd thrown away her last chance to make him see *her*. In all this time, she'd never been able to get him out of her head, not properly, and now here he was, with a ridiculous offer of hope. He clearly had no idea how desperate the situation was.

'I know she is. And the last thing she needs right now is you in the way again, being stuck and blocking the road. Just get in your vehicle, turn around, and go back to wherever your life is now.'

Harsh, but honest, she told herself.

'Please, Tracy, I need to get through. Dani won't

make it through the night. You know that. I need to at least try and find her. What have you got to lose by letting me pass?'

Tracy held her ground. 'And what makes you believe you can find her? You don't know where to search, and you won't be able to stand up, let alone make progress in this weather. Even if she's two metres in front of you, she might as well be two hundred, because you'll never see her in the whiteout. Are you trying to prove yourself? Because if you are, it's a bit late for that!'

Nicholas hadn't considered anything beyond going up the mountain and looking. He had to act; the why and how didn't seem to matter.

'I don't know, Tracy! I haven't thought that far ahead, and you know what? You might be right, I might not get past the first bend; look at it, you can hardly see the road down here, let alone up there.' He stopped for breath and then rushed on, determined to make her see what was so clear to him. 'What I do know is that right now I can either take a step closer to finding someone who's in real trouble, or I can take a step in the opposite direction. But what would Dani do? If she were standing here and we were up there, what would she do for us?'

He looked different from the Nicholas she recalled. The one who had remained passive when publicly humiliated by his father. The one she had seen on the night of his twentieth birthday, battered and beaten. And the one who remained silent when she had walked up and berated him in front of his friend. This version of Nicholas seemed determined, even if his idea was ridiculous.

He looked straight at her. 'I didn't ask for any of this, Tracy, and I know it's easier to turn and run away. I've done plenty of that in my time. But how far would I have to run to escape the knowledge that Dani had died on the mountain, and I'd done nothing to help her?'

In that one phrase, even amid the turmoil of their situation, Tracy understood, and it frightened her in a way she had never felt before. Suddenly, all the official procedures that had previously protected her in the face of other people's tragedies melted away, exposing her looming fear of being abandoned, without her best friend and without Nicholas, who had always exerted such a powerful pull on her emotions. Guilt rushed in. *Why am I always so vindictive towards him? Why am I trying to hurt him yet again? It's never made him like me.* And there was real danger here, now. Nicholas was right. As absurd as it sounded, this was likely to be the only chance that Dani had. And she remembered Dani's support when she'd needed it. But what about Nicholas, out there on the mountain? She looked at his determined face, and saw a confidence that had never been there before. She reached out and rubbed his arm, then, wondering what had possessed her, abruptly pulled back.

'I'll open the gates for you, but please, Nicholas, take care.'

She was about to move when he stopped her. 'Could you do me a favour? It's Sandy. Can I leave him with you? It would be unfair to take him out in this weather, and if I leave him in the vehicle all night ...'

'Who's Sandy?'

Nicholas went to the rear of the Land Rover, fiddled in the back, and out jumped an energetic young German Shepherd on a lead.

'How am I supposed to explain this?' she asked, visualising a scene at the station in which she was trying to explain why another person was lost on the mountain and how she came to have possession of their dog.

Nicholas resolutely held out the lead. 'I need to go now, Tracy.'

'I'll think of something,' she muttered, taking it from him.

With the dog in tow, Tracy drew open one of the gates and, as Nicholas drove through, she gave a little wave of encouragement. *What the hell am I doing?* she wondered. *Letting him go out there to risk his life? How can he survive that storm, let alone find and save Dani?* He returned the wave and smiled, then disappeared, the sound of his engine drowned out by the wind.

She drew the gate shut and stood for a moment. It felt almost as though Nicholas had never been there. Then she looked down at Sandy, his presence confirming that for a moment, he had been. 'Come on, Puppy,' she said, opening the passenger door of the police vehicle and conscious that once again, she had allowed Nicholas to vanish.

Frenzied questions crowded Dani's mind: *how much*

air do I have? How deep am I? Who knows I'm here? In pitch darkness, powerless to move and unable to tell up from down, claustrophobia loomed. A demon that would drive a cycle of self-destruction in which she would hyperventilate, lose consciousness, then suffocate. She tried to move, gently at first, wriggling her body, then straining violently, but what had once been delicate snowflakes had sintered into a solid mass.

Her straining sent bolts of pain from the torn knee. Opening her mouth to cry out, she gulped in wet snow and unable to move her head or hands, found herself gagging as the large glob of half-frozen matter entered her throat. With the little air left in her lungs, she coughed out a stream of slush, the mixture running over her cheeks, into her eyes and stinging them shut.

Powerless against the grip of her frozen tomb and in the knowledge that no one knew of her situation, she stopped moving, allowing her laboured breathing to return and wondering just how long she could endure.

With four-wheel-drive engaged, Nicholas pressed on. Drift after drift, chains gripping, slipping, and then regaining traction to send judders and jolts through the vehicle. It took everything the engine had to punch a way through, with Nicholas acutely aware that loss of momentum in a drift would render him stranded, just as Tracy had predicted.

Remember the bends, left, now right, keep into the bank but not too far. It seemed an age since he'd last ascended here – and never in such conditions. Shearing wind sent horizontal streamers of snow that blurred in the headlights and accumulated on the side window and windscreen, clogging the wipers and threatening to snap the arms from their spindles. Unable to see through the smearing mess he stopped to clear it and was shocked to see a hairpin straight ahead. Another six feet and he would have plunged over the edge.

A moment's reassurance when he passed a familiar sign, but it was short-lived as a series of gusts buffeted him sideways. The slow progress and intense concentration toyed with his perception of time and distance, but after what seemed an eternity, the Car Park sign appeared. He crossed a wilderness of swirling snow, reached the far side and turned off the engine. Leaning forward onto the steering wheel he took a deep breath. *Right, that's the easy part done.*

Accepting her fate, Dani's mind transcended to a world of calm and cherished memories: her father and the image of a woman in a floral-patterned dress on the sideboard at their home in Inverness. 'Mum,' she whispered, knowing that whatever came next, she wasn't alone.

She worked through the situation. Marshall would have phoned for help and be looking for her. Perhaps he'd see the tracks from the avalanche and use the transceiver as she had instructed. She then considered the significance of the liquid running from her mouth, across her cheeks and into her eyes.

It meant her feet were slightly elevated. She thought about how she had gagged. *I must be face-up too, otherwise that wouldn't have happened.*

Her mind turned to her priorities: getting air and staying warm. Although her left arm was trapped out to the side, her right had movement, but the glove was missing, making her hand numb with cold. Working it up her bodyline by pressing down her jacket and excavating the snow, she reached her neck and pushed the hand behind her collar to warm. With feeling returned she continued clearing the snow from above her face until at nearly an arm's length she felt the movement of the storm above.

Inching open the Land Rover door Nicholas felt the grab of the wind try to wrestle it from his grasp. He pulled it closed, then looked behind to a ghostlike glow from a distant floodlight and the temptation of sanctuary in a building. But then he thought of Dani and, taking the map he'd used earlier that day from the dashboard, he laid it open across the steering wheel. *Right, what might Dani have done? She's a good skier, so even in these conditions she should have made it down.* Then there was the boyfriend, the guy Ryan had referred to as Marshall. Despite being disorientated, he had made it down. If this was his first time up here and they had become separated, Dani would have stayed and looked for him. Surely, at some point, she would have realised it was futile and sought help? What might have stopped her from doing that?

Running his finger along and between the

contours on the map, he imagined the terrain, tracking ridges and slopes, looking for areas with both an easy exit and a hazard. There seemed to be three such places. To cover one would be an enormous challenge, two would be impossible. *Come on, Dani, where are you?* Turning to the empty passenger seat he imagined Jerome sitting there. *Sometimes all we can do is follow our instincts and hope for the best. But remember, we and others bear the consequences of our decisions.* If he got this wrong, Dani might perish, her father would lose his daughter and his mother could lose him.

Within the first area, Dani and Marshall were unlikely to have become separated: the terrain was too closed-in Within the second, the doglegs on the descent would have been too much for Marshall to negotiate alone. This left only the ridge, with its notorious slope into the corrie.

Reaching back, he retrieved a compass from the top of the rucksack and with a pencil and the aid of the base plate, drew three straight lines on the map then determined their distance and bearing. He calculated times and paces for what would be incredibly slow progress, jotting them onto a pad and transposing the key numbers onto the back of his hand with a biro.

Time to move. Keeping downwind, he worked his way to the back of the vehicle and using a cord to keep the door from fully opening, wedged himself into the gap. Through habit, he picked up his avalanche transceiver, switched it on and secured it to his body. Then, with the aid of a head torch, he continued his preparations. The rucksack was full of karabiners, slings and other mountaineering gear. However, none of that would be needed tonight, so he replaced it with extra clothing, a sleeping bag and a large survival bag. That done, he packed an orange sleeve containing the thin interconnecting rods of an avalanche search probe, and a collapsible shovel. Thankfully, the top pocket was already stocked with an assortment of energy foods. Finally, he rummaged for his snowshoes and walking poles. *I didn't think I'd be using these again so soon.*

Donning his windproof jacket and goggles, he slung the load onto his back, flinching under its weight. *At last, ready to go* and within seconds, holding a compass in his mitted hand, Nicholas had disappeared into the storm.

The wind continued its relentless attack, pounding him as it had the Land Rover, the stronger gusts knocking him to the ground, holding his body prone and pushing his face into the snow. He imagined the weight of his father bearing down and mocking his efforts, and he knew that if he lay there, he would die. Determined to deny the man that with which he had always taunted his wife – the death of her son – and knowing that Dani was on her own, he hauled himself back onto his feet.

At times the head torch reached no further than his snowshoes. His goggles required constant wiping, but when he tried removing them, the blast of icy particles was blinding. They stayed on. Following the bearing, he crossed what he thought to be a snow-covered stream then traversed a precarious slope, his snowshoes snagging on clumps of exposed turf, peat hags and rocks. Despite the way they spread the pressure, he frequently found himself thigh-deep in snow, necessitating an awkward crawl to get out.

He urged himself on, counting his distance in groups of ten paces. At nine hundred paces, he paused to catch his breath. Bracing against the poles, he stuffed a glucose jelly into his mouth, savouring its sweetness, before setting a new compass bearing and continuing forwards.

After two hours of tortuous passage and further changes in direction, the route intersected the avalanche zone. His thoughts turned to Corinne, the despair he had seen in her eyes at the loss of Alexander, and what she would be saying to him now. And he thought of what must have been going through Alexander's mind, caught in this same position. With increasing frequency, the extra loading on the unpredictable slope fractured the snow beneath his feet: a faultline that threatened to unleash its mass. And each time, he froze, praying it would go no further, before moving on. 'Dani! Dani!' he called into the chaos.

Fifteen minutes later an outcrop appeared on which two years before he had stood with a friend as an avalanche cascaded past – a chastening experience that had sent them scurrying off the mountain. The stance wouldn't protect against a significant slide, but it offered a footing from which to work.

This has to be it.

The head torch scanned, occasionally probing a little further through tantalising breaks in the weather to offer glimpses of the slope, only for it to close like a stage curtain the moment Nicholas tried to peer through. Examining the ground, he saw churned snow resembling whisked egg whites. The fresh fall sought to disguise the evidence, but this was definitely recent avalanche debris.

Making awkward passage, he swept the slope back and forth, a U-turn at each end as he searched for clues that failed to emerge.

Sinking onto his knees, his head dropped as the folly of his actions became clear. *How could I believe this would work?* Everything Tracy had said made sense. *Dani could be anywhere: up on the ridge or over by the piste. She might even have returned to the valley. And I've put myself in an impossible situation, trying to be someone I'm not.* It was too late to turn back: he would never make it. *I should try and find shelter. If I survive the night, I'll face the consequences of what I've done and leave Auchenmore for good.* The storm seemed to deride his efforts, and with it came the feeling of failure that had once been so familiar. With his spirits deflated, the cold and fatigue quickly stole what was left of his energy. *Perhaps I should just lie down in the snow and wait ...*

Then his mind returned to Dani and her situation. He thought of how far he had come on his own despite everything that life had thrown at him, and he remembered Calum, the boy whom life had treated so harshly, refusing to give up as he hung from the trapeze. He smiled at the memory of Calum's shoe falling off and his determination to try again. He recalled Geoff's words. *If you think something is possible, then it probably is.*

Getting back onto his feet, Nicholas continued to search. The falling snow was increasing the chances of a second avalanche, and if Dani was here, it would bury her deeper. Something caught his eye, a short length of what seemed to be webbing tape. Tugging hard, a ski pack with a broken strap emerged. A lucky spot.

I wonder, I wonder? Opening his jacket, he retrieved his transceiver. *Come on, Dani, remember what you said to me, 'Always wear a transceiver when skiing off-piste.'*

With raised hopes, he switched the device to receive, only to get a return of No Signal.

'Switch it on, Dani,' he urged, then acknowledging the absurdity of his request.

He continued back and forth, the transceiver held at his side. A sound caught his attention, a high-pitched beeping. In disbelief, he lifted the device, almost dropping it in his haste, to see *22 Metres* fill the display.

'Yes!' as he followed the arrows on the screen. The pulses quickened and the distance dropped: 20 metres, 18, 16, 12, 13, left a bit … 12 … 8, 6 and 4 … Beep! … Beep! Beep! … Beeeeeeep! A continuous tone blared but looking down, he could see only white.

Having marked a cross in the snow, he assembled the probe, then pushed it gently down, working the area until he found a point of resistance. With the shovel he carefully dug, excavating enough to complete the task by hand. *It isn't deep, so if it is Dani, that's promising. But if it's her, how long has she been buried?* He knew from the depth of the fresh covering that considerable time had passed since the avalanche and that survival rates plummeted after fifteen minutes, and again after thirty. But there was always hope. People had survived being buried for much longer, and Dani would have been well dressed and physically fit. With thoughts of the harsh conditions, fatigue and the risk to his own life forgotten, he continued, desperate to reach what lay below.

Then, there she was, her body inert. 'No!' he shouted. 'No!'

'Dani, come on, it's time to get up.' She pulled the duvet a little higher to escape the draught. The bedroom always seemed so cold in winter. 'Come on, Dani, you'll be late for school and your porridge is getting cold.' *Why is Dad always so persistent?* Then her sleepy mind started to wonder. *Is it Dad, or is it, Marshall? It's Marshall, he's found me! But why is he speaking with Nicholas's voice?*

'Dani, Dani, wake up. It's Nicholas. I've come to take you home.'

But I am home.

Struggling to make sense of it, she tried to open her eyes but failed. *I'm dreaming,* moving her head slightly to escape whatever was touching her face.

'Be still, Dani. Your eyelids are frozen shut. I'm

warming them.'

Soon, they flickered open. 'Nicholas?' the word barely audible through her frozen lips.

He nodded and smiled, then started digging the snow from around her. 'We need to get somewhere safe.'

More questions filled her head but her numb lips rendered her mute. Seeing her concerned look, Nicholas stopped and leant down close to her so she could hear him. 'Marshall's safe – he's back down in the valley.'

She relaxed, her drowsiness lulling her in and out of sleep, and her limbs lightening as Nicholas continued to free them from the avalanche's clutch.

'You've lost a glove,' he said, slipping one onto her hand. 'I'm going to clear some of this from your clothes.'

She lay helpless as he brushed snow off her jacket and from around her neck. 'Now, Dani, we need to get down the slope to shelter.'

He tried to lift her but each time failed, the effort pushing him down into the snow; try as she might, Dani was powerless to help.

'I'll drag you,' he said, locking his arms under her armpits and using his body weight to haul her backwards. They started down with frequent stops as Nicholas stumbled, pulling them to the ground. 'Sorry,' he would say, getting up and carrying on.

The terrain eased, then flattened, but Nicholas continued, hauling Dani away from the slope. Reaching an area of boulders she sensed him looking around with his torch while still holding on to her.

'We can shelter over there,' he said as they set off towards a substantial rock.

With Dani sitting in the shelter of its lee, Nicholas stopped to catch his breath and allow the blood to return to his burning muscles. He knew it was imperative to reverse Dani's heat loss, but warming her too quickly could send cold blood from her extremities back to her core, leading to further cooling and possible cardiac arrest.

Taking the orange survival bag from his rucksack, he released the sleeping bag into it, and then laid an insulating mat on the base. He wanted Dani inside, but her jacket was caked in ice and her ski boots would never fit in. The left boot released without fuss, but as he pulled on the right she cried out in pain. 'I'm sorry, Dani. Let's get this done and you into the warm,' gripping her ankle and pulling the boot firmly against his hold.

With her now able to offer limited assistance, he removed her jacket, then fed her into the sleeping bag, replacing her helmet with his woollen hat. 'I warmed it up for you,' he said, climbing into the survival bag himself, and positioning the rucksack as a barrier against the elements.

It was past midnight when he sent a 999 text, receiving a reply minutes later.

'Expect a land team or helicopter at first light or sooner. Will update.'

Dani was warming and starting to communicate. 'I can't feel my hands.'

'Let's put these on them,' slipping his glove liners onto her fingers then drawing her sleeping bag cord to trap the heat. He set the torch to low power and positioned it near their heads, creating an orangey-red glow. Opening his down jacket, he wrapped it around Dani as far as he could and snuggled close to share their precious warmth.

He wanted her awake until he could be sure of her recovery, uneasy that she might drift off into eternity. However, he was feeling better about their situation. The shelter was protecting them, and Dani was responding. She was more alert and complaining about the pain in her hands as the blood returned to the damaged tissue.

'They'll be a wee bit sore, but that's a good thing. It means they're warming,' he encouraged.

'Do you think we'll be alright?' she asked.

'We'll be fine. We just need to wait until daybreak and we can do that, can't we?' Then taking the packet of glucose jellies from his pocket he popped one into her mouth. 'Try this, it will give you energy.'

'That tastes good,' she said, as it melted on her tongue.

He fed her sweets and talked to keep their spirits up: his trip to France, his work, Sandy, and his friends, Corinne and Jerome.

Then she asked him a question. 'I don't understand, Nicholas. Why are you here on your own? Where are the others?'

'They'll be along by morning.'

And as she looked at him, he could see her eyes fill with fear. 'I wouldn't have lasted that long.'

With her exhausted but recovering, and in the

knowledge that any sleep would soon be interrupted, he let her doze. It felt strange to be so close to her again. He recalled their night at Waterfall Bothy, how they had kissed from the confinement of their sleeping bags and how he had wanted her to climb inside his with him but left it unsaid for fear of taking things too quickly for her. Tonight there was no mention of that or the subsequent events that had torn them apart. It was as though none of it had happened. But it had, and this was temporary; tomorrow, Dani would be gone. He looked at her sleeping beside him, watching her breathing gently with whatever thoughts she had.

'I'm so sorry for messing things up,' he whispered, then closed his eyes.

The world was silent. *A lull perhaps,* but the peace continued, so Nicholas stuck his head out and looked around. *It's over, the storm has passed.*

Shaking the snow from the survival bag, he climbed out, careful not to disturb Dani, then stood up and stretched – his body stiff and sore from the night. It was early, but the approaching dawn was awakening a spectacular world shrouded in a blanket of white. He looked towards the loch and beyond to Auchenmore, where the yellow and white lights of habitation twinkled; a comforting sight after being so remote. Far below, the blue light of an emergency vehicle was winding its way up the mountain. He turned towards the slope they had descended the previous night, but all trace of their passage had vanished.

Dani stirred. 'The storm is over,' he said. 'It will soon be morning. I need to make sure the rescuers can see us,' and busied himself with clearing snow from around their shelter.

'Can I look out?' she asked, 'I want to see where we are, and get some air.'

'Of course, let me help you.'

Keeping Dani within the sleeping and survival bags, he sat her up against the boulder and crouched beside her.

They stared at the world below, Dani taking in her beloved Highlands, Nicholas content being in the moment, and the two of them together, as it had been before.

She then looked at him and saw the faraway expression on his face. 'Nicholas?' she asked. He turned towards her, but the moment was lost to the sound of an approaching helicopter. Dani's eyes followed him as he stood up and waved his head torch slowly back and forth. As it got closer the pilot illuminated an enormous searchlight, did a small circle then stopped to one side of their position. Snow swirled in the downdraught, and Nicholas, fearing for Dani, held her tight, keeping their heads down.

In a beautifully choreographed procedure, a winchman and stretcher descended on the wire. Reaching the ground, the winchman unclipped, looked up and signalled the helicopter to pull away.

'Hello, I'm Lewis. How are you both?' he said warmly, his eyes scanning and assessing their condition.

'Surviving,' Nicholas replied, with a faint smile. 'It's been a long night. Dani's warming up, but she's hurt her knee.'

'Hello, Dani. We'll have a quick look at that and I'll check you over. Then it's off to Inverness for breakfast. How does that sound?' making a trip to the A&E department sound like something one wouldn't want to miss out on.

She nodded obediently, familiar with the way the emergency services spoke to normalise the worst of situations.

Lewis beckoned Nicholas. 'If you could give me a hand?'

They unzipped the sleeping bag and assessed Dani's condition, immobilised her leg, and then lifted her carefully onto the stretcher. Lewis secured the ties, offering reassurance like a parent taking their child to the doctor.

Nicholas heard him radio the helicopter and watched it arc back towards them.

'Let's move her into the open … Ready to go, Dani?' Lewis asked.

Looking apprehensive, she nodded again.

'You'll be fine,' he said, sensing her anxiety.

He then turned to Nicholas. 'Are you coming, too?'

'No, I'll clear up here. You get going; you'll be faster that way.'

'Are you sure? There's plenty of room,' his eyes going from Nicholas to Dani as though they were a couple. Dani's mind spun.

'Yes, I'm sure, but thanks anyway,' Nicholas

replied, embarrassed at what Lewis had presumed.

'OK. Well, there are a couple of chaps coming to help you home. One of them says he knows you.'

Lewis clipped on to the wire that had once again been lowered, and signalled for the lift. The basket started up quickly, with Nicholas holding it steady. Lewis gave a signal to let go. Dani looked at Nicholas with urgency in her face, 'Nicholas, Nicholas,' she was saying. He moved towards her, still holding the stretcher.

'Let go!' shouted Lewis, fearful of what would happen if he didn't.

Nicholas did and the stretcher ascended, taking Dani and her words with it.

An arm appeared to assist them aboard, and with a sideways swing, the ensemble disappeared inside. Lewis's head reappeared moments later. He gave Nicholas a final thumb-up then returned inside and the door closed. The helicopter rotated slowly towards the valley, dipped its nose then started on its journey home.

Nicholas stood watching Dani disappear once again from his life. To the east, a chink of sun had emerged from behind the hill, washing the valley in gold. With the pressure of the storm past, he thought once again of Jerome, who had given him the skills that had saved his and Dani's lives. He thought of Alexander, who had lost his life trying to help others, and of Corinne, left to bear the pain but now determined to honour Alexander's memory. He thought of his mother, who had paid a heavy price for protecting him, and then he thought of his father, the brutality he had meted out, and how he had only ever served himself.

CHAPTER 9

Nicholas was repacking the sleeping bag when two people came into view, plodding laboriously through knee-deep snow towards him. They stopped and waved. Returning their greeting he recognised one of the men as his friend Geoff from the outdoor centre, and the other, Drew, who worked in the local medical practice.

'Hello, stranger!' Geoff said, in his cheery way. As they hugged and the stress of the previous night dissipated, Nicholas found himself struggling with his emotions. 'I understand,' said Geoff, giving him time to collect himself.

Drew took a large flask from his rucksack and the three of them drank sweet tea and ate chocolate biscuits and energy bars before setting off back to the car park. The path formed by Geoff and Drew's outward passage made the return easier. Nicholas scanned the mountainside for signs of the previous night's trek, but it was as though he had never been there, and the great battle with the storm had been a figment of his imagination.

As the car park came into view, he saw a Suzuki four-by-four next to his Land Rover. It flashed its headlights, then Tracy got out, followed quickly through the same door by an unmistakable Sandy. Picking up Nicholas's scent, the dog came bounding towards him through the snow, followed by Tracy walking in a more dignified manner.

'It looks like you have a reception committee,' said Geoff to Nicholas. 'We'll leave you to it, mate, but make sure you call in and see us.'

'That's kind, but I don't know my plans yet. I was meant to be back in Edinburgh yesterday.' He shook Drew's hand and then Geoff's. 'Thanks for helping me back …' but Geoff raised his other hand to stop him.

'No Nicholas, it's us who are thankful. What you did last night was exceptional. I'm proud of you, son,' and with that, they headed off towards the far end of the car park, giving Tracy a wave as they went.

Seconds later, Sandy arrived at Nicholas's feet. He bent down and ruffled the excited dog. 'Hello fella,' then looked over to Tracy, who had caught up. No longer in uniform, she was dressed in warm black leggings, snow boots, a big beige jacket with a furry hood, and a beanie from which her hair flowed. Despite the time of day, she had applied a little make-up. Sandy, feeling he had received all the attention he would get from Nicholas for now, turned towards her. She willingly obliged – thankful of the diversion while she thought about what to say after their encounter the previous evening.

'Looks like you two have made friends,' Nicholas laughed. 'I hope you haven't been waiting long?'

'No, not really,' she said, making light of what had been a tense night. 'We wanted to see if you were OK … or needed anything.' She was floundering for words. She knew she had to be here but hadn't processed why. Reuniting Sandy and Nicholas made a good excuse, but there was more to it. At the end of her shift, she'd taken Sandy to her flat, where they'd held an anxious vigil. A radio borrowed from the station had kept her posted with snippets of operational news and at around 5 a.m., after hearing of Dani's evacuation and Nicholas's return on foot, they had headed out to meet him.

Now she found herself standing before him with a complex mixture of feelings: relief, embarrassment and something more significant that until recently she had deceived herself into thinking was behind her. She knew now that it was still very much alive, but what to do next didn't seem so straightforward. All the breezy sentences she had rehearsed felt utterly inappropriate.

'You had me worried, Nicholas,' she said, struggling to find the right tone. 'Worse than that, I thought I was going to lose you both. Don't do that again,' as her hand gently thumped his chest. Nicholas could see that she was upset and put his arms out to console her. She held him, pressing her face against his chest, fearful she might lose him yet again.

'It's OK,' he said, lightly patting her back. 'It's been a difficult night, hasn't it?'

She nodded.

'Yes,' she eventually replied.

Relaxing, she let go of him and took a tissue out to blow her nose. Aware that her make-up had run she dabbed under her eyes, then taking control, reached out her hand. 'Give me your rucksack, I'll take it,' as a parent might when meeting their child from the school bus.

'Are you sure?' he asked, not wanting to undermine her, but aware of its weight.

'Yes, I'm, sure,' beckoning it with her hand.

Nicholas obliged, helping her heft it onto her back. Struggling under its weight she led the way towards their cars with Sandy running in huge circles through the snow, as though this were a day like any other.

'I phoned the hospital. Dani's fine,' she said. 'They'll be keeping her in, but nothing to be concerned about. You did well, Nicholas. Better than I thought you would,' teasing him.

Arriving at a frozen stream, she stopped and looked warily at the ice-covered rocks. Nicholas crossed first and asked her to pass him the rucksack and then put out his hand to help her. She didn't object when he discreetly shouldered the backpack and carried it the remaining distance.

With his gear back in the Land Rover and his boots exchanged for trainers, Nicholas turned to Tracy. 'Thanks for looking after Sandy and bringing him up here. I hope I didn't get you into trouble?'

She shook her head. 'No, it was fine.' Having contradicted her sergeant's orders by letting Nicholas through the gates was now the least of her concerns. 'What are your plans now?' she asked, aware that he was about to leave again.

He looked into the distance. 'I'll head down to Edinburgh, I suppose. I'm staying with a friend who has a flat there. We were meant to head back yesterday. Maybe we can rest in the centre for an hour or two. No matter, I'll sort something.'

'No,' she said. 'You can rest on my settee, Sandy's already agreed. But before that, we can stop at the centre. You can get changed and leave your stuff in the drying room, and then I'll treat you to breakfast in Auchenmore. Follow me.'

They entered the café, drawing a friendly welcome from Tony, the owner, as he stacked crockery on a shelf.

'Hello, Nicholas, I haven't seen you about these parts for a while. How are things?' he asked, acknowledging Tracy with a more familiar nod and smile. It was as though he was awaiting Nicholas's return.

'Fine, thanks,' said Nicholas, for want of a better reply, and Tony directed them to a corner booth.

They removed their coats then sat on opposite sides of the fixed table, Sandy settling underneath.

With his shelf-stocking complete, Tony came over. 'Would you like a cuppa to get you started?'

'Tea please,' said Tracy, and Nicholas nodded his agreement.

She took off her wool hat and ruffled her red hair to return its volume.

Nicholas looked around the place that for a while had been a regular haunt.

Tracy read his thoughts. 'What does it feel like to be back?'

'I'm not sure. It's all a bit of a whirlwind.'

Two large mugs of piping hot tea appeared and Tony took an order pad from his pocket. 'What can I get you?'

Tracy didn't need the menu. 'My favourite is the Egg Muffin, but today I think we should go for it,' and with Nicholas's tacit consent she ordered two house favourites, Highlander Breakfast Specials.

They sat with their hands clasping their mugs, Nicholas mindlessly watching Tony mop the floor by the entrance where the snow from their boots had already thawed, and Tracy looking at Nicholas, wondering what was going on inside that mysterious head of his.

She broke the silence. 'Nicholas, I want to say I'm sorry for how I spoke to you last night.'

His eyes shifted to meet hers. 'Oh, don't worry about it, Tracy. I must have looked quite stupid standing there.'

'No, you didn't look stupid, and I was unkind.' She paused, wondering whether to mention the other time, when she had seen him with the pretty girl, but decided to leave it.

She continued. 'I think it was because last night I was scared. Scared about what would happen to Dani, and to you. The whole situation felt out of control and there was nothing anyone could do about it. Except you, that is. You decided to do something, didn't you?'

'That out-of-control feeling is horrible,' he said.

'I know all about it.'

Breakfast arrived and they chatted as they ate. Small talk of everyday things in life: the weather, the season's snowfall and the new budget hotel taking shape at the end of town.

Tracy looked over to the counter with the sauces and cutlery. 'I'm going to get ketchup. Would you like some?' but instead of answering, he slid off his seat and went himself.

'One or two?' he called over, holding a sachet up.

'Two please,' she replied, eyeing their minuscule size.

Nicholas returned to his seat, carefully tore off the corners then handed the sachets to Tracy.

'Are you not having any?' she asked.

He smiled and shook his head. 'I'll tell you a funny story some time about me, ketchup and France, but for now, let's just say that I'm wary of it,' and Tracy felt comfort in knowing that from her mundane desire for ketchup he had shown her kindness, joked with her and intimated that they would be talking again.

Hearing him mention France, she recalled Claire telling her of his departure to Chamonix. Beyond that, nobody seemed to know much. She was curious. 'Tell me what you've been up to, Nicholas. You just disappeared. One day you're here, the next you're gone like snow off a dyke.'

He thought about her question and what to say. Should he tell her the real reason? How an abusive father, a personal crisis and the death of a dear friend had left him feeling the need for a new start? Or should he say he'd gone to France because it had seemed like an interesting life move?

He chose the middle ground. 'Things weren't working out for me here. My fault, I know, but I realised that I needed to find a different path for my life.'

'Do you think you've found it?' knowing something profound lay behind his smile. When he didn't answer she felt disappointed. 'That means you're still looking, doesn't it?'

'I know that I don't want to return to where I was, and it worries me that if I don't sort things out, I might,' he said, looking around as though to reassure himself there was nothing to be fearful of.

'You mean here? You don't want to return here?'

'No, that's not what I meant. My problems were never with Auchenmore.'

She thought about what he had just said and the openness with which he was speaking.

'You know, Nicholas, you're nothing like I thought you would be.' *If only I had known.*

'What were you expecting?'

'I meant that you're easy to talk to. Much easier than I used to think.'

He cast his mind back to how little they had spoken in the past and supposed it was the shame he'd felt that had held him back – embarrassed about how his father had treated him in front of her on their first meeting, the father adept at making people look and feel worthless. How could he have had any dignity in front of her after that?

However, Tracy had been talking of herself. To

her, Nicholas Fraser had been out of reach and as such, she had shunned him to protect herself. Until yesterday, when by chance everything had changed.

A man Nicholas recognised entered the café, a stiff-faced individual called Ron who owned a local ski-hire shop. With his austere reputation together with his being an acquaintance of Dani, Nicholas wasn't surprised to receive no more than a perfunctory nod of acknowledgement. Tony disappeared into the kitchen and returned with a white plastic bag. 'Six bacon rolls,' Nicholas heard him say as he put the bag down on the counter. From the hushed conversation that followed while Ron was paying and the furtive glances cast in his direction, Nicholas suspected they were talking about him.

Tony cleared the plates without them noticing, and fresh mugs of tea arrived.

Sensing that Tracy was still pondering his reply, Nicholas took a deep breath then looked down at his now clasped hands, thumbs playing with each other. 'Perhaps I should explain why everything seemed so difficult when I was here before.' In a moment of contemplation, he lowered his guard. 'I was a bit of a mess, Tracy. Sometimes a person can become somebody they don't want to be as a way of coping.'

She reached forward and touched his hand. 'It's OK, Nicholas. You don't need to say anything more.'

He smiled, and the atmosphere lightened as he ran through his time in the Alps, the climbing, the skiing, washing dishes, clearing snow and cutting wood. As he had with Dani in the bivouac he spoke of the people he had met, Jerome, Corinne, and that Sandy had been one of Corinne's husband's dogs, but he didn't elaborate.

'Sandy has so much potential.'

Tracy looked down at the sleeping dog, 'I think you're right. He's so … well … human! Last night I found myself talking to him, and it was as though he was talking back to me.'

'I find myself doing the same.'

In return, Tracy told Nicholas of her life: her job, college, her bad experience with the creep, O'Doile, and her voluntary work with the police.

'I was thinking of joining the regulars, like Dani, but I don't know. I like my job, and I like being a Special. I guess I have the best of both worlds.'

'Sounds like it, and you seem happy. I'm glad for you. How about Dani? I'm surprised she's in the police, I thought the mountains meant everything to her. Is she happy in her new career?'

Seeing Tracy's uncomfortable look, he broached the subject. 'I hear she has a boyfriend?'

Tracy nodded, relieved that he knew. 'Yes, the guy she was skiing with yesterday. He was a colleague, well, still is but I haven't met him.' Then she took a sudden interest in her nails. 'I suppose you have a girlfriend.'

He let out a little laugh. 'No, I don't. No one would have me.'

'Me neither,' she said, immediately regretting it. 'I mean, I don't have a boyfriend.'

Her expression became curious. 'Last night, how

did you know where to look for Dani? I mean, you had so many choices – it's such a big area.'

'I didn't know for sure. There were places where I thought she might be, but in deciding I used my intuition. Maybe I just got lucky.'

She shook her head and her eyes went back to the table. 'No. I think we make our own luck. You wouldn't have got lucky if you had listened to me, would you?'

'I did listen to you. I was careful, well, sort of anyway, and that's what you asked me to do, wasn't it?' and she smiled. Then he looked directly at her. 'Would you mind doing something for me?'

'Of course, what is it?'

'When you see Dani, would you tell her that I'm sorry for the way I behaved in the past? I wanted to tell her last night, but it wasn't the time.'

Tracy sat bolt upright. 'No, Nicholas. You need to do that yourself,' shaking her head to emphasise. 'You're not honestly saying that after last night you're going to up-and-off without seeing her?'

He shifted on his seat. 'I don't think seeing Dani is a good idea.'

But Tracy wasn't having it. 'I think you need to get this sorted out once and for all. Dani *was* hurt by whatever happened between the two of you. However, things have changed since then. After last night, how will she take it if you leave without seeing her? Don't you think she might be hurt again? You have no idea about girls, have you, Nicholas Fraser?'

Seeing his reluctance, Tracy decided for him.

'Right, so it's settled. You can get a few hours of sleep at my place, then this evening you go to Inverness and sort things out with Dani. Sandy and I have things to do here.'

They gathered their coats and Tony came over to collect the mugs.

'This one's on me,' said Tracy, going for her purse, but Tony intervened.

'No need for that. Ron's paid for you both.' Then looking at Nicholas, 'He said to tell you "good effort last night".'

***

The automatic doors swished open. Nicholas passed through them, then along a wide corridor to join the reception queue. He waited in line while the receptionist dealt with those ahead of him.

When his turn came, he enquired as to the whereabouts of Dani Bruce.

The receptionist glanced at him indifferently. 'Visiting is restricted to family and close friends. Do you fall into either of those categories?'

'No, I'm afraid not,' he replied.

'I see,' her attention drifting to the next in line.

He hesitated. 'I assisted with the rescue last night, that's all. I wanted to see how she's doing, but perhaps I'll leave it.' He turned to go.

Quickly, the receptionist rose from her seat, lifted the hatch and came through to where he was standing. 'Sorry, I should have known. I'm Jane. I was at school with Dani. I went to see her this afternoon. She's doing well,' and without further ado led Nicholas to the stairway. 'Next floor up and you'll see ward 9 straight ahead. She's in bed number 12; don't forget to use the disinfection point at the door.'

'Of course, thanks,' he said, looking up the stairs.

Jane leant forward and gave him a peck on the cheek. 'Thank you for what you did,' then turned and walked hurriedly back to her post.

Rubbing sharp-smelling sanitiser into his hands, he pondered the wisdom of what he was about to do, then, mindful that he'd come this far, he entered the ward. It was like any other hospital ward he had visited. The atmosphere was stiflingly warm, and a stuffy smell hung in the air: disinfectant, the evening meal and something of bedclothes. It bustled with people. Visitors with patients who were either seated or in their beds, restless children entertaining themselves with whatever mischief they could conjure. Older couples sat close – life companions coming to terms with the inevitability of time. Some patients talked enthusiastically, others lay passive, too weak to participate and longing for seven o'clock, when calm would return.

Nicholas made his way warily past the cubicles, looking at each number and receiving the occasional glance from an inhabitant. As he approached number 12 his stomach started to churn. *Perhaps I should turn around.*

Then there she was, sitting propped up in bed supported by numerous pillows, her bandaged hands out on top of the sheets, her face a little puffed and her lips chapped. However, she was smiling and chatting with her visitors. That morning she had looked entirely different – weak and vulnerable – but here she was, back again, the Dani he remembered: confident, smart and easy-going.

As soon as she saw him, her face lit up. 'Hello, my hero, I hoped you'd come. I wanted to call you but my phone was damaged last night.'

He wondered whether she still had his number. However, it was too much to process so he let it go. He registered that her visitors were watching him from the periphery, but his attention remained fixed on her.

An older man stood up. 'Hello, I'm Rory, Dani's father,' he said, shaking Nicholas's hand. 'And this is Marshall.'

Marshall stood up and gave Nicholas a confident smile, coming round to shake his hand. 'Well, Nicholas. I have to thank you for succeeding where I failed. I was over an hour looking for Dani before concluding that the sensible thing was to descend until I got a mobile signal to alert Mountain Rescue. I wish now that I'd continued the search.'

Nicholas looked at Marshall: calm, confident and at ease with people. So different from how he saw himself. It was no wonder that Dani had fallen for him.

'Come and sit down,' said Rory, offering Nicholas his seat. 'I'll fetch another one,' and with a bound that belied his age, he headed off.

'Thank you,' Nicholas replied after him, then

took off his down jacket and looked for a place to lay it.

'Just put it there,' said Dani, gesturing to the floor next to her locker.

He complied, then sat awkwardly on the chair that Rory had vacated, his back straight and his hands on his lap, as though ready to depart.

He glanced over at Marshall, who had returned to his seat, and then back at Dani. 'How are you?'

'It's not as bad as it looks,' she replied in a perky voice. 'I tore a knee ligament, but they can do a keyhole job to speed up the recovery, and my fingers got a bit cold. The doctor says they'll be better in a few weeks.' She held them up, looking at each in turn, fully bandaged like boxing gloves. 'I'll not be able to eat finger food,' she joked. 'I just need to keep them warm. I feel a bit washed out, but I'm fine. Honestly, I am.'

Rory returned with the extra chair and sat down next to Nicholas. He put his hand lightly on Nicholas's arm. 'I want to say how grateful we are for what you did last night and—' but Nicholas cut in.

'Please, there's no need. I appreciate what you're saying, but honestly, it's OK.'

'As long as you know,' Rory added.

Nicholas nodded. 'Thank you, yes, I do … I needed the exercise,' trying to make light of it.

Marshall gave a good-humoured laugh at the turn of phrase, and repeated it. 'He needed the exercise! I like that. Have you guys known each other long?' looking between Nicholas and Dani.

Dani spoke first, 'Yes, we're old friends,' conscious that this would be news to Marshall and hoping it would satisfy his curiosity. Nicholas was just too intimate a part of her life to be discussed.

'Not that old,' Rory intervened, but Dani pushed the conversation on.

'So … where are you headed next?' she asked, eager to know of Nicholas's intentions.

'I'm not sure. I was thinking of staying around Auchenmore for a day or two until you're better, but I can see you're fine. Maybe I'll head back to Edinburgh in the morning. I've got a few things on the go.'

That caught Dani by surprise. After all this time away, Nicholas was about to disappear from her life again.

'Why not stay up here for a few days? Dad could put you up?' looking to her father for acknowledgement.

'Um, yes, of course. I'd be delighted to. Marshall is staying, but we can figure something out.'

'No, that's alright, my things are at Tracy's.'

Dani looked curiously at him. 'She's a good girl, Tracy, isn't she?'

'Yes, she's great, really nice,' he replied, sensing that she was probing.

Then he went quiet and his eyes dropped to stare at the side of the bed as though contemplating the weave of the blanket, and as Dani watched him twiddling his thumbs she realised there was something on his mind.

'Could you give us a bit of time to ourselves?' she

asked, looking at her father and Marshall in turn.

'Of course,' said Marshall, rising to his feet. 'I'm sure you need to digest your adventure. Come on, Rory, let me buy you a cup of tea and a sandwich. It was a tough night for everyone.' Then, turning to Dani, 'Can I get you anything from the shop?'

She shook her head. 'No, I've got everything I need,' and Marshall made a point of bending over and kissing her.

Nicholas remained as he was, still focused on the weave of the blanket and fiddling with his thumbs. Dani caught the eye of a passing nurse who, without fuss, drew the curtain around the bed.

Realising his demeanour was unlikely to change, Dani asked, 'What's wrong, Nicholas? We're fine now, aren't we?'

'Yes, I suppose we are,' he replied, but without conviction.

'What is it then?'

She could tell from the way he'd brushed off her father's thanks that this wasn't about the previous night, when he had put himself on the line to save her. Without his act of selflessness, she would have met with the same end as the poor soul she remembered from years before, who unbeknown to anyone had been avalanched, and whose body was only discovered with the spring thaw.

When his silence reached a point where no further evasion was possible, Nicholas looked up. 'I've come to ask you something, Dani.'

'Well go ahead and ask,' she replied, but he didn't respond, and she realised her tone was inappropriate.

He started again, but stopped, then looked around as though seeking an exit and making Dani fearful he would get up and leave, as he had on the night of his birthday.

But he stayed, gathered himself then looked at her. 'I want to ask if we can be friends again. I know it won't be the same as before, but if we could just …'

It was Dani's turn to choke up. *How could he doubt that after what we've just been through togther?*

She nodded several times, biting her bottom lip as Nicholas waited, anticipating her answer.

'Come, give me your hand,' she said, reaching out with her bandaged paw for him to hold. 'It's about what happened at the chalet, isn't it?'

He nodded slowly, his eyes welling. 'Yes … I hurt you. I didn't mean to say what I did. It was because I was struggling with everything. I knew you were disappointed and that I was the cause of that.'

She smiled at him. 'You're probably right, Nicholas. Shit does happen, and it wasn't just you that night. It was me also, and how I felt. I was scared of my feelings. Between the two of us … well, it just went wrong. But good things can come from bad things can't they? Let's put it behind us and move on.'

She reached out her arms and beckoned him towards her. They embraced, Nicholas sensing her warmth towards him.

'Thank you for saving me,' she whispered.

He rested her on the pillows, then pulled back the curtain from around the bed and sat back down on the seat beside her. A nurse went by, her concern dissipating as she saw the two of them sitting peaceably.

Dani laughed. 'Do you remember that night at Waterfall Bothy when you brought all that food and wood?'

'Better than the menu last night,' he joked, and they shared memories of skiing, bikes and happy times in each other's company.

After twenty minutes or so they anticipated Rory and Marshall's return.

'Would you mind visiting me again?' Dani asked. 'Come a little earlier, so we can have time to ourselves for a proper catch-up. It's been so long.'

'I'd like that. Tracy's offered to put me up for tonight but tomorrow I need to check with Geoff for a spare bed at the centre.'

'I don't think that will be necessary,' said Dani with a cheeky grin, but Nicholas wasn't getting it.

She watched him leave the ward, confident. So different from the beaten young man she had seen walk away in Auchenmore, and the drunken mess she had witnessed the night of his party. He stopped at the door, turned around and gave her a friendly smile and wave, and Dani once again felt a flutter inside. She looked furtively around, self-conscious that someone else might know of her feelings, and realised the elderly woman in the bed opposite had been quietly watching.

'You like that laddie, don't you?' the woman said.

'He's just a really good friend,' Dani replied.

'Ah, like that is it?' replied the woman, with half a wink.

CHAPTER 10

The communal door onto the street banged shut, alerting Tracy to Nicholas's return. Anxious not to appear too eager, she waited for his knock before opening the door to her flat.

He took off his boots in the hall, placing them neatly on the doormat.

'How did it go?' she asked, leading the way through to the sitting room.

'Good, thanks. Do you mind if I sit down? I'm exhausted.'

'Of course not,' she replied, moving a small pile of unironed washing she had dumped on the settee. 'Sandy's asleep in the kitchen. He's had his walk. Do you want to go out for something to eat? Or I can fix us something here?' noticing him slump into the seat.

'Oh, something here would be great, if it's not too much trouble?'

'It's not. I'll make us cheese on toast.'

'Perfect. And thanks for encouraging me to visit Dani. I'm so glad I went and put things to rest.'

'I'm pleased for you,' she said, plumping a cushion as a diversion whilst wondering what it all meant. Nicholas spoke as though what he had done on the mountain was peripheral, and it was she who had done him a service. She knew that since their meeting at the snow gates, and the subsequent rescue, all their worlds had changed, but making sense of how would take time.

When she returned from the kitchen with a plate of cheese on toast in one hand and two mugs of tea gripped in the other, Nicholas was fast asleep. She put the plate and mugs down on the coffee table, and hesitantly lifted his legs onto the cushions, wondering what to say if he woke, then covered him with a blanket. Sitting in a chair to one side and eating the two servings, she glanced across at him, watching in the way that one is drawn by curiosity to a stranger in a public waiting area, cautious in the knowledge that at any moment they might notice your gaze and seek an explanation. Then she realised that after their turbulent twenty-four hours, she too was exhausted.

Tracy was woken by the first light of day gleaming through the curtains. She lay pondering the events of the past thirty-six hours until the phone alarm sounded, reminding her that work started at eight. Pulling on her dressing gown, she entered the sitting room expecting to see Nicholas asleep. But he was gone, his blanket neatly folded and left to one side. The kitchen was no different, with the old rug donated to Sandy placed tidily in a corner. It all felt uncomfortably familiar, as if the circus had briefly visited then left, leaving her behind, and in so doing, dashed her hopes. However, what those hopes were, she couldn't fathom. It was time to get ready for work and hope the routine of life would distract her.

Turning the shower temperature a little higher than usual as a comfort, she attempted to think through the day ahead of her. But her thoughts kept coming back to what was becoming a huge disappointment. Wrapping a towel around her wet hair and another around her body, she returned to the bedroom. *Perhaps he will phone me later* ... then, realising that he didn't have her number, she rebuked herself. *What was I thinking? I invited him to stay a night, he was thankful, but it's not as if* ... Now he would be making his way back to Edinburgh, or as she regretted saying at the snow gates, to wherever his life was now.

'We're back,' Nicholas called from outside the front door. Sandy bounced up to her when she rushed to open it.

'Sorry about this,' Nicholas said, as he tried to juggle a cardboard carrier, a paper bag and retrieve the excitable animal whilst averting his eyes from the half-dressed girl before him. 'I've bought us some breakfast.'

She tried to look as if she'd guessed as much. 'Ah, I thought you might be doing something like that.'

He retreated to the kitchen, removed two lattes from their carrier and placed them on the table. From the bag he took two egg muffins with cheese – Tracy's favourite, he recalled from the previous morning. Once dressed, Tracy joined him. They chatted as they ate, Nicholas doing most of the talking as he told her of his plans for the day ahead. 'I'm taking Sandy for a walk, then going to see Geoff. This afternoon I'll visit Dani.'

Tracy looked at her watch. 'I'd better go, or I'll be late,' but she didn't move. Shifting her gaze from the cup in her hands, she looked at him.

'Nicholas, why don't you stay here for a few days?'

It was an exploratory question presented in an entirely different manner from the assertive tone she'd taken the previous morning. Her reasons for asking were complex. There was the obvious: Nicholas had loose ends to tidy up. However, there was more to it. Tracy knew that if there was to be any chance of something between them, they would need time to get to know one another.

He didn't answer, so she continued. 'Is there somewhere else you need to be, perhaps?'

He thought about Edinburgh and his mother. Then, by association, his thoughts turned to his father and everything that the man represented. 'There are things I need to do in Edinburgh. Important things. But I would like to stay, if you don't mind – just for a few days.'

The day was crisp, with a bright blue sky broken by occasional puffs of cumulus carried on a light westerly breeze. As Nicholas pulled into the car park he saw a boy clearing snow from the path leading to the High Ropes. The boy stopped what he was doing and looked over, using a raised hand to shield his eyes from the sun. As Nicholas opened the back of the Land Rover for Sandy to jump out, the boy dropped his snow shovel and came running towards them. At first, Nicholas didn't recognise him, dressed in his centre jacket, outdoor trousers and boots, but as he got closer the glasses, albeit new ones, gave him away.

'What are doing back here, Calum?' he asked as they shook hands.

Calum turned his attention to the dog, stroking his head. 'It's half-term. Geoff invited me up to help out. He says that if I get my Highers, he'll take me on for the summer!'

'Well, you know what you need to do then, don't you?'

Calum nodded and smiled. 'I thought you were gone for good but then I hear you're up the mountain chasing after girls.'

'Well, one girl and she isn't just any old girl, Calum. She's a special girl.'

'You have a girlfriend then?' Calum asked, with that head-tilted quizzical expression of his.

'No. Not like that. But we're good friends.'

Seeming to ponder what he had just heard, Calum looked out towards the mountain, then back to Nicholas. 'Like me and my mum,' with a fondness Nicholas understood was born from shared adversity. 'What's your dog's name?' he asked.

'Sandy. Would you mind looking after him while I speak to Geoff?' And with Sandy in tow, Calum returned to his snow clearing.

Nicholas entered Geoff's office. It was as untidy

as ever, with piles of paper on the desk, and the floor cluttered with outdoor equipment. Against one wall was a small table hosting the paraphernalia for making tea and coffee.

'Fancy a brew?' asked Geoff, as he preemptively flicked the kettle switch and dropped teabags into mugs. 'If you want to stay, we can probably find a bed for you. Or maybe you're back at the chalet?'

Nicholas shook his said. 'No, I'm not returning there. Thanks for the offer, but Tracy Shaw says I can stay at her place for a few days.'

The kettle boiled and switched itself off with a loud click, and Geoff poured the water. 'She's a nice lass, that Tracy Shaw. She and Claire spend time together doing their police thing.' But Nicholas wasn't listening, his thoughts elsewhere as he stared out of the window.

'What's on your mind?' asked Geoff, handing him a mug. 'Is it about going it alone on the mountain? If it is, forget it. You won't get any comeback.'

'No, I hadn't even thought about that again. It's coming back to Scotland. I'm not sure I've done the right thing.'

Geoff gave him a shrewd look. 'I don't think Dani would agree with you.'

'I suppose not. It's just that when I was in France everything seemed clear. I'd return and put to rest all the things that sent me away in the first place. But now I'm back it all seems much harder than I thought it would be.'

Geoff sat down at his desk and looked around. 'A

bit like tidying this place, I suppose. I need to decide whether I'm serious about wanting it tidy, or if I'm just kidding myself. Then I need to figure the end goal and steps to achieve it.'

Nicholas continued to stare into the distance. 'I want to get closer to my mum, and I want to free us both from the curse of my father.'

Now Geoff was also looking out of the window. 'Have you discussed this with her?'

Nicholas shook his head. 'We haven't talked properly for years. I don't know where to start, and when I try, it's as though the words just won't come out.'

'Why not start with simple things, like "What did you do today?"'

Nicholas turned to Geoff with a look that was appreciative but also doubtful. 'Thanks for listening. I'd better be moving. I promised I'd head back up and see Dani.'

'Any time, Nicholas. And if you're looking for part-time work, just let me know. It's the usual gig: rubbish pay but the craic's good. Oh, and you get to do something useful, which is a rare thing in this day and age.'

'Is everything OK, Tracy?'

She turned to see a colleague trying to get past with a restocking trolley. 'Oh, sorry. Yes, I'm fine. My mind was somewhere else,' as she stood aside to make way.

Her colleague stopped. 'It sounds as though that was a close shave Dani had on the mountain. Is she alright?'

'Yes, but she was lucky to be found the way she was.'

Her colleague scratched the back of his head as though trying to work something out. 'The guy who went looking for her, I heard he's one of that Edinburgh crowd who used to hang around up here?'

'He knew them, but wasn't part of their set,' she replied, conscious that this wouldn't have been her answer a week ago.

'Well, I'm glad it ended well,' he said, resuming his journey to the cereal aisle.

Tracy continued her day with a sense that this evening there was something to look forward to, but also aware that Nicholas's absence that morning had confirmed there was also, once again, something to lose. She wondered how he felt, and whether she appeared too eager or expected too much.

As the shift moved towards a close she glanced at the entrance, wondering when he would be back from Inverness and if he might come to meet her. By the time she'd bought a few groceries, he was waiting by the door with Sandy. The dog saw her first and gave a loud bark, triggering a row of checkout staff to peer from their stations.

'Can I help you with the trolleys?' he joked, referring to their first meeting at this very place. She smiled awkwardly. 'Let me carry that for you,' he continued, taking the shopping from her.

They made their way along the pavement, avoiding the slippery patches missed by the gritter.

'How was your day?' she asked, looking across

the road at a young couple laughing as they entered a shop, and wondering how she and Nicholas appeared to others.

'Good. I went to see Geoff, then up to visit Dani.'

'How's she getting on?'

'Fine. They're going to do a little knee operation tomorrow and she'll be out the day after to recuperate at home. She said that Marshall's taken time off until the weekend to look after her.'

Tracy reached out her hand. 'I'll take Sandy's lead if you like?'

'Thanks.' He passed her the lead and, sensing the change, Sandy glanced back indifferently. Tracy thought how easily the three of them fitted together.

'Do you think she and Marshall are serious?' Tracy asked.

'Probably, but she didn't discuss him with me. It's not my business, is it?'

'Does it bother you, seeing as how you used to be quite close?'

'No, it doesn't. Whatever we had was part of that time. I'm glad we're friends again – that did bother me – but I'm also pleased that she's with someone who makes her happy. Anyway, I've got an idea. How about I take you for dinner? My treat.'

'You don't need to do that,' Tracy replied.

'But I'd like to.'

'In that case, I accept.'

As her train crossed the viaduct, Dani peered out of the window and down to the burn below, etching its way through a snowy landscape punctuated by gorse.

A roe deer looked up curiously from where she was grazing dwarf shrubs with her kid. Dani thought of her call to the viaduct down south, how her career in the police had pivoted around the encounter with Jason, and the evening afterwards when she, Marshall and a few others had gone for a drink.

She realised that taking him skiing off-piste had been a mistake. The confidence he'd exuded hadn't been matched by ability. Despite the early onset of the storm, if he had been able to keep up, they would have been clear of the ridge; by the time she'd realised he was struggling, it was already too late. The storm had arrived and although they hadn't been far apart, the whiteout had made it impossible to find him. If only they had managed to stick together, they would both have made it down.

And then there was her father's flippant remark after Nicholas had left the hospital. How could he dismiss what Nicholas had done out there on the mountain so easily, and say that she would most likely have been rescued anyway? He wasn't the one who'd been buried alive. He had tried to detach himself from what he'd said, 'I'm sorry, Dani. I didn't mean it that way,' but she knew he had, and she knew why. Could he not accept that Nicholas wasn't the reason she'd left for Thames Valley?

Her eyes lifted to the mountains and her thoughts turned to all they meant to her. *Cianalas*, the longing for the place of your birth – it was with her always. She looked at her gloved hands, trembling again, as they had during those difficult early days with her police career.

The public address system crackled. 'Next stop: Auchenmore. Please remember to take all personal effects with you,' and Dani manoeuvred her crutches into the aisle, ready.

Hobbling onto the platform she saw Nicholas and Tracy waving as they came towards her. Tracy hugged her tight, 'I'm so glad you could make it, Dani. I really wanted to see you before you head back down south.' Dani looked over Tracy's shoulder to see Nicholas standing there, smiling.

They crammed into the front of the Land Rover – Dani seated by the door and Tracy straddling the driveshaft tunnel – and made their way to the flat.

'That's my mess,' said Nicholas, seeing Dani eye the bedding in the corner of the sitting room. 'Tracy's let me stay here while you were recovering, but I'm off to Edinburgh for a couple of days tomorrow.' And for a moment Nicholas felt an uncomfortable sense of déjà vu: a trip to Edinburgh, his father and uncertainty as to where it would lead.

Dani thought how strange it felt. The last time the three of them were together had been the night of Nicholas's twentieth birthday – nearly two years ago, and so much had happened to them all since then. She remembered how fractious Tracy had been. Now it seemed that, like her, Tracy was at peace with him.

They ate huge jacket potatoes with fillings of grated cheese with chives, egg mayonnaise and tuna. 'I raided the deli counter,' admitted Tracy. Then she gave Dani a present from her mum. 'Knitted specially for you,' she said, putting the scarf around

Dani's neck, the hat on her head and showing her the mittens. Dani's eyes filled with tears and Tracy hugged her again. 'Come on, Dani. Be strong.'

For dessert, they headed out for milkshakes in the newly opened American Diner. Taking a booth, they chose from the menu and Tracy went up to place their order at the counter. 'On me,' she insisted.

'How do you feel about going back?' Nicholas asked Dani as they waited for Tracy to return.

'I just need to get on with it, don't I,' she replied, in a way that left Nicholas doubtful.

He noticed her hands shaking and remembered when as a child his hands had done the same. 'Are you sure you're OK?'

She forced a smile, then seizing her moment asked him. 'You won't forget me will you, Nicholas?'

'Of course I won't,' he replied, standing up to help Tracy, who had arrived with a tray bearing three tall glasses of brightly coloured milkshake.

When he next looked at Dani, her eyes were still on him, her expression unchanged, as though hoping for more. He looked at her questioningly, and she looked back with an uncertain smile, then picked up her milkshake.

Tracy raised her glass. 'Here's to the three of us.'

CHAPTER 11

Crossing George Street, Nicholas glanced up at the statue of William Pitt the Younger, complete with an ill-tempered looking seagull perched on its head, then descended to Princes Street. Having turned right towards Lothian Road he looked left to the castle – its battlements blending into the low-hanging cloud.

He reflected on how he felt. Rescuing Dani had been frightening, but it had come upon him so quickly there hadn't been time for it to sink in. With his father, it had been different. From an early age, he had been conditioned to live with fear. Fear for himself, but mostly for his mother. All that had changed with the crises his father had set in motion. Left with nowhere further to fall, but everything to think about, Nicholas was slowly rebuilding himself, and with that came a growing sense of resentment at what the man had subjected them to.

Approaching the office – an impressive edifice of concrete and glass with a wide set of steps in front – it occurred to Nicholas that he had never before set foot inside. He had seen it aplenty but it never crossed his mind that one day he would enter it.

Mounting the steps in twos he reached a revolving

door, following it until he was deposited inside a huge foyer reaching six floors up to a glass roof.

Further forward sat a line of access barriers and beyond that, a large reception island staffed by three corporately dressed women.

A receptionist looked in his direction, then across to a listless security guard sitting at one side. With a leaden walk, the guard made his way over. 'Do you have an appointment?' he asked, casting a disparaging eye over Nicholas's jeans and hoodie.

'No, I'm afraid not.'

'Well, if it's work you're after, I suggest you look at our website, and if you do get an interview, think about a haircut and a suit.'

'No, I'm not looking for work. Not here, anyway. I've come to see someone. If you'd be kind enough to pass them a message?'

The guard sighed. 'Well, give me your name and that of the person you're looking for.'

'My name is Nicholas and I wish to speak with my father, Mr Fraser.' The guard returned a blank look so Nicholas assisted. 'Mr Hamish Fraser?' The barrier miraculously opened.

Having signed an electronic tablet and been issued a printed name badge, Nicholas made his way to the visitor waiting area, smartly laid out with facing settees separated by coffee tables. He took a phone from his pocket, set it on the table then sat down and waited.

Fifteen minutes or so later he watched a woman in a neatly fitting skirt and jacket approach the reception desk, ask a question and have Nicholas pointed out to her.

'Hello, I'm Sam Montgomery, Hamish's PA …'

Nicholas stopped listening as he wondered whether or not his father had slept with her – or perhaps he was still sleeping with her?

'Is that alright?' she asked, awaiting his reply.

'I'm sorry, I drifted away for a moment. What did you say?'

'I was saying Mr Fraser is busy all day with meetings. But he will speak to you this evening.'

'In that case, I'm afraid it's not alright, although I rather expected that answer.'

Ms Montgomery looked uncertain and Nicholas wondered whether it was the contradiction of her master's instruction that unnerved her or the thought that she would have to go back and tell him as much.

He retrieved a prepared note from his pocket. 'Ms Montgomery, I'm going to give you a note to pass on to him and then I'm going to wait for …' he looked up at the six floors above, with their balconies looking onto the atrium. 'What floor is he on?'

'The sixth,' she replied.

'In that case, ten minutes, and after that my next appointment will be at Torphichen Place.' She looked blankly back. 'The police station?' Ms Montgomery disappeared.

Nicholas watched as Hamish strode into the foyer, stopped and searched the faces of the waiting visitors. In his right hand was the note. He appeared as Nicholas had always known him to be: sharp-suited and exuding an aura that affected those around him. Voices hushed, the three women at reception took a sudden interest in their computer screens and the apathetic security guard discovered new resolve in diligently patrolling the barriers.

For a split second, Nicholas felt the onset of the fear that had previously accompanied his father's presence. But then he remembered what had brought him here, and found himself fighting back anger that threatened to erupt and destroy that purpose.

He didn't try to attract Hamish's attention but waited until their eyes met. For a moment they stared at each other as people might when seeing a familiar face in an unexpected place, but then Hamish made his way over and stood imposing himself over Nicholas.

'Your mother told me you were back,' his voice compromised by the need for privacy. He held up the note. 'What's the meaning of this?'

His personal space encroached on, Nicholas shuffled sideways along the settee. 'We can do this standing up or sitting down,' he said.

Hamish glanced about and sensing prying eyes watching them, moved to sit on the edge of the settee opposite, his forearms on his thighs and hands clasped.

Fixing Nicholas with a hard stare he slowly tore the piece of paper in two. 'Do you think I haven't been threatened before?' Then, noticing the phone on the table, he picked it up and pressed the power-down button. 'You won't catch me that easily, laddie,' he smiled grimly as he put the phone back, 'and I can't see your mother standing up in a court of law and saying her husband is a tyrant who beats her and her son. If she were going to do that, she would have done it a long time ago. But she's weak, Nicholas ... and always will be.'

'What about *my* word?' Nicholas asked.

Hamish leant further forward, closing the gap between them.

'And a court will believe you? I hope you've got a good lawyer advising you on all of this because you're playing a dangerous game here.'

'Who said anything about a court?' Nicholas replied. Hamish remained expressionless so Nicholas gestured around with his hands. 'Your power over all of this, it's what you get off on, isn't it? How would that change if I told the world about how you've treated your family for all these years? What would you be left with?'

He could see the man's arrogance turn to anger. 'Don't cross me, Nicholas.'

'Or what? You'll hit me again?' he replied, in a slightly louder voice that once again drew eyes. 'Or perhaps you'll get him to do it,' he mocked, indicating the security guard.

Hamish's eyes darkened. 'I should have hit you harder when I had the chance, but let's cut to the chase, shall we? What do you want? Money for that half-baked idea of yours?'

'No. I don't want your money. I want you to disappear from our lives.'

A sour grin appeared on Hamish's face. 'She put you up to this, didn't she?'

Nicholas shook his head. 'No, she didn't.'

'Ah, in that case, she knows nothing about it.

You're doing this on your own, aren't you?'

Nicholas sensed that the man was angling to get the upper hand. 'I'm putting you on notice that if anything happens to Mum, anything at all, I'll make sure your world comes crashing down.'

Standing up, he retrieved the phone from the table. 'For my French SIM,' he said. Then taking another from his pocket, 'And my UK one. You didn't say everything I wanted you to, but it's a start.'

He left the building and headed down Lothian Road and back onto Princes Street, from where he could see the gloom over the castle had lifted. *A good omen*. He considered how, for the first time in his life, he had stood up to his father and left his mark. *But will it be enough to keep Mum safe?* Tomorrow, he would be returning to Auchenmore to give Geoff a hand and develop his idea for an outdoor centre. *Will that man take advantage of my absence?*

***

Tracy was taking her after-work shower when someone knocked at the front door.

'I'll get it,' called Nicholas.

'No, I will,' she called back, with an urgency that, had Nicholas heard, would have warned him.

But she was too late. 'Hello, I'm Mary,' said the woman before him. He stood without speaking, trying to place her. 'Tracy's mum?' she added, with an unimpressed look.

'Oh, sorry,' he replied, stepping aside to let her in.

Tracy rushed into the hall, a hand towel grabbed in haste wrapped around her. 'Mum!' she exclaimed, her eyes flitting between them, then down over her own half-naked body.

'Yes, it's me. I thought you might have forgotten who I am.'

'Oh, I've been so busy at work,' Tracy replied, as she took in how things might seem. 'I'm just in – I was taking a shower. This is—'

But Mary interrupted, 'Nicholas, I know. It would have been nice if you had told me about your new arrangement yourself, rather than leaving it to village gossip.'

Nicholas adopted as contrite a look as he could muster. 'I'm sorry, Mrs Shaw. I didn't mean to cause you any problems …'

'Ms, but don't worry. Call me Mary.'

Tracy scurried off to get dressed and Nicholas took Mary's coat and hung it by the door. 'This is Sandy,' he said, wondering how she would react to the addition of a dog.

Her face softening, she reached down and stroked the dog's head. 'Hello, Sandy.'

Feeling like an impostor, Nicholas led the way through to the kitchen. 'I was just making tea. Would you like a cup?'

'Yes, that would be nice,' said Mary, as her eyes scanned the kitchen surfaces, sink and table, then relaxed as though what she had seen met with her approval.

Thank goodness I tidied up. He glanced at Mary, trying to make sense of her familiarity. Without make-up and with tight curls of blonde hair, she was a naturally attractive woman. There was a resemblance to Tracy, but it was subtle: her facial proportions and mouth. She seemed young compared to his mother, then he realised it was more to do with how she was dressed – soft jeans, ankle boots and a lambswool jumper.

Mary sat down. 'Oh, I should have offered,' said Nicholas, but she didn't seem put out.

'Do your parents still have the chalet?' she asked.

He stopped what he was doing and in an uncertain voice, asked, 'We've met before, haven't we?'

By now, having pulled on a pair of jogging bottoms and a sweatshirt, Tracy was standing barefoot at the door.

Mary looked at her daughter, then back at Nicholas. 'Surely the two of you remember?' But they returned blank looks. 'I used to babysit for your parents. It was a long time ago.'

And it all came flooding back to him: the day his father was stabbed and the kind lady and her daughter who had looked after him until his grandfather arrived. A thought played across his mind, *Just how much of that night is she about to revisit?* But Mary put him at ease. 'We looked after you for a few hours when your mother was taken poorly.'

Tracy sat down at the table. 'I don't know why we didn't figure this out ourselves.'

'Me neither,' said Nicholas, 'but I recognise you now – both of you.'

He finished making the tea and Mary turned the conversation to everyday topics: the hotel where she worked, the improvement in the weather and arranging for a joiner to repair a unit door in the kitchen.

'I can probably fix that,' offered Nicholas.

'Could you? Why don't the two of you come for supper this week?' she asked.

'Great. I'll bring a few tools with me,' said Nicholas, before Tracy had a chance to make their excuses.

Mary turned to her daughter. 'Give me those things you wanted mending and I'll have them ready,' and when Tracy left the room to collect them, Mary took her opportunity.

'How is your mother doing? I remember her as such a kind woman.'

From the way she asked, Nicholas could tell the question ran deeper than common courtesy. 'That's a difficult question, Mary. Not much has changed since the last time we met. But I want it to.' Unsure why he felt so open with a woman he had only just re-met, he added, 'I want Mum to have the life she deserves.'

Mary seemed understanding. 'I remember you as a nice boy, Nicholas.' Then she looked at her fingers, the way Tracy did when thinking. 'Tracy is very special to me.'

'Are you concerned about me being here?' he asked. 'Because if you are, I promise there is nothing for you to be worried about.'

'I know that. It's just that people can be so easily hurt.'

Tracy returned before Nicholas had the chance to reassure her, but he gave an understanding nod.

Mary smiled back and stood up. 'I'd best be off. And you two, no more surprises, alright?'

Nicholas squeezed the Land Rover past yet another oversized rental motorhome that had half-pulled into the already small passing place, a ritual that heralded the start of the summer holiday season.

With relief, they reached the car park. Tracy opened the backdoor. Sandy jumped out and took an immediate interest in tracking scents along the ground. The trio set off through a metal swing gate and along the path that led through the pine forest surrounding the loch. Stopping at the far end, they sat on a bench to admire the view. Nicholas took out a water bottle, a couple of cereal bars and an orange from his pack. He peeled the orange and handed it to Tracy.

'Are you not having any?' she asked, offering him a piece back.

'No, you have it; I know how much you like them.'

She stared down the loch, remembering the day before she left home and she and her mother had sat here. 'This is where Mum and I talked about my dad. I wish I could say not knowing him doesn't bother me, but it does. I don't think about it all the time, but it's always there in the background as though my life isn't quite complete.'

Nicholas put his hand on hers. 'You could have mine, but I wouldn't wish him on my worst enemy. Why would anyone make it their life's work to be evil? I used to be scared of him, but now I just feel hatred. I'll never forgive him for what he's put me and Mum through.'

'But at least you've moved on,' she said.

'No. I've changed, but I've not moved on.'

'But you're no longer frightened of him.'

He took a deep breath. 'Perhaps. But is feeling angry any better? I'm hoping he will decide there's nothing more he can take from us and move out.'

'Do you think he'll do that?'

'I'm hopeful.'

Sandy's attention was drawn to two ducks enjoying the evening sun as they splashed playfully in the reeds at the water's edge. 'Leave them be, Sandy,' said Nicholas, thwarting his plans.

Tracy called the dog over, then asked Nicholas, 'Is that how you felt when you went looking for Dani on the mountain – hopeful?'

'There wasn't a choice then, was there? he said. 'I had to try and find her, whatever it took.'

'I know, Nicholas. I've been thinking about it.'

She started to inspect her fingernails.

'What is it?' he asked, having learnt in the short time they had been together that this signalled something was bothering her.

'I was thinking that if the storm hadn't arrived, you would have gone home and we wouldn't have met again. And if Dani wasn't with Marshall, perhaps …'

'Perhaps what?' he asked

'Perhaps you would be with her.'

He considered the what-ifs that had shaped his life and those of the people around him. *What if I hadn't found Dani? What if Alexander hadn't tried to help the buried climbers? What if Tess hadn't been in that car?* And the biggest what-if of all, *What if, as a child, I hadn't intervened when my father was bleeding to death on the kitchen floor?*

Reaching into a pocket he retrieved his phone, opened the picture gallery and started thumbing through photos. 'Life's full of what-ifs, Tracy.'

Curious, she looked down at the screen: familiar pictures of herself, of Sandy, and one of Nicholas and another person on top of a dome-shaped snowy mountain. 'Where's that?' she asked. 'Mont Blanc,' he replied. There were more pictures of her, Dani in the hospital, and his mum.

He paused. 'She used to say, "Your past doesn't need to determine your future".'

'Who?' Tracy asked, but her question hung as he continued thumbing through.

Finally, he stopped at an image and tipped the phone slightly so Tracy could get a better view of the screen.

'Pretty, isn't she?' he said.

Tracy immediately tensed up. It was the girl who'd been with Nicholas the night she'd challenged him. Slightly older than Nicholas, with straight dark hair tied back, she was looking wistfully out over a loch. And yes, she was pretty – she'd thought so back then, and she hadn't been wrong.

'Why are you showing me this?' she asked, her indignation clear.

'Come on, don't be like that,' he replied.

'Well, isn't it odd to show me a picture of one of your ex-girlfriends? Or maybe you're still …'

Nicholas looked at her. 'You don't know who she is, do you?'

'Yes, if you must know, I do. She's the girl you were with that night, isn't she?'

'That's not what I meant. Tess was a friend from Edinburgh. A good friend, but not a girlfriend. She came to help me when everything fell apart.'

Tracy picked up on the past tense.

'Where is she now?' she asked.

'I'm sorry, I thought you knew. She died in that terrible accident on the A9, not long before I left here.'

Shocked, she took the phone gently from him and looked at the picture. 'No, it should be me apologising. I remember the accident, but I didn't know she was involved. I feel terrible about what I just said.'

Nicholas put a comforting arm around her, then told her how Tess had helped him, what had befallen her and the impact her death had had on the lives of her loved ones.

'You know, Tracy, a lot of local people made assumptions about the accident. They thought I was somehow connected to it. But the people in the car weren't staying with me that weekend. The ski season was over and they had rented a place further north. I don't think there was much sympathy from some. They saw us as a bunch of spoilt rich kids. But I can tell you, they weren't like that. Do you know how many people spoke to me about what happened?'

Tracy didn't answer. She knew that she hadn't said anything, and neither had Dani.

'Two people: Claire and Geoff. Claire came to the chalet to tell me about the accident, and Geoff was a listening ear.'

'I didn't know that either. Claire didn't say that she had been to see you, only that you were working with Geoff and later that you'd left for France.'

Her mind went back to her feelings at that time: the resentment she had harboured towards him. 'Nicholas, there's something I want to tell you. It's been preying on my mind, and I need to get it out, but I'm worried you'll think badly of me.'

'I'm not one to judge. What is it?'

'It was that night when you were with Tess, what I said to you, those horrible things.'

'Oh, don't worry about that. To be honest, I don't remember much about it.'

'No, I need to tell you anyway. I have to. Not what I said, but why I said it.'

She looked down then her eyes lifted to his. 'I wanted to hurt you. I did, Nicholas. I wanted to hurt you so badly ... because I was hurt.'

'Was it because of what happened with Dani and me?'

She shook her head. 'No. It gave me an excuse. Dani was upset, but it wasn't the real reason. It was because I felt you had shunned me. It was painful, and I wanted to hurt you back. It sounds so wrong when I say it now.'

'Please, Tracy, don't beat yourself up. I didn't talk to you, did I? It was because I was embarrassed.'

Her eyes fell again. 'I thought you were. Was it because I'm not like your friends?'

'No, it was nothing like that. It was because of what you saw at the supermarket ... how my father treated me in front of you. I was the one who was ashamed.'

'Oh. Looking back, that was how I felt about myself.'

'Tracy, you asked me if I would be with Dani. It's not a case of whether I *would* be with her, but whether I now *want* to be with her. I'm not very good at these things, but I think we make a good team, you and me, don't we?'

She smiled, took a tissue from her pocket and blew her nose. 'Yes, I think we do.'

Nicholas continued. 'I do worry about Dani, though. Being buried by the avalanche must have been traumatic. When she left, her hands were shaking. It's what my hands did when I had my problems. I hope she's over it now. I know you two are good friends and you'll be watching out for her.'

Tracy squeezed his arm. 'We're not in contact as much as we used to be, but I'll make a point of calling her. And thanks for listening to me.'

CHAPTER 12

Suspecting it would be Mum, Nicholas took his phone from his pocket and glanced at the screen. He'd spent years avoiding her calls; the stress of making forced conversation had been more than he could cope with. But in the six months since the rescue, things had changed. She would now chat about this or that, and he would indulge her with more than a cursory reply. It was as though they were practising in a safe environment for a far more complicated conversation still to come.

And then there was his father, who was yet to show his hand since Nicholas had warned him off.

He had tried to reassure his mother. 'All I said to him was that we weren't prepared to be abused any longer. I had a right to say that, didn't I?'

'Of course you did, Nicholas. I should have said it myself a long time ago. But that doesn't change what he's like, does it?'

Nicholas could tell that, like him, she was wary of where Hamish's threats would lead.

He answered quickly, caught between his need to know she was safe and not alerting her to his fears. 'Hi, Mum.'

'He's gone, Nicholas. He's taken his bags and gone.'

Nicholas fell silent as it sank in. And as it did, he felt himself lighten, as though a sinister presence had been expelled from his body.

'Are you alright, Nicholas?' she asked.

'Yes. Yes, I'm fine. I just can't believe it.'

'Neither could I.'

'Did he say or do anything?'

'He did what he's always done and turned it on me. But that's a small price to pay.'

'I'm pleased, Mum.'

'And thank you, Nicholas, for your support. Your visit to his office changed everything. I know it did. Why don't you come down to Edinburgh for the weekend? The Festival is in full swing. You could see one of those comedy things you like.'

He hesitated. 'I don't know, Mum. I promised someone here—'

She cut him short. 'Bring your girlfriend with you. I'd love to meet her. And don't worry, I'll not say anything awkward.' He didn't respond. 'Don't you think I can tell, Nicholas? I'm your mother, after all.'

Tracy handed him her bag. 'Remember, Nicholas, I'm doing this for you. Don't leave me on my own with your mother or I'll be on the next train home to spend the weekend with Mum and Sandy. Is that understood?'

He took the bag and they stepped out onto platform 15 at Waverley Station. 'You'll be fine, I promise. Now, follow me.'

Although she'd never met Miriam, Tracy had formed an image of a severe woman who would look down contemptuously on her son's unworthy partner. With Mary's support, Nicholas had persuaded Tracy to come, albeit with her strict conditions attached.

They arrived outside the terraced house at seven in the evening. Part of the New Town development in the 1800s, the Georgian building looked imposing as its sandstone blocks rose to meet the sky. Broad steps bordered by wrought-iron railings straddled a basement to reach a large black front door with an impressive brass letterbox. Above the door sat a glass fanlight on which was written 33 Moray Circle. Across the road was a fenced area of grass, trees and shrubs. From somewhere within came the voices of people lingering in the evening sun.

Tracy looked up at the door, then further still to two storeys of tall sash windows, their ornate balconies also painted gloss black, and wondered whether Nicholas was playing with her. Was this a hotel of some description? However, the familiar way he took the steps, reached the door and opened it with his key, said that this was a place he knew well. She joined him and they entered together.

'Mum, we're here,' he called.

Tracy felt apprehensive as she took in the high ceilings with intricate cornices, the crystal chandelier and a large vase of fresh white lilies on the marble-topped side table. To her left a wide staircase with balustrades curved its way up to a landing. It seemed more like a set from a period drama she would watch on a Sunday evening with Mum than a place where people actually lived.

Miriam appeared from what Tracy took to be the kitchen at the far end of the corridor and came towards them.

'Hello Nicholas, you're right on time,' she said with a warm smile.

'Mum, meet Tracy.'

Miriam moved forward to kiss Tracy on the cheek, but Tracy misinterpreted her intention and put out her hand.

'Nice to meet you, Ms Stewart,' recalling what Nicholas had said about his mother's return to her maiden name.

'Nice to meet you too, Tracy. Please, call me Miriam.'

Miriam moved to the door and closed it, making a point of turning the mortise lock. 'You must be tired. Come, I'll show you up to your room. Be careful on the stairs, they can be quite daunting.'

Gripping the bannister, Miriam led the way up. Tracy followed as Miriam bore right at the top and past two closed doors to a spacious bedroom at the front of the house. Miriam went to the king-size bed and brushed her hand across the white duvet to remove an invisible crease. 'I hope you're comfortable, Tracy. Margaret prepared the room this afternoon. Let me know if you need anything at all. I'm a little out of practice as a hostess, but I'll do my best.'

Tracy didn't reply, fully preoccupied with taking

in the room. Miriam turned on a light in the en suite bathroom to discreetly indicate its presence and then left.

The girl from Auchenmore stood looking around. She pressed the bed with her hands as she had seen them do in films. At the end was a freestanding wooden rail with three fluffy white towels, and on a dressing table were more fresh flowers in a vase, together with a carafe of water and a glass.

She looked up to another high ceiling with another elaborate cornice, painted white to contrast with the autumn sun-coloured walls, and then towards the tall windows, framed by long yellow-and-white striped curtains. Net drapes fluttered gently in the breeze. Venturing to the window she pulled the drapes to one side and looked out across the road to the little park still bathed in sunlight, and smiled. 'Who will buy my sweet red roses?' she whispered, remembering the musical, *Oliver!* that she and Mum would watch at Christmas, then turned and went back to sit on the edge of the bed.

Nicholas appeared at the door and came to sit next to her. He looked around, as though seeing the room for the first time.

'Is everything OK for you?' he asked, not thinking beyond the immediate practicalities.

She didn't answer his question but continued to look around in wonder at the vast room – larger than her sitting room and kitchen combined.

'Who's Margaret?' she asked.

'Mum's housekeeper.'

'What was it like living here, Nicholas?'

'Lonely,' he replied.

They descended to the kitchen, where lights blazed from suspended wire tracks, tempting Tracy to flick off a switch or two from habit.

To the right sat a solid wood kitchen table with six leather button-down dining chairs. The wall behind was papered in a grey nutmeg pattern: neat rows of the little shapes on an off-white background adding to a regimented feel. The preparation area looked straight out of *Dream Kitchens*, with few signs of real-world use. Dark grey base units topped by granite work surfaces and interspersed with full-height wall units.

Tracy looked at the ceramic two-bowl sink with its extravagant tap and wondered whether it cost more than her car. Apart from a wooden block housing a conspicuously expensive set of kitchen knives, the surfaces were bare of any item that might identify the inhabitants, except to confirm their affluence. She walked across to Miriam, who was struggling with the top of a foil tray.

'Can I help at all?' Tracy offered.

'If you could open this for me, that would be kind of you. They insist on making them difficult to break into, don't they?'

'I'll fix us a drink,' Nicholas announced. Tracy questioned Miriam about Edinburgh and the Festival, easy conversation to keep things going while Nicholas took out three large crystal glass tumblers and laid them on the surface next to the sink. He retrieved a strangely shaped bottle of gin from the freezer.

'An old trick,' he said, seeing Tracy's questioning look, then poured a generous measure into each glass. With tonic from the concealed refrigerator, he topped the glasses. Ice cubes ejected noisily from a dispenser into a bowl and having rinsed the cubes under the cold tap, he placed two into each tumbler. Finally, he sliced a lime taken from the refrigerator, dropping a segment into each glass, and handed the finished articles to Miriam and Tracy in unison.

'Cheers,' he said, raising his drink.

Miriam took a sip. 'Mmm,' then took another before announcing, 'Nobody makes a G & T like Nicholas,' and sitting down contentedly.

Tracy was sceptical. She had sampled enough overpriced, warm and tasteless gin and tonics in the pub not to expect much from this pantomime, but took a sip anyway to confirm her reservations, then stopped and looked at Nicholas. 'You never told me you could make these?'

Not to be outdone, she discreetly turned down the oven, thus preventing the incineration of the ready meal, and prepared the salad that Miriam had contemplated but not started.

Nicholas took out his mobile. 'I want to give Herb a quick call,' calculating that with drinks in hand, he could safely leave them for a few minutes.

Miriam and Tracy gelled immediately, with Miriam keen to catch up on the news from Auchenmore and Tracy more than happy to share the gossip. Miriam recalled many of the details concerning people and places and was unsurprised at how little the town had changed.

'How is Mary's drawing these days?' she asked.

Tracy was puzzled. 'I don't remember Mum drawing.'

'Ah, it was probably just a passing thing then,' Miriam replied, getting up to set the table.

The meal heated, Miriam commenced the rigmarole of getting Nicholas to the table and wasn't surprised to hear his response of, 'Coming.'

Minutes later, Tracy called up with an uncompromising, 'Are you coming, or what?'

'I need to go, mate, supper's ready. See you tomorrow, eh?' they heard, as he approached the kitchen still holding the phone to his ear.

Better than I could do, thought Miriam.

The next day, as they were finishing breakfast, the doorbell clanged.

'It'll be Herb, I'll get it,' Nicholas said.

'Not taking any chances, are you, mate?' Herb remarked, having heard the mortise lock, bolt and chain.

'It's Mum. She's freaked out over security. There was a break-in up the road or something.'

Herb tugged again on the old bell-pull, drawing the wires, pulleys and directional turns that reached through the walls and up to the ceiling to jangle the large brass bell on its coiled spring. 'I love this thing,' enticing Nicholas to try the same.

'Leave it alone, children,' Miriam called with feigned tedium, and then turned to Tracy. 'They've always done that. I think being together brings out their mischievousness.'

Herb and Nicholas entered the kitchen, Herb with a laptop bag slung over his shoulder. He kissed Miriam on each cheek and then did the same to a half-standing and unprepared Tracy.

Ah, that's what you do, she thought, seeing the ease with which Miriam reciprocated.

'Nice to see you, Mrs Fraser,' Herb added, triggering an exchange of awkward glances.

'Just call me Miriam,' she replied, as she busied herself at the sink.

'Ah, OK. Sorry.'

She glanced around. 'There's nothing to be sorry about, Herb,' putting him back at ease and then returning to her task.

Herb took a seat at the table and cast his eyes over Miriam from behind as she proceeded to make the coffee.

'I must say you're looking well … Miriam. Something's agreeing with you,' he said, hesitating over the unfamiliar use of her first name.

Herb's comment drew Nicholas's attention to his mother, and he realised there was, indeed, a difference in her. Since his father's departure, a youthfulness had started to emerge; he was embarrassed to catch himself thinking she was actually rather attractive. Miriam didn't answer, but it was apparent that she was flattered.

'How is your mother keeping, Herb?' she asked, reinstating the 'friend's mother' relationship.

'She's well, and sends her regards.'

'That's good, be sure to return mine. Tell her we

need to meet for a catch-up sometime. It's been so long.'

'I will,' he replied, then tasted the coffee she had given him, 'Wow, that's fantastic.'

Tracy watched Herb and Nicholas exchange grins and shook her head as if to say, *Grow up*, then announced that she was heading out for an hour or so, to look around the shops in Stockbridge while they did whatever it was that was so important.

'Would you mind terribly if I joined you?' Miriam asked with overstated deference. 'Oh, and don't think I don't know when these two are teasing me.'

As soon as Nicholas and Herb were alone, the mood changed. Herb took out his large laptop, put it on the kitchen table and turned it on.

'How's Dani getting on?' he asked while they waited for it to boot up.

'Fine. Why do you ask?'

'I'm curious, Nicholas. I know how much you liked her, and then there was that business at your party which put the kibosh on it.'

Nicholas looked uncomfortable. 'And?'

'Well, you shoot off to France then come back and save the girl's life. But rather than the two of you getting back together, you take up with someone else. Don't get me wrong, I like Tracy – what I've seen of her.'

Nicholas glanced at the screen in the hope it would move them on. No such luck, it was still waking up.

'I think Tracy's wondering about that herself. Dani's a friend and I'm pleased I was able to help her, but we've both moved on with our lives. I'm now with Tracy and I've got this to concentrate on,' he said, pointing to the screen, which was finally awaiting a password. 'And Dani's got her career and the guy she's seeing.'

Herb typed in his password and they pulled their chairs in close, forgetting everything else as Herb clicked a file named 'The Grand Plan'.

'I've done some 3D modelling. Let me run through it with you, and we can list any changes. Then I'll get some plans printed out on the plotter at uni,' Herb said, as Nicholas waited to see the realisation of his dream.

'Stop it, you're embarrassing me,' Tracy hissed, sliding down in her seat and jabbing him in the ribs.

The Kilt and the Caber was an intriguing title, but when it turned out to be a comedy based on the Highlanders of Scotland and a set of quips at their expense, Tracy saw red. Nicholas, however, found it hilarious – even the parts that fell flat with the rest of the audience – something he demonstrated through solitary but raucous laughter.

'They made us look like a bunch of Teuchters,' she said, as they made their way from the venue towards Bristo Place.

'It was satire,' Nicholas laughed, swinging her arm.

'Aye, right,' using the two positives to express her scepticism.

Her eyes caught a little statue. 'Look, there's Bobby. I love that wee Skye Terrier.'

'So do I. I still have the storybook at home. Come on, let's make a wish.'

They crossed the busy junction then stood looking at the bronze figure painted black – except for his nose, which had been polished to a golden sheen by thousands of hopeful fingers.

'It wasn't like that when I was a child,' said Nicholas. 'People touch it for luck but I'm sure he doesn't like it – what dog would! Just make a wish and he'll hear you.'

Tracy closed her eyes, then opened them.

'Have you made your wish?'

She smiled and nodded, 'Have you?'

'Of course.'

They headed down Candlemaker Row, with its quirky shops and cafes, to the Cowgate. As they walked, Nicholas told the story of how John Gray, a night-watchman, had died and was buried in the nearby kirkyard.

'Bobby watched over his master's grave and was taken into Edinburgh's heart for his devotion.'

'You know the story so well.'

'I read the book a few times. Bobby was such a loyal little dog; I admire that.'

Tracy held his arm a bit tighter. With Nicholas's talk of loyalty, it seemed that Bobby had heard her wish.

At the bottom of the hill, Nicholas pointed to a padlocked door covered in graffiti.

'That's a nightclub. We used to go there when the

pubs shut. It's pure mental,' he said, suggesting more went on in there than met the eye.

Tracy looked at her watch with relief; it was still a few hours before closing, by which time she would make sure they were well clear of this place.

Up to their right sat a building where the George IV Bridge straddled the Cowgate.

'That's the library where I used to study for my exams. I couldn't concentrate at home. I was there every night and still failed. Twice, in fact. What a waste.'

'Well, look on the bright side, at least you know what you're rubbish at.'

He laughed, 'I don't think it was that. I think it was because it was all theory and I'm a practical type of person.'

'You mean you're street smart, rather than book smart?'

'I love the way you keep things simple,' he said.

They entered the Grassmarket and joined the throng in a standing-room-only pub, eventually drawing the attention of bar staff adept at evading all but the most dazzling displays of attention-seeking.

'I'll get them,' Tracy said, ordering Nicholas a pint and a spritzer for herself. They then stood yelling at each other over the noise and defending their drinks from being sploshed by the jostling crowd.

Deciding to move on, it was back out into fresh evening air and a climb up the curve of Victoria Street with its patchwork of brightly painted shops and then left, crossing the Royal Mile to descend the

Mound.

The lively notes of ceilidh music caught Tracy's ear. 'Where's that coming from?'

'Oh, over there somewhere,' said Nicholas, pointing vaguely in the direction of Mound Place.

Tracy wasn't deterred by his indifference. 'Come on, it sounds fun, we might be able to get in.'

'Why?' he asked, associating Scottish Country Dancing with his school days and compulsory dancing to the reedy notes of a listless accordionist.

She tugged his arm. 'Don't be so boring, it'll be fun.' He hoped it would turn out to be a private function.

Two large open doors spilt music, whoops and shouts of laughter into the night.

'Come on,' she said, drawn like a moth to a flame.

Nicholas paid the requisite entry fee, and the two of them melted into the crowd just as a reel concluded. There wasn't a kilt in sight, just a typical Festival mix of nationalities dressed in jeans, shorts, T-shirts, summer dresses and leggings.

The room was called to order by a girl on stage wearing a black dress and holding a fiddle. 'Take your partners for a Strip the Willow.'

Nicholas shook his head and pulled back, but Tracy was having none of it.

'Ah, ah,' she said, wagging a finger, 'I did that excuse for a comedy, so you're doing this. Stand over there and do what I say.'

It seemed he had no choice.

The girl with the fiddle talked the hapless eights

through their steps. 'Women on this side and men on that.' A simple enough request, but apparently beyond the comprehension of most in the room. Next, she explained a series of manoeuvres requiring turns, partners, the linking of arms and 'stripping' down the line, all of which sounded fascinating but unworkable in practice.

'One final thing: nobody moves until I say. Is that clear?' She looked around to a floor preoccupied with the formulation of survival strategies. She repeated, 'I said "Is that clear"?'

'Yes,' replied the more optimistic.

A lone piper commenced a slow, poignant skirl, filling the room with an innately Scottish sound that spoke of heritage and pride. The girl on the fiddle started her piece, constructing a rhythm and rehearsing a repetition in the minds and bodies of the dancers.

Nicholas looked across at Tracy smiling back at him, preparing for the explosion of movement to come. 'Ready?' she mouthed, with a look to caution him.

He nodded, hesitantly. The bass guitarist joined the fiddle, followed by the drummer. Then an electric guitar played several chords, holding the final note in an extended reverb. 'GO,' shouted the girl, releasing the dancers to their fate.

The first pair was off, dancing down the line to become the fourth couple.

'Now,' Tracy called, and taking Nicholas firmly by the arm, she birled him through the twirls with a centrifugal force that had him fearful lest she let go and he found himself hurled across the city.

Tracy danced down the line, her red hair flying. Around a man and back to Nicholas, around the next and back, and again. He could see the expectation on their faces as they awaited their chance to dance with the lass. All he wanted now was Tracy back with him, taking control and swinging him around. Then his turn. Around a lady and back to Tracy, around the next and back, and again. The band took the dance to a frenzied crescendo then stopped, collapsing the floor into an exhausted mêlée.

'That was amazing,' he said, throwing his arms around Tracy and drawing her towards him. He kissed her hard on the mouth, feeling her hot body through his shirt, and then brought her even closer.

It was the wee small hours when the ceilidh concluded.

'Shall we get a taxi?' he asked.

Tracy looked across a still bustling Princes Street. 'Can we walk?'

'Sure.'

Their arms locking together, they resumed their descent of the Mound, passing oncoming revellers labouring with the climb, but high-spirited enough to share greetings.

Tracy's eyes took in the brightly lit scene with the Walter Scott Monument to the right. 'What a great place to call home. It looks so exciting compared with Auchenmore.'

He looked around. 'I guess it is, but I'm not sure it's home anymore.'

'Where's home for you, then?' she asked,

hopefully.

'I'm not sure now,' he replied, then changed the subject.

Hearing someone enter, Miriam called through, 'Nicholas, is that you?'

'Yes. It's just us,' and she joined them with a look of relief that Nicholas recalled from his childhood.

'Did you both have a good evening?' she asked.

Tracy's face beamed. 'It was brilliant.'

Miriam looked happy for them. 'That's good. I'm off to bed. I'll see you in the morning.'

Nicholas and Tracy went into the kitchen and turned on one of the lights, dimming it in the manner that the early hours encourage.

'Fancy a cuppa ... and some cheese on toast?' he asked, having already started to prepare it.

Tracy gave a naughty grin and a nod.

Kettle on and the toaster set about its task, Nicholas's mood quietened. He once again put his arms around Tracy, his hands moving to the bottom of her back, then below. Looking into his eyes, she put her hands around him to match and they kissed each other softly on the lips.

Having returned to collect her forgotten reading glasses, Miriam crossed the darkened hallway. Looking towards the kitchen she caught sight of her son holding the girl he was so fond of and her mind went back to a time long ago, when she too had briefly found love.

Sunlight streamed through the open curtains that had

afforded a stunning nighttime view of the Edinburgh skyline, awakening Tracy from a confused dream. She reached over and then remembered Nicholas had slunk off back to his room just before dawn. As she lay looking at the rays, her mind went back to the ceilidh, how they had kissed in the kitchen, their cuddle and the view they had finally gone to sleep with. She thought of everything she had learnt over the last two days. Before their visit there had been an Auchenmore version of Nicholas: she had once met a vile father, viewed a chalet from the outside and heard of a beleaguered mother. Now she had seen inside Nicholas's other world and found it different from what she expected: the city, his home and his mother. It raised questions about their relationship. Was it for real, or just a passing phase in his life? Today they would go back to her home, Auchenmore and the flat, but it wasn't his home. He had inadvertently told her that as they descended the Mound. How quickly would he tire of their arrangement when there were so many alternatives for him? The answer seemed elusive so she got up, washed and dressed for the day.

She peered into his darkened bedroom. 'Nicholas, are you awake?'

The duvet inched higher and from beneath came a muffled voice, 'I'll be down in a bit.'

Miriam was sitting at the kitchen table, deep in thought. 'Oh, Tracy, have a seat. I'll make coffee,' she said, getting up.

'Thanks, that would be great. What were you thinking about?' Tracy asked as Miriam popped a coffee capsule into the machine.

'Well, if you must know, I was thinking about a green gardener's shed. But never mind that. Tell me about your evening.'

Tracy told her all about the ceilidh. 'It was great, Miriam. You would have loved it.'

Miriam smiled, appreciative that Tracy saw her as someone who could go and take joy from the world, rather than the embattled soul she felt herself to be.

'Mind you, Nicholas's comedy thing was a bit weird.'

Miriam wasn't surprised. 'Yes, his Fringe choices are somewhat of an acquired taste.'

She handed Tracy the perfect cup of Columbian, prepared another for herself, then sat down at the table. They had just taken their first sips and were about to put their cups down when a loud clatter sounded from the front door. Miriam jumped, tossing her coffee over the table, causing Tracy to recoil and do the same.

Miriam apologised. 'I'm sorry; I seem a little on edge. It's just the Sunday newspaper,' and got up to clear the mess.

Tracy recognised the reaction from her encounter with the creep, O'Doile – that sense of being anxious and overreacting to the unexpected.

'Is everything OK, Miriam?' she asked.

But Miriam brushed her off. 'Yes, I'm fine. I'm just being silly,' as she set about remaking their coffee.

'Nicholas tells me you're a Special Constable. That must be exciting?'

'Some of the time. The rest of the time, it's more interesting than exciting, but you do feel you're helping others.'

'Perhaps that's what I need to do, something useful … once I get things sorted out.' She didn't say what those things might be. 'Tell me, how's Dani getting on?'

The mention of Dani came as a jolt. *This is my world, not Dani's. Why is she asking about a girl she hasn't even met?*

'She's back down south with her boyfriend, Marshall.'

'Oh, what does he do?'

'He's a police officer as well.'

Miriam returned to the table with their remade coffee. 'I should have guessed, with a name like that! And Dani's fully recovered from the incident on the mountain? It must be, what, six months or so now since it happened?'

'About that, yes. And I think so – at least, she hasn't said there's a problem.'

'I'm glad. Nicholas never told me properly what he did that night. I read about it in the paper – it sounded quite an adventure – but when I asked him, he said it was nothing and that the newspapers had overplayed it.'

'It wasn't "nothing", Miriam, it was a big thing he did, a huge thing. He saved Dani's life, risking his own to do it.'

Miriam sipped her coffee. 'I suspected as much.'

Tracy went quiet, her fingers playing with her cup.

'What is it, lass? What's on your mind?'

Tracy felt flustered, unsure whether to say anything. Eventually, she spoke. 'It's just that I sometimes wonder … I know I shouldn't, but I wonder, if Nicholas hadn't stayed in Auchenmore to rescue Dani that night, would we be together?'

'I think you're talking about fate. It's such a shame that with love comes the fear of loss.'

Tracy looked questioningly and Miriam acknowledged her.

'Yes Tracy, I was in love once.' She looked down at the cup she held so carefully. 'There was a boy who took the same bus as me home from school. I always sat upstairs on a seat next to the window so I could look down to the pavement. He used to look up, and when he saw me, he would get on, come upstairs and smile as he walked past. I would dare myself to look back at him, and when I did I would feel flutters inside. I think that's what love feels like, isn't it?'

Tracy looked at her in agreement as she remembered the first time she met Nicholas, and Miriam continued. 'Eventually, we said hello. Then one day – the 14th of February it was – he gave me a card. Inside, in beautiful handwriting, he had written three lines from a poem. "The dance gaed thro' the lighted ha,' To thee my fancy took its wing, I sat, but neither heard nor saw …".'

'That's from "Mary Morison", by Robert Burns, isn't it?' Tracy ventured. 'We studied it at school. That's so romantic. What did you do?' she asked, keen to hear the rest of the story.

'We met once, secretly of course. It was a Saturday afternoon. He took me for a walk in the Botanic Gardens and then we went to the house of one of my friends – a girl called Dorothy. She also had a boyfriend, but her parents were easier than mine about such things. Anyway, her parents were away for the weekend. It was like a big adventure. We watched a film then cooked something to eat, but it all went wrong.'

'What happened?'

'We lost track of time, my parents panicked and when I got home there was a police car outside. My mother thought I had been kidnapped or something stupid like that. She was furious and spoke to Dorothy, forcing her to confess about the boy as though I had sinned. Then she forbade me from ever seeing him again.'

Miriam looked pensively back at the cup still between her fingers.

'My mother found the card that he had given me in my bedroom and threw it away, but I retrieved it. After that, I was too frightened to talk to him again. It's strange, the hold that parents can have over you. A year later I met Hamish and married him. My mother said that it was for the best.'

'What do you mean by, "for the best"?'

'Oh, it doesn't matter, it was complicated.' But Tracy knew it did matter. She had seen it with her mother – things of the heart that were yet to be reconciled.

'And you never saw the boy again?'

'No. I know that he became a writer. Short

stories, that type of thing.'

'Do you still have the card?' a question to which Tracy already knew the answer.

Miriam's face brightened. 'Would you like to see it?'

Keen to share her secret, she lifted her handbag from a chair, removed the card and handed it over.

Tracy's eyes scanned the faded poem and the signature at the bottom before handing it back to Miriam's waiting hand.

'I don't know why I've started to carry it again. I think it's to remind me that not all men are the same. You won't say anything to Nicholas, will you?' she said, putting it safely back.

'Don't worry. Your secret is safe with me.'

'And you don't need to worry about Nicholas. He's a kind boy. That's why it hurts me so much to think …' but Miriam couldn't go on.

'It's OK, you don't have to say anything more,' Tracy interjected, as she had with Nicholas at the café. 'Perhaps one day you could talk to him about these things. Get to know each other better.'

'I'm trying to do that. And Nicholas has been a great support since he came back from France. But I don't think either of us is ready to confront all that's happened. There are so many painful memories – I wouldn't know where to start.'

'You'll find a way, I'm sure you will,' she said, then reached over and hugged Miriam.

Miriam gathered herself. 'I haven't helped you with your conundrum, have I?'

Tracy looked confused again.

'About what would have happened if Nicholas hadn't stayed to rescue Dani.'

'Oh, that one,' Tracy answered, remembering where their conversation had started.

'Why don't you talk to him about it?' Miriam suggested, then realised it was the same advice she had just received.

To both women, it felt too soon by the time Tracy and Nicholas were at the front door, ready to depart. Even Nicholas was aware of the friendship starting to form between them.

'Will you be OK, Mum?' unsure why he had chosen that turn of phrase.

'I'll be fine, don't worry about me. Just give me a call from time to time, will you?'

He kissed her on the cheek then slung the rucksack onto his back and picked up Tracy's bag in his right hand.

'Don't worry, Miriam. I'll make sure he does,' Tracy assured as she leant forward and kissed Miriam on both cheeks, the way she had seen Herb do. They had started down the steps when Tracy stopped, turned and ran back. Throwing her arms around Miriam she hugged her tight, just as she had done with her mother the night of her first wage packet, and Miriam realised she was crying.

Tracy eventually let go and wiped her eyes with a tissue. 'I'm sorry, Miriam. I don't know what happened there.'

'There's nothing to be sorry about. You'll come and visit again soon, won't you?' giving a final hug to the girl who now felt like the daughter she'd never had.

'She's always done that,' said Nicholas as they stood waiting for their bus.

'What?' Tracy asked, unsure if they were thinking the same thing.

'Protected me, but I know she's worried and it will be to do with that man I used to call my father.'

'Don't get angry, Nicholas. It won't help. Anyway, I've got a bone to pick with you.'

'Oh, what have I done now?' he asked

'Your mum, she's lovely; nothing like you said she was.'

'Eh? I never said that.'

She smiled. 'Put your bag down for a moment, will you.'

'Why?' he asked.

'Just put it down.'

He conceded and she wrapped her arms around him and kissed him on the cheek. 'Thanks for bringing me to Edinburgh, and sorry I was reluctant to start with.'

'That's OK.'

Then she looked thoughtful. 'Perhaps I shouldn't ask, but do you know there was once a boy your mum was in love with?'

Nicholas picked up Tracy's hand. 'She's never mentioned it directly, but I've always had my suspicions. I think it's what's given her hope for all these years.' He looked down the road and saw a number 30 bus approaching. 'This is ours.'

CHAPTER 13

As Tracy finished the call, she wondered why
Nicholas had made such a point of suggesting they
go out tonight, and why he hadn't just waited till
they saw each other after work. *If he has something
important to say, why does he not just say it? Why go
for a bar supper?* She ran through the possibilities.
*He's got funding for his idea. Maybe he's found a
site – or perhaps he has something special to ask
me! No, that won't be it,* and her initial excitement
waned.

When they arrived at the familiar haunt, she could
barely wait until they were seated before asking,
'Are you going to tell me now?'

'Let's order first.' His reticence made Tracy feel
he was stalling for time.

She gave him a questioning look then shrugged
and was about to browse the menu when she noticed
how distracted he was.

'What's up? Don't tell me you're not hungry?'

'I was just thinking that this is where you, me and
Dani sat on my birthday.'

Her mind returned to that night and how badly it
had ended. She visualised him sitting there with the

same pensive look he wore tonight, then getting up and leaving. She put down her menu. 'What is it, Nicholas? You look as though something's worrying you.'

'Tracy, I want to talk to you about us living together in the flat.'

'What's there to talk about?' An uneasy feeling started to grow.

'It's been great. I'm so grateful to you for taking Sandy and me in, but it's small for two people and a dog.'

'What are you saying?'

'I've been thinking about what you asked me in Edinburgh, about where my home is.'

'Nicholas, when I asked you that I was only—'

But he interrupted. 'Listen for a minute and I'll explain. I've been looking at a place on one of the local estates. It was accommodation for seasonal workers, but it's been empty for a couple of years. It's called 'The Bothy' – not very original, I know. I looked it over this afternoon. It needs a bit of work done to make it habitable again, but I think if I get stuck in I could have it ready for winter. It would benefit from a wood-burning stove, and the décor sorted out, but all that is straightforward enough. I'm sure Mum has some spare furniture – there's a whole load of stuff in the Edinburgh basement.'

Tracy's eyes were on him but her mind had wandered to the evenings they'd spent together in the flat. It was small and not very welcoming, even with the effort she had put in. Built as a concrete box in the early seventies, and not hers to alter, it was difficult to do more. However, they had been happy there, and it was their home, wasn't it?

Nicholas continued his monologue. 'There's a bedroom, a kitchen-cum-sitting room, a crummy bathroom-type thing ...' He finally noticed Tracy's absent look. 'Tracy, are you listening? This is important.'

'What?' she asked, as she struggled to divide her attention between him and the profusion of emotions welling inside her. *Some evening this is turning into.* She fidgeted on her seat, tempted to get up and walk out. No,she needed answers. She drew in a breath to ask him what this was really about, but the lump in her throat checked her voice and before she could gather herself he was off again. *I was right all along,* she thought. *He arrived, left, returned and now he's leaving again. When will he shut up and give me space to get a word in?* She stared blankly, waiting. Holding in the tears as her insecurities came flooding back, insecurities she realised had never gone away. *All that talk about us being good together and the way he held me in his arms the night of the ceilidh – all just lies.*

'Could you at least think about it?'

Think about what? She wanted to fight back, but couldn't and despite her efforts, the tears welled.

Eventually, she choked out the words. 'Why are you doing this to me, Nicholas? What have I done to deserve it?'

Nicholas jerked back in his seat. *What?! What does she mean?* Panic took hold, taking him back to so many previous episodes of helplessness.

'You haven't done anything wrong! I'm not trying to hurt you, honestly. Why would I do that?' He tried to claw back a situation that had somehow gone awry. 'I'm making a mess of this, aren't I?'

Tracy couldn't help agreeing, and Nicholas reached over and took her unresponsive hand. He looked into her sad eyes, trying to make her see how much she meant to him.

'I haven't explained why to you, and that's important. It was when you asked me "Where is home for you?", and I didn't have an answer. I realised then what I've been missing: a place to call home. I've been trying to figure out what makes a home. I think it's a place where you feel happy and secure. A place you put your mark on. A reflection of who you are. Somewhere you share with the people you love. I know now that I've never had any of those things before, not properly, and I want to try and make up for it.' *Why is she just sitting there saying nothing?*

He carried on. 'I'm sorry if I've confused you. I know this is a big thing I'm asking. But I love you, Tracy. You know that, don't you? I'd like us to have a place of our own – you and me. Somewhere we can call our home together. But if you'd prefer to—'

She jumped to her feet and ran round to his side of the table, her chair clattering to the floor, and he stumbled to a halt.

Taking his head in her hands, she kissed him on each cheek, the way he always did with her.

'Is that a yes?'

She pulled her head away and looked at him,

nodding frantically, unable to say anything, knowing that if she did, she really would be brought to tears. Then still holding him, she looked straight into his eyes and landed a massive kiss on his mouth.

***

Pushing her bike up the slope, Dani looked into the woods, taking comfort from the Scots pines and their sweet earthy-wood fragrance.

Marshall stopped and called ahead. 'Dani, please slow down.'

Without looking back, she waited for him to catch up.

'What's wrong?' he asked. 'I thought we were coming up to Scotland for some time together, but you've hardly spoken to me.'

She hesitated, unsure whether it was the words she was lacking or the courage to speak them.

'What is it?' he prompted, but she shook her head.

'Leave it, it doesn't matter. Let's go or we'll be late.'

They reached the rendezvous – a little glen where two streams met – but the others hadn't arrived yet. Placing their bikes against a tree they sat down next to each other on a gentle slope looking down to the water. Dani lay back on the grass and closed her eyes. She could sense Marshall looking at her questioningly – seeking answers as to what was happening with their relationship – before lying down on the grass beside her. She inadvertently reached out her hand to the side and he instinctively took hold of it, receiving a slight squeeze before she let go. *I need to tell him this isn't what I want.* But it was difficult. She tried once again to make sense of it all. *Was it the avalanche that changed everything? Or is Marshall unable to give me what I had hoped for?* It now felt awkward when it was just the two of them. Yet blaming him felt wrong, especially if, as he said, he had risked his life on the mountain to try and find her. And then there was her irrational but lingering hope that something from the past might rekindle – that she'd be able to return to the Highlands, and share a life in the outdoors with Nicholas, for whom she had a myriad of contradictory emotions.

'I wonder where the others are?' she asked, her eyes still closed as she basked in the warmth.

'They won't be long,' he replied, sensing the unease in her voice.

She started to doze, and from the confusing land of half-sleep, heard Nicholas and Tracy approaching. Nicholas was talking and laughing, as he used to do with her, and Tracy sounded happy, as she had once been.

Dani got to her feet. 'Where did you get to?' she asked them.

Nicholas and Tracy smiled guiltily at each other, but Dani didn't respond, leaving them to regret their lack of tact.

They sat down together, talking until Mary and Rory arrived.

Mary joined them on the grass and looked out across the heather to the mountains. 'Isn't it incredibly beautiful? What a good idea of yours, Nicholas,' she said.

Rory passed her a water bottle. 'I think it was Dani's idea.'

Dani sighed and challenged him, unable to keep her irritation out of her voice. 'Dad, what difference does it make whose idea it was?'

'I'm just saying it wasn't Nicholas's idea, that's all.'

Everyone could tell he wasn't going to give Nicholas credit he didn't believe was due to him.

Mary defused the tension with a brief, 'Leave it, Rory,' and he backed down.

They handed round the food from their bags, Nicholas indulging Tracy and Dani with the things he knew they liked. Rory was watching him. 'Don't spoil it,' whispered Mary. Rory's grudge against the boy had become very obvious.

When they'd finished eating, Nicholas went down to the stream, removed his shoes and socks and put his feet in the water. Marshall took out his phone and started to scroll through his messages.

Dani stood up. 'I'm going to sit over there and look at the view,' then moved to the shade of an old Scots pine. She sat with her knees pulled up tight to her chest, held by the wrap of her arms as though fearful she might fall apart. Nicholas gave her a carefree wave and a smile. Dani acknowledged him with a flutter of fingers, released for the purpose but quickly returned. After everything they had been through, they seemed closer than ever, connected by something deeper than she understood. Yet Dani had the impression that all the things that shaped her heart and had once given meaning to her life – the Highlands, Nicholas and her dreams – were moving further and further from reach.

She looked out to the mountains with their little patches of snow that had endured through the summer, clinging on to their final moment of 'being,' and wondered if it was now inevitable that, like the snow, her moment had passed.

Tracy noticed her solitude and came to sit beside her, putting her arm comfortingly around Dani's shoulders.

'How are you, Dani?' she asked.

'I don't know, Tracy. I feel so lost – I don't know who I am anymore.'

Dani sipped her tea then looked around the mess room; a Police Scotland version of her home station. There was an alcove kitchen equipped with a sink, kettle, communal refrigerator and cupboards with team numbers on their doors. The main room hosted a double table surrounded by chairs and walls adorned with the mandatory Federation posters informing of pensions, members' rights and the local rep. A TV in the corner displayed a silent game show and on the wall beside it was a pinboard with pictures drawn by local children thanking officers for their school visit.

Claire returned clutching a piece of paper and sat down beside her.

'This is just for your use, isn't it Dani?' she asked. 'Although to be honest, I can't see any great secret surrounding any of it.'

Dani nodded. 'I just need to be clear in my head what happened that day.'

Claire looked sympathetic and put the piece of paper on the table. Then, with Dani looking on, she ran through the timeline with her finger. 'You can see this was when the storm struck. Calls started to build quickly but if you want to be even more accurate, go online and look at the mountain weather station. The archive will show you a sudden increase in wind speed.' Claire continued down the listing, reaching an entry with an asterisk. 'This is the call made by the climbers who came across your companion forty minutes later.' She looked sideways at Dani. 'Does it put your mind at rest?'

'Not really,' Dani replied, slumping back in her chair.

Claire looked confused, so Dani elaborated. 'If Marshall had spent an hour looking for me as he says he did, he wouldn't have been with the climbers forty minutes after we became separated, would he?'

'I suppose not,' said Claire, looking again at the timeline for anything she'd missed but drawing a blank.

Then she looked at Dani more searchingly. 'What you went through was traumatic. Have you considered speaking to someone about it? A professional?'

Dani glanced at her watch. 'I'm fine, Claire. Thanks for your help. I'd better push on … I've arranged to pick something up from Artair's workshop.'

Claire suppressed a sigh, nodded and showed Dani out. Watching her walk away, she was heartened to see that Dani was moving quickly, as though looking forward to something. Maybe things weren't as bad as she'd sensed.

Dani opened the workshop door and entered. Artair was at the far end, engrossed in what he was forming on his lathe. Twirls of wood fed from a chisel as he worked his way up and down a spinning piece of oak. The workshop had always intrigued her; a wooden building with a tin roof, and heated by a stove fuelled by Artair's offcuts. Below a long window of small glass panes sat a bench with various power tools: a sander, drill and saw. At the rear of the bench was a raised shelf with holes to accommodate chisels of every imaginable shape and size. Stacked against the opposite wall were numerous pieces of wood collected by Artair during local forages. All from native species, some were straight and proud, others knurled and knotted as though having reached a point of utter confusion in their growth. Strangest of all were the blackened roots, retrieved from bogs and dating back to the great Caledonian Forest.

It was said that Artair's true gift lay not in carving, but in revealing what time held within the wood. Dani remembered as a little girl visiting with her father. She recalled lifting a piece of wood from the bench, turning it in her hands and wondering what it would become.

Artair had crouched down beside her. 'Can you see the story in there, Dani?' but despite her efforts, all she beheld was an unusual shape. Running his fingers over the wood he explained, 'There's a little girl in here. She's looking up to the stars and dreaming. Now I just need to use my tools to let her out.'

That Christmas she had unwrapped a strange package from under the tree, and there she was, the little girl. Artair had even attached a star with a thin wire.

His mother had been known throughout the district and beyond for her palmistry. People would visit her cottage, sit at the lace-covered table and have their destinies revealed. Young Artair would be parked in the corner working a piece of wood with his knife and taking in his mother's 'gift'.

The lathe eventually powered down and Artair came across, collecting a package wrapped in brown paper from a shelf as he passed.

'Let me show it to you,' he said, but Dani shook her head. 'No, that's OK. I'm sure it's beautiful.'

She expected him to hand over the package, but he stood looking at it in his hands. Then his eyes met Dani's, their blue at odds with his ruddy face. 'I've known your family for many years, haven't I?' but Dani didn't answer, knowing this was a prelude. 'I remember you coming here as a little girl, and carving that figure for you.'

Dani smiled. 'I still have it in my bedroom in Inverness.'

'Aye, that's where she is, right enough,' as though confirming it to her. 'And it was an easy enough task to find the wee lass in the wood.' Then he scratched his chin with a leathery hand. 'This was another matter altogether. I've made it as close as I could to what you wanted, but I can't hide the truth, Dani.'

'I'm not sure what you mean.'

'Aye, well, you'll know soon enough. I hope your boy from the mountain finds it to his liking.'

'I never said …'

But Artair had turned away. 'I'll send you the bill when I have time,' he called, restarting the lathe and inspecting the tip of his chisel.

Nicholas was stacking wood when Dani arrived at the Bothy.

'Where's Marshall?' he asked.

'He's helping Dad in the shop today. I wanted a bit of time to myself.'

'Ah.' Lifting a couple of small logs, he added, 'It seems I've made a career of stacking wood. You should have phoned and I'd have picked you up.'

'I know you would have. I needed the walk, and it gave me a chance to think.'

She sat down on the bench beside the porch, holding the package from Artair on her lap, and watched him work.

'I'm nearly finished,' he said, glancing at what she was holding

'Take your time.'

He looked up and smiled at her, and she smiled

back – a sad smile.

'Are you OK?' he asked, placing the last pieces of wood.

'Yes. I'm fine … Dani's always fine, isn't she?'

Surprised by her tone, he came and sat beside her. 'This isn't like you, Dani. What's up?' But she didn't answer his question. Instead, she handed him the package.

'This is for you.' She looked tearful, leaving Nicholas unsure how to respond. 'Open it. I had it made specially. I've never thanked you properly for everything you've done. This can be something for your home that you can remember me by.'

'You're part of this as well,' he said, gesturing around, but it didn't seem to register. So he proceeded to carefully unwrap the package. Inside was a beautiful plaque in ornate wood. About eighteen inches wide and twelve inches tall, it was carved with numerous images that he recognised from Auchenmore and their time together. There were the mountains, little trees, a stream, a deer and the ptarmigan they had seen. There were two bikes, two pairs of walking boots hanging from their laces, two climbers roped together and three little pairs of skis: an inconsistency, he thought. Engraved in the bottom right corner was a single word: *cianalas*.

His fingers ran lightly over the carving, his eyes taking in the detail. 'This is beautiful. It's incredible how the character of the wood matches the figures.' Then he looked into her hazel eyes. 'Just beautiful,' and for a moment he was taken back to the time when all this had taken place. A time of immense pain and confusion, but also burning desire for the girl now sitting next to him.

'Where's the wood from?' he asked.

'Artair found it beside the loch: driftwood, just like me.'

Then she started to cry, a tragic sight, her arms by her sides and big tears streaming down her cheeks. It was as though she was emptying the last piece of herself. Seeing her distress he put an arm around her shoulder.

'Come on, Dani,' he whispered.

She didn't say anything, so he stood up, brought her to her feet and reached out with both arms, hugging her tightly. He could feel the contours of her body as she pulled herself towards him and he felt for her sadness, but more profoundly, he felt startled by other feelings emerging within him. Feelings he'd thought had been put to rest.

Eventually, she let go and wiped her eyes.

'I'm sorry, this was meant to be a happy occasion.'

'Don't be. I guess it's the thought of going back, is it?'

'Yes, that'll be it.' she replied, without conviction.

'Let me go and fetch us a cuppa. You sit here. I'll take this inside to keep it safe,' his eyes on the carving but his mind on what had occurred.

Dani sat down again and looked around as Nicholas prepared the tea.

'There,' he said, handing her a mug and a couple of biscuits and sitting down beside her again.

She leaned her head against his shoulder and with her face turned to the sun, she started to doze.

'Do you trust Marshall?' she asked, her eyes still closed.

'That's a strange question. Why, do you not? He certainly seems keen on you.'

'He says he is, but I'm just not sure anymore. I'm not sure about anything.'

'Is it Marshall, or is it something else?'

She took her head off his shoulder and looked around, as though seeking the answer, then turned to Nicholas. 'I can't help thinking what life would have been like if we hadn't messed up that night at the chalet.'

Nicholas picked up one of her hands in his. 'Don't think that way, Dani. That night was bound to happen in some shape or form. I was a complete mess myself, and I'm sorry for what I put you through, you know that.'

'I suppose so, and you've got Tracy now, haven't you?'

'Yes, Tracy and I are together.' He felt her hand go limp in his. 'But that doesn't mean I don't care for you.'

'I know that. And I'm not looking to get in between the two of you. I think I'm looking for some positives in my life.' She took her hand back and straightened. 'Can you show me the plans for your project?'

Nicholas stood up and took her empty mug. 'Sure. Let me show you around and then we can look at them.'

She had visited the Bothy before but never had the official tour. 'This is beautiful,' she said, looking at the wall panelling he had completed in the main room.

He ran his fingers along the wood as if checking his work. 'I got most of my ideas in France. This wood is from an old barn on the estate. It was just a case of brushing it and cutting the pieces to size.'

Her eyes darted around and then stopped on the wood-burning stove.

'We bought that second-hand. I've blackened it again with a special polish. The stone it's sitting on comes from a derelict mill. Do you like it?'

She nodded. 'And over there?' pointing to two doors at the end of the room.

'Two bedrooms. If you ever need somewhere to stay for the night ...'

She looked questioningly, then shifted her eyes to the kitchen table.

'That was already here. I spruced it up. We've still to get curtains. Mum's got a load in Edinburgh, I just need to collect them, and Mary's offered to do the alterations.'

Hearing him mention Edinburgh, Dani asked, 'Have you heard from your father?'

He immediately tensed. 'No, and I don't *want* to hear from that evil ...' then, looking contrite, he apologised.

Dani gave him a knowing look. 'Don't let him take any more of your life, Nicholas. He's not worth it.'

'But after what he's done, it's difficult not to get

angry.'

She nodded, 'Dads can be hard work,' then looked to change the subject. 'Anyway, you've still not shown me your plans.'

'No, and you can't go back without seeing them.'

They sat down at the table and Nicholas opened a scroll of paper, holding the ends down with two pebbles he had for the purpose.

'Here it is, Dani. "The Grand Plan", as we call it.'

Dani's eyes ran across the impressive drawings as Nicholas explained his ideas for an outdoor centre. There would be traditional pursuits together with more novel offerings: programmes in Gaelic, cookery, music, wildlife, digital photography and crofting.

He seemed to have covered every angle: the build, activities, costing and marketing, and his enthusiasm brought it to life, just as it had when he'd first shared his dream with her.

Dani was astonished. What she had believed was a fantasy was becoming a reality, exactly as he had described it to her three years before.

'When did you do all this?' she asked.

'I don't think there's been a day that's gone by when I haven't thought about it. Is this not what we talked about?'

Dani nodded; indeed, it was … just as he had described and as they had imagined when they first met.

'What does Tracy think?' she asked, still staring in awe.

'That's her bit, there,' pointing to a largish-looking part at the side of the building. 'A retail area with artisan food, but best ask her. She has an amazing business head.'

Dani thought how, despite having so little, Tracy always seemed to get by and have a bit extra left.

'And what are those little buildings?' pointing to what looked like two small chalets off to one side.

'Those are cabins: retreats for families.'

She looked at him for further explanation.

'Coming up here was never what it should have been for my family, but that was because of us. It would be nice to be able to help families who need a break. A place where they can spend time together writing a positive future.'

He thought about his mother's suffering, of what Tracy had told him about Mary's tribulations and about how his return to Auchenmore had enabled him to find a place to call home. 'I want to do good things, Dani. To help people.'

She smiled and rubbed his arm. 'You're good at that, Nicholas. You have the heart to help people. Have you seen any sites?'

'There are a few building plots around. The land is costly, though. Especially if you want a view.'

'How will you pay for it?'

'I'm still working on that one.'

'Doesn't it scare you?'

'Big challenges always look scary, don't they? But if you want something badly enough, you'll find a way to make it happen.'

Dani thought of his aspirations, and her mind wandered to her own heart.

'Nicholas, do you think it's possible to make *any* dream come true?'

'I do – if you want something badly enough. You need to make a plan and put in the effort, but yes, we can make dreams come true. You have to be brave though, Dani.'

'Like you?'

'I'm not brave. I've only done what I've thought was right, and tried to make up for my past mistakes.'

He reached out, put his hand on top of hers and squeezed it hard, and she thought about how he had faced up to the storm, and how, by contrast, she felt so scared of everything now.

'Look at us, Dani. It was my biggest hope that we would be friends again. That's what I wanted more than anything, and it came true! All this, it's just stuff compared to that,' he said, gesturing around the room.

She looked down at his hand still clutching hers, and thought about what she had learnt from the letter she'd found at her home two days before. The letter from Nicholas that her father had hidden from her.

'Nicholas?'

'Yes?'

'Can I share my dream with you?'

He held her hand tighter now, leaning towards her and looking deep into those beautiful hazel eyes that were desperately trying to communicate.

'Go on, tell me your dream,' he encouraged.

'My dream is to come home … and be part of this … but I can't see how,' and her tears returned.

From the knoll, Nicholas looked around then down at the idyllic view of the Bothy, its bright red corrugated iron roof and wood smoke drifting lazily from the chimney.

With Sandy settled beside him, he was in no hurry to move as his mind contrasted the tranquillity of his surroundings with what he'd seen Dani go through the previous afternoon. By the time Tracy had returned from work, Dani was feeling a little stronger, her tears having purged the turmoil he now knew she was suffering. He had left the girls to spend some time together, then Tracy had dropped her off at the station to catch the train back to Inverness, with a promise to call in to say a final goodbye today.

He heard Marshall's car arrive, doors opening and closing and Tracy greeting them. He could just make out her words in the still air. 'Nicholas has taken Sandy for a walk. He won't be long,' and somehow wasn't surprised to see Marshall tramping up the hill towards him. He watched his approach, a dejected spectacle in his long coat, his hands thrust deep in his pockets. Gone was the swagger that Nicholas had observed when they'd first met in the hospital nine months ago.

Sandy remained with his head on Nicholas's outstretched legs, one ear pricked up.

Nicholas waved and Marshall lifted a hand, but his face betrayed that this wasn't a social visit.

'Hi, Nicholas,' he said, looking down on him, and Nicholas could see the police officer: polite but to the point and keen to stamp his authority.

'Marshall,' replied Nicholas from his seat on the ground.

Marshall looked around, surveying the scene. 'It's a nice place you and Tracy have here. I can see why Dani's so taken with it.'

'Is she?' replied Nicholas, his tone questioning Marshall's motives.

Marshall drew in a breath. 'I want to have a word with you, Nicholas. Just the two of us. You know that we're all grateful for what you did on the mountain, but Dani's father is pretty fed up with the negative effect you're having on her.'

'Is this you trying to warn me off?' Nicholas asked. Sensing Marshall's hostility, Sandy got to his feet, his eyes fastened on the visitor.

Marshall glanced at the dog then fixed Nicholas with a look he might have used on a suspect in an interview room. 'Apparently, things didn't end that well between you and Dani the first time around?'

Nicholas looked towards the mountains. 'Is that what Rory said?'

'In so many words, yes. And I have to say that from the little I've seen of the two of you together, I think he's right. Dani needs to be left to get on with her life without you stringing her along.'

'Stringing her along? Is this about Dani, or is it about you?'

'Primarily about Dani. But I have to say, your intrusion isn't helping my relationship with her. Now, let's go down to the others and say our goodbyes in a civilised fashion, shall we?'

As Marshall turned to leave, Nicholas rose to his feet. 'What happened up there?' he asked nodding towards the mountain, and for the first time he saw Marshall's cool waver.

'We both looked for Dani, you got lucky, I didn't, which makes you the hero. Satisfied?'

'Is that why you think I did it?' but Marshall had turned and was making his way back down.

Once there, Marshall got back into the car while Dani put her arms around Tracy's neck.

'I love you, Tracy,' she said, patting her on the back.

'Bye-bye, lovely lass,' Tracy replied.

She then went to Nicholas, and with her eyes closed, put her arms around him, hugged tight, then abruptly released him with an air of finality. Without saying another word or looking back she got into the car, closed the door and Marshall pulled away.

'She's not well,' said Tracy.

'I know.'

They watched the car go down the track and turn, its roof bobbing along behind a hawthorn hedge. As they watched, Nicholas asked Tracy, 'What does *cianalas* mean?'

'It's a Gaelic word. I think it means yearning for your home or your roots.'

He watched as Dani disappeared, just as she had in the helicopter, only this time, with the ominous feeling that her storm was still to show its worst.

CHAPTER 14

The bar teemed with busy-young-things – aspirants from the financial sector doing their best to out-look, out-smart and out-impress their peers. By seven o'clock they would be gone, back to their over-mortgaged new-build flats in Leith, Edinburgh's wannabe new New Town.

Rachael entered the fray, her raised coat collar and large sunglasses undermining her attempts at anonymity.

A smartly dressed man in his mid-thirties standing at a tall bar table looked over to her and waved an iPad in the air. Without responding, she made her way towards him.

After a furtive glance around, she spoke. 'Garth Holloway?' He nodded.

She looked him up and down – the impeccable white shirt, silk tie in a half Windsor, pressed trousers and polished shoes – her eyes coming to rest on the glass of sparkling mineral water. 'You don't look like a reporter.'

'What were you expecting? A whisky-soaked hack with nicotine-stained fingers, wearing a trench coat?'

'Something like that,' she said, fiddling with her bag.

'If it's any consolation, you don't look like a so-called HR professional. More like someone from the Stasi. But there again, in my experience, there's not much difference between the two.'

Thrown by his candour she attempted to assert her authority. 'How do you know I'm in HR?'

'LinkedIn?' he said, indicating the iPad and with a sceptical expression that cast doubt on her intelligence. 'Now, are you going to tell me what this is all about or not, because quite frankly, I don't like the smell of the company in these places.'

She sniffed the air as though testing his assertion, then went into her bag and retrieved a folder.

'You specialise in bringing people down, don't you?' she said, as though seeking confirmation.

Garth took a final drink from his glass and picked up his things to leave. 'Sorry, I'm afraid you've got the wrong person. I'm a business journalist, not a hitman. Now, if you will excuse me.'

Her eyes darted around the bar as though seeking a reply, then back to him. 'So you're not interested in corporate corruption?'

He glanced at his watch. 'You've got precisely ten seconds and then I'm walking.'

She swithered while his patience morphed into a foot-to-foot shuffle, a sigh and then a final look at the watch. 'OK, that's it, I'm—'

Her resolve stiffened and she cut in. 'Hamish Fraser.' Garth paused.

'Do you know him?' she asked, confident that he

would.

Garth put the iPad back down on the table. 'Everyone who's in Edinburgh's corporate clique knows Hamish Fraser, and not for the right reasons.'

She lifted the document file and Garth looked keenly at it.

'So, what's your beef with him?' he asked.

Her face hardened. 'I've put years of my working life into covering up his crap, and when a promotion finally appears, he gives it to someone else. Someone less qualified, whose knickers he wants to get inside.'

Garth cocked an eyebrow. 'Not very PC of HR speaking about one of their colleagues like that.' She gave a nonchalant shrug but said nothing. 'What was the job?' he asked.

'Head of Talent.'

He returned a scoffing laugh. 'Head of Talent. You couldn't make this stuff up. Sounds like the type of job that old letch would come up with.' Rachael's mouth pinched shut. 'Oh, I get it,' he continued. 'You and Herr Fraser had something going, did you? Please accept my sympathies.'

She didn't look amused. 'I'm not here to discuss my life with you. Do you want this or not?'

Garth put out his hand and she gave him the folder. 'I'll take a look, but understand what you're starting here. If he's been up to something and it goes public, his career is toast.'

She gave him a piercing look. 'I know the power of dirty laundry.'

He once again gathered his things, making sure

the folder was secured. 'I'll be in touch.'

Garth looked up through the pillars to the huge
pediment of the Queen Street venue, then headed
inside and on towards the conference suite where
pull-up banners on either side of the doors
announced the AGM. Despite massive chandeliers,
the large room seemed underlit and the air freshener
liberally applied that morning did little to mask the
stale smell betraying the suite's use the previous
night.

The main floor was set with rows of gold-framed
banqueting chairs upholstered in royal blue velvet,
an Annual Report placed on each. In front ran a
room-width stage, deep enough to accommodate a
full dance band and with steps either end, well away
from the insurance claims of exuberant dancers.

On the stage were two covered tables with a row
of chairs behind, affording their occupants a
commanding position over their audience. And on
the rear wall a screen displayed a rolling film, a
cringe-worthy affair pulled together by the
propagandists in Corporate Communications, and
choreographed to woo investors – much as the
manufacturer of some ghastly pollutant might
portray its virtues.

He was one of the first to arrive, keen to get a
prominent seat and ensure his request to speak would
not be ignored. A voice from the wings or the back
could easily be overlooked or brushed aside with the
familiar, 'Any further questions? No? Excellent,
drinks are served in the foyer.' Game over. He chose

carefully, then sat down and waited.

The room slowly filled with institutional investors, retired males fantasising about a corporate career that had eluded them, the curious and members of the press – several of whom Garth inconspicuously acknowledged.

With the attendees settled, the chair – clearly nothing more than a respectable mouthpiece – took to the stage and opened proceedings. It was a typical AGM. A cosy affair at which nobody wanted to rock the boat. *We've all done very nicely this year, haven't we? But don't ask how.* They ran through the usual agenda items: minutes, reports, a fait accompli for the re-election of the self-congratulatory board, and then to close, the mandatory but nugatory 'Any Other Business,' with its opportunity for questions from the floor.

Garth knew the type of thing to expect: lazy, comfortable questions asked by those keen to hear the sound of their voice, rather than anyone with anything of value to add.

Somebody had an inane query about the company logo, which the CEO floored with great decorum. Words to the effect of *a good question, we'll think about that, thank you. Now go away.*

Then a sycophant from within the company, a fellow bright enough to know that no one was promoted on ability, but too dim-witted to have figured out the cronyism, asked a stupid question in a last-ditch career play. *Oh almighty ones, may I ask how you sleep at night, shouldering such awesome responsibility?* Or triteness to that effect. The board purred at the adoration, and then rejected the imbecile's overtures as irrelevant while making a mental note to put him on the list for Rachael from HR.

The AGM was almost over and the board was looking complacent. It was time for Garth to break cover. Looking down at the report to hide his face, he put his hand up. Careless in his choice, the mouthpiece signalled in Garth's direction and an attractive assistant handpicked from the pool of executive PAs made her way over with the microphone.

Garth tapped its wire mesh, confirming functionality and wakening the wilting audience with a resounding thud from the two stand-mounted speakers.

'Garth Holloway, Business Section, Zurich Brothers News Agency. I have a question, please, for the FD.'

Cornered by the attention of the audience Hamish Fraser stood up and looked cagily at Garth.

Game on.

'CFO, I'd like to ask how you can justify the board awarding themselves eye-watering year-on-year salary increases, and qualifying for disproportionate bonuses and pension contributions, when for the last seven years your share price has been tanking?'

The chummy cabal behind the table no longer looked so chummy, sending Hamish glares with *Shut him down now* written all over them. Hamish gathered himself to deliver a healthy dose of 'No story here, let's move on'.

'Ah, yes. Garth Holloway. I've read some of your reports. You're getting quite a reputation for your sensationalist stories, aren't you? However, I'm afraid there's no scoop to be had here. If you'd bothered to look at the dividends our shareholders are enjoying, and our pipeline of future work, you would have saved yourself a journey. Sadly, another case of sloppy journalism.'

There was some belly-laughing at Garth's expense, and believing his short shrift had hit its mark Hamish made to sit down.

But Garth wasn't finished. 'Mr Fraser, how do dividends compensate for a year-on-year drop in share value, and how are you funding them? It appears that your balance sheet has become increasingly ambiguous. You've rebranded then sold company assets for below their market value, while renaming and increasing the value of others to give the impression that the business is still worth what it was. I can see the debt burden has doubled in two years with nothing tangible to show for it. The pipeline of work you refer to seems to comprise long-term contracts won at unsustainable bid prices, the consequences of which will be borne by investors when you are long gone. It's not all stated where I would expect to find it, but it doesn't take a doctorate in business forensics to find it. Look, it's all here on page one hundred and twenty-four,' he said, holding up the report and sending the audience scurrying to the said page. 'I'm also given to understand there are several, shall we say, sensitive

HR issues looming for you,' halting the audience in their tracks with the hint of something salacious.

Hamish raised his hand to stop the proceedings, while frantically signalling a geeky audio-visual technician to kill the sound. Caught on the opposite side of the room, the technician stumbled between chairs to retrieve the microphone, adding to the sense of drama and the perception that the board had something to hide.

'Right, Holloway, you've had your moment of glory,' Hamish shouted, as the technician tried to grab the mic. But Garth kept his back turned, moving deftly from side to side to avoid his lunges and creating an even more compelling spectacle. He continued his attack, his amplified voice drowning out the protestations from the stage.

'FD, investment decisions are about confidence, and you have a serious problem in that department. Feel free to read about them in tomorrow's editions.'

With his headline secured, Garth handed over the microphone and left.

Hamish tried to dismiss it with his usual bluster – political uncertainty, long-term investments, strong headwinds, regulation and blowback from the Brexit fiasco. However, nobody was listening as they resumed their search for page one hundred and twenty-four while simultaneously pressing their speed dials.

***

Tracy looked at her watch, then coquettishly back to Nicholas and kissed him. 'This is down to you. I had all afternoon, and now I'm late.'

'I'm happy to take the blame,' he said, grabbing her playfully and hugging her again.

She squirmed from his grasp. 'I'll see you tonight,' then disappeared off to her late shift.

'Come on, Sandy. Let's go for a walk.' They had just set off when his phone sounded.

What's she forgotten? Pre-empting, he answered, 'Is this to tell me that you love me?'

'Nicholas, he's at the door!'

Terror shot through him at the sound of his mother's panicked voice. 'He's in a rage, Nicholas. Worse than I've ever seen him. I'm so scared. He'll kill me, I know he will.'

He could hear banging and shouting in the background. 'Miriam, you open this door now, or I swear I will break it down, and when I do I will come in and give you such a beating you'll regret you were ever born.'

He visualised his mother petrified on the other end, her arms tight around her body, preparing herself for the nightmare she had been through so many times before. Hit about the head, pushed to the ground, kicked and strangled to within seconds of her life – perhaps this time it would be final.

What have I done? Nicholas knew this was the culmination of events he had allowed to perpetuate years before by saving Hamish Fraser's life and stoked through provoking the man at his office.

'Mum, have you called the police?'

'I can't, Nicholas.'

It sounded irrational, yet wholly predictable. For Nicholas, the thought of standing up to the tyrant had been inconceivable before his crisis had forced him to break free. It had only been with the help of friends – at the centre, in France and back in Auchenmore – that he had learnt to question his norm, to challenge its efficacy and reconstruct himself. Eventually, his anger had made him confront their abuser. However, his mother's path had never changed. Until today, when as a consequence of his actions she would have to face the full wrath of Hamish Fraser.

'You need to phone them now. Or I will. Please, Mum, do it for me. Do it for your—' But the phone had gone dead.

Tango Romeo Four Four sat at the red lights on Lothian Road, en route to the Edinburgh city centre after a wearing shift. Speeders were rare these days; the congestion took care of that. However, there were bumps aplenty as drivers chose to ignore stationary traffic in favour of mobile devices during the relentless stop-start cycle.

'Fingers crossed,' said Colin, hoping that no calls would come their way. Tonight was the tiebreak between his Jambos and St Johnstone. A sharp finish would allow for a swift pint before he headed to the turnstiles.

'I'll think of you as I go through my routines,'

Leah replied, mindful of the gruelling Body Step classes she now regretted having signed up to. Just the thought of the 'fat-burning' forty-five minutes made her long for a soak in a hot bath accompanied by scented candles and a generous glass of red wine.

The officers' earpieces chirped into life.

'Control to any unit able to attend a priority incident ongoing at 33 Moray Circle.'

A unit from their panda, 'Five One will attend from Leith Walk.' Short and concise.

'Five Three will attend also, from Dalry Road.' A van unit this time.

With crews dispatched, Control elaborated. 'The caller is the female occupant of the property. She says her husband is outside behaving in a threatening manner, trying to break down the door to enter the property.' A pause as Control switched screens. 'There's a warning marker on the address for a female abuse victim,' the change in timbre divulged an increased level of concern. 'There are also conditions applied to the husband, prohibiting him from approaching her or the property.'

The local cops were used to reports of 'persons behaving suspiciously' (which usually meant a lost soul looking for an address), Sunday morning reports of damage to vehicles and the occasional theft of shopping while the occupant unloaded their car. However, incidents of domestic violence were rare. It was just not what one reported in such a privileged part of the city.

Colin's forefinger tapped the steering wheel, and Leah stared straight ahead as they visualised a scene in which a terrified woman was about to face her tormentor.

'They'll never make it through the traffic,' said Leah, knowing that although it was not their beat, they were the best chance the caller had. The pandas were nimble and their crews blue-light trained. However, their cars were nothing special, and the vans were slow and cumbersome, better suited to lifting drunks on the weekend night shift.

Tango Romeo was in a different league. The German SUV, with its powerful engine, was highly visible, very fast and manned by a crew trained to exacting standards.

Without a further word, Colin pressed 999, activating a blaze of flashing, flickering blue lights and alternating headlamps, then pushed the centre of the steering wheel to activate the siren.

'Tango Romeo Four Four will attend also, from the junction of Western Approach and Lothian Road.'

Tonight, the Jambos would have to be put on hold.

BANG ... BANG ... BANG. 'Open this door NOW, you BITCH!'

Control could hear every detail of the horror unfolding.

'Is there a room you can lock yourself in? Can you get out of the back door? A unit will be with you in two minutes. Try to stay calm.'

'I don't think I've got that long,' replied the terrified caller. 'I want this to stop, he'll kill me, he'll kill me. I know he will.'

'Units attending Moray Circle. The caller reports the male is about to enter the property and is concerned for her life. Be mindful of officer safety.' The situation was now critical.

Four Four hurtled towards the stationary traffic at the foot of Lothian Road. Colin pressed the horn button again, switching from the rising and falling siren to a barrage foreground klaxon.

Pulling into the oncoming lane they swung right and sprinted along Princes Street, circumventing a line of maroon double-decker buses then, forming a perfect arc between the herds of pedestrians poised on either pavement, turned left into South Charlotte Street.

A silver Astra pulled out without looking or listening to overtake a bus. Suddenly noticing the police vehicle behind, it stopped dead in its tracks, blocking the lane. Four Four deftly took the gap formed between the Astra and oncoming traffic, then darted across Charlotte Square.

A man in a business suit intent on his phone stepped heedlessly off the pavement. Colin saw the hazard, and a burst of klaxon awoke him with a jump.

'Control to all units attending Moray Circle: the assailant has now entered the property. We have lost contact with the caller but can hear shouts and screaming.'

They sped down North Charlotte Street, braking hard at the junction, then right onto Albyn Place for a sprint into Queen Street. Red lights. Activate klaxon, brake, brake, brake, pushing the officers into their seat belts. Klaxon off and sharp left for a short dash down to Moray Circle.

Tyres squealed in protest as the vehicle came to a halt. 'Four Four, on scene,' as they jumped out and raced up the steps to the gaping black front door.

'He's going to kill me,' gasped the terrified woman as they burst in. She was trying to pull down the assailant's choking arm from around her neck – and losing the battle.

'Release her and stand back,' Leah shouted, but the man held fast, dragging the woman down the corridor, her face turning blue. Colin got in close, attempted an arm lock but failed and was pulled along with the ensemble. Leah tried also, but the assailant blocked her path, using the woman as a shield. Pulling out her incapacitant spray Leah hunted for a line to his eyes, but he turned away and a burst to any other area would have little effect. Meanwhile, Colin was still trying to grab his arm.

The ruction entered the kitchen. Leah saw the man's wild eyes check for something. She shouted, 'STOP ... PAVA,' but he lunged towards a block of knives. From two metres she released a burst of the liquid into his face, hitting him directly in the eyes. She was sure it would halt him, but it didn't. Shouting deliriously and unable to fully open his streaming eyes, the man fumbled with his free hand to make contact with a knife while still holding the now limp woman around her neck.

Leah drew her baton and was about to strike the outstretched arm when two other officers entered.

With the combined might of four, they felled the man to the ground as if he were some giant monster brought down by a massed army. The woman collapsed to one side and a pair of officers worked to get the assailant's hands close enough to cuff behind his back. Two others lay across his legs, finding themselves bounced as they secured his knees then ankles with hook-and-loop fastening straps. Trussed up, and with his adrenalin levels dropping, the man capitulated but his disjointed threats to the woman, whom Leah was now assisting, continued.

'You bitch, you worthless fucking bitch. I'll kill you and that boy of yours. Don't think this is the end of it. I'll tell him about everything you did. Everything!'

He then spat venomously in her direction, compelling an officer to pull a mesh hood over his head.

Held by Leah, Miriam cowered in a corner, her hands covering her face. She knew what he was threatening. It had been his ultimate menace throughout their pitiful marriage, and now with nothing further to lose, he would unleash his weapon.

'Are you OK?' Leah asked.

'I think my arm's broken.' She then turned to her husband who, spent of energy, was lying on the floor, his mouth foaming into the hood as if he were a rabid dog. 'Why do you persist in wanting to hurt us, Hamish? What *is* it that you want?'

A tradesman's van and a police car were parked

outside. Nicholas made his way up the steps to where a joiner was sweeping up sawdust and wood-shavings. 'That's me finished, Mrs Fraser. Safe as houses again.'

A police officer gave him a stare that questioned his tact and hastened his departure, then looked at Nicholas in the doorway.

'It's alright, he's my son, Nicholas,' Miriam said.

The officer acknowledged him then clipped her handheld device to her stab vest. 'Well, Ms Stewart, if you're sure that everything's OK, I'll leave you to it.'

'Thank you. You've been very kind. I'm sorry to have put you to so much trouble.'

'Not at all,' said the officer, who turned to Nicholas and added, 'Take care of your mum.'

Nicholas gave a thin smile and the officer left, closing the door behind her.

Now just the two of them, the feeling of dread that had once been so much a part of his life re-emerged. His mother looked utterly beaten, her arm suspended in a sling, the bruises on her face and around her neck testament to the brutality she had yet again endured. It was as though all she had hoped to become had been cruelly taken from her.

As she spoke he read shame in her eyes. 'The easiest thing would be for me to say I tripped and fell down the stairs or walked into a door, wouldn't it? Then we could pretend everything was normal. But somehow I don't think you would believe that now, would you, Nicholas?'

Falling down the stairs, the instrument with

which his father had held her to ransom. 'You can't do anything right can you, Miriam?' he would taunt. 'You can't even fall down the stairs and get it right.'

As a child, Nicholas hadn't considered its meaning, beyond it being a way to hurt her. Later on, he had his suspicions but never lingered on them, held back by the subconscious fear of what it might mean. Until the night his father had struck him around the head. Then he was forced to see what his mother was being accused of. His flight to France and their subsequent attempts at reconciliation had kept it suppressed, but it was time – past time – for it to be brought into the open.

He could see she was desperately trying to hold herself together for him. 'I have to face up to this, Nicholas, to deal with it, and I need to try to explain things to you.' But after hearing her terror on the phone, it was as though her words no longer made sense. 'I'm alright, Nicholas,' she continued, the way she had when he was a small boy and upset at what he had witnessed. 'Honestly, I am.'

Hearing her plead, he could feel his compassion build, as it had with Corinne when she had told him of her loss. 'Mum ...' he started, but once again the words refused to come.

She touched his arm. 'It's OK, you don't have to say anything,' just as Tracy had said, and just as the two of them had always been – silent in their shared misery.

But he knew it wasn't OK, and she wasn't OK.

Dropping to a whisper to bypass a voice stifled by emotion, he tried again. 'When the phone went dead today I thought I had lost you. This is my fault, all of it. I'm so sorry.'

Shaking her head slowly, she reached forward and hugged him close. And as she held on, he could tell that like him, she was crying, as though they had finally given each other permission.

'Put your things upstairs, Nicholas, then we can talk in the kitchen.'

Having left his bag and coat in his bedroom he went through to the bathroom to wash his face. As he waited for the hot water to make its way through the pipework, he looked at himself in the mirror. Although his eyes were reddened and his cheeks streaked by tears, it was no longer the face of a frightened child that he saw. Searching deep into his eyes, beyond the sadness he felt for his mother, was someone he didn't recognise – a young man who frightened him – and he knew that had that version of himself been in the house when Hamish had arrived, the outcome would have been very different.

Leaving the bathroom and passing his mother's bedroom, he glanced in. He could see that in her haste to find something she had scattered the contents of her bag on the bed. Items lay strewn on the floor and as he reached down to pick up her purse, he saw a card had slipped under the bed.

'Nicholas, is everything alright?' she called up to him.

'On my way,' he replied, closing the card and putting it into her bag.

They sat at the kitchen table with cups of tea and

an untouched plate of sandwiches between them.

'Are we ready to talk?' she asked, and Nicholas nodded.

'Let me start by telling you where things currently stand. After Hamish moved out, I spoke to lawyers about making our separation permanent.'

'A divorce?'

'Yes, a divorce. When I laid out my case, I was advised to get an injunction served to stop him from coming back here. It meant speaking to the police, which I didn't want to do. But I was frightened, Nicholas. Frightened that he would do what he did tonight. I did speak to them, and they warned me that in abuse cases certain things can trigger an escalation of violence, for instance, if the abuser feels they are losing power over the victim. Last week Hamish was put on a leave of absence by his work. I suppose he couldn't handle both that and having to relinquish his hold over me. I don't know what he hoped to achieve by coming here today. I dread to think what would have happened if the police hadn't arrived when they did.'

'Where is he now?'

'He's been arrested. The police assure me he will be remanded. They say that after what they witnessed he could be charged with attempted murder.'

Nicholas shook his head. 'I would say it was unbelievable, but how many times has he struck out, and how many times were you lucky not to have been killed?'

Miriam was quiet as she thought about what they

had endured and how she had accepted Hamish Fraser's brutality as being their lot in life.

'What happened with his work?' Nicholas asked. 'He always gave the impression of being invincible.'

'He's being investigated for, amongst other things, financial misconduct. It started with a reporter at the AGM. It's in the papers, if you want to look. Who would have thought the mighty Hamish Fraser would be brought down by a reporter?'

Nicholas caught her mocking tone, something she would never previously have dared.

'I just wish I had been more courageous that day at the chalet,' she said.

He felt a rush of fear at this reference to the event that had defined his life, yet never been spoken of since.

'I didn't attack him, Nicholas. I don't know if you remember, but when we returned to the chalet there was a woman there – one of Hamish's ex-mistresses. She worked for him and threatened to expose his affairs and something financial that he had done, so he hit her. But unlike me, she fought back and stabbed him. I tried to stop it, but couldn't. That day I was going to take you away but what happened in the chalet changed everything. I told the police what I knew but Hamish contradicted me.'

'What did he say had happened?'

'He said that there had been an argument between him and the other woman, Rachael, but he had accidentally inflicted the knife wound on himself.'

'Did the police believe that?'

'Probably not. But it was my statement against their suspicion. If he had said it was her, she would have said he struck the first blow – which he did – and exposed all the other goings-on, whatever they were.'

'Could you not have left him then?'

'It was difficult. Do you remember after the incident staying with your grandparents for a few weeks?' Nicholas nodded. 'Well, I was stuck here with him while he recuperated, and during that time he slowly ground me down. He said that if I caused trouble for him, he would do the same to me. He said that Rachael had calmed down and if required, she would act as a witness against me. I could be locked up and you would be left in his care. I couldn't let that happen, so I didn't argue with his story and stayed with him. And then, of course, there was the stigma … what people might think,' she added, confirming the shame she felt with her situation.

They sat in silence, contemplating what Miriam had finally shared. It was almost too much to comprehend, and yet at the same time, this dreadfulness was no more than they had come to expect from a man they knew was monstrous.

'You know Nicholas, he's always had a hold over me, and I don't think I'll ever be able to shake it off.'

'I know what he threatened you with, Mum. It's what he said the night he hit me, isn't it? But you don't need to worry. From the way you've protected me all these years, I know you would never have thrown yourself down the stairs to hurt your baby. I know you wouldn't have wanted that. And I also know you have nothing to be ashamed of.'

She took his hand, 'I've spent a lifetime wondering what you would think of me when you found out. I think it's why I've been so scared to get close. I've been worried that when you knew, I would lose you.'

He looked down at his hands. 'And I thought it was because you blamed me.'

'Blamed you for what? What have you ever done other than try to survive?'

'For saving his life. If I hadn't done that, our misery would have been over a long time ago.'

Her tone changed. 'Look at me, Nicholas. Look at me,' and his eyes rose slowly to meet hers. 'I would never want you to have let him die. Your kindness is what makes you so special. If anyone's to blame, it's me, for intervening when I did. Perhaps I should have let the Rachael woman get on with the job. But like you, I couldn't just stand by.'

'You're wrong about me, Mum. Perhaps I was once that person, but not now.'

'Of course it's you.'

He shook his head.

CHAPTER 15

Encumbered with a paper bag containing his possessions, and to a background of echoey shouts between inmates, Hamish followed the prison officer. Well built, with a shaven head and folds of skin behind his neck, the officer was the type of man who commanded respect in a world where an inadvertent look could rack up a heavy price. Hamish noted his bulled shoes, pressed black trousers and meticulously ironed shirt. He pondered the significance of the alphanumeric epaulettes. *Rank, tenure or some random number?*

They climbed a set of steel checker-plate stairs then made their way along the level 2 landing. Hamish looked down through the railings to the suspended net below: another escape route blocked to those who sought an exit.

From outside, the prison looked modern, with a well-appointed car park, visitor centre and glass-fronted reception area. However, behind the façade, the building was much the same as when it was built in the 1800s. With its rows of uniform arched entrances, reinforced doors and complicated locking devices leading into diminutive cells, the layout suggested a macabre doll's house. Each cell was painted gloss and contained a bunk bed on one side, a rudimentary writing table on the other, and in the far corner, a small, stainless-steel toilet. High up, in the middle of the end wall, a heavily barred window gave a tantalising glimpse of the sky.

As they trod the landing, Hamish browsed the cells with the display of entitlement that had distinguished him throughout his corporate career. Through the first door, two ghoulish figures stared back with haunted eyes.

Through the second, he caught the eye of a disturbed-looking specimen lying on a bunk. The man sat up – quick and rigid – and emitted a spittle-laden hiss. Accustomed to receiving a diffident response, Hamish recoiled with a start.

'Quieten down, Snake,' said the officer, unsurprised by the occurrence, then without looking back, he addressed Hamish. 'Mr Fraser, you would do well to keep yourself to yourself in this place. Try not to stand out. If your fellow inmates think you have something they want, you'll be pressured until they have it.'

They stopped by an open cell door and a wiry little man with fading ginger hair stood up from where he had been sitting on the edge of the bottom bunk, staring at something indiscernible on the wall opposite.

'Archie, meet Mr Fraser. Mr Fraser, meet Archie.' Then turning to Hamish, 'Archie is well versed in the ways of this place: he'll tell you everything there is to know. I suggest you listen to him. And Archie, no slapping. Do you hear me, son?'

Archie cast his eyes submissively to the concrete floor and Hamish looked him up and down: the thin, stubbly face – aged before its years – fleece-covered arms decorated with crudely drawn tattoos and the tired white T-shirt, grey jogging bottoms and dirty white plimsolls. On the back of his right hand was tattooed the name Lizzy.

'Right, gentlemen,' said the officer. 'I'll leave you in peace to get to know one another.'

Archie extended an enthusiastic hand. 'Welcome, Mr Fraser,' but Hamish ignored the gesture and walked to the back of the cell, his eyes exploring the little else there was to see, then coming to rest on the seatless toilet pan.

'I cleaned it this morning,' said Archie. 'That's why the cell smells of disinfectant.'

Hamish adopted a supercilious expression as his eyes toggled between Archie and the toilet. 'I won't be staying here long, so let's skip the introductions.'

But Archie was undeterred and gestured towards the bunk. 'I'm on the top, but if you have a preference?'

Hamish put his bag down at the end of the bottom bunk, climbed onto it and lay still, his hands stacked on his stomach and eyes closed.

In a well-practised manoeuvre, Archie deposited himself up above and assumed a similar posture.

'Find a spot to focus on, Mr Fraser. I have a mark on the ceiling up here. If you look carefully at the bedsprings above you, you'll see a wire with a bend in it. If you use your imagination, you can turn it into a door. Then if you think hard enough, your mind will take you outside to wherever you want to be.'

Shut up little man, thought Hamish, then opened his eyes and sure enough, there was the wire. Within five minutes his imagination had taken him back to a life quite different from this.

***

From her seat at the rear of the briefing room, Dani kept her eyes fixed on the series of slides: mug shots of menacing characters – either wanted or newly released – and the lost and vulnerable of society whom officers might happen across during the shift. However, her mind was elsewhere, filled with intractable questions about people, places and predicaments. *Why did I get involved with him, how did I end up here and how do I get out of this mess?* One by one, pairs of officers stood up and left the room until she realised it was just her and her sergeant, Sandra Cameron.

'Odd number today, Dani. Let's get a coffee shall we?'

A euphemism for 'I'd like a word with you'.

They descended the stairs with Sandra leading the way, and passed through a corridor lined on one side by trophy cabinets to reach the canteen. Curious eyes picked them up but had lost interest by the time they reached the coffee counter.

Sandra took out her card. 'My treat. What would

you like?'

'Americano, white, thank you,' Dani replied.

With coffees in hand, Sandra chose carefully, taking a table on the periphery and seats not so turned as to raise suspicions but far enough around that their conversation remained private.

'Well, Dani. Are you going to tell me what's up?'

Dani looked at her sergeant, then at her cup. 'Has there been a complaint made against me?'

'No, nothing like that. But you don't need to be in CID to work out that there's something wrong. Of course, you don't have to tell me if you don't want to.'

'It's nothing to do with Marshall, if that's what you're thinking,' Dani replied, mindful of the guidance relating to intimate relationships between officers.

'No, I wasn't thinking that. But I heard that the two of you are an item.'

'Were ...'

'Oh, I'm sorry,' but Dani was indifferent.

'As I said, it's nothing to do with Marshall.' With her hands still on her cup and leaning back, she looked at Sandra. 'I just don't think that any of this is me. It's not who I am.'

Sandra looked sympathetic. 'No, it's not who you are. It's not who any of us are. It's what we do. Sure, some people seem better suited to the uniform than others, but the days of the typical cop are long gone.' Then, seeking to build rapport, she leant back to match Dani's posture. 'If I said that I think it's to do with what happened to you up in Scotland last winter, what would you say?'

'I'd say that's my business.'

Sandra's face tightened and Dani realised she was treading a narrow line.

'I'm sorry, Sarge. I didn't mean to be rude. I know you're trying to help, but honestly, there's nothing you can do.'

'I can arrange an appointment with occupational health for you? They have people you can talk to. Or perhaps a few days off?'

Dani shook her head. 'What would I do with a few days off down here?'

'You could get a flight or a train up to Scotland?'

'No, that would just make matters worse. I'll get on with my work and try to be more positive.'

Sandra looked uncertain. 'OK. But let's check in with each other, shall we?'

Dani nodded. 'But if I do decide that I've had enough, I presume there's nothing to stop me leaving?'

'Just the notice period. But Dani, don't be hasty. You're a good officer. Don't throw that way.' Then she looked at her watch. 'I need to dash off to a meeting but stay and finish your coffee.'

Sandra left and Dani took out her phone. There was another text from Tracy. 'Hi Dani, I've been trying to reach you. Is everything OK?'

'I'll call tonight. Promise.'

***

'What are you writing about, Mr Fraser?'

'That's none of your business.'

Archie shrugged and headed for the cell door.

Conscious that his cellmate was his only means of understanding this world, Hamish turned abruptly towards him. 'Where are you going?'

The wiry little fellow gave a wry smile. 'I should say, "That's none of your business, Mr Fraser", but if you must know, it's teatime. Would you like to join me?' and without a further word, Hamish slipped the piece of paper he was writing on into a folder, got up and followed.

As they made their way along the landing Archie cautioned in a hushed voice. 'We're not all on remand here. There are some real bad bastards around – lifers with little to lose. At one time, these places were full of old lags, and there was respect for each other, but that's long gone. There are people in here from all over the world and some of them are connected to serious crime. Don't make eye contact with anyone, stay close to me, and you should be fine.'

They stood in a silent queue, collecting a plastic compartmentalised food tray from a stack as they passed and adding a plastic fork and spoon. Arriving at the servery, a man in chef's whites whom Hamish assumed to be an inmate and practised at distancing himself, added portions of stew, mashed potatoes, half a tomato and fruit jelly.

'No jelly for me,' said Hamish, but the server

chose not to hear.

'Just take it,' Archie encouraged.

They took a seat at a bench-type table anchored to the floor, with stools equally firmly attached, and Archie started to devour his meal as though it would be taken from him at any moment.

'Not with them,' shouted an officer from across the hall and Hamish looked up to see two large men with closely cropped hair, blue jogging bottoms and T-shirts break off their approach and go to sit next to each other at another table.

Once seated, they looked across and grinned, 'clocking' Hamish to make it known they had taken an interest in him. One displayed a toothless grin as if proudly offering proof that his top incisors were missing. The other bore a badly healed scar on his cheek.

Hamish peered back at them while chewing yet another piece of gristle. 'Keen to introduce themselves, are they?'

Archie kept his eyes on his food. 'They're called the Weans. Don't look, though. It will only encourage them.'

'Weans?'

'Yes. They're from Glasgow and that's what people there call young children.'

Sure enough, with their pale complexions and flabby bulk, the Weans had the appearance of a cross between marauding England supporters in some tawdry Spanish resort and overgrown babies, but vicious ones.

Hamish commented, 'That's a hell of a scar he

has on his face.'

Archie started on his fruit jelly. 'He'll have been attacked with a Stanley knife. They use two blades with a match stick between them so that it's hard to stitch. It won't bother him though. He'll think it makes him look hard.'

Hamish gave Archie an incredulous look which he didn't acknowledge.

'What business do they think they have with me?'

'Drugs probably.'

'Well, if they think that I'm a potential customer they can think again,' he said.

Archie shook his head. 'They'll want to use you to smuggle drugs in for them.'

'Well, they can forget it and if they have a problem understanding that, my lawyers will take care of them.'

Archie let out a deep breath. 'I hope you're joking, Mr Fraser, because if you're not, you have a lot to learn about these places. People like the Weans don't come to you with a proposition – at least not the type you want to hear.'

***

Tracy pushed in the bottom damper on the woodstove and the roaring flames subsided to a soothing curl from the mixture of burning gas and wood.

With a satisfied look, she settled onto the settee, her feet tucked under her and Sandy on the floor below, then took the phone from the table beside her.

'Hi, Dani. How're things?'

'Oh, same old. You know me, nothing much changes in my life.'

Tracy felt tempted to tease her, *oh, cheer up*, or something like that. But the situation had moved beyond jovial comments, and in an attempt to find easy ground, she asked, 'How's Marshall?'

'He's fine … I think … We're having a break from each other.'

'Oh, sorry. Do you want to talk about it?'

'There's not much to say. It was my decision. What have you and Nicholas been up to?'

'He's down at his mum's for a couple of days. But I've got some exciting news for you. Guess what it is.'

Dani felt as though the last shred of her old world was about to fall through the floor: *He's proposed to me, or worse still, I'm expecting.*

'Please, Tracy, don't play games with me. I'm not up to it.'

'Sorry, Dani. And I suppose it's not that interesting anyway, but I might be getting a promotion. There's a shift manager post coming up, and I've been asked to apply.'

'That's nice,' Dani whispered, and with her emotions in turmoil the dam finally broke and she started to cry.

'Oh Dani, I knew there was something wrong.'

'I need to go, Tracy.'

'No. Don't hang up. You don't need to say anything. Just stay on the line and I'll talk to you.'

***

Following a listless escort, Hamish made his way along the corridor. He'd come to realise that prison life was universally accepted as monotonous and that any deviation from the established routine would risk protracting the already slow passage of time. Both inmates and staff initiated any activity with a pause, in the knowledge that moving quickly would only encourage its ending and the inevitable boredom to follow.

Quite different from the fast-paced efficiency he had experienced with the police. From the moment he'd been taken, handcuffed, from the cage in the back of their van and placed into custody, he'd been part of a smooth machine. Identification and state of mind checked, clothes and wallet removed and stored, even a humiliating body-check for concealed items. Then the official interview, where he'd followed the advice of his barrister, Anthea Strachan, supervening the detectives' questions with a curt, 'No comment.' The whole process from arrest to charge had taken a mere five and a half hours. *At this rate I'll be out by tomorrow*, Hamish had smirked. *Anthea will see to it.*

They entered one of the sparse rooms reserved for inmates to meet with their legal representation. Dressed in a well-cut dark suit, white shirt and cobalt-blue tie, Gregor Lochty was waiting at the table with papers prepared. In his thirties, with neatly cut hair, a round face and wire-framed glasses, he seemed to have mastered the aura of the consummate professional incumbent on his trade.

The escort directed Hamish to the chair opposite the lawyer. 'I'm not an imbecile,' Hamish snarled, but as with the other prison staff, the escort seemed impervious to goading and moved to take a seat further back in the room.

As someone accustomed to using dress to display status, Hamish was aware that, despite being the client, his jogging bottoms and sweatshirt put him at a serious disadvantage. He looked for signs of contempt from Lochty, a flickering glance to the wrong place or a trace of condescension in his eyes, but there was nothing.

'Mr Fraser, Gregor Lochty. I'm one of the partners assigned to your legal team,' he said, proffering a hand.

Brow furrowed, Hamish moved a little further back in his seat, leaving Lochty to make an awkward reach across the table. 'Where's Anthea Strachan? I asked her to lead my case, not a stand-in. And why did I need to wait until 4 p.m. for someone to get here?'

Lochty remained composed. 'I understand, Mr Fraser. Ms Strachan is leading the case. She sends her apologies but she's in court today. She said that she had made that clear to you?'

Hamish huffed but yielded and Lochty continued. 'We've made a good start on your behalf.'

'So you've spoken to them?'

Seeing his lawyer's uncertain expression, Hamish glanced back at the escort, who was looking down at his twiddling thumbs, then leant forward, fixing

Lochty with a stare. 'I haven't got time for this, Lochty. The board. The bloody board. Has she spoken to them? I want to be reinstated or for them to agree to the terms of resignation I've put forward. I mentioned it to Anthea again yesterday?'

Lochty sat back in his chair, puffed up his cheeks and looked out to the side, playing for time as he considered his approach.

'Mr Fraser. The board is dissociating itself from the claims being made against you. They are taking the line that whatever surfaces was carried out without their knowledge. They have appointed a legal firm who specialise in HR law to look into claims that you've behaved inappropriately towards female staff members.'

Hamish let out a sarcastic laugh. 'Bloody hypocrites. Virtue-signalling, that's all it is.'

Lochty's expression changed.

'What?' Hamish snapped.

'Mr Fraser …'

'For Christ's sake man, let's drop the false deference. Call me Hamish, if you must.'

But Lochty stuck to the formal. 'Mr Fraser … I think we need to consider the priorities here. The board will do what they're going to do, and if you choose to, when the time comes we can look at how to defend you. But right now there are much more pressing matters.'

Hamish looked at the piece of paper in Lochty's hand. 'It's the charge sheet, isn't it? That bitch,' he muttered, and for the first time he saw Lochty wince in disapproval. 'Oh. You're not going to tell me that you believe her story are you?'

Lochty gathered himself. 'It's not a case of whose story to believe. You've appointed us to represent you and that's what I'm here to discuss.'

'Well, let's discuss how you're going to get me out of this place and have those charges dropped.'

Lochty looked at the sheet again. 'The team have been through the detail of your arrest and your subsequent treatment. At the moment there's nothing to suggest anything untoward in the process. Abuse cases are too high-profile these days for the police to make careless mistakes.'

Hamish grunted dismissively and folded his arms.

'Mr Fraser. I need to be sure that you fully appreciate the gravity of the charges being made against you. Attempted murder, systematic abuse and aggravated assault. We can't just wish these away.'

Waiting for a response, Gregor Lochty put the piece of paper down on the table and Hamish stared at it. Then, as though having come to a plan, Hamish once again looked to see if the escort was listening before leaning forward.

'Come on, Gregor. Off the record here. Are you married?'

Looking wary, but prepared to concede that much of his private life, the lawyer returned a weak nod.

'Children?'

'One. A little girl.'

'Well, you're not going to sit there and tell me that things have never become heated between you and your wife, are you?' Hamish said, giving a conspiratorial wink.

The lawyer looked uncertain. 'What's this to do with your case?'

'It has everything to do with my case. I need to know what type of man you are. I need to know that you are on my side.'

Lochty looked at the papers then at the wall and finally, having come to a decision, at the client sitting expectantly in front of him.

'Yes, my wife and I are only human. We've had our differences. But I've never hit her or my daughter, and I never would.'

'Bullshit.'

Lochty gathered the papers and stood up. 'I'll speak to Ms Strachan this evening and have a colleague replace me on the team. Now, if you'll excuse me, Mr Fraser.'

He left the room and Hamish sat in silence, staring at the table until a voice behind him reminded him of where he was.

'If that's you finished, I'll take you back to your cell.'

＊

The settled weather had brought a chill to the November day. By early evening, a navy sky speckled with a thousand glinting stars had paved the way for a covering of hoarfrost.

From where she was watching television tucked up on the settee, Tracy looked over to Nicholas working on his laptop.

'That's what you'll look like twenty years from now,' she said, referring to the face of a man on an article he had displayed on the screen. He moved the page on and Tracy went back to her TV. She flicked through the channels and then turned it off, simultaneously sounding a theatrical huff and chucking the remote to one side.

'What's up?' Nicholas asked.

'Nothing,' she answered, so he returned to his screen.

She tried again. 'If I say something, it will look as though I'm needy, insecure or whatever, but if I don't, I'll regret it, won't I?'

Nicholas stopped and turned towards her.

'What do you mean? Is there a problem at your work?'

'Why do people always think that if there's something wrong it's to do with my work?'

'Well, what is it then?'

'OK, seeing as you're asking. What do you intend to do when Dani comes back?'

His looked changed. 'What do you mean by "do" and what do you mean by "comes back"? Has she said something?'

'She doesn't need to. It's obvious she'll come back to Scotland, and it's obvious she likes you … and you like her, don't you?'

He looked at her calmly. 'Why do you say that?'

Tracy pointed towards the carving that Dani had given him, now fixed to the wall away from the heat of the stove. 'Because of that.'

'Because she gave me a present? You know why she gave me that.'

'Come on, Nicholas, I'm not stupid. There's two of everything on there. Two! You and her,' she said, pronouncing the 'two' loud and slow as though he was thick.

For a moment he was tempted to correct her and mention the three pairs of skis, but something told him it might not be a sensible move.

She broke off eye contact and looked down at her hands, straightening her fingers and inspecting their freshly painted nails from afar.

'That's just the way it's been carved, Tracy. It would look a bit odd with one of everything, wouldn't it?' But it failed to convince even himself. 'Maybe what you're asking me is, would I leave you for Dani. Is that it?'

She carried on scrutinising her finger so he persisted. 'Well, is it?'

'Maybe.' His question wasn't exactly what she had in mind, but it was close enough. Nicholas got up from the table and sat down beside her.

'Firstly, I wouldn't even be here if it weren't for you, Tracy. Secondly, my friendship with Dani was never like ours is.'

'You're naïve, Nicholas. Dani likes you. I'm not sure why she ever went with Marshall. He's a nice enough guy I suppose, but he isn't her type and doesn't have what she needs.'

'And what do you think Dani needs?'

'She needs to be loved, and in the place she loves. She needs to be at home. She needs to be in the

Highlands. She's like the little ptarmigan on the mountain. Do you think she's happy down there? She's hurting, Nicholas. You know that, don't you?'

He looked thoughtfully at the flames in the stove. 'Yes, I do.'

Then he remembered how Dani had hugged him on her last visit, the profile of her body against his. 'Well, just supposing Dani does "like" me, whatever that means, it doesn't change things between you and me, does it?'

Tracy didn't answer, so Nicholas took hold of her hand.

'I know that this is difficult for you, Tracy. You and Dani are friends and I didn't get off to the best of starts with you, did I? I'm fond of Dani, just as you are, but not in the way I love you.' He looked at the carving. 'After everything me and Dani have been through together, I do feel a bond. And you know as well as I do, we can't abandon her, can we?'

Tracy looked across at the carving and shook her head. 'No, we can't.' Then, searching his face for intent, she asked 'And how do you feel about me?'

'I love you more than anything, but perhaps I'm not good at showing it. Otherwise you wouldn't have the doubts that you seem to. You need to trust me, Tracy.'

She smiled. 'I do trust you, I'm just being silly.'

'Should we get an early night?' he asked, with that particular look on his face.

She looked back at him flirtatiously. 'Yes, let's do that.'

***

From where he was perched on his bunk, Archie put down the week-old red-top and looked curiously over to Hamish working at the desk.

'You write a lot, don't you Mr Fraser?'

'I don't have time for chit-chat, Archie. Go back to that rag of yours and leave me in peace.'

But the wiry little fellow persisted. 'Oh, I only read it to keep myself occupied. By the time I get them, they're a week old. Is it your court case? Is that what you're working on?'

'Something like that.'

'Mmm. Sounds as though you're up to something. Don't let the Weans get wind of it. Those two are paranoid.'

Hamish banged his pen down on the desk and swivelled on his seat. 'What are you in here for, Archie? Annoying people? Is that what it is?'

But Archie either missed or chose not to pick up on the sarcasm. 'I've never been out of these places. Not for long, anyway. But if you must know, this time it's for carrying drugs.'

Hamish gave him a hard look. 'Oh. Brilliant. So they've shacked me up with a drug dealer. That will be something to talk about in the club when I get out of this damned place.'

Archie turned on his side, his head propped on his hand. 'No. It was nothing like that. I was on probation and trying to look after my Lizzy. She's my daughter, you see. She has a drug problem, and I thought if I helped, I could make it easier. Keep her away from the dealers who drag her back each time. But I was stopped by the police and charged with possession. Being on probation, I ended up back inside, and now she's on her own.'

Hamish could sense the man's anguish. 'I thought perhaps it was for slapping people?'

'Oh, that. No, I was already in here when that happened. It was your predecessor. He touched me and I hate people touching me, ever since I was a little boy.'

For once unsure what to say, Hamish didn't reply.

'What about you, Mr Fraser? What's your story? Men like you usually have expensive lawyers who get them bailed or sent to some cushy countryside retreat to grow vegetables. What did you do so wrong as to end up here with me?'

'Oh, it was a financial thing. A misunderstanding, that's all.'

'OK, Mr Fraser. A financial thing we'll call it, if that's what you prefer.' Archie then took a deep breath. 'I meant what I said before. You need to be careful in these places. People are talking about you. They think you're up to something.'

'What do you think, Archie? Do you think I'm up to something?'

Archie drew air through his teeth. 'Just keep away from the Weans.'

A clatter reverberated around the hall and an angry voice shouted, 'You clumsy fuck!,' followed by an argument and the sound of footsteps running along the landing.

From where he was sitting at the end of the bunk, Archie's eyes shot to the cell door as though expecting something fearsome to appear, his body tensing in alarm. Hamish, who was sitting at the desk, immediately felt Archie's anxiety.

'What is it, Archie?'

'It might be a diversion to get the officers off the landings. Their numbers are low today.'

And then they entered – the Weans. One behind the other, their shadows blocking the light from the hall. Archie curled into a ball, covering his head, but instead of receiving blows, he found himself lifted and thrown to cower in a far corner.

Hamish felt a huge fatty damp arm wrap around his neck, threatening to choke him, then the smell of cheap deodorant as his body was pulled in against the man's chest, his lower back arched over the protruding belly. In a practised routine, a sock was wrapped across his mouth and tugged tight by a knot to the rear, gagging him.

The man released the chokehold while the other grabbed both of Hamish's wrists from behind and hauled hard, pinning his back against the upright of the bunk.

Struggling to free himself, Hamish saw a blow advance towards his stomach, followed by another. The air rushed from his lungs and with a wave of nausea he crumpled forward. The assailant caught him by the hair, pulled his head up and back, then systematically struck his face with an open hand. Side to side, strike after strike, wearing him down to the edge of consciousness.

Then, as fast as they had entered, they were gone. Hamish slumped to the floor and Archie scampered over to him.

'Are you OK?' Archie asked, taking a plastic water bottle, pouring some of the contents onto a T-shirt and wiping Hamish's face. His eyes rolling, Hamish came round and Archie helped him onto his bunk.

'What is it with those bastards?' Hamish groaned.

'They're just two bully boys who want to get control over you. They'll be working for someone, but they enjoy their job. Holding power over people. You only have to see what happens when they enter a room to know the effect they have on everyone here.'

Hamish gave a knowing nod. 'Why the continued interest in me?'

Archie shrugged. 'I'm worthless to them. Assaulting someone risks getting caught. In my case, what for? The prize for beating the wee guy who's already beaten? I don't own anything and my daughter's too ill to visit so it's not as if they can get her to bring stuff in. But you, Mr Fraser, I'm afraid they see you as useful. Either that or a threat.'

Hamish lay back on his pillow and closed his eyes. 'This place is a bloody nightmare, Archie. How can anyone survive here?

'It's difficult at first, Mr Fraser. But after a while, you stop questioning and accept this as being your lot in life.'

CHAPTER 16

Now in her pyjamas, Dani lay staring at the ceiling, exhausted by a wave of crying, and fearful, knowing that the next bout would bring her closer to something worse. Her despair felt intolerable and sleep impossible with the unimaginable horrors it brought.

Desperate to outrun her misery, she had spent the evening pacing the streets, moving fast through a sea of anonymous faces, letting the bitter cold of the night reach past her unzipped jacket as a punishing means of coping with her overwhelmed mind.

Outside, an unruly group of passers-by were shouting and cursing. One of them banged on the door but she ignored it. An object hit the window with a loud tap. A few seconds later, it happened again. Any harder and the glass would shatter, but at least it was a diversion from her thoughts. Hesitantly, she peered around a curtain, and then threw it wide open, staring with foreboding at the image standing on the kerb below sent to taunt her. A figure that she knew would soon disappear, as it had in all her other nightmares.

Wake up, you must wake up, pinching her arm in

the hope of breaking free, but he kept looking. *Don't do this to me,* she implored, closing her eyes tightly. *Think about something else.*

An image flashed before her: the young man sitting on the edge of the viaduct looking to escape his torment. She considered running at the glass, through the window and onto the pavement. Borrowing against an all but spent will, she opened her eyes, resigned to the emptiness that would follow. But he was still there, waving his arms and mouthing the words, 'Open the door, Dani.'

With nothing more to lose, she went down the stairs, opened the door a crack, then when she saw Nicholas was really there, started to cry. Nicholas put his arms around her, his familiar down jacket against her face with the dear smell she recalled, that inimitable combination of the freshness of his aftershave and woodsmoke.

Alarmed by how fragile and cold she felt, he moved her into the hall and closed the door. 'It's OK, Dani. I'm here. Let's get you into the warm.'

Moving her up the stairway and into the bedsit, he sat her on the settee. 'It will be OK now. I promise you,' he said, covering her with a blanket and propping a pillow behind her head.

She stared into his face as though he were a ghost, and with a breaking voice, finally told him of her pain. 'I'm so lonely, Nicholas. I'm surrounded by people, but I feel so alone.'

It was a pain he recognised. The feeling of utter emptiness, the questioning whether such a life was worth living.

'How did you know?' she asked.

'Tracy and I both knew.'

Seeing her shiver, he took off his jacket, covered her with it then turned on a fan heater that was lying unplugged. 'I'm going to make something to warm you up.'

'No, don't go,' she pleaded.

'I'll only be through there,' he said, pointing to the kitchenette.

He kept talking as he prepared tea, then handed Dani a mug and sat back beside her.

Looking at her sympathetically, he asked, 'What's happened, Dani?'

She started to sob again, and pushing the words out as best she could, she tried to explain.

'I can't cope anymore.'

She told him of the constant nightmares and daytime flashbacks. Harrowing scenes she had witnessed in which she thought it her duty to act but was powerless: the cyclist crushed under the rear wheels of a lorry and the young man whose corpse she had seen half-submerged in the sludge of the Thames, his face eaten away by rats, a ghoulish image that filled her mind whenever she closed her eyes. In another horror, a young man was clutching her hand and trying to pull her into space as he jumped, while she desperately tried but failed to grasp the outstretched hand of another boy trying to save her.

Knowing from her pleading eyes that she was referring to him, Nicholas took her hand. 'I'd never fail you like that, Dani. I'd make sure I got hold of your hand, whatever it took,' and as if to affirm it, he squeezed her hand in his a little tighter.

'You don't understand, Nicholas. It's not about my hand; it's about a reason to be here. A reason to live. There's nothing left for me. I've looked, but everyone and everything has gone from my life and all my dreams are dead. You don't know what I'm feeling,' she sobbed. 'You should have left me to die on the mountain.'

He wondered whether he had inadvertently abandoned her, a word his mother had used when trying to explain her neglect of him. Had he been so preoccupied with the goings-on in his own life that he had failed to see Dani's suffering?

'The things you dream of are still possible, Dani. You just can't see them at the moment. Do you remember when that happened to me, that night of my birthday? It's what I thought, but I was wrong. Together we can sort this.'

'Do you honestly think that's possible? Everything seems so broken now.'

'I *know* it's possible.'

They talked for a long time. She told Nicholas about finding the card and note he had sent to her home in Inverness. The three-year-old note in which he had written of his regret and his feelings for her, and she talked about how her father had colluded with Marshall against her.

Nicholas thought about what he had seen of Marshall. How his bravado at the hospital had evaporated into the pitiful plea for him to back off. 'I don't think Marshall's a bad person, Dani. I think in his own way he cares about you, and I think he's scared of losing you.'

Her face tensed. 'He left me, then lied about it, Nicholas. That afternoon on the mountain I stayed and searched for him. If I hadn't, I wouldn't have been caught in the avalanche. He said he spent an hour looking for me, but that's impossible. I've seen the timelines. He headed straight down, but he won't admit it.'

'So you've spoken to him about it?'

'Yes, and he just sticks to the same story every time.'

'He would have been scared, Dani. The conditions up there were terrible and from what I gather, he was completely disorientated. Don't be hard on him for that.'

She started to play absently with the empty mug in her hands, her thoughts elsewhere.

'What is it?' he asked.

'There's something else I need to tell you, Nicholas ... I thought Marshall would be ...' then she stopped.

'Come on, Dani, tell me. You thought he would be what?'

'I thought he would be like you.'

Nicholas shook his head. 'No, you're wrong, I'm nothing special. I'm really not.'

'You are to me,' she whispered.

So much of what Dani had described reminded Nicholas of his childhood: the nightmares and flashbacks, the feeling of panic, the lack of belief in the future, and the indescribable emptiness. He recalled the fear he always associated with his father. Crying himself to sleep and hoping he would never wake up. He'd felt trapped in a never-ending cycle of despair … until he met Dani.

Rubbing her arm, he looked at her with empathy for how she felt and sadness for what they had both suffered in life. 'I think we both know that there is more to this.'

'I'm not well, am I?' she said, her eyes widening as she anticipated how the world would respond to her confession.

'Not at the moment. I think you're suffering from post-traumatic stress, but we'll get through it,' taking her hand again and lifting it for her to see.

He looked around at the anonymous bedsit, so far from Dani's home in the Highlands. 'You can't be working when you're like this, and you can't stay here on your own.'

She suddenly became agitated. 'I'm not going back to stay with my father. Not after what he's done.'

'It's OK,' he said, trying to calm her. 'You don't need to do that. I'm going to make us something to eat, then we'll get some sleep and tomorrow, once we get things sorted out with your work, we'll go back up to Scotland together. You'll come and stay with us at the Bothy for as long as you need to. We'll look after you. Would you like that?'

She threw her arms around him, making it clear that it was what she had desperately hoped for.

***

Like a man on a mission, Archie swung himself down from the top bunk, went over to the table where Hamish was writing and slapped the newspaper down in front of him.

'To think I felt sorry for you when the Weans gave you a hiding. You're just as big a bastard as they are.'

He then left the cell and Hamish picked up the paper and flipped his way through, scanning the columns until he reached a heading on page 5. *Edinburgh Executive Held for Systematic Abuse and Attempted Murder.*

He read the short article as though it was the tale of a stranger then looked at the door. The cell felt quiet and he realised that since his arrest, this was the first time he had been alone.

Putting the newspaper down, he picked up his pen again and continued to write an account of a board meeting during which they had collectively agreed on something. However, his hopes of reinstatement were waning as the reality of his situation slowly sank in. From the rejected business sections of the other inmates' newspapers, he had read of the board's recovery plan, which included selling off more assets and green-washing the business, accompanied by the creation of an 'ethical' bond. The head of HR had even brought in a PR company to roll out a set of phoney values – all the usual hocus-pocus used to woo investors back into the fold. In so doing, they had justified Hamish Fraser's relegation to that of yesterday's man. However, they would soon know that he was still capable of making waves.

An officer stuck his head in the door. 'Everything alright, Mr Fraser? I saw your friend in the recreation area. The two of you haven't fallen out, have you?'

'Friend? I don't have any friends in this place. Now if you will excuse me, I have work to do.'

The officer hesitated as though about to say something more, then changed his mind. 'As you wish, Mr Fraser,' and departed.

Hamish put down the pen, stood up and paced the cell. He picked up the newspaper again and had another read of the article, his mind considering how he might present a different interpretation of it, or whether he should just wait for Archie's return then brush it off. Eventually, he threw the newspaper into a bag they used for rubbish and left the cell.

Archie was sitting alone on a bench, mindlessly watching two inmates entertain themselves with a makeshift game of deck quoits. Encouraged by an audience who seemed to have more than a casual interest invested in the result, the players were meticulously measuring the distance between their rings of spliced rope and circles chalked on the floor. As Hamish approached, Archie glanced briefly in his direction then returned to the game.

Hamish took a seat on the bench a little way apart from him but remained silent.

Without shifting his eyes from the players, Archie spoke. 'You know, Mr Fraser, I always thought that wealthy men like you had happy families. Like on the television. They would be safe and do things together. I used to dream of a life like that for my wife and daughter, having a place to call home, but things didn't work out for us.'

'What went wrong?'

Archie shrugged. 'Life, I suppose. I was a teenager when I was first locked up. It was for stealing car stereos. I mean, you wouldn't be able to give those away now, but it started the revolving door. When I came out I swore I would never end up back inside. I got a job in a garage, met my wife, Trina, and not long after that Lizzy was born. With all the expenses and one thing and another, I did something stupid. After that, it seemed easier and easier to find my way back here and harder and harder to stay away.'

'Is Trina waiting for you?'

Archie shook his head. 'No. She died five years ago. They said it was the drink. I was given day release to go to her funeral. What about you? If you and your wife weren't getting on, surely you had enough money to go your separate ways? You didn't need to hurt her, did you?' He then stared hard at Hamish. 'Or are you one of those men like the Weans?'

The quoits players had declared a winner, the audience were either celebrating or rueing their involvement and the next pair were making their first throws.

'Call me Hamish, if you like.'

'As you wish, but it doesn't change what you did,

does it? I'll not say anything, but soon enough everyone here will know. You can't keep secrets like that in a place like this. Perhaps you should speak to the chaplain – Brian. He's a nice guy and you'll get a decent cup of coffee for your efforts.'

'What is there to talk about?'

'I don't know, Hamish. But if I had done what they are accusing you of, I think I'd need to talk it over with someone.'

The laughter in the room stopped and the players went to gather the rope loops.

'That will be the Weans arriving,' said Archie, getting up to leave.

***

Tracy pulled the pillow over her head. 'For Pete's sake. This is becoming a nightly ritual. I've got work tomorrow.'

Nicholas swung his legs over the edge of the bed. 'Come on, Tracy. She can't help it,' as random screams and shouts came through the walls from the spare room. In the two weeks since Nicholas had brought her to their home, Dani's night terrors had not abated. Tracy was finding it more challenging than she had imagined when they had first talked of trying to help their friend, and as he pulled on his trainers and fleece, she tried to squash the niggling thought that Nicholas didn't seem to be finding it quite so difficult. He patted her absentmindedly and left the bedroom, quietly closing the door behind him.

By the time he had turned on a table lamp, Dani was standing at her bedroom door. Her face wore a look of dread as her wide eyes tried to take in and explain to her confused mind where she was.

'It's OK,' said Nicholas, going towards her and gently taking her arm. 'You just had a bad dream. You're safe, here in the Bothy with us.'

She didn't answer but closed her eyes and moved her head as though trying to clear it of the demons that tonight's fractured sleep had conjured.

'Come and sit in the warm,' he whispered.

Dani sat on the edge of the settee and Nicholas opened the stove door, put in a log then pulled the damper, the draught quickly bringing the smouldering embers back to flame.

'Put your feet up and I'll make us a hot chocolate,' he said, moving a couple of cushions for her to lean against then covering her with a travel rug.

Sandy moved from his blanket across the room and lay down at Dani's feet. She caressed his head while watching Nicholas busy himself putting milk in two mugs then setting them to warm in the microwave. With his eyes fixed on the timer as it counted down from two minutes, his finger hit the stop button with five seconds to go, avoiding a loud ping and ramifications from Tracy.

'Thank you,' she said, accepting the mug from him and sipping from it.

Nicholas sat down at the table and restarted his laptop. He looked at Dani and she looked back at him and smiled, her face lit by dancing flames, just as it had been years before at Waterfall Bothy.

He got up, came over to her and adjusted the blanket. 'I'm going to do some work. You get some sleep and when you wake up, I'll be here.'

She reached out with her free hand and rubbed his arm. 'Thank you.'

***

As he entered, Hamish looked at the sign on the door – *Entry Strictly By Appointment With The Chaplain.* An officer sitting at one side spoke up. 'Brian will be along soon. Take a seat,' indicating a table on the right with two cushioned chairs.

Hamish obliged, subconsciously choosing a seat facing a high window, and cast an eye around the room. On the left, two inmates were playing a well-practised game of table tennis, the tiny ball firing back and forth in a blur. At the far end were bookshelves where another inmate was patiently pulling out books one at a time, noting their reference number against a sheet, then wiping them with a duster before returning them to the shelf. In the centre of the room was a semi-circle of chairs laid out for a group session, a chair at one end set slightly apart.

'Mr Fraser?' came a cheerful voice. He looked round to see a friendly-faced man in his late thirties dressed in jeans and a polo shirt approaching with a plastic cup in each hand.

The table tennis players called out 'Hi Brian,' but continued their game.

He handed Hamish a cup. 'As you just heard, I'm Brian – the prison chaplain. If you're wondering where my dog collar is, I don't have one. We're multidenominational.'

Hamish didn't answer, then, drawn by the aroma, looked down at the cup and remembered Archie's comment about decent coffee.

Brian gave a knowing smile. 'Yes, filter coffee from the machine in my lair. Nothing to do with enticing people, you understand. Do you take sugar?'

Hamish shook his head then sipped from the cup, the rich taste reminding him of the world outside that was becoming increasingly distant. Drawn by the noise, he looked across at the two ping-pong players, laughing and joking as one levelled the score on the other.

'How can they be so happy?' he asked. 'Are they about to be released?'

Brian leant back on his seat. 'I can't speak directly about them. Anything anyone discusses with me is confidential. But I can tell you that the biggest jailer is not the four walls, but our failure to come to terms with our past. The road from here is found in being optimistic that our lives can be put to better use in the future.'

'Is that so,' said Hamish, making it obvious he didn't believe a word of it.

Brian sipped his coffee, looked towards the ping-pong players, then back to Hamish.

'This is a difficult place for people to find

themselves in, especially if they don't have visitors. Would it be helpful for you to have a listening ear? Someone to talk to?'

Hamish sighed. 'Oh, I see. Archie Gow's been talking to you, has he? Tell me, Mr Do-Good-Chaplain, do you have a fucking clue what it's like to be incarcerated here?'

Putting his cup down, the chaplain leant towards him. 'First off, Mr Fraser, Archie Gow has nothing to do with this. Secondly, if *you* want to talk with me, then let's show each other some respect, shall we? Otherwise, this session is over. And yes, I do. I spent two years in a place very similar to this. It's no secret: I was greedy and while I had more than most people could ever dream of, I wanted more. To get that I crossed the line and in so doing, lost everything: my wife, my career and the people who I thought were friends. So, shall we start again, or shall we call it a day?'

Hamish looked unseeingly towards the inmate dusting books and then back to the expectant chaplain.

'Your choice, Mr Fraser. A non-judgemental conversation, or I'll leave you free to continue your day.'

Conscious of the stark choice, but savouring the relative familiarity and comfort of a coffee and space, Hamish gave a resigned sigh. 'Let's try the conversation.'

Brian returned a conciliatory smile and relaxed into his seat. 'Look, Hamish,' deliberately switching to his first name, 'I'm not here to give unwanted advice. Just to help where I can. Is there anything in particular you'd like to talk about?'

Hamish took another sip of coffee, then shook his head. 'Not really. I'm not the type of man who talks about himself, and what there is to know about me wouldn't meet with your approval.'

'It might not now, but that doesn't mean I haven't been there. You're one of Edinburgh's finance guys, aren't you?'

'Was. It rather looks as though all that has been brought to a close,' said Hamish, looking at his cup. 'But finance isn't why I'm in here. You know that, don't you?'

Brian gave a nod. 'I read the papers. It's for the courts to decide where you go next, and for you to think about where this experience takes you as a person.'

'I'm not sure I want to go anywhere. Perhaps I'll just stay here and be who I am.'

'Do you think that's sustainable?'

Hamish shook his head. 'No. If I'm honest, I'm too attached to the person I've always been and the life I had, to be able to accept this in the long term.'

***

Miriam led the way through the scent-laden atmosphere of 'Make-up, Fragrance and Skincare' and on to the lifts from where she and Tracy ascended to the fifth-floor restaurant. Tracy noticed how the staff acknowledged Miriam, something commonplace in Auchenmore, but to see such intimacy in a busy Edinburgh store surprised her.

'It's the couthy atmosphere that makes this place unique, and why I go nowhere else,' Miriam commented.

Stepping from the lift Tracy paused to take in the spectacular view over the New Town to the Firth of Forth and Fife beyond. To her left, in its signature red-oxide paint, stood the Forth Rail Bridge. Beyond sat the dreary-grey Road Bridge, looking like something built from a cereal box, and just visible behind that, the Queensferry Crossing, resembling an upended stringed instrument.

Miriam gestured to one of the more popular tables by the window. 'Let's take that one. I think it's a little cool for the terrace today.'

'Do you mind if we sit over there instead?' asked Tracy, pointing towards an out-of-the-way corner.

'Of course not,' Miriam replied, hoping this would give Tracy the confidence to finally say why she'd come all the way down to see her, and by herself.

They sat down in small semi-circular leather chairs at a generously proportioned table, and a waiter came to take their order.

'A pot of tea for two and two pieces of your delicious banoffee pie, if we may?' requested Miriam, displaying the deference that comes with status.

'I remember that was one of your favourites last time you were down here – you didn't mind me ordering on your behalf?' she asked, once the waiter had departed.

'Oh no, of course not,' Tracy replied, but having taken none of it in.

Miriam gave an understanding smile. 'Come on. Tell me what's bothering you.'

'Am I that obvious?'

'I'm afraid so.'

Tracy looked thoughtfully across to the windows, then back to Miriam. 'I just need someone to help me make sense of everything that's going on at the moment.'

Miriam's expression turned to one of concern. 'It's not to do with Hamish and the court case, is it?'

Tracy shook her head. 'No. It's Dani coming back to Scotland and staying with us.'

'Oh … Are things not working out between the three of you?'

Tracy released a sigh. 'It's more complicated than that … at least, it is for me.'

Miriam held her peace while Tracy searched for her words. 'I feel as though Nicholas always puts Dani before me, or maybe it's Dani I'm bothered about. The fact that she seems to just turn up, click her fingers and get what she wants.'

'Is Nicholas behaving differently towards you?'

'Well, he's bound to. Dani's around all the time now, watching his every move with those big doe eyes of hers. As soon as he leaves the room she's anxious for his return. I can tell, even though she tries to cover it up. Even Sandy doesn't do that!'

Their order arrived and Miriam poured the tea, speaking as she did so. 'You know why Dani does that, don't you?' Receiving no reply, she continued. 'Because she feels vulnerable. Did you agree to her staying with you?'

Tracy gave a one-shouldered shrug. 'I didn't feel I was given a choice in the matter. If I'd said "no", it would have looked as if I didn't care about my friend, so I agreed.'

'But in your heart, you didn't want her there?'

Tracy shook her head, muttering shamefacedly. 'No, I didn't.'

'Because you think that she and Nicholas will somehow side-line you?' Tracy nodded.

'Have you shared your concerns with Nicholas?'

'He says there's nothing for me to worry about and that Dani is our friend and we should be helping her, as though I'm in the wrong. I know she's our friend, but …'

Miriam took a sip from her cup and made a half-hearted approach to the banoffee pie, then changed her mind and put the spoon back down.

'I want to tell you something, Tracy. Something I think you need to know. Do you remember Nicholas's first winter in Auchenmore?'

Unsure where Miriam was taking this, Tracy shifted her eyes around the table. 'Sort of. I didn't really know him then.'

'Well, let me tell you something that happened. Nicholas came down to Edinburgh asking for my help …'

She stopped and Tracy became aware that whatever it was that Miriam was trying to say had suddenly become difficult for her.

'Are you alright, Miriam?'

Miriam gave a confirming smile. 'What I want to tell you is that I didn't help him when I could have. I'm not saying that I would have given Nicholas everything he asked for, but I effectively washed my hands of it, deferring to Hamish. Doing that has been one of the biggest regrets of my life, and believe me, Tracy, I've had a few.'

Tracy picked up the napkin from the table and played with it gently between her fingers. 'I remember him coming back to Auchenmore. It seemed that after that, everything just went wrong.'

Miriam nodded. 'Nicholas bore a heavy price for what I didn't do, and I have a feeling that Dani was involved somewhere along the line.'

Tracy put the napkin back. 'Yes, she was. They wanted to set up a business together. When it didn't happen she was – well, disappointed – and Nicholas has told me he felt as though he let her down.'

Miriam's look said she had suspected as much. 'I don't think Nicholas is trying to share himself between the two of you. I think he feels the same affection for you that he did before. But I also think he doesn't want to let Dani down again. He wants to help her in the way that Tess helped him.'

Miriam saw the surprised look on Tracy's face at the mention of Tess. 'You do know about Tess, don't you?' Miriam asked.

'Yes, I do. She sounded like a lovely person.'

'She was a selfless girl, Tracy. Nicholas still keeps in touch with her parents.'

Tracy sat back in her chair. 'You're making me

feel guilty.'

'I'm not trying to do that. I care about you very much and I don't want you to have regrets concerning Dani. Helping people can be at the least inconvenient, and at worst near impossible. But what's the alternative?'

Seeing Tracy's resigned look, Miriam tried to encourage her.

'I know you mean a great deal to Nicholas, even if he's not the best at expressing his feelings, and I understand that things are difficult for you. If you feel he's being unreasonable then you need to speak to him about it, but be sure of your motives.'

'Thanks, Miriam,' Tracy said, taking a sip from her tea. 'I need to work it all through in my head.'

'That's alright. I'm glad if it was of some help. Come on. Let's get finished up here and we'll go down to the clothes department. There's someone I'd like you to meet.'

Taking the stairs one floor down to 'Ladies Designer and Fashion,' they entered what felt like a profusion of glass: full-length windows allowing natural light to flood in, and a plethora of mirrors creating a sense of spaciousness. Discreetly recessed lighting on gimballed mounts added to the ambience with the precise illumination of distinct items. Despite the glass, it felt uncluttered – almost sparse. Informally situated hanging racks, topped by the names of design houses, displayed limited numbers of pieces, adding to the uniqueness of any given purchase, and little pigeonholes with glass shelves boasted bijoux accessories.

A friendly-looking girl with a heart-shaped face and straight shoulder-length fair hair approached them. Of medium build, she wore a snug-fitting suit in black, grey and white Prince of Wales check, the two-buttoned jacket overlapping a skirt that ended just above the knee. On her feet were grey, low-heeled shoes. Tracy's eyes rested on the lapel badge: Sally Brown, Personal Assistant.

Miriam reached out and lightly shook her hand. 'Hello, Sally. Nice to see you again. I'd like to introduce you to Tracy. She's accompanying me today.'

'Hello, Ms ...' Sally hesitated, floundering as she tried to recall her manageress's instructions on how to address the VIP customer formerly known as Mrs Fraser.

'Yes, it's awkward, isn't it? It's Ms Stewart now, but why not call me Miriam?'

Sally smiled and turned to Tracy. The two felt an immediate connection as they exchanged hellos.

Miriam continued. 'Sally's been with me for several years, haven't you, Sally? She knows what I like, which makes things so much less complicated.'

'I suppose I do,' Sally replied in response to their time together, but avoiding any reference to Miriam's taste in clothing.

Then Miriam got down to business. 'Well, here's the brief, Sally. I have a rather important engagement with a certain somebody. It will be an afternoon arrangement, and will, no doubt, involve a short walk.'

Tracy looked knowingly at Miriam, and Sally

looked at Tracy, whereupon the two girls exchanged subtle smiles which Miriam chose to ignore.

'I'm looking for something special. Shall we get to it?' and with that Miriam set off in a familiar direction, followed by an obedient Sally.

While Miriam and Sally busied themselves rifling through sizes on a rack labelled Town and Country, Tracy wandered over to the windows and gazed out over another breathtaking view, this time Princes Street and beyond. To her right, she could see the Scott Monument, and further on, the Mound, reminding her of the night she and Nicholas descended it arm in arm after the ceilidh. She recalled her question about where home was, her disappointment with his answer and subsequent joy at moving into the Bothy with him.

How did this happen? she wondered, thinking of how Dani's arrival had thrown it all into disarray.

Hearing Miriam's voice, she turned to see her standing in front of a tall mirror, Sally slightly behind and to one side. For a moment, Tracy thought Miriam was still wearing the same tweed jacket and skirt in which she had arrived.

'Yes, that's me,' she was saying to Sally as Tracy joined them.

'That's your style, Miriam. That's what you like, isn't it?' Sally replied.

Miriam carried on inspecting herself in the mirror, turning this way and that to check the fit.

'What do you think, Tracy? Do you like it?' seeking approval before completing her purchase. When there was no response, she looked at Tracy in the mirror.

Tracy was staring back at the outfit, a troubled expression on her face.

'What's wrong, is it the fit?'

'No, it's not the fit.'

'Well, what is it then?'

'I don't know what you're doing, Miriam,' Tracy blurted out, flustered and lost for words. 'You look as though you're going to … I don't know …' her face communicating her incredulity, 'a grouse-beating thingummy or something!'

There was silence. Miriam looked shocked, and Sally turned pale.

Then Tracy burst into laughter, and unable to contain herself, Sally followed suit.

'Come on, Miriam,' said Tracy, putting an arm around her. 'You're beautiful. Many women would die to have your figure. Make the most of it,' she encouraged. 'What do you think, Sally?'

Sally gave a reluctant nod. 'I've always thought that, Ms Stewart,' she replied, returning to the formal.

When Miriam next looked in the mirror, she saw the crusty old manageress from the floor lurking to the rear in the pretence of spacing garments on a rack.

'Everything alright?' she asked, giving Sally a look of reproach.

Miriam fixed the manageress with a similar look. 'Yes, everything's quite alright. Come on girls, I'll get out of this … grouse thingummy, and we'll see what else there is.'

They browsed racks of unremarkable clothes: dresses, tops, combinations, and separates. Sally would give her spiel and Miriam would glance, occasionally feel the fabric, but remain indifferent. There seemed to be nothing that excited her. Then reaching a quiet corner, Sally looked around to check the coast was clear before addressing her client.

'The problem is that many of these items appeal to a particular clientele. They are well thought out, beautifully made and can be chic when worn the right way, but I'm not sure that they suit your character. There's a collection we're trialling with some Scottish designers. Well, I'm trialling. The materials are sourced in Scotland: Harris Tweed, lamb's wool, cashmere, etc. I'm not supposed to promote them over the other design houses, but if you ask me?'

'Lead the way, Sally.'

The girls pulled an outfit together and Miriam retired to a fitting room.

As they waited, Tracy cast an incredulous eye up and down a scantily dressed, size zero mannequin, with impossibly contorted Bambi-esque legs.

'I know, it's ridiculous, isn't it?' agreed Sally. 'Are you related to Miriam?' her curiosity getting the better of her.

'No, her son, Nicholas, is my boyfriend,' she replied.

Hearing the lack of conviction in Tracy's voice Sally changed the subject. 'I like your outfit. Where do you buy your pieces?'

Tracy smiled. 'Charity shops, mainly.'

'Really? That's what I do. My dream is to establish a boutique, specialising in Scottish designers. I've been here for five years and learnt so much. However, I think it's time to make the jump, but I'm not quite sure how to go about it.'

'Would you like to have a coffee sometime and chat it through?' asked Tracy. 'But I don't want to impose myself.'

'I'd love to,' Sally replied. 'We'd need to figure out how to keep away from stuff like that though,' her eyes back on the asinine mannequin.

There was something about the word 'we' that thrilled them both.

Then Miriam reappeared, embarrassed at her excitement. She stood in front of the mirror, and they all stared at her reflection.

It was Tracy who spoke first. 'Miriam, you look *amazing*.

CHAPTER 17

The Land Rover bumped its way across the gravel car park, splashing muddy water from potholes overflowing with the persistent rain of a dreary day. *And it's probably about to get much worse,* thought Nicholas. To the left sat Rory's tired-looking four-by-four, with its predictable cycle rack and a rear window sticker proclaiming his aspirations for Scotland's future. Nicholas turned right and pulled into a parking bay defined by logs secured to the ground. *When this all goes horribly wrong, I want to be walking in the opposite direction from Rory Bruce.* Grabbing his baseball cap from the passenger seat, he got out and headed for the entrance.

The Highland Pantry and Restaurant was another local business with an intentionally bland name to inform tourists precisely what it offered, but differentiated by being rather good at its trade. To the right was an all-weather walkway between small paddocks with goats and sheep for the children to pet, and at the far end, a wooded area with benches set amongst native saplings: rowan, silver birch, alder and, of course, Scots pine.

The building had a quasi-rural look: larch-clad,

with large windows looking out to the mountains and a steel roof painted green. The interior was divided into a shop selling local crafts and produce, and a café specialising in light but wholesome meals. Contemporary vivid paintings of Highland cows with cute fringes, deer, and capercaillie adorned the walls above seating and tables constructed from heavy wood. At the far end was a U-shape of leather sofas facing a wood-burning stove, lit to add cheer to the gloomy day.

As he entered, Nicholas spotted Rory sitting on one of the sofas, a mug of something hot on the table in front of him. The big clock on the wall read 10.55. Nicholas cross-checked with his watch. *Five minutes early, in case he starts on my timekeeping,* then made his way over.

Hearing the door, Rory looked around then rose awkwardly from his sunken position on the sofa. He smiled at Nicholas as he approached but Nicholas remained expressionless.

He offered his hand. 'Hello, Nicholas.'

'Mr Bruce,' he replied, ignoring the attempt at physical contact.

'Come and sit down,' said Rory, gesturing to the sofa, but Nicholas stayed where he was. He noted that the man looked gaunt and tired. He had lost weight and no longer seemed to have the spring in his step that had always belied his age.

'I don't have long, Mr Bruce; I need to get back. Tell me what it is you want to say. Perhaps you're here to ask me why I'm not working today. Is that it?'

Rory sat back down. 'I suppose I deserve that. How is Dani doing?'

'Why don't you ask her yourself? She's your daughter.'

The man looked beaten. 'You know why, Nicholas,' and try as he might, Nicholas couldn't bring himself to attack again.

'She's taken Sandy for a walk around the loch.'

Rory gave a gentle smile, 'She'll like that,' and Nicholas made his way cautiously to a seat, took off his cap and sat down. A young man wearing a navy apron appeared and Nicholas ordered a latte. 'Would you like a cake to go with that?' the waiter asked, hopeful of an upsell. His appetite having taken flight, Nicholas shook his head.

They sat in awkward silence, Rory looking at the young man who had saved his daughter's life, fiddling with his hands, his face expressionless, careful not to give himself away, but at the same time telling Rory everything he needed to know.

'You don't need to worry, Nicholas. I'm not here to have a go at you.'

'I'm not worried, Mr Bruce. I'm confused. You've been rude to me since the first time we met. You don't like me; you've made that blatantly clear. But now you're going to ask for my help, aren't you? You want me to patch things up between you and Dani. Is that not the case?'

Rory sat passively, thinking through his response as the waiter put down the latte without Nicholas noticing.

Then Rory sighed. 'Let me try and explain, even

though I don't think I can. It's because I feel guilty. I've always felt guilty – ever since Dani was born – and I took it out on you. To start with, it seemed as though you gave me an excuse. You hurt my Dani, didn't you?'

Nicholas didn't answer, but he knew the man was right.

'And then, despite you making amends, I couldn't let go of it. You see, I was jealous of you.'

'Jealous of my friendship with Dani? She's your daughter, for goodness' sake! I was never a threat to you.'

Rory shook his head. 'No, it wasn't that. I was jealous that you made amends. You were able to save Dani, but I wasn't able to save her mother, Isla.'

Nicholas looked with confusion at the tormented man before him. 'I don't understand.'

'It was when Isla was pregnant with Dani. There was a gathering on the beach. I was keen to go, but Isla said she was feeling unwell. She had pains in her stomach and wanted to stay at home. I said the fresh air would be good for her. So, we went, and when we were there, Isla collapsed … and died in hospital shortly afterwards.'

Nicholas had heard the story, but never quite like this. Dani had said her mother was taken unwell in childbirth and there was nothing anyone could do for her.

'But surely that wasn't your fault?'

'That's what the doctors said, what everyone said, but I can't help thinking, "If only I'd listened to her." Since then, I've spent my life trying to get back to the past. Back to a time before Isla died, to make amends. But I can't do that, can I?'

Nicholas looked at the fire, then back to Rory. 'I can't say I know what that feels like, Mr Bruce, but I have learnt that it's important, for the sake of the future, to come to terms with the past.'

'I know that now, Nicholas. I think I've known it for some time, but I've been in denial. So, you see, none of this is your fault. And now it seems I've lost not only my wife but my daughter also.'

'If you supported Dani instead of trying to run her life, I think you would see things change. Dani should be your pride and joy. Instead …' but he didn't finish.

'Instead, I've made her unhappy. That's what you want to say, isn't it?'

Nicholas shook his head. 'No, I think it would be unfair to put all of Dani's problems down to you, but I don't think you've helped her either.'

Rory rubbed the back of his neck as though easing the tension. 'I blamed you for her leaving, but I now see that I drove her away, while you, Nicholas, you brought her back. Twice. I'm not sure that I can ever repay you for that. And I'm sorry about holding on to your letter and getting Marshall to speak to you. He didn't want to do it. I should never have done either of those things. Will you accept my apologies for the way I've behaved towards you?'

Nicholas remembered the pain he'd suffered when, as her friend, he had let Dani down. *Just how unbearable would that be for her father?*

'You don't need to apologise to me, Rory. You

and Dani need each other.'

***

Two officers arrived at the cell door and stood watching Hamish engrossed in his writing. The prisoner who had arrived so full of himself now appeared tired and drawn. His cheeks hollowed by weight loss, and the curly black hair now lifeless.

An officer cleared his throat. 'Mr Fraser, would you like me to book you an appointment with the medical centre?'

'That won't be necessary, thank you,' he replied, barely hiding his irritation at their intrusion.

The officer shrugged and Archie looked on from the top bunk. Something had changed in his cellmate, a man whom even the prison officers referred to by his formal title.

'Anyway, you need to come with us, Mr Fraser. The Governor would like a word.'

'Two of you?' Hamish replied, his eyes roaming between them.

'Standard practice, that's all.'

He stood up with a sigh, gathered his papers from the desk and put them into the folder. 'Look after this would you, Archie?'

Archie made a show of placing it under his pillow for safekeeping and the officers handcuffed themselves to Hamish's wrists. Watched by inquisitive eyes, they made their way along the landing to a double security door operated by staff in a toughened-glass booth. *Buzz, clunk, bang*, sounding their arrival, the unlocking of the door, and once through, its closure.

Reaching the management wing, Hamish searched for familiar signs of corporate life, but there were none. It was a dismal affair compared with his old domain; a conspicuous absence of plush carpets, executive kitchen, and subservient PAs on hand to gatekeep, pamper and fawn.

Continuing down a wide corridor, they reached a double door with a plastic seat on either side and a Formica sign into which the words *Prison Governor* were engraved in a font from a bygone era.

An escort knocked cautiously and received a booming reply of 'Enter'. The generously-sized office had once been painted magnolia but was now a grubby cream, except for random rectangles where pictures had once hung. At the far end was a large table, behind which sat the Governor. A man in his mid-sixties and weighing over twenty stone, he wore a pink nylon shirt that clung unhealthily to the contours of his flabby anatomy. His bald head glistened with perspiration, and his round face with its flat nose had a porcine look – a heavy nasal twang adding to the impression of swine.

Without looking up from his desk he addressed the escorts. 'Thank you, gentlemen, you can wait outside: I'm sure Mr Fraser and I understand each other.'

The officers released the cuffs, beckoned Hamish to sit on a simple plastic chair in front of the desk, then turned pointedly and left the room.

Hamish noticed a woman in her late fifties whom he assumed to be a secretary seated to one side. Having given up the fight against greying hair, and wearing a thick cardigan with sleeves pulled down to warm the backs of her hands, she stared through winged spectacles at a monitor while typing on a clunky keyboard.

The Governor rifled through the documents on his desk – simultaneously snorting his ennui at the task – then picked up a sheet of blue paper.

'Mr Fraser, you and I are not dissimilar,' he said, flaunting the use of a double negative. 'We have both had careers as custodians of power. I have power over time, and according to this, you once bore power over those unfortunate enough to depend on you.'

From his uncomfortable seat, Hamish found himself irritated by the display of primacy. However, the Governor hadn't concluded his dramaturgy. 'In six months, my sentence will be over and I'll retire to seek forgiveness from my sadly neglected allotment. Forty-seven years, I will have served. That's more than two life sentences. But strangely, I'm going to miss all this. The allure of power, I suppose.'

Hamish was aware that the man was playing with him. Posturing with dominance, just as he had done over his subordinates and family.

'I'll get straight to the point.'

'Please do,' Hamish replied.

For the first time, the Governor looked up, fixing Hamish with a cold stare. 'Careful, Mr Fraser,' then lifted and read what Hamish saw to be a hand-written note. 'It seems our esteemed chaplain is concerned about your wellbeing. He believes you are …' He re-read the note then quoted, '"Lacking purpose and therefore vulnerable", although I daresay he wouldn't condone my brevity. In any case, I'm now required to run through a list of questions. My assistant will note your replies.'

The Governor laboured through the list and the secretary noted Hamish's monosyllabic replies. Once complete, she printed out a piece of paper and brought it over to the Governor, who in turn beckoned Hamish forward to sign it.

Hamish recognised the man's indifference. He was following a process, and the remand prisoner, Hamish Fraser, was an anonymous inconvenience, just as Hamish himself had always considered those who served under him to be.

'I believe we are finished, Mr Fraser,' the Governor announced, bringing him back from his thoughts, and as if by psychokinesis the door opened and the officers entered to escort him back to his cell.

***

Tracy didn't return Nicholas's smile but instead looked over at the Land Rover to see if he was alone.

'I thought I'd come and meet you,' he said

'No. You came here to speak to me,' she replied.

He looked resigned. 'Yes, you're right. We need to talk away from the Bothy.'

Tracy folded her arms and gave a dismissive tut. 'What? We go somewhere for a cosy tête-à-tête with a nice cup of tea and get tongues wagging? Don't you think there's enough of that already, Nicholas, with you moving your ex into our house?' He looked taken aback.

'I'm sorry, I didn't mean that,' she added before he could find the words to protest. 'But I am fed up with all of this.'

'I think you did mean it, Tracy. None of this is what I intended, and I agree that things can't go on this way. We could go for a hot chocolate, or a walk if you prefer?'

They ended up in a hotel bar, alone except for a weather-worn man in bright orange overalls nursing a half pint and nip while making inane conversation with the barman.

Tracy took a table at the far end of the room while Nicholas bought them a couple of soft drinks. Arriving at the table with them, he shrugged off his coat. 'Are you cold?' he asked, seeing that she had kept hers on.

'No,' shaking her head, but the coat stubbornly remained where it was.

He moved to the edge of his seat. 'I want to clear the air.'

She looked across the room, her face tight, then back to Nicholas. 'I just don't think it's working, having Dani around. I thought it would, but it's not.'

Nicholas looked at his drink, then at Tracy's hand holding hers, and finally at her face. 'Do you feel that I'm paying Dani too much attention?'

She shrugged before turning it into, 'Perhaps.'

He nodded to show he understood. 'She's not going to be with us for long. As soon as she patches things up with her dad, she'll be back up to Inverness.'

'How soon will that be?'

He gave Tracy a hopeful look. 'Soon,' then reached forward and held her fingers lightly in his. 'You know that I love you, don't you?'

'You've got a strange way of showing it. Have you thought about how all this makes me feel?'

His face dropped. 'What have I actually done wrong? We both agreed that Dani should stay with us for a while. Not permanently, just for a bit while she gets her strength back and sorts things out with her father. I had a very awkward meeting with him to help that along. Yes, I do spend time with her – but only to help her. I'm not picking up from wherever it was that we left off. That's all in the past. I'm just helping her find herself again. If it makes life easier I can get off the pitch and go down to Edinburgh for a few days. Give the two of you time together?'

For a moment Tracy wavered, but then the peeved look that had occupied her face since shortly after Dani's return to the Highlands reappeared. She gulped down her drink. 'Oh, you head off to Edinburgh. That would make me look great, wouldn't it.'

***

Anthea entered the room in a flurry, dumped her leather attaché case on the table and peeled off her coat 'Before you comment on my timekeeping, Hamish, let me tell you that I have some excellent news for you.'

Hamish leant back in his chair, taking in her expensive business skirt and jacket combination. In her mid-forties, with impeccably applied make-up and shoulder-length hair dyed jet black, Anthea Strachan was one of the few women he respected, although he had never told her so. Armed with an astute legal mind and a razor-sharp tongue, her ability to hold adversaries to account had given her a fearsome reputation.

Hamish sighed. 'Let me guess. This is all some type of drug-induced hallucination and I'm about to wake up in the year 1999.'

'Why that year?' she asked, always the inquisitive lawyer.

'It doesn't matter. Go on. Tell me the latest.'

'Well, the reason I'm running behind today,' glancing at her Rolex, 'is that I was asked in to see your ex-colleagues.' She noted his dissenting look and made a play of it. 'Yes, Hamish, I said ex-colleagues. They've agreed to your terms! I think they've come to realise that if they're to have another ride on the gravy train, they need you off their backs.'

'Paying me off to keep their nasty little habits out of the press.'

Conscious of Hamish's lack of discretion, Anthea cast her eyes over to the escort.

'Don't worry about him,' Hamish advised without looking back. 'He'll be on autopilot. I've concluded that everyone in here is. It's how prats like the Weans get away with what they do.'

Her jaw dropped in mock-horror. 'Crikey, Hamish. This place has certainly expanded your vocabulary. I haven't heard that expression since my student days in Glasgow. Who are the Weans when they're at home … or in this case, not.'

'Oh, just a couple of halfwits who run a racket here and go out of their way to make everyone's life a misery.'

She gave Hamish a knowing look.

'You don't need to tell me,' he replied. 'Anyway, have the board handed over the money?'

She smiled, opened the attaché case and removed a document and a pen. 'Yes. It's in a holding account pending your signature. Have a read through this then sign it, and as soon as I'm back in the office I'll have the funds released into your account.'

He leant forwards, spun the document and applied a rapid signature.

'You don't want to read it?' she questioned.

'What for? If I've got everything I asked for I don't need to read what's attached to getting it, do I?'

'I suppose not,' she said, returning the document to her bag.

That matter concluded, she leant back on her seat to match Hamish's posture. 'How many years have we worked together, Hamish? Fifteen? Or is it more than that?'

He thought for a moment then made a face to intimate he neither knew nor cared, so she enlightened him.

'It was the Dublin deal. And as I recall you tried to get me into bed with you.'

'But you didn't bite.'

She shook her head. 'No. I'm afraid your reputation in that department preceded you. Besides, I knew you needed me to close the deal, so declining your advances wasn't going to cost me my career.'

He gave her a questioning look. 'How could you be so certain?'

'Because Hamish Fraser has always put getting to the top before everything else. Your tenacity is something I've admired.'

He noted her eyes break contact with his, a thing she rarely needed to do.

'What?' he asked.

Drawing a couple of short breaths in preparation, she looked straight at him. 'I think the need to win at any cost can desensitise a person. There's a difference between fighting amongst your peers and how we deal with the other people in our lives.'

'You're talking about this business with Miriam, aren't you? Don't tell me that you're about to do a Lochty on me?'

Her mouth tightened and her eyes half-closed. 'Yes. I still have him to deal with, don't I?'

Hamish looked at one of his fingernails. 'Don't punish the guy for being honest. It's a rare commodity these days,' and she returned to his question. 'No, I'm not going to do a "Lochty", as you so eloquently put it. But I have to say I am taken aback by the allegations being made against you. Your wife didn't have a reputation for setting the heather alight, but neither did she seem to pose much of a threat to you. And your marriage certainly didn't get in the way of your extra-curricular activities. So what brought all this on?'

'Brought what on?'

'This,' she said, lifting her hands and looking around the room.

He thought for a moment, conscious that she was waiting for some profound reply.

'Inevitability,' he said.

'Inevitability? What the heck do you mean by that?' Her look said she wasn't buying it.

He nodded. 'Inevitability.'

'Well, I can't see that working when we stand up in court. Let's think of a different approach, shall we?'

He sat upright and lifted two envelopes he had brought with him. 'I'd like to leave that for another day. But there are a couple of other matters I want to talk to you about, Anthea.'

***

Nicholas sat in the usual place on the knoll: his back against one of the Scots pines that had been there since long before he was born. Tracy and Dani's argument the previous evening played across his mind; everything had become so difficult.

He saw Dani walking up the slope towards him, looking uncertain of her welcome.

'Do you mind if I join you?' she asked.

He smiled and gestured, and she sat down beside him, crossed her legs and started playing with a small pine cone as a distraction.

'I didn't mean to snap at Tracy last night, but she seems to have a go at me all the time now. I'm in the way, it's obvious.'

'I don't think she means to hurt you, Dani. She just needs reassurance.'

'Reassurance that I'm not here to take you away from her?'

'Something like that,' he replied, uncomfortable that what he was saying could be construed as disloyal to his girlfriend. 'Shall we head down?'

When they got in, Tracy was getting ready for work. From a standing position, she poured cereal into a bowl, added milk and started to eat, propping herself against the Welsh dresser to catch the last of the heat off the stove.

'What are you two up to today?' she asked.

'We're going to have a look at a piece of land,' replied Nicholas.

Tracy rinsed the bowl under the tap and then put on her coat and a beige knitted hat. She looked in the mirror and arranged the air protruding from underneath, then picked up her bag and went over to where Nicholas was sitting. He stood up intending to give her a quick peck on the cheek, but she made a point of kissing him on the mouth, knowing precisely what Dani would make of it.

'I'll see you later,' she said to Nicholas, then more abruptly added, 'Bye, Dani. Have a good day.'

Dani looked up from her pretence of searching for something on her phone.

'We will,' she said, deliberately using the collective as Tracy closed the door.

Nicholas looked at Dani and shook his head.

'Well, am I just supposed to take that from her?' He let out a sigh. 'I know.'

Sandy jumped into the back of the Land Rover and Nicholas closed the door. Dani climbed in on the passenger side, pulling her door to with a clatter, and Nicholas took the driver's seat.

They headed north along a minor road and after several miles started to look for the turning on the right they'd been told about.

'It should be close,' Nicholas said, pulling over and taking out his phone. 'Ah, according to this, it was that overgrown gate we passed.'

He swung the vehicle around, making several cuts to compensate for the limited turning circle, and headed back to the gate. Dani jumped out, untwisted the piece of rusty fence wire that held it closed, then lifted it off the ground and pushed as best she could against the undergrowth that had filled in behind.

Nicholas edged the vehicle through the gap, stopping for Dani to jump back in. Peering ahead in anticipation, they crept along the overgrown track, avoiding as many of the protruding Sitka spruce branches as possible, until they reached the edge of the forest. There, they stopped and gazed in awe through the windscreen. To the left, a burn ran down to a small lochan and beyond sat a copse of mature woodland. Further still, heathers, rough grass and rocky outcrops led to a spectacular vista of the mountains beyond.

'It's just perfect,' Nicholas said, and Dani nodded.

They wandered around the site, took some pictures then headed back, excited by what they had seen. Dani chatted away about all the things they could do there until ahead they saw the flashing blue and red rear lights of a stationary police vehicle.

'The road will be closed for about an hour,' the officer advised. 'A trailer's shed a load of bales. We're waiting for a tractor with a front loader.'

'I guess we could cut through the forest onto the other road?' suggested Nicholas.

'I guess you could if I don't know about it,' the officer replied, and with that, they turned around, reached the forest turnoff and took the rough track for a mile before exiting onto the back road.

Dani continued to effuse about opportunities for the site until she noticed that Nicholas had gone quiet. Then she realised they were approaching the lane that led to his family's old chalet.

'Just keep going, Nicholas,' she advised, but he slowed and turned in.

'Look at how run-down they are,' he said.

'Is this a good idea?' Dani asked. 'What do you hope to achieve here?'

He knew she was right. It made no sense to stop, and yet he felt compelled – as though he needed to be here to prove he was able.

Pulling up on the weed-strewn drive, the two of them stared at the chalet where it had all gone wrong. 'You know, Dani, all of this seems so long ago now, but it still has a hold on me,' he said, referring to a past that still seemed impossible to reconcile with.

They got out of the vehicle and Nicholas walked towards the front door – just as he had done in that first winter of exile – then stopped on a little area of rough grass and looked down at it thoughtfully.

Dani was now beside him. 'What is it?' she asked.

'This is where as a child I made a snowman. It was that snowman who taught me how to run. I got very good at that, didn't I?'

She didn't comment but took his hand in hers.

'You know, Dani, I spent years running away from that man I called my father. Until everything changed and I was no longer scared of him. I thought that would be the end of it, but it hasn't been. Now I want to run *at* him. I want to hurt the fucker, for all the pain he has caused Mum and me.'

She looked into his eyes and saw a mix of anger and fear. But this time the fear was of himself, of what he might do, and Dani realised that just as when she had hugged him beside the wall in Auchenmore almost three years before, Nicholas was on a collision course with something monumental.

'You need to let go of it, Nicholas. This anger

will eat you up.'

'I can't, Dani. I have terrible dreams. I'm arriving home and he's in the kitchen with Mum, hitting her. I take a knife and stab him in the stomach … over and over. I keep going and when I wake up I'm disappointed that it was only a dream!'

His face revealed his confusion. 'I was never like this before. Never. Why do I think such things? Everything seems to be a mess.'

Looking at the chalet she remembered the evening they had fallen out, how she had left him and how despite that, he always came to her aid. 'Me being around is making everything more difficult for you, Nicholas. You've been so kind to me, you've always been kind to me. But I need to stop taking from you. Give me a few days to sort things out with my dad, and I'll be gone.

CHAPTER 18

'The Weans won't listen to you,' Archie pleaded.
'It's not the way they work.'

Hamish gave him a reassuring pat on the arm.
'Believe me, Archie, I know exactly how men like
the Weans work. All I'm going to do is see if there is
a way forward, and all you need to do is let me know
that the coast is clear to do that. We won't be
entering the dining hall together, we won't sit
together: apart from us sharing a cell there will be
nothing to say that you are a part of this.'

Archie shook his head. 'No good will come of it.
You'll just make matters worse.'

But Hamish wasn't for changing his plan. 'As
much as I admire your fortitude Archie, I don't see
how matters can be made any worse. Now, I'm
heading down. If you decide to help, then you know
what to do.'

Hamish worked his way along with the queue,
presenting and retracting his tray as appropriate to
get a meal, if not to his liking, then at least of his
choice.

Taking a table by himself, he picked away at the
chips and a piece of batter bereft of the fish it was

supposed to coat.

The hushing of voices heralded the Weans arrival. Hamish watched as an inmate stood back to let them cut into the front of the queue then lingered steps behind, cautious to avoid entering their space. With a sleight of hand, the server dropped what appeared to be a small package into a compartment on one of their trays then slopped a dollop of mashed potatoes on top and the Weans moved on.

Hamish glanced across to see Archie now in place and gave him a wink but received nothing in reply. Shortly after, Archie was talking to the duty officer. Tray in hand, Hamish stood up, walked over to the Weans table and took a seat facing them.

He had wondered what their reaction would be, but they just sat looking at him with blank expressions.

'I'm here to lay it on the line with you,' he said.

The Weans looked at each other, as though searching for inspiration as to 'what next?' then back to Hamish.

'You know I've been to see the Governor, don't you?' he asked, their lack of response confirming they did. 'Well, it was about your little racket.' Again, blank looks. 'You know the one I mean? The deal you have with the guy in the kitchen over there,' his head gesturing towards the servery and then to the now-upturned mash potatoes. 'I wasn't sure how you did it, but now I know. Very clever. Tomorrow, I'll go back and fill the Governor in on the details.'

They were about to speak when Hamish lifted a prominent finger. 'One last thing. Is it a mother or father that you two have in common? Because whichever it is, they sure as hell fell out of the ugly tree.'

The Weans' faces reddened as they set to move on him, but stopped, aware that someone was now standing beside them. 'Interesting combination,' said the officer, and Scarface finally found his words. 'You're deid, Fraser.'

With Archie engrossed in tidying his bed, Hamish slipped a note into his pile of clothes, then returned to the desk.

'Shall we go for breakfast, Archie?'

'Sure. But let's keep away from the Weans until we know the outcome of your negotiations.'

Hamish smiled. 'Don't worry about those two buffoons. Keep your attention on getting out of here and helping Lizzy.'

'I will, but I'm not as hopeful as you about that happening.'

'Sure you are. Come on, let's go.'

Hamish stood up, then paused and rubbed his chin as though in thought.

'What is it?' Archie asked.

'I was thinking, the first time we met I didn't shake your hand, did I?'

'Oh, don't worry about that,' but Hamish put his hand out and Archie took it.

The next moment, Archie found himself hurled out of the cell to strike the railings and fall to the ground. He looked back in astonishment at Hamish, who was now screaming. 'Help! Help! Someone help!'

There were calls from the end of the landing then the sound of running boots coming towards them.

'That little bastard just attacked me,' Hamish cried, a slap mark now visible on one side of his face. 'You knew he was dangerous and yet you put me in a cell with him. You've failed in your duty of care. Just wait until my barrister hears of this.'

The officers grabbed Archie by the arms. 'Right, Gow,' one of them scowled, 'you knew the score, two strikes and you're out, and you've just had the second.'

Archie protested, 'But I didn't do anything,' as the officers frogmarched him along the landing.

Hamish called after them. 'Search the cell, I saw him on a mobile phone,' and then slipped quietly out of the door.

The washroom was deserted while inmates took their breakfast. Hamish stood facing a mirror above a sink and waited, in the knowledge that the Weans would notice his absence from the dining hall and take their opportunity. Their menacing figures entered but hesitated as they saw him watching their approach through the reflection in the mirror.

'Get on with it,' he said matter-of-factly, then closed his eyes.

The Weans exchanged looks, then rushed forward. Hamish felt a massive blow and fell to the floor.

An inmate entered the shower area, saw Hamish lying unconscious in a pool of blood, turned and left.

The cell search team found the note tucked

between Archie's personal effects and realised they had been set up.

'Find Fraser, quickly!' shouted one of the team, knowing it would be too late.

***

Nicholas looked at the bowl of breakfast cereal that Dani was eating then turned to Tracy sitting in her usual place on the settee.

'Using the last of the milk isn't a big deal. If you're that concerned I'll go and buy some more,' he said.

Tracy snapped back, 'Oh, taking her side are you?'

'No, I'm not taking anyone's side. I just want us to get along. If we keep looking for fault with each other that's never going to happen.'

Dani stood up, took her mug of coffee across to Tracy and placed it firmly down on the table beside her. 'There. If my finishing the milk has deprived you of your coffee, take mine. And don't worry, I haven't touched it so you won't catch anything.'

Nicholas rose from his seat. 'For goodness' sake,' and lifting his mobile phone from the table, headed towards the door. 'Come on, Sandy, let's go for a walk.'

The girls carried on ignoring each other, Dani feigning interest in something on the back of the cereal box, and Tracy tight-faced, staring at the floor.

Dani spoke first. 'Go on, tell me it's my fault and

that I shouldn't be here.'

'Your words, not mine.'

'But it's what you're thinking. I've known you a long time, Tracy.'

'Maybe you don't know me as well as you think you do.'

'Perhaps. But I know when you're seething. It's how you behaved when I used to go skiing with Nicholas and you felt he had ignored you. Strange, isn't it, now you have him, but you're still doing the same thing.'

'No, I'm not doing the same thing, but I think we've reached a point here. You know what they say: "three's a crowd".'

Dani went to the sink and as she rinsed the plates with her back turned she spoke to Tracy. 'Well, at least you're being honest with me now. And to think we were once so close.' She turned to face her and held out a trembling hand. 'Look at me, I'm a wreck, but it's all about you, isn't it? I'll pack my things and leave you to get on with your life.'

Tracy stood up and looked at Dani now leaning over the basin. For a moment she was going to say something more, that they still were friends and that she hadn't meant what she'd said, but something burning inside stopped her. 'Leave the dishes, I'll do them later,' she said, and left for her bedroom, closing the door behind her.

She lay on the bed, thinking. Twenty minutes later the front door opened. *Nicholas will be back from his walk and start talking as though nothing has happened, the way he always does, hoping to gloss over the obvious.*

'I don't know what you're worried about, Tracy,' he would say, 'Dani's not a threat, she's our friend and needs our help. You know that.'

But the Bothy remained quiet. *Perhaps he'd gone out again?* Then there was a knock on the bedroom door and Dani entered, looking concerned.

'Tracy, I think you need to come through. Miriam's phoned. Hamish is in hospital.'

Nicholas was sitting at the table, ashen white.

'What happened?' Tracy asked him, but Dani answered in his place.

'He was attacked in prison. He's in a coma. They think he hasn't got long to live.'

Tracy didn't respond.

'What do you want to do, Nicholas?' Dani asked.

Leave him alone, thought Tracy, *I should be helping him, not you.*

'I'm going down to Edinburgh, but I need to feed Sandy first,' he replied.

It was one of those things that people did when traumatised: search for something familiar, an anchor, like making a cup of tea or tidying up. Tracy and Dani had seen it as the bearers of bad news during their police work. 'Would you like a cup of tea?' the bereaved would ask, as though it were the officers who needed comfort. Dani recalled Stuart Murdoch's wife talking of their forthcoming trip to Dunkeld while her husband lay dead on the caravan floor.

Nicholas left the room and Dani looked at Tracy.

'What?' Tracy asked.

'Are you not going to Edinburgh with him?'

'To see that man? No, I'm not. Nicholas can't stand the sight of him, so I'm damned sure he doesn't mean anything to me.'

Dani shook her head. 'You're unbelievable. This isn't about you or Hamish. It's about Nicholas,' but Tracy remained resolute.

Nicholas returned to the room. Dani gave Tracy one final look and then turned to him. 'I'm coming with you. I'll get our things together,' and left to pack.

Tracy looked at Nicholas's dazed, unfocused face. 'What was I meant to be doing today?' he asked.

Unsure whether it was to stop Dani or help Nicholas, Tracy changed her mind.

'Leave it, Dani. I'll go with him. We can take my car.'

She shoved some things into an overnight bag and they headed out to her four-by-four.

Nicholas sat in silence as they drove down the A9. Tracy glanced across at him as she tried to make sense of it all. *Why are you doing this, Nicholas? Why can't you just let him go?* She wanted to ask, but her anger with Nicholas and Dani stood in the way. By the time they reached Perth, she regretted her decision not to let Dani get on with it.

At four o'clock they reached the Edinburgh city bypass. Nicholas texted his mother, informing her that they would be arriving shortly, and at four-thirty they entered the Royal Infirmary.

As they made their way down the long corridor towards the Intensive Care Unit, Nicholas caught sight of his mother standing with a small group of people – hospital staff and a prison officer.

Miriam saw him and broke off to meet him. 'Oh, Nicholas, are you alright?' she asked, putting an arm around him.

He nodded, and they were ushered into the Relatives' Room, Tracy trailing behind. Miriam asked the neurosurgeon the obvious question.

'It's not good,' he replied in a calm and practised manner. 'I'll tell you what I know from a medical perspective. We admitted Mr Fraser unconscious at nine-thirty this morning. He had sustained a serious head injury and was bleeding from a scalp wound. We ran tests: he has a Glasgow Coma Score of 3 and his pupils are not reacting to light stimulus.'

At their uncomprehending looks, he elaborated. 'That's the way we measure a patient's level of consciousness and brain function, and I'm afraid that 3 is a deep coma or brain dead.'

He paused to allow the information to sink in.

'How is he now?' Nicholas asked.

'We've intubated him. That means we've inserted a tube to help his breathing, and he's on a ventilator. The CT scan of his head shows a severe diffuse brain injury, that's to say, it's injured in multiple places and the damage is too extensive for us to operate on. His scalp wound has been sutured and bandaged.'

'But what does all this mean?' Miriam pressed.

'I'm afraid it means there are no longer signs of life, other than a heartbeat, which could keep going for an uncertain period. But brainstem testing confirms that the brain is dead.'

The surgeon didn't wait for their next question. 'Our advice is that it's futile to continue the current measures. It's in Mr Fraser's best interest to withdraw further treatment.'

'Are you going to leave him like that?' she asked.

He shook his head. 'He's brain dead. We advise switching off the ventilatory support. I need to ask if you agree with this, and if so, would you like to be present when it's done?'

Miriam was struggling to comprehend it all but at the same time, she knew she was still legally Mrs Fraser and as such, Hamish Fraser's next of kin.

'Would you allow me time to speak privately with my son?'

'Of course.'

As they entered Hamish's room, Nicholas was struck by just how powerless the man he had called his father looked. His heavily bandaged head made him look like a mummy, and his slightly opened eyelids like slits through which he might be peeking out at them. His mouth had fallen open to accommodate the breathing tube, giving it the long, grotesque look of Munch's *The Scream*. Nicholas immediately felt guilt at the association and pushed the image from his mind.

The rhythmic sound of the ventilator brought a slight movement to Hamish's chest, and a faint beep from a cardiac monitor, accompanied by its green wave pattern, said there was a heart beating, but beyond that, nothing.

A nurse bustled about, checking the various tubes

and wires sustaining him, and fussing with the
blanket in a caring way that would make no
difference to anyone except her.

Nicholas stood back from the bed, staring at the
hand lying limp and helpless on the sheet, and
wondered how it had ever been possible for that
hand to strike them. It was a hand they had both
feared, but which now aroused an entirely different
feeling within him.

Tracy sat down on a seat near the door, unable to
make sense of the scene before her. It was only the
second time she had seen Hamish Fraser, and yet she
knew so much about the mark he had made on his
family.

Then Miriam stepped forward to within a foot of
the bed and looked at the man lying in front of her:
the man she had married and who had brought her so
much disappointment and pain. Nicholas wondered
whether she might reach forward and touch him one
final time, his hand perhaps, but she stayed where
she was.

'Goodbye, Hamish,' she said, in a voice devoid of
emotion, and then turned to Tracy. 'Tell Nicholas I'll
be waiting down the corridor,' and with that Miriam
left her husband for the last time.

Nicholas stayed where he was, and from where
she was sitting, Tracy could tell his eyes had filled
with tears. He stepped closer to the bed. The nurse
glanced in his direction and without a word, brought
a chair over for him to sit on.

He sat down, and with both his hands took the
hand of the man before him, holding it gently in his

own. Although the doctor had said that, in a medical sense, he was dead, Nicholas wondered whether his soul was still in there and if he could sense what was going on.

'Can you hear me?' he asked.

Tracy found herself overwhelmed by the contradiction between how she was responding to the challenges in her life and what she saw in front of her. *Why are you bothering about him, Nicholas? After everything he's done to you and your mother, why do you care?*

More people entered the room – medical staff to carry out the various roles required when life is to cease.

'Would you like to stay?' a nurse asked Nicholas.

'Yes, I would. May I say something to him before you turn off the ventilator?'

The nurse discreetly signalled the others to stand back, which they did, tactfully attending to their preparations to give Nicholas his privacy. He stood up, leant forward and whispered into the ear of the man whose life was about to end. From where she was sitting, Tracy listened in disbelief to the words: 'I forgive you.'

He sat down again, and the staff asked if he was ready. He nodded and held the hand gently in his own as they went about their work. Tracy quietly left, unable to contend with all that was happening in the room, and within her. She had seen death before, but never as intimately as this.

Thirty minutes later, Hamish was pronounced dead, and Nicholas placed the hand gently back onto the sheet, then he too left the room. He made his way solemnly down the corridor to where his mother and Tracy stood waiting.

'It's over,' he said, and then he saw Tracy's look of utter confusion – a look he took to be contempt.

'What was I supposed to do?' he asked her, 'I couldn't let him die with things as they were … if you want to leave me, then just go. I don't care anymore, Tracy.'

Nicholas poked at the food on his plate, turning it with his fork and wearing the look his mother recalled from their strained suppers at this very kitchen table: a look he used to communicate his discomfort with her company and his wish to be anywhere but here. She put out her hand to touch his. 'I know, Nicholas. Tonight was difficult for you,' but he withdrew his hand sharply, stood up and glared between her and Tracy.

'Neither of you knows anything about it.'

They heard him climb the stairs and the bedroom door shut. Tracy knew from the sombre look on Miriam's face that all her previous fears had re-emerged, but worse. There had been the hope of something better between her and Nicholas: an accommodation with their past and a brighter future. However, tonight had demonstrated just how fragile that was.

Tracy put her fork and knife side by side on the plate. 'I'm sorry, Miriam. I shouldn't have come here. It's not my place. I'm in the way, and Nicholas doesn't want me.'

Miriam was exasperated. 'How many times have you told me that? Perhaps you should be asking yourself what it is that *you* want. You saw what happened tonight. He couldn't leave Hamish to die alone in the same way that he couldn't turn his back on Dani. It doesn't mean he doesn't care about *you*. It means he cares about them too. But it's too much for him. It's simply unbearable for me to see it happening again.' Looking straight at Tracy she asked, 'What's happened between the three of you?'

Tracy stood up and started to clear their plates, but Miriam stopped her. 'Leave them, I'll do it. Off you go to bed. I need a bit of time to myself, if you don't mind.'

Tracy left the room, the confident girl in her having once again taken flight, but this time it was worse. Like Nicholas and Miriam, she had started to experience something better, which made the pain of this loss all the harder. She stood at the foot of the stairs, an outsider in this house that had been so welcoming. It was now as Nicholas had described on that first visit when they had sat together on the edge of her bed. 'Lonely.' She longed for the comfort and love that had become so natural before Dani's return. Comfort and love that had since evaporated, to be replaced by a profusion of anger, resentment and what she now recognised as jealousy, eating away at her, as Nicholas's rage at Hamish Fraser had eaten into him. Yet tonight, after what she had seen in the hospital, even that had gone, leaving her utterly empty.

She thought of the bedroom where she and

Nicholas had lain together staring at the Edinburgh skyline. Of how he had held her and how in the morning, she had wondered whether the dream could last. The thought of going upstairs, back to the guest room instead of joining Nicholas, and lying alone waiting for the dawn when she knew that she would leave on her own, was too much to contemplate.

It was cold outside: a frigid cold that crept up the Forth from the North Sea, chilling her to the bone. She sat on the uppermost step in front of the black door, looking down to the pavement and across to the park. An older couple walked peacefully by, making their way home from a concert or restaurant, their arms linked as if they'd spent a lifetime together, whispering to preserve the tranquillity of the night.

She took out her phone, stared at the screen and then pressed the familiar key.

'Dani, it's me. I need to talk to someone. Everything's just gone so wrong between us all.'

Dani didn't seem surprised to hear her. 'I tried to call Nicholas but there's no answer. That's so unlike him. What happened?'

Tracy struggled to find the words, as though the subject required an unfamiliar language of its own.

'I saw something tonight that I didn't believe possible. I've made a huge mistake, Dani, and I think it's too late to go back. Nicholas won't talk to me now. He won't talk to anyone.'

'It's what he does when he can't cope,' Dani said. 'Don't be surprised if tomorrow he runs away to escape from it all, as he did before.'

'I know; I can see it coming. He's pushed Miriam and me out. I know he doesn't want me here, but what else can I do? If I leave now, I'll never see him again, and I'd sooner sit here and freeze than let that happen.'

As if she'd heard Tracy go outside, Miriam appeared with a shawl for her shoulders and a mug of hot chocolate. 'Lock the door when you come in, I'm off to bed,' she said, before retreating indoors.

They talked at length. Tracy told Dani what she had seen at the hospital, and how it made her previous feelings back at the Bothy irrelevant. 'You know, Dani, this whole relationship thing with Nicholas seems to have brought out the worst in me. I wanted to feel happy, but instead it's made me and everyone else miserable. I'm angry and resentful all the time now. I love him, but it's as if I've been trying to hurt him again, and I know I've been horrible to you.'

'It's not all your fault, Tracy,' Dani replied. 'I've been thinking about it too. I've allowed what I've been through to make me a burden on Nicholas, and that's unfair on both of you. What are you going to do now?'

There was a pause, and then Tracy replied. 'I'm not sure there is anything I can do.'

As she went back into the house and locked the door, she thought of all the measures taken to protect this family from the person meant to be their protector. Hamish was no longer a physical threat, but in death, he still haunted them. Turning right at the top of the stairs, she reached the guest bedroom.

To make it welcoming, Miriam had drawn the curtains, turned down a corner of the duvet and switched on a bedside lamp. But Tracy knew she was now alone, shut firmly out of Nicholas's life. Taking off her clothes and putting them on a chair, she went naked through to the bathroom and splashed warm water onto her face.

From the overnight bag she took the white slip nightie bought as a treat for Nicholas back when it had seemed they couldn't keep their hands off each other. Her silhouette looked back at her from the long mirror, the arms and legs covered in goosebumps and the face telling of its disappointment in her. It was only then that she realised she was shivering from the cold and recalled Dani's words when she had returned from England, and they were still on speaking terms. *I used to go outside at night and make myself as cold as possible to punish myself. The pain was a distraction from how miserable I felt*, and the tears started to descend Tracy's cheeks. 'I'm sorry, Dani,' she whispered, 'I didn't understand,' then made her way along the landing to Nicholas's room.

She called softly from the door, 'Nicholas, can we talk?'

Despite his silence, she sensed he was awake, taking refuge under the duvet, just as she had when Dani came to her aid after the O'Doile episode. And she knew that, like her on that day, he was in pain. It was hard to believe he was the same boy who had overcome the demons of his past, fought the storm on the mountain to save Dani, and on this night put aside his bitterness and anger to forgive a brutal father so that they might find peace.

Moving into the room, she sat down on the edge of the bed, head bowed and hands limp on her lap.

'You don't like me anymore, do you, Nicholas? I don't blame you. I don't think I like myself now.' He didn't move, but she could tell he was listening.

'I'm hurting so badly. I know you are too. It's as though all the bonds we have with the people we love are coming apart. I know I haven't shown it lately but I love you so much. I've loved you from that very first time we met. Do you remember when we were little, and you came to our house that evening? I knew then that you were someone very special to me and later I realised that I had fallen in love with you. I've never wanted anyone else.'

In his mind, he pictured her handing him her closest companion, Floppy Rabbit, in the knowledge that at that moment, his need was greater than hers.

'Then Dani came back, and I felt as though the two of you didn't want me there. I felt shut out and became resentful and angry, but now I feel cold and alone. I know we agreed to help Dani, but if I'm honest with myself, I'm not a confident person and have always felt second-best in life. I get so scared of being hurt. So scared that I end up hurting myself and others. My heart's breaking. Love seems to be such a painful thing. I'll leave you alone now.'

She stood up, went to the door, opened it, and then paused. 'I'm sorry for being such a bitch, but you have a strength that I find difficult to match. You can forgive people. Perhaps one day you can forgive me.'

'You're not second best,' he called.

Closing the door, she tiptoed across the room. He lifted the duvet and she climbed under it, next to him. Taking her in his arms, he kissed her softly as she lay with her head on his chest.

'I had to do what I did tonight, Tracy. I had to let my anger go and let him die in peace.

'I know that now, Nicholas. You did the right thing.'

CHAPTER 19

'Cheer up Archie,' said the officer, but Archie stayed as he was, perched on the edge of the bottom bunk, staring at the wall opposite. The officer tipped his head to see what he was looking at. 'You won't see it,' said Archie. 'It's gone.'

'What has?'

'It doesn't matter. I was fooling myself to think I would ever get out of here.'

The officer was sympathetic. 'It's about Mr Fraser, isn't it? I understand. I'm sorry about what happened yesterday. It was a nasty business. Still, some good has come of it. The Governor has split up the Weans. He's shifted one to Bar-L and the other to Aberdeen. From what I hear they were quite upset about it – their human rights and all that malarkey.'

Archie wasn't interested. Someone had fleetingly entered his life and for some reason, given him hope. *Why did I think that things could change?* It was obvious now, Hamish Fraser the wife-beater had lied. All that talk about hope for him and Lizzy and negotiating with the Weans – a smokescreen while he planned his escape.

'Anyway, son, life goes on. Your barrister is here

to see you.'

Archie's eyes shifted to the floor. 'I don't have a barrister.'

'It seems as though you do now. Let's go, I haven't got all day.'

Archie followed abjectly as they descended the stairs and made their way to the meeting room.

The officer gestured him to a seat at the table then took up his position some distance back. The two of them waited in silence, Archie looking absently down at his spindly arms with their gingery fleece and the officer staring up at the ceiling, waiting for another monotonous shift to end.

Ten minutes later an intense-looking woman with an expensive leather attaché case but no obvious enthusiasm was ushered in by a prison escort. She sat down briskly on the opposite side of the table and glared across at Archie.

'Mr Gow? Mr Archie Gow?' Her exclusive Edinburgh education rang through her accent.

'Yes, that's me. Who's asking?'

'I'm Anthea Strachan, your barrister.'

'I wasn't aware that a barrister had been appointed to my case. And I sure as hell can't afford one,' he replied, pushing himself back in his seat away from her.

She pursed her lips and looked keenly at him. 'Your acquaintance—' then stopped as though re-evaluating. 'Hamish has asked me to represent you, and if so required, the needs of your daughter.'

Archie looked incredulous, and then became agitated.

'Is this some kind of joke? If it is, you need to stop right now,' he said, getting up from his seat.

The officer behind moved towards him, putting his hand gently on Archie's shoulder. 'Sit down and listen to the woman, Archie. See what she has to say.'

'I'm sorry,' he said, and the officer retreated.

Coming to terms with the presence of a client very different from her norm, Anthea looked slightly more at ease. 'That's quite alright, Mr Gow. It's not a joke. I can understand why, after the last twenty-four hours, you might be finding it difficult to comprehend all of this. I certainly am. If it helps, I can show you the paperwork?' She held out a document but Archie didn't move as his mind struggled to make sense of it all.

'Mr Gow, I've pushed for a court appearance this afternoon because I'm informed the particular sheriff on duty favours rehabilitation. I'm confident that we have a strong case for bail. Don't worry, the cost is taken care of,' seeing his doubtful expression.

'There's something else,' she went on, unsealing a brown envelope and reading a document taken from within. 'It seems that Mr Fraser has arranged accommodation for you.' Flicking on to the next page, her eyes caught something to which she paid keen attention. 'It's what he describes as, "A place to call home".' She pronounced each word separately. 'A furnished two-bedroom flat in the Viewforth area of town. He's also provided you with a weekly allowance for your subsistence until you get "back on your feet" as he puts it, and for your daughter's treatment. There are several other items, but we can cover these in detail once we've finished with the court.'

Her eyes continued to scan the brief.

'Mr Fraser has instructed me to read you a message. I quote, "I know life won't be easy for either you or Lizzy, but you're a good man, and you'll make it work. Good luck to you both. Hamish".'

Anthea looked into the air, and Archie Gow stared at the door, each working through the significance of what they had just heard.

It was Anthea Strachan who moved first.

'Well, Mr Gow, it seems that we have a busy afternoon ahead of us, don't we?'

***

At midday, the sun broke through to announce a bright Highland afternoon. Dani picked up her phone and looked at the incoming message.

'It's from Tracy to wish me luck.' Then putting the phone back into her pocket, she added, 'I can't believe I feel so nervous about seeing my father.'

Nicholas reached over and rubbed her arm. 'He only wants to talk to you, Dani. I honestly don't think there's anything to worry about.'

'I know. But even before this there was so much left unsaid between us. My mum, my feelings … his feelings.'

They drove on in silence, Dani fiddling with the

pair of bright blue approach shoes Nicholas had insisted on buying her, and he thinking about everything that had been left unsaid between him and his mother.

Ten minutes later the Highland Pantry and Restaurant came into view. Dani spotted her father sitting in his black four-by-four with the bicycle rack on the roof.

'He's already here,' she said, taking a deep breath.

Nicholas pulled up in the same place as before.

'Are you ready?' he asked.

She nodded, forced a smile, got out and closed the door. Rory came over and said a few words to her, pointing to the restaurant, but Dani shook her head and gestured towards the all-weather walk. Nicholas watched discreetly as they reached the seating area at the far end. Rory took off his coat and laid it on the damp bench for Dani and him to sit on. She was doing most of the talking, animated as she vented her frustration; no doubt telling him of the price she had paid for his meddling. Dani, the girl Nicholas had longed for and who he now knew had felt the same about him. In the chaos of finding that truth, they had slipped through each other's fingers.

'Come on, Sandy, let's go for a walk,' he said, keen to move on from his thoughts. They ambled through the woods on the opposite side of the car park then Nicholas put Sandy back into the Land Rover and bought two hot chocolates to take away. Returning to the vehicle, he saw Rory and Dani on their way back.

Dani opened the Land Rover door, climbed in, and Nicholas handed her the hot chocolate. 'Thanks' she said, taking a sip then placing it in the cup holder attached to the dashboard.

He started the engine and they left. After a couple of miles they passed a sign: *Lay-by and Picnic Area 500 yards.*

'Do you mind if we stop?' she asked, and Nicholas pulled in. He carried on past a cylindrical concrete litter bin and stopped short of an overhanging silver birch, still dripping from the earlier rain. Dani wound down the window and breathed in the crisp air.

'Are you OK?' he asked.

'I was feeling a bit queasy, but I'm fine now.'

'Not enough cream in your hot chocolate, perhaps?' he said, with that sense of humour that always made her laugh.

She chuckled, then looked out of her window into the distance and asked what she knew would be a difficult question for both of them.

'Nicholas, do you love Tracy, or do you feel sorry for her?'

'Why would I feel sorry for her?'

'Because she's vulnerable, and I know you look after the vulnerable. I think it's because you know what it feels like, don't you? You know what it's like to suffer. We all do.'

'That doesn't mean I don't love her, Dani.'

'I'm sorry. It was a stupid question.' She continued to stare into the distance. 'You've changed so much since we first met. There's part of you that I no longer understand. Something I want to get a hold of, but don't know where to start. You've moved on, but I'm stuck where I was when we first met.' The frustration was clear in her voice.

'You're not in the same place, Dani. Look what you've achieved. What you just went through was a blip, nothing more than that. We all have them from time to time. I had to move on. You can remember the mess I was in. But nothing's changed between us.'

The absurdity of what he had just said was obvious to them both.

Then she turned to him. 'My dad asked me a question. It was a painful question because I knew that, whatever the answer was, it wouldn't be what I wanted.'

'What did he ask?'

'He asked whether we would be together if he hadn't taken that letter you sent me … Was there ever any hope for us, Nicholas?'

'I don't know the answer to that. Neither of us does. But let's think about what we do have. The three of us have sorted out our differences, and we know that we'll always be here for each other.'

'I suppose so. You've been so kind, coming to my aid when I needed you most … putting me before yourself – and before Tracy. I'm lucky to have such a friend. I've agreed with Dad to move back home for a while. I'll be leaving the day after tomorrow.'

'Well, tomorrow night the three of us will go out for something to eat. Not a celebration, but to have fun together.'

'That would be nice. Thank you.'

***

Miriam put the document down on the kitchen table. 'Sorry, girls, I'm a little distracted today. But I love the plans and think we should go ahead. Do we shake on it? Is that how these things are done?'

Sally and Tracy looked at each other for an answer but failing to find one opted instead to jump up and down with excitement, then all three shook hands and kissed cheeks. Miriam recalled the time her nineteen-year-old son had come looking for her support and laid his plans on this same kitchen table. She remembered deferring his request to her husband then standing by and watching the man denigrate, assault and finally break the boy. 'You're a fucking embarrassment,' he had said. The same 'fucking embarrassment' who had held his hand and offered forgiveness at the end of his life. For a moment, her sense of regret once again threatened to overwhelm her.

Sally handed round a box of handmade patisseries.

'Keep one for me, I'll have it later,' Miriam suggested.

Tracy picked up on her uncertain tone. 'Don't worry, Miriam, it will be fine, you look great, he'll be blown away.'

It wasn't her appearance that worried Miriam, however, but what she knew she would have to share. She stood still while the girls fussed about her, straightening the neatly cut dark blue and green Black Watch plaid blazer.

'Soft shoulders are better,' Sally had advised. 'Less intimidating. And don't wear a thick necklace – especially a gold one. A silver chain would work. The idea is to look elegant; it's not a display of wealth, which always looks pretentious.'

They tidied her layered bob, Tracy applied some light make-up and to finish, Miriam puffed her Acqua di Parma Magnolia, filling the air with a fragrance of citrus, white flowers and musk.

Tracy drew in the scent, looked at Miriam and smiled. 'Perfect,' she said.

'You'll be able to model for us,' Sally suggested.

'Now you're being silly, stop it,' Miriam replied, sneaking another quick look to test Sally's suggestion.

'Meeting anyone in particular?' the cabbie asked, looking to ingratiate himself with the well-dressed lady in the back. A bit of extra effort usually paid off if the customer looked like a good tipper, and short fares such as Moray Circle to the Botanic Gardens needed a sweetener to be worth the effort.

'Oh, just a friend,' Miriam answered, struggling for an appropriate set of words to describe something that had begun as exciting but was now daunting.

The cab made a characteristically tight U-turn into the semi-circular drop-off area on Arboretum Road and Miriam took out her purse.

'Keep the change,' she said, reaching awkwardly

through the security slot and anxious to rid herself of the distraction.

The cab departed, its diesel engine rattling like a shaken bag of bolts and leaving a hush broken only by the sound of leather on willow from the field opposite.

Fiddling with her handbag, she made her way towards the entrance. Then looking up, there he was. The recognition was immediate: an older version of the boy who had given her the card, the boy who had met her in this same place all those years ago, and an everyday familiarity she had known ever since. For a moment, the two of them stood speechless, and then Miriam became flustered, unable to process what to say or do.

Dressed in a blue Harris Tweed jacket, a heather-coloured shirt and navy trousers, Darroch stepped forward and kissed her lightly on the side of her cheek.

'Hello Miriam,' he said, with a kindness that settled her. 'I've waited over twenty years for this day.'

She looked at him, her turmoil dissipating.

'Hello Darroch,' her heart aching to say so much more.

He put out his arm for her. 'Shall we take a walk? It's such a pleasant afternoon,' and they strolled through the foyer and out onto a path.

'I had forgotten just how beautiful this is,' Miriam said, looking across the grassy expanse, populated by a wealth of trees: deciduous, evergreens and conifers of varying size and age.

Sunlight penetrated their foliage – throwing beams of light – and where it couldn't, it left its mark with an abundance of shadows, creating an intricate collage on the ground. The air hung full with the rich, sweet scent of azaleas and a welcoming chorus of birdsong emanated from all directions. People sat or lay in sunny havens, taking the time to talk, read, or just relax during this tranquil interlude in their lives.

Darroch said, 'I would ask, "Do you come here often?" if it weren't so predictable. But then again if you did, no doubt I would have seen you. This is one of my favourite haunts.'

'No doubt you would have,' she replied. But this place had been too full of regrets for her to visit.

They continued their stroll, making small talk about the Edinburgh they'd known before the invasion of tourists and tartan tat. They touched on books, writers, the trams and the various plants and trees they passed. Darroch paused at a beautifully formed silver lime. 'Did you know this has medicinal properties? But don't give me credit,' he confessed as she read the plaque for herself. 'As I said, I visit here often.'

They stopped on a little bridge and watched the water cascading over rocky steps to a pond, then moved on.

Miriam said, 'I'm going into business with two young ladies. One of them, Tracy, is the girlfriend of my son, Nicholas. She comes from Auchenmore in the Highlands. We want to specialise in Scottish Designer Clothing for women. I'm what you might call a sleeping partner, although I hope to be a little more useful than that. They have such energy and ambition.'

'It's a boutique then?' he asked, seeming not to notice the reference to her son.

'Yes, that's right, a boutique.'

As they continued, it occurred to Miriam that this was like a work of fiction. They were talking about the present as though that was all there was, when underneath the past threatened to show through, and with it would come a crushing disappointment.

'I was married, Darroch.'

It was an out of place statement, said in the hope of evoking a question she would be forced to answer.

He nodded. 'I read about what happened to your husband. I'm sorry,' and in so doing, removing another layer of discomfort.

'Were you ever married? Perhaps you still are?' she asked, looking to broach something they both knew was hanging over them.

'For a short time in my early twenties. But it didn't last.'

'Why?' she asked, instantly regretting her spontaneity.

'Oh, one thing and another, I suppose. She was a girl I met at university. I'm not sure why we married. It just seemed to be what people did. But I could tell from very early on that I was a disappointment to her.'

'I can't believe that.'

'You're very kind, Miriam, but I was. She was ambitious, working in one of those big corporate places, and I was just starting. Writing my socks off but getting nowhere. After nine months, I think she had had as much as she could take. I don't blame her. I was on the verge of giving up myself, but I was too late.'

He only needed her silence for permission to tell more.

'I knew she was seeing someone else. They say you can always tell these things.'

Yes, you can, and each time it's more painful than the time before. I've lived a life of it, thought Miriam.

'I'm sorry to hear that.'

He gave her hand a little squeeze. 'It's wasn't all bad, though. She was the muse that gave me something compelling to write about. A short story. It was published in one of the broadsheets, and with that, I started to build my name as a writer.'

'I suppose we've all had our up and downs,' Miriam said, thinking of her own story still to tell.

An approaching couple looked knowingly towards them. The woman whispered something to the man then flicked her gaze back and forth between Miriam and Darroch, a hint of envy in her eyes that only another woman would sense. Darroch held Miriam a little tighter as though proud of her, and Miriam felt warm inside – conscious that it was the first time a man had made her feel that way. As they went by, Miriam noted the familiarity with which they and Darroch acknowledged each other.

'Do you know them, Darroch?' she asked.

'Not in person. I'm afraid you might need to get

used to that. However, don't be alarmed. My followership is of an amiable type.'

They carried on, Miriam taking slight comfort from his indirect reference to their future. Then there it was: the site of the green gardener's shed, the structure long since removed, but the mark it had made on their lives still palpable. It was the first and only time that Miriam Stewart had made love the way it is supposed to be.

She pulled up sharply on Darroch's arm, taking him by surprise.

'Yes, we were young, weren't we?' he said, hoping to ease what he took to be embarrassment.

'No, it's not that, Darroch. Would you mind if we sat for a while? There's something I must tell you … something you need to know about me. I'm not the person you think I am.'

They made their way in silence over the grass to a bench with a view across a lily pond. Miriam could see Darroch was uneasy about what he might hear, and resigned herself to her past once again dashing her hopes. They sat down next to each other, Miriam clutching the handbag on her lap, her elbows drawn close.

'What is it?' he asked.

'I got pregnant …' He nodded, but before he could say anything, she rushed on. 'It's about what I did with my unborn son … I was so lost and confused, I don't think I knew what I was doing. Looking back, it's as though I was another person entirely. But I'm not making excuses, and believe me, my husband made sure I never forgot.'

'What did you do, Miriam? What could torture you like this?'

'I had thoughts of getting rid of my unborn child – Nicholas. To rid myself of what seemed to be at the centre of all my problems. I don't even remember doing it, but I must have, otherwise I wouldn't have ended up there, would I?'

'Where?'

Her eyes widened at the thought of what she was about to expose.

'At the bottom of the stairs.' Miriam looked out across the pond and back twenty-two years. 'I remember being at the top, thinking "Wouldn't this be easy?" and I remember being at the bottom, but I honestly don't recall anything in between. I was suffering from dreadful morning sickness, and under so much pressure from my mother. I ended up in hospital.'

'Miriam, you wouldn't have done that deliberately.'

'How do you know that, Darroch? How do you know what I'm capable of?' she said, clutching at a hope.

'Because I know you. You've lived in my heart since the moment we met, and I know you would never do such a thing. It's cruel of anyone to suggest otherwise. I can't see why your husband would have done that.'

'To control me, and make me feel worthless.'

Darroch took her hand. 'You've been through a lot. I can see that.'

She looked at him with wide eyes. 'Will you be

honest with me? Why did you want us to meet? Did Tracy speak to you? She's the only one who knew about us.'

He leant forward, his forearms on his lap and still holding Miriam's hand.

'I promised not to say anything, but after what you've shared, I think you need to know. Your son, Nicholas, contacted me. He came to a reading I held in Inverness and sat at the front. I immediately noticed something familiar with him.' He smiled and gave a half-laugh. 'That, and the fact he was half the age of anyone else in the room. He came to speak to me at the end and when he told me who he was, I realised it must have been you I was seeing in him. He said that he had come across a card with my name on it, and thought it was time for us to catch up. I asked whether he had discussed it with you and he said he didn't need to: he knew it would be the right thing to do. To be honest, I wasn't sure whether to call. I think it was fear of being rejected a second time that made me hesitate.'

'So why did you?'

'Because I had an even greater fear, the fear of you passing me by again. He's a nice young man.'

Then overwhelmed by the need for truth, she told him.

'Darroch, Nicholas is our son: yours and mine. From that last time we met.'

They sat in silence for several minutes. Darroch took a tissue from his pocket, wiped his eyes, and turned towards Miriam.

'Does he know?'

'I think so, it must be why he came to see you.'

'He's a child born of love, Miriam.' Then he stood up. 'Shall we continue our walk? There's a nice place a bit further on where we could have tea.'

He reached out a hand to help her up and then gave his arm for her to take once again.

'Don't worry,' he said. 'Things will be better from now on. I promise.'

***

They sat opposite each other on modern tan-coloured sofas, separated by a glass coffee table and in what for some reason had become an awkward silence, broken only by the slow ticking of a clock on the mantelpiece.

Nicholas looked around. It was a big office – intended to impress. At the far end was a large desk, and behind that, a tall sash window with a commanding view of Edinburgh Castle. The floor was carpeted with a plush claret pile and the furniture a mixture of contemporary designer pieces and a few tastefully placed antiques.

Above the mantelpiece sat a sizeable portrait of a tweed-clad gentleman bearing large whiskers.

'I had that restored some time ago,' said Anthea, sensing Nicholas's curiosity. 'I've only just got around to having it hung. He is my great-great-grandfather and one of the founders of this practice.'

Nicholas looked further into the picture, searching for a resemblance with Anthea Strachan; he couldn't see her there, except perhaps the eyes.

She continued. 'He was a good man. A man with principles,' as though Nicholas might have doubts.

On a shelf inside a glass-doored Edwardian display cabinet sat several certificates in frames: Anthea Strachan QC's credentials. On another shelf were two photos. One was of Anthea taken some time ago, holding a baby at the seaside. She looked happy, and the large hotel in the background made Nicholas think it might be the beach at St Andrews. The other picture was more recent, of a boy, perhaps eight years old, wearing a school uniform. The boy looked familiar and then it registered – the uniform – they had attended the same prep school.

He looked back at Anthea and was about to comment on the coincidence but noticed she was staring into her coffee cup. It seemed that the confident barrister had departed, leaving an altogether more human-looking woman lost in her thoughts.

Raising her eyes to meet Nicholas's, she spoke. 'I find this whole business with Hamish so distressing. To be murdered in prison. I mean, what was he doing in the washrooms on his own? He must have known the dangers, surely? And how did he end up in prison? How can a man keep something like that hidden from the world? I always knew he was a tough cookie when it came to business, and a womaniser, but when I found out how he treated his family I was truly shocked. I mean, I had no idea that any of that was going on.'

'Really?' Nicholas asked, his scepticism clear.

'He was a violent man, Ms Strachan, so I'm not at all surprised to hear that he died the way he did. And you want me to believe that during all the time you knew him you thought he was a kind and loving husband and father? People close to him would have known exactly what he was capable of. At the very least they would have had their suspicions. They just didn't want to get involved.'

She adopted what he took to be an apologetic look. 'I can understand why you're doubtful,' she said and was about to say more when there was a gentle knock on the door.

Without waiting for a reply, a smartly-suited young man entered. He crossed to where Anthea was sitting and handed her a brown A4 envelope.

'Thank you, Simon,' she said, giving him leave to go.

She cast her eyes to the envelope in her hand. Nicholas could see her finger – its perfectly manicured nail painted flamboyant red – running along the join made by the flap: a join marked with the signature of Hamish Fraser.

Then she handed it to Nicholas and he opened it, taking out a piece of paper from within. His eyes followed the writing, going back several times as he worked through its meaning. Finally, he gazed past Anthea, and out of the window to the castle beyond.

His eyes returned to hers. 'I suppose you know what's written here?'

She nodded. 'It's a lot of money for a young man.'

'No. I wasn't referring to that,' he said.

She looked apologetic. 'I'm sorry. That was presumptuous of me. You're referring to his regrets. Are you surprised?'

'No, not now. I always knew that he didn't want to be my father. When I was young I desperately wanted him to be, but it was something he seemed incapable of. I know that biologically he wasn't, but that's not what I'm referring to. However, when I sat with him and watched his life end, I'm certain his soul was trying to tell me something, and regardless of what went before, it was something positive. I'm no longer angry the way that I was – it's burnt itself out – and I'm sure the encounter had something to do with that. So to hear that he had regrets doesn't surprise me and I think he understood when I said that I forgave him.'

He looked around the office again, its opulence speaking of power and privilege, and then turned back to Anthea. 'There's nothing wrong with any of this,' gesturing with his hand. 'It's how you treat people as you get it and what you do once you have it that counts. Nothing is inevitable.'

Anthea smiled. 'Hamish said it was inevitable, so it gives me hope to hear you say otherwise.' Then she looked at the picture of her great-great-grandfather. 'It's time for us to return to something meaningful here as a law firm – time to put something back. I'm sponsoring one of the partners to look into it.'

'I wish you luck with that,' said Nicholas and his eyes returned to the picture in the cabinet. 'And don't forget your son. He looks like a nice boy. A good person. Now if you'll excuse me, I've arranged to meet Mum and my girlfriend, Tracy, for lunch.'

The End

ABOUT THE AUTHOR

Having moved to Edinburgh as a child, Oliver fell in love with Scotland and the great outdoors. After studying Outdoor Education in Liverpool, he returned north to pursue a career as an outdoor instructor.

Always with an eye open for the next adventure, his journey has taken him into the worlds of business, policing, academia and chalet building.

Now based in Perthshire, he spends his time sharing adventures through writing, tramping the hills, sailing, kayaking and lecturing.

Printed in Great Britain
by Amazon

79002109R00234